山东大学出版基金（SDUPF）资助
Shandong University Publication Foundation
山东大学自主创新基金（IIFSDU）资助
Independent Innovation Foundation of Shandong University

U0147315

青少年健康 与 发展研究

双语 Bilingual

Adolescent Health and Development Studies

中文主编（Chinese Chief Editors）　　臧渝梨　Yuli Zang
　　　　　　　　　　　　　　　　　赵　勇　Yong Zhao

英文主编（English Chief Editors）　　臧渝梨　Yuli Zang
　　　　　　　　　　　　　　　　　罗杰·华生　Roger Watson

人民卫生出版社
PEOPLE'S MEDICAL PUBLISHING HOUSE

图书在版编目（CIP）数据

青少年健康与发展研究/臧渝梨等主编.—北京：
人民卫生出版社，2011.12
ISBN 978-7-117-15086-6

Ⅰ.①青…　Ⅱ.①臧…　Ⅲ.①青少年－健康教育
Ⅳ.①G479

中国版本图书馆 CIP 数据核字（2011）第 231351 号

| 门户网：www.pmph.com | 出版物查询、网上书店 |
| 卫人网：www.ipmph.com | 护士、医师、药师、中医
师、卫生资格考试培训 |

版权所有，侵权必究！

青少年健康与发展研究

主　　编：臧渝梨　赵　勇　罗杰·华生
出版发行：人民卫生出版社（中继线 010-59780011）
地　　址：北京市朝阳区潘家园南里 19 号
邮　　编：100021
E - mail：pmph @ pmph.com
购书热线：010-67605754　010-65264830
　　　　　010-59787586　010-59787592
印　　刷：潮河印业有限公司
经　　销：新华书店
开　　本：710×1000　1/16　　印张：23
字　　数：420 千字
版　　次：2011 年 12 月第 1 版　2011 年 12 月第 1 版第 1 次印刷
标准书号：ISBN 978-7-117-15086-6/R·15087
定　　价：55.00 元

打击盗版举报电话：010-59787491　E-mail：WQ @ pmph.com
（凡属印装质量问题请与本社销售中心联系退换）

顾　问		
Kathleen Fritsch	Patanjali Dev Nayar	Jeffrey Fuller

主　编		
臧渝梨	赵　勇	罗杰·华生

副主编		
刘化侠	甄广军	吴之明
郝玉玲	班　博	宋　洁
孟庆慧		

编审委员会

主任

臧渝梨（山东大学）	赵　勇（山东大学附属中学）

副主任（按姓氏笔画排序）

刘化侠（泰山医学院）	吴之明（大连大学）
宋　洁（山东中医药大学）	孟庆慧（潍坊医学院）
郝玉玲（滨州医学院）	班　博（济宁医学院附属医院）
甄广军（山东大学附属中学）	

委员（按姓氏笔画排序）

Alison Hutton（弗林德斯大学）	Julian Grant（弗林德斯大学）
王道远（山东大学附属中学）	刘文英（山东大学附属中学）
刘鹏飞（济宁医学院）	李秀艳（潍坊医学院）
杨　青（山东大学附属中学）	张　雯（泰山医学院）
张　寰（山东大学附属中学）	陈　欧（山东大学）
柳　宇（山东大学附属中学）	扈丽萍（山东省立医院）
唐永云（滨州医学院）	鞠小莉（威海卫生学校）
霍　苗（大连大学）	

作者（按姓氏笔画排序）			
王丽媛	王春美	刘茜	刘婷
刘静	刘晓燕	关持循	江宁
李娜	李云峰	杨黎	杨红霞
宋洁	张雯	陈林	孟庆慧
侯晓红	唐永云	扈丽萍	蒲林哲
臧渝梨	潘尧云	霍苗	
曾经写作贡献者（按姓氏笔画排序）			
王伟学	王笑蕾	刘鹏飞	李蕾
佘燕朝	张雪芹	钟丽丽	韩扬扬

Kathleen Fritsch
世界卫生组织西太平洋
地区办公室　护理顾问

Patanjali Dev Nayar
世界卫生组织西太平洋地区
办公室儿少卫生　技术官

Jeffrey Fuller
澳大利亚弗林德斯大学
教授

主 编

臧渝梨，女，香港理工大学哲学博士，副教授，硕士研究生导师，山东大学护理学院副院长。主要研究方向为护理信息标准化、创新护理教育与临床（灾害、残障、青少年健康）。先后在世界卫生组织瑞士日内瓦总部及其驻菲律宾马尼拉西太平洋办公室做护理学者，获兵库海外研究网资助在日本兵库大学做访问学者。近五年来，先后主持十余项国内外交叉学科课题，以第一作者或通讯作者发表 SCI 等高水平论文约40 篇，副主编双语教材一部，主译大量世界卫生组织资料，在国内外学术会议上作报告 20 次，主管亚太区突发事件及灾害护理协作网（APEDNN）网络平台的研发。学术兼职有：世界灾害护理学会顾问，APEDNN核心委员，全球护理及助产联盟指导委员会委员，世界灾难与急救医学会护理分会执行理事，中国残疾人研究会理事，山东省标准化技术委员会委员，还担任 *Journal of Clinical Nursing* 和 *Journal of Nursing and Health Sciences* 编委，以及《中华护理杂志》、《中国实用护理杂志》和《中华护理教育杂志》审稿专家，是华夏高等护理教育联盟 *Journal of Clinical Nursing* 摘要译员。

赵勇，男，山东大学附属中学校长，党总支委员，中学地理高级教师，山东省济南市地理教学研究会副理事长。参与山东省"初中地理图像程序教学研究"、《初中地理——渗透环境教育参考资料》研究，并获山东省第四届中小学教育科研优秀成果一等奖；主持教育部"十五"重点课题"课程资源开发和利用研究"子课题"生活中的地理"；现作为核心课题组成员参与山东省"十一五"课题《网络环境教育》研究。在各级教育报刊上发表多篇文章；先后参编由省市教研室组织的《地理学习目标与检测》、《地理基础训练》和《中国地理问题解答与同步训练》的编写。

Roger Watson，男，博士，英国谢菲尔德大学教授，《临床护理杂志》(*Journal of Clinical Nursing*)总主编，香港理工大学名誉教授，西悉尼大学兼职教授，澳大利亚昆士兰大学名誉教授，台湾慈济技术学院客座教授，英国斯特林大学名誉教授。首位当选美国护理科学院院士的英国护士，2009年成为英国皇家护理学院成员，2010年成为爱尔兰皇家护理与助产学院成员。

刘化侠，女，教授，硕士研究生导师，泰山医学院护理学院院长。1993～1994年获得笹川医学奖学金赴日本研修临床护理。2000年毕业于中国协和医科大学护理学院，获得医学硕士学位。研究方向为护理教育和护理管理。近5年来承担科研课题13项，其中厅级以上课题4项。科研获奖15项，主编卫生部规划教材3部，副主编人民卫生出版社创新教材1部，参编教育部和卫生部规划教材2部。在省级以上刊物发表论文46篇，获得专利2项。现担任全国高等护理教育分会和华东地区高等护理教育协会的理事，山东护理教育委员会副主任委员，《护理研究》、《中华现代护理杂志》、《中国实用护理杂志》的编委，山东泰安市政协委员，泰安市泰山区人大代表。

甄广军，男，中学高级教师，山东大学附属中学政教处主任。曾获全国优秀课评比一等奖、山东省教学能手、山东省教育系统技术能手、山东省教学基本功一等奖第一名、济南市体育学科带头人、历下区百佳教师、市说课一等奖、历下区特殊贡献先进个人、课余训练先进个人、历下区优秀德育工作者、省中学学科培训专家等荣誉称号。有10篇教育教学论文获得省、市、区级一等奖，并在多种刊物发表，先后参与编写中学教材、教参8本。参与济南市教育科学研究重点课题《体育教学运用"掌握学习"的操作研究》、《微型课研究》和《以发展性评价，促进教师成长的策略研究》。

吴之明，女，大连大学护理学院常务副院长，教授。主要研究方向：高等护理教育与临床老年护理等。近五年，先后主持十余项省部级教育教学改革与老年护理等课题，以第一作者发表论文十余篇，主编教育部国家级规划教材5部，在国内外学术会议上作专题报告5次。学术兼职：全国高等医学教育学会护理教育分会理事，中华护理学会辽宁省分会常务理事及辽宁省护理专家，辽宁省高等学校教学名师，辽宁省普通高等学校专业带头人等。

郝玉玲，女，滨州医学院护理学院副院长，副主任护师。1986年在滨州医学院附属医院从事护理工作，1998年担任护理部副主任职务，2000年主持护理部工作，2007年担任滨州医学院护理学院副院长职务。主要研究方向为护理管理、临床护理、护理教育。获省级科研成果奖励3项，厅局级科研成果奖励8项，在省级以上核心期刊发表论文二十余篇，主编著作5部。学术兼职为华东地区高等护理教育学会理事，山东省护理学会理事，滨州市护理学会常务理事，滨州市医学会康复医学专业委员会副主任委员。

班博，女，医学博士，教授，主任医师，硕士研究生导师。现任济宁医学院护理学院院长，济宁医学院附属医院副院长，山东省内分泌学会副主任委员，天津医科大学护理学硕士生导师，山东大学及天津医科大学内分泌专业硕士生导师，济宁市第三批有突出贡献的中青年专家。致力于护理管理、糖尿病及其并发症的研究。主持参加了国家自然科学基金、卫生部优秀青年基金、山东省自然科学基金资助的多项糖尿病研究课题，其中7项科研成果获得山东省及济宁市科技进步二、三等奖，发表学术论文40余篇。

宋洁，女，山东中医药大学中西医结合基础专业博士，副教授，山东中医药大学外科及急救护理学教研室主任。主要研究方向为老年护理、急救护理。2010.9～2011.2 在英国爱丁堡内皮尔大学做护理访问学者。近三年来，主持 3 项厅级以上课题，以第一作者发表核心期刊论文约 10 篇，主编急救护理学、老年护理学及急危重症护理学各一部。

孟庆慧，女，潍坊医学院护理学院人文护理教研室主任。2004 年硕士毕业于北京大学医学部护理学院，为山东大学 2009 级在读博士。曾于新加坡国立大学医院工作学习 2 年，于北京和睦家医院工作 1 年。主要研究方向：老年护理、护理教育与护理管理。主讲课程：护理管理学、护理教育学、护理专业英语、护理研究、护士礼仪与修养等。主持山东省自然科学基金等科学研究与教学研究课题 5 项，发表论文 20 余篇，主编、副主编、翻译、校译国家级规划教材等 7 部。为山东高等教育护理教育分会委员，潍坊市医疗事故鉴定专家。

Alison Hutton，博士，弗林德斯大学护理与助产学院高级讲师，荣誉护生项目负责人。当前工作主要为：青年健康促进和伤害最小化，年轻人的行为和人生自我决策，并发表多篇相关文章。同时是澳大利亚儿少卫生学会理事会青年代言人，*Child Health and Paediatric Nursing Journal* 杂志副主编，4 个国际护理杂志审稿专家，青年儿童学院南澳分院院长；近期荣获南澳 2010 社区安全奖。

Julian Grant，博士，澳大利亚弗林德斯大学护理与助产学院高级讲师。主要研究方向为：儿少家庭健康护理，初级卫生保健，反思实践，人类文化学视频方法学，避难所卫生，文化能力与跨文化交流。

王道远，男，曲阜师范大学硕士毕业生，研究生学历，山东大学附属中学教师。

刘文英，女，同济大学硕士毕业生，研究生学历，助教，山东大学附属中学教师。发表核心期刊论文1篇。

刘鹏飞，济宁医学院护理学院教学管理科科长，基础护理教研室主任，主要方向为护理教育及慢性疾病管理。现已在核心期刊发表论文7篇。

杨青，女，山东师范大学硕士毕业生，现任山东大学附属中学生物教师，"青少年性别认知与浪漫关系研究"课题组山大附中负责人。在核心期刊及国家级期刊发表第一作者论文2篇，第二作者论文2篇，并参与多项校级课题。曾获历下区班会评比课一等奖、历下区新苗新秀优质课一等奖、济南市课件评比一等奖、山东省中学生创新实验大赛指导教师一等奖、历下区教育论文评比二等奖等荣誉。

陈欧，女，山东大学护理学院讲师，主要方向为儿科护理学及急救护理学。发表论文6篇。参与翻译《轻松儿科护理》、《轻松护生成功之路》。作为副主编及编者，参编教材及著作9本。承担并参与省部级课题8项，获省教育厅高等学校优秀科研成果奖一等奖一项，二等奖一项，山东省医学会奖二等奖一项。

　　张雯，女，山东中医药大学硕士毕业生，现在泰山医学院护理学院内儿教研室工作，主要研究方向为中西医结合儿童病的护理及健康评估。在核心期刊及国家级期刊发表第一作者论文6篇，主持并参与多项校级课题，指导大学生课题两项。先后获得校级及院级教学能手等多项荣誉称号，并作为山东省优秀青年教师国内访问学者于2010.9～2011.7在北京协和护理学院研修学习。

　　张寰，女，山东大学护理学院毕业，大专学历，主要研究青春期知识和保健。

　　李秀艳，女，中国科学院心理研究所与菲律宾圣托马斯大学心理学博士学位。为护理学、心理学研究生导师，国家高级心理咨询师，兼任中国高等护理教育学会理事、山东省心理卫生协会护理专业委员会副主任等职务。主讲生理学、护理心理学、护理管理学等课程，是护理管理学省级精品课程负责人。主编教材14部，发表学术论文90余篇，承担教学科研课题20余项，其中以首位人员承担省部级教学科研项目5项，其中省部级教学成果二等奖一项，科研成果二、三等奖5项，获得科研经费160余万元。

柳宇，女，山东师范大学毕业，现任山东大学附属中学英语教师，国际交流项目负责人。本科方向：生物教育；研究生方向：英语语言与教育。曾获济南市电教课一等奖，历下区优质课一等奖，国际汉语教师中国志愿者荣誉证书，美国语言学会高级英语能力证书。曾在包括耶鲁大学、崇德私立高中等在内的两所美国高校和多所优秀高中任教。2006～2008 年任《汉语世界》（国内邮发代号：80-570，国外代号：BM4956）专栏作者。现主持校级课题一项，参与校级课题两项。

唐永云，女，2004 年毕业于滨州医学院护理学院，获学士学位，同年留校任教，内儿护理学教研室教师，承担《急救护理学》、《重症护理学》、《护理学基础》等多门课程。主要研究方向为急危重症护理及青少年健康，近年来以第一作者发表学术论文 6 篇，参编著作 5 部。

扈丽萍，女，山东大学附属省立医院注册护士，主管护师，保健心血管病房护士。目前为山东大学护理学院 2008 级研究生。2001 年毕业于山东大学护理学院，同年分配至山东省立医院工作。先后在神经外科、保健心血管科工作，参加山东省立医院 ICU 护士培训，获得证书。大学时就通过英语六级考试，工作后在省级以上杂志发表论文 5 篇，参编著作两部。

　　霍苗，女，中国医科大学攻读护理学硕士学位，师从李小寒教授，研究方向为护理教育。2008 年参加由教育部、国家自然科学基金委员会主办的"2008 年全国研究生暑期学校（护理学）"，被评为优秀学员，2009 年 7 月被评为"中国医科大学优秀毕业生"。同年就职于大连大学护理学院，人文护理学教研室教师兼任护理学院教学秘书，承担《护理学导论》、《护理科研》、《护理教育学》等多门课程。近两年，参与省部级课题 5 项，核心期刊发表学术论文 1 篇，参编专著 1 部，2010 年被评为"大连大学优秀教师"。

　　鞠小莉，女，1994 年毕业于山东医科大学护理系，2008 年取得山东大学护理学院硕士学位，讲师，威海市卫生学校护理教研室主任，主要研究方向为护理教育，2004 年底至 2005 年 5 月赴澳大利亚昆士兰州南岸职业技术学院做访问学者。近年来，已在核心期刊发表论文数篇，参编著作多部，并多次获得"威海市先进教育工作者"、"师德标兵"等荣誉称号。

作 者

王丽媛，女，山东大学护理学院 2011 级推荐免试硕士研究生，现就读于山东大学护理学院，本科期间曾获得国家奖学金、国家励志奖学金、山东大学优秀学生奖学金、三好学生、优秀学生干部、优秀共青团员和山东省优秀毕业生等荣誉称号。现主要研究方向为护理信息学和青少年健康服务。

王春美，女，山东大学第二医院普外科护士长、主管护师。2000 年毕业于山东大学护理学院，获本科医学学士学位。先后在山东大学第二医院小儿内科、普外科工作。2009 年 9 月考入山东大学护理学院攻读硕士学位。现已在核心期刊发表论文篇，参编著作多部。

关持循，女，2003 年毕业于哈尔滨医科大学护理学院，获得学士学位，同年进入吉林大学护理学院任教；2005 年调入大连大学护理系任教，职称讲师，2011年毕业于辽宁医学院护理学院，获得硕士学位。主要研究方向为护理教育、护理心理、外科护理及护理英语，发表学术论文 5 篇，参编教材 1 部。

刘茜，女，山东大学护理学院本科在读，多次获得山东大学优秀学生一等奖学金、国家奖学金，荣获山东大学优秀共青团员、山东大学优秀志愿者等荣誉称号，获"五四论文"二等奖，曾在日本和歌山县立医科大学交流学习。

刘晓燕，女，山东大学护理学院 2007 级推荐免试硕士研究生，主要方向为护理信息学、护理管理学。研究生期间，共在核心期刊发表论文 5 篇，荣获山东大学优秀学生干部，山东大学优秀共青团员，山东大学社会实践先进个人等荣誉称号。曾在香港理工大学、台湾成功大学交流学习。2010 年毕业后就职于济南市天桥区卫生局。

刘婷，女，山东大学护理学院硕士毕业生，现在澳大利亚弗林德斯大学攻读博士学位，主要研究方向为护理信息、青少年健康与发展。硕士期间发表核心期刊论文 10 篇，参编译著 1 部，曾获得国家励志奖学金、山东大学校长奖学金、十佳共青团员、全面发展标兵、山东省优秀毕业生等荣誉称号，多次获优秀学生一等奖学金、优秀研究生奖学金。

刘静，女，山东大学护理学院 2007 级推荐免试硕士研究生，主要方向为护理信息学、护理管理学。研究生期间，共在核心期刊发表论文 5 篇，曾获山东大学优秀研究生，山东大学优秀共青团员，山东大学社会实践先进个人等荣誉称号。2010 年毕业后就职于山东省立医院。

江宁，女，山西医科大学护理学院硕士毕业生，研究生学历，助教，泰山医学院护理学院内儿教研室教师，主要研究方向为内科护理、健康评估。发表核心期刊论文 4 篇，国家级期刊论文 2 篇。主持校级课题 1 项，参与市级课题一项，省级课题 1 项，参编双语教材一部。于 2010 年参与山东省红十字会主持的急救师资培训班，获得救护培训师资格。

李云峰，女，山东省大学附属千佛山医院注册护士，主管护师，儿科病房护士长。目前为山东大学护理学院 2010 级研究生。1996 年 6 月通过山东省高等教育自学考试获得高等护理大专文凭。1997 年 6 月至 8 月赴以色列 Dina School of Nursing 参加国际儿科护士学习班。1999 年 4 月通过新加坡卫生部注册护士考试赴新加坡国家心脏中心心胸外科病房进修学习 2 年。2005 年 8 月赴北京大学新生儿监护室进修 NICU 3 个月，并于 2005 年 12 月通过山东省高等教育自学考试获得护理学本科文凭及学士学位。自 2002 年以来，一直在大中专院校教授儿科护理学和医学英语。2008 年 6 月通过美国 NCLEX-RN 考试，2008 年 11 月参加雅思考试并取得总分 7 分和口语 7.5 分的成绩。申请国家实用专利两项，作为成员之一参与省级科研项目一个，在省级以上杂志发表论文 5 篇，作为副主编出版专著两部，作为副译审参与 ICNP 汉语术语翻译校对工作。

李娜，女，山东大学护理学院 2009 级推荐免试硕士研究生，曾多次获得山东大学优秀学生奖学金及优秀学生荣誉称号、社团活动先进个人称号等。现已在核心期刊发表第一作者论文 2 篇。参与翻译《轻松护生成功之路》和《国际护理实践分类》（第 2 版）。英语水平较高，顺利通过新托福考试。

杨红霞，女，山东泰山医学院硕士毕业生，现在山东省泰山医学院工作，主要方向为儿童护理。自参加工作以来，发表论文6篇，主持一项校级课题，参与课题多项。

杨黎，女，硕士，讲师，国家二级心理咨询师，中国医科大学护理学本科毕业，泰山医学院护理学院硕士毕业。现在泰山医学院护理学院工作，主要方向为护理心理及护理教育。硕士期间，主修心理咨询，熟练掌握青少年常见心理疾病的诊断、咨询与治疗。在核心期刊发表论文4篇。

陈林，女，山东大学护理学院硕士毕业生，现在山东省立医院工作，主要方向为护理信息及灾害护理。硕士期间，在核心期刊发表论文7篇，参与导师硕士课题多项。大学及研究生期间，曾先后获得三好学生、国家奖学金、优秀研究生、优秀学生干部、优秀志愿者等荣誉称号。2010年1月，曾前往日本参加国际学术会议，并用英文在大会上作报告。

侯晓红，女，山东大学护理学院硕士毕业生，现在山东省立医院工作，主要方向为护理信息学。硕士期间，在核心期刊发表论文6篇，参编人民卫生出版社创新双语教材1部，参译著作1部，已通过雅思考试。参与导师硕士课题多项。大学及研究生期间，多次获校级奖学金、校三好学生、省级优秀志愿者、校十大优秀女大学生、优秀研究生、优秀学生干部等荣誉称号。

蒲林哲，女，武汉大学 HOPE 护理学院 2010 级推荐免试硕士研究生，现就读于山东大学护理学院，本科期间曾多次获得武汉大学优秀学生奖学金、优秀共青团员和三好学生等荣誉称号，多次参加英语征文及表演比赛，成绩优异。现主要研究方向为护理信息学和青少年健康服务。参与翻译《国际护理实践分类体系双语词典》。

潘尧云，女，山东大学护理学院 2009 级推荐免试硕士研究生，主要方向为护理信息及青少年健康服务。现已在核心期刊发表论文 3 篇，另有 2 篇论文接收待刊。参与翻译《专业护士及助产士起点教育全球标准》、《轻松护生成功之路》及《国际护理实践分类体系双语词典》。曾获得山东大学优秀共青团员、山东大学优秀学生党员、山东省"省级优秀学生"等荣誉称号，多次获得山东大学优秀学生奖学金。已顺利通过英语雅思考试。

王伟学，男，山东中医药大学中医内科心血管专业硕士，现在山东省泰山医学院工作，主要讲授内科护理学、健康评估等课程。

王笑蕾，女，山东大学护理学院硕士毕业生，现在山东省泰山医学院工作，主要讲授内科护理学、老年护理学。

佘燕朝，女，大连大学护理学院讲师，主讲专业英语、护理科研。于2007年7月毕业于天津医科大学护理学院并获得硕士学位，主要方向为护理教育。已在核心期刊发表论文3篇，在澳门护理杂志上发表1篇英文文章。在学期间与翻译公司合作兼职医药笔译。

张雪芹，女，山东青岛大学护理学院硕士毕业生，现在泰山医学院护理学院工作，主要方向为社区护理及心理护理。硕士期间，在核心期刊发表论文 3 篇。工作后在核心期刊发表论文 5 篇。

李蕾，女，泰山医学院硕士毕业生，现在泰山医学院护理学院工作，主要方向为外科护理及疼痛护理。在核心期刊发表论文 7 篇，承担校级课题 2 项，参加省市级课题多项，参编教材 3 部。

钟丽丽，女，延边大学护理学院硕士毕业生，研究生学历，讲师，大连大学护理学院人文护理教研室副主任，主讲科目为《护理学导论》、《护理管理学》。发表核心期刊论文 2 篇。主持校级创新课题 1 项，参与市级课题 2 项，省级课题 3 项，国家级课题 1 项。参编"十二五"规划教材辅导用书 1 部。参加国际学术会议 2 次，参加全国护理学教师暑期培训 2 次。

韩扬扬，女，中南大学湘雅医学院硕士毕业生，研究生学历，助教，泰山医学院护理学院外妇护理学教研室教师，主要研究方向为临床护理学、护理管理学。发表核心期刊论文 6 篇。主持校级和市级课题各 1 项，参与省级课题 1 项，市级课题 1 项，校级课题 3 项。

寄　语

非常高兴在此向大家引荐即将在中国出版发行的双语《青少年健康与发展研究》，我不禁想起 2007 年 8 月在新加坡举行的第十四届双年度校园护士国际学术会议，在此会议期间，山东大学和香港理工大学首度就《青少年健康与发展》三个教学模块资料的英译汉进行会谈。此后，臧渝梨博士开始在中国内地发挥引领作用，分析青少年健康发展相关课程薄弱点，并在山东大学试教选修课，最终共有六所大学护理学院参与到相关活动中，这些学校是：大连大学、泰山医学院、潍坊医学院、济宁医学院、滨州医学院、青岛大学。所开展的活动包括但并不局限于：发展教学资料、探索适宜的教学方式方法以培养本科生和研究生，不止是针对卫生保健专业的学生，还培训医院、社区卫生服务中心的卫生工作者和学校教师，目的是提高青少年健康发展服务能力。在此期间，弗林德斯大学也成为合作伙伴之一，主要关注城市化对青少年健康发展的影响。

作为世界卫生组织西太平洋地区护理顾问，我见证了臧博士以及她的团队在过去几年里所做出的具有战略意义的各种努力：她们表现得坚定而坚决，不断将所获得的其他地区的研究发现和最佳实践经验与当地的具体情况结合起来，促进大学护理及更多学科的教育（包括继续教育）发生改变，且改变要具有持久性。现已设计并成功实施了校园和社区青少年健康发展干预活动，主要是教育性干预，迄今共有 8 名护理硕士研究生在不断开展相关项目的工作，已发表硕士学位论文一篇、专业学术论文六篇、新闻报道数篇及英文学术论文一篇。山东省卫生厅及山东大学附属中学在后勤保障、行政管理及现场干预方面都给予了大力支持。大家的共同努力使我深信：本书是在对当地形势及青少年健康发展状况有清晰认识的基础上编撰而成的。

本书共有十个章节，呈现了青少年健康发展基本知识、信念和态度，是所有可能接触青少年服务对象的卫生工作者及学校教师的必备读物，可帮助解答青少年对青春期和其他关注的问题，该书也有助于卫生保健专业大学生和青少年更好地理解青少年健康发展，提高自身的健康发展能力。

愿您在阅读此书时能乐在其中！我确信，臧博士和她的团队盼望收到您的反馈，而您的意见和建议都将被融合到未来各版本中。

Kathleen Fritsch
世界卫生组织西太平洋
地区护理顾问

在中国出版中英文的《青少年健康与发展研究》真是令人欣喜！对于作为教育工作者的我们，它标志着我们职业生涯的巨大飞跃，超越了语言、学科和国界的限制。

在过去三年里，我们与山东大学护理学院副院长臧渝梨博士（副教授）密切合作，主要领域是青少年健康促进和积极青年发展，尤其是在青少年早期。始终激励和鼓舞着我们的是心中的一种热望，那就是，通过教育改善青少年的健康与发展，在此过程中充分结合学校管理者、教师、父母或其他主要监护人、专业卫生人员以及科研工作者的力量。我们已经充分认识到：目前尚没有多少证据能够帮助我们更好地理解处于青春期及所伴随心理社会发展巨变中的中国青少年及其家庭，正是这种认识引导着我们去研发行之有效的干预方案。

对中国的青少年及其家庭而言，他们最主要的压力是学业，因为良好的学业是美好未来的重要保障。我们必定要承担责任，也就是，为青少年及其家庭提供支持，以促进其应对此类挑战。我们也有义务去发展技能和实力，从而与青少年及其家庭充分合作，促进青少年在社会生活的所有关键方面达到作为人类个体所能达到的最高标准。正是出于这样一种热望，我们才组建了这个包括山东大学护理学院、山东大学附属中学、弗林德斯大学护理与助产学院以及其他护理学院（校）在内的国际化团队，从而深入研究青少年健康与发展相关能力，并探索在家庭和校园条件下增强提供最佳青少年服务的方式方法。

从不曾有不劳而获！双语《青少年健康与发展研究》的出版发行，是我们跨学科、跨机构、跨国合作的重要里程碑。此著作的出版，将有助于缩小中国与国际社会在青少年健康发展领域的差距，也有助于拉近青少年教育与卫生服务的距离，它所呈现的基础知识将为拓宽和深化青少年健康发展领域的合作铺平道路。

青少年是人类社会的未来，是最有发展前景、最具发展潜能的个体，我们虔诚地请求：所有致力于改善青少年教育与卫生服务工作的人们，请支持我们或与我们合作！在我们共同的努力与和谐的行动下，青少年才有可能克服困难，从容面对学业压力和青春期变化，为应对美好未来之路上所面临的诸多挑战做好准备。

弗林德斯大学护理与助产学院
Jeffrey Fuller 教授

山东大学附属中学校长
赵　勇　副教授

致 谢

在编撰这本双语著作的漫长过程中,有很多人让我们深怀感恩和感激。

首先我们要衷心感谢世界卫生组织西太平洋地区办公室护理顾问官 Kathleen Fritsch 女士。若不是她,我们不会去如此深入地研究青少年健康与发展的有关问题,也不可能克服工作中遇到的那么多的、始料未及的困难和挑战。她鼓励我们积极进行护理及其他相关领域的探索与合作,这也是过去几年的国际合作得以成功的原因所在。

我们也非常感谢世界卫生组织西太平洋地区办公室儿少卫生技术官 Patanjali Dev Nayar 博士,他引导、支持我们组织回顾和强化护理课程,促进开展青少年健康发展能力需求有关活动。

我们对所有的参加单位和活动参加者深怀感恩,将永远铭记那些在我们需要时给予支持帮助的人们,现谨在此向他们表达我们诚挚的敬意。若没有他们,我们不可能顺利完成这些教育性资料的准备,也不可能实施任何校园或家庭干预。

我们也永远不会忘记山东大学护理学院的研究生们所做的出色工作:她们中有些已经毕业,有些在国外继续深造,还有一些仍跟我们密切合作着,当然不止限于青少年健康与发展领域。学生们个个都非常优秀,因其自身的聪慧、勤奋克己、敬业奉献以及对青少年教育及健康发展的浓厚兴趣。

最后,我们要对家人、朋友和所在机构的领导表达敬意与感激,是他们组成了最强大的支持网络,也正是在这样的支持网络中,我们才得以精力充沛和快乐地对所感兴趣的领域进行自由的科学探索。

通向成功的道路仍旧漫长,充满挑战和不可预测性,但我们有信心,在大家的支持和帮助下,我们终将成功。

青少年健康与发展小组

目 录

引　言

　　10～19 岁是青少年由稚嫩逐渐走向成熟的时期。在此期间,他们要挖掘自身潜能,完成从孩童到成人的角色转变。因此,不论在生理上还是在心理上,此期的青少年都会面临着显著的转变和严峻的挑战。

　　健康和人类发展生物生态学理论表明,塑造和影响青少年健康与发展的社会环境主要是家庭和学校 [1-3]。因此,家庭、学校和社区中就需要一些具有丰富卫生保健知识的人员来提供足够的优质服务。这些服务可以帮助青少年顺利完成从孩童向成人的转变,促进养成健康的生活方式(如合理膳食和充足的锻炼),预防和减少健康危险行为(如不良的饮食习惯、吸烟、酗酒、过早性行为及抗劝),并帮助青少年监测和治疗慢性病(如哮喘、糖尿病和癌症)[4-7]。

　　一般认为,在青少年可能出现的各种环境中,包括医院和社区,护士是实现上述目标的主力军,因为护士可提供综合性的服务,包括诸如健康与发展评估与管理、健康教育、疾病预防、健康辅导、转诊、人员协调、人员培训等 [4, 8-10]。为加强护士在这些方面的能力,世界各地都做出了很多努力,包括对卫生工作者进行职前培训、继续教育、培养终身学习习惯 [11-14]。然而,目前的服务体系仍然普遍缺乏青少年健康与发展服务,对残疾青少年的服务更是薄弱,对校园护士也缺乏培养培训 [7, 15-18]。

　　在医院、教育机构和社区进行的一系列研究表明,我国目前的卫生和教育体系也存在上述类似问题 [19-25]。虽是如此,这些研究也反映了海内外在解决这些问题中所做出的不断努力,包括与香港(如香港理工大学)和澳大利亚(如弗林德斯大学)伙伴的合作,而这些合作都离不开世界卫生组织(World Health Organization, WHO)官员的指导,如 WHO 西太平洋地区办公室(或称WPRO)的 Kathleen Fritsch 女士和 Patanjali Dev Nayar 博士。

　　亟待本著作能用于普遍提高卫生工作者(尤其是护士)的基本能力,以满足应对青少年健康发展主要问题的需要,实现根据发展状况提供亲青卫生服务的目标。第二章是青少年健康与发展概述,第三章具体描述与 WHO 指导性框架一致的亲青卫生服务（AFHS）的特征，第四章至第七章，主要围绕青少年的主要健康与发展问题进行论述，分别涉及青少年生长发育（第四章）、心理社会发展（第五章）、健康危险行为（第六章）、性生殖健康（第七章）和伤害（第八章）。继之则是两个相对独立的章节，第九章是残障青少年，第十章是结篇，提供了一些可用于监测青少年健康与发展状况的工具，使本著作更加实用。有关如何与关键人员（包括青少年、青少年的父母及老师）进行沟通的内容则可以参考相关章节，如第五章。

（王丽媛，臧渝梨）

参 考 文 献

[1] Bronfenbrenner U. Making human beings human: bioecological perspectives on human development[M]. Thousand Oaks, California: Sage, 2005.

[2] Kickbusch I. Approaches to an ecological base for public health[J]. Health Promotion International, 1989, 4(4): 265-268.

[3] Simpson AR. Raising teens: a synthesis of research and foundation for action[EB/OL]. Harvard School of Public Health, 2001[2011-5-11]: http: //www.hsph.harvard.edu/chc/parenting/report.pdf.

[4] Keeney BG, Cassata L, McElmurry JB. Adolescent health and development in nursing and midwifery education[EB/OL]. World Health Organization, 2004[2011-7-25]: http: //whqlibdoc.who.int/hq/2004/WHO_EIP_HRH_NUR_2004.1.pdf.

[5] Michaud P, Suris J, Viner R. The adolescent with a chronic condition. Part Ⅱ: healthcare provision[J]. Archives of Disease Childhood, 2004, 89(10): 943-949.

[6] Suris J-C, Michaud P-A, Viner R. The adolescent with a chronic condition. Part I: developmental issues[J]. Archives of Disease in Childhood, 2004, 89(10): 938-942.

[7] WHO. Strengthening the health sector response to adolescent health and development[EB/OL]. 2010_[2011-6-12]: http: //www.who.int/child_adolescent_health/documents/cah_adh_flyer_2010_12_en.pdf.

[8] Fritsch K, Heckert KA. Working together: health promoting schools and school nurses[J]. Asian Nursing Research, 2007, 1(3): 147-152.

[9] Levenberg PB. GAPS: an opportunity for nurse practitioners to promote the health of adolescents through clinical preventive services[J]. Journal of Pediatric Health Care, 1998, 12(1): 2-9.

[10] Smith S. Adolescent units--an evidence-based approach to quality nursing in adolescent care[J]. European Journal of Oncology Nursing, 2004, 8(1): 20-29.

[11] CSH. Role of the School Nurse in Providing School Health Services[J]. Pediatrics, 2008,

121（5）：1052-1056.

[12] Reuterswärd M，Lagerström M. The aspects school health nurses find important for successful health promotion[J]. Scandinavian Journal of Caring Sciences，2010，24（1）：156-163.

[13] St Leger L. Health promotion and health education in schools：trends，effectiveness and possibilities[M]. Noble Park North，Victoria：Royal Automobile Club of Victoria （RACV），2006.

[14] Yoo IY，Yoo MS，Lee GY. Self-evaluated competencies of school nurses in Korea[J]. Journal of School Health，2004，74（4）：144-146.

[15] McConkey R & Kelly M. Nursing inputs to special schools in N. Ireland[J]. International Journal of Nursing Studies，2001，38（4）：395-403.

[16] Moore G，McConkey R，Duffy M. The role of the school nurse in special schools for pupils with severe learning difficulties[J]. International Journal of Nursing Studies，2003，40（7）：771-779.

[17] Park MJ，Adams SH，Irwin Jr CE. Health care services and the transition to young adulthood：challenges and opportunities[J]. Academic Pediatrics，2011，11（2）：115-122.

[18] WPRO. A Framework for the Integration of Adolescent Health and Development Concepts Into Pre-service Health Professional Educational Curricula WHO Western Pacific Region[EB/OL]. 2002[2011-7-17]：http：//www.wpro.who.int/NR/rdonlyres/88E71899-5915-4932-AD47-A78EF3D8E7FB/0/ADHframework.pdf.

[19] Hutton A，Grant J. Expanding the role of nurses for a rapidly urbanising China[J]. RCNAreport：nursing news，views & attitudes，2011，（2）：6 [2011-8-6]：http：//www.apnedmedia.com.au/email/rcna-report-feb-11-web-ready.pdf.

[20] 鞠小莉，臧渝梨，娄凤兰，等. 开设青少年健康与发展课程必要性的探讨 [J]. 中华护理教育，2009b，6（9）：401-403.

[21] 刘婷，潘尧云，臧渝梨. 护士对青少年健康与发展能力的认知调查 [J]. 护理学杂志，2011，26（3，综合版）：53-56.

[22] 潘尧云，刘婷，臧渝梨. 青少年健康与发展课程融入本科护理教育初探 [J]. 护理学杂志，2010，25（9，综合版）：64-66.

[23] 潘尧云，刘婷，臧渝梨. 青少年健康与发展能力认知与需求测评工具的构建及应用 [J]. 护理学杂志，2011，26（2，外科版）：65-68.

[24] Zang YL，Zhao Y，Yang Q，et al. A randomised trial on pubertal development and health in China[J]. Journal of Clinical Nursing，2011，20（21-22）：3081-3091.

[25] 鞠小莉，臧渝梨，刘文，等. 青少年健康与发展课程在中国的适用性研究 [J]. 护理教育研究，2009a，24（2，外科版）：8-10.

第二章

青少年健康与发展概述

人们越来越重视卫生工作者尤其是校园护士的青少年健康发展（adolescent health development，AHD）能力，WHO 提出了旨在加强卫生部门应对 AHD 的"4S 框架"，即收集和使用具有战略意义的信息（S1）、发展有科学依据的支持性政策（S2）、增加卫生服务和卫生用品供给（S3）、加强其他有关部门（尤其是教育和青少年部门）（S4）[1]。根据青少年健康发展指导原则（即初级卫生保健原则）开展了一系列全省性和全国性的活动，这些活动揭示出，现有教育和卫生部门在培养卫生工作者和教育者发展 AHD 能力方面显然比较薄弱。本章旨在为更好地理解青少年健康发展提供必要的知识，包括在国内所开展的有关活动和研究。

"青春期"一词对卫生工作者意味着很多，本部分主要介绍青春期定义、青少年发展特征、青少年阶段的发展任务以及有助于青少年健康发展的重要议题。

青春期定义

"青春期"一词源于拉丁文 *adolescere*，意思是"长大成为成年人"[2]。在任何社会，青春期都是指从稚嫩依赖的儿童期进入相对成熟独立的成年期的过渡阶段，涉及显著的生理变化以及与社会期待和社会感知相一致的社会心理和经济条件的变化。身体上的生长发育往往伴随着性的逐步成熟和亲密关系（尤其是恋爱关系）的发展[1-4]。此期的健康状况与发展水平将为个体发挥潜能、获得最佳生活铺平道路。对青少年健康发展进行投资，将有助于改善青少年自身今后的生活，使下一代受益匪浅，并有助于提高社会生产力，促进社会繁荣[1]。增强青少年的社会责任感，包括孝道，是有力应对社会（尤其是在我国）老龄化和慢性病增加的一项必要措施。

鉴于青春期的分界较为模糊，许多社会是结合年龄和生活情景界定何为"青少年"，导致出现各种不同术语，如青少年（adolescent）、青年（youth）、年轻人（young people），均用于描述同一生命阶段的人类个体[5]。以我国为例，目前尚没有统一的对青少年的定义，仅提议采用 14～28 岁年龄段定义，从而与党领导下的共青团员的政治化年龄界定保持一致[6]。为此，WHO 倾向于采用年龄段定义，以促进各国和不同学科在此概念上的可比性和相互理解："年轻人"是那些处于合并年龄段内的 10～19 岁的"青少年"和 15～24 岁的"青年"[4, 5]。

就我国而言，政治上的考虑对国家统计和学术领域中"青少年"的年龄段界定，尤其是年龄下限，有着重要的影响。中国共青团，是中国共产党领导下的先进青年组织，规定了团员的年龄资格是 14～28 岁，因此 14 岁始终被认为是青年的年龄下限，而那些不足 14 岁者则被称为儿童和少年[6-8]。尽管没有对"青少年"或"青春期"的年龄界定，中国政府习惯于沿用联合国（包括WHO）的定义、建议和立场声明。因此在本著作中，"青少年"统一指 10～19 岁群体，以反映第二性征（如面部痤疮、体毛、女孩乳房和月经、男孩睾丸和阴茎）在早发育、迟完成方面的变异。

人口社会与经济特征

采用上述年龄段定义，估计 2000 年全世界共有 11 亿多青少年，大约每五人中就有一名 10～19 岁者[6]。根据世界银行 2002 年的报告，全球 17 亿青少年中，大部分（86%）生活在发展中国家，通常是占当地人口总数的 30% 甚至更多[5]。

据我国卫生部 2008 年调查显示，10～19 岁的青少年大约有 1.94 亿，占总人数的 14.6%（抽样人数为 1 178 521，抽样率为 0.887‰），男女比例为 115 : 100[9]。按照此青少年人口比例和 2010 年国家统计局人口普查数据（总人口 1 339 724 852）推算，截至 2010 年 11 月初，我国青少年人口为195 599 828[10]。

影响青少年健康发展的最主要因素是教育、就业和贫困。教育对于达到所期望的社会经济发展状况至关重要，因为教育可以提高获得经济增长的机会，正规教育对青少年的发展更为重要。学校不仅是青少年获得技能、培养读写、计算和思维能力的重要环境，更是获得健康教育和指导的主要源泉，并能为健康筛查和卫生服务提供安全便利的环境。

尽管我国已全面实施九年制义务教育，许多青少年（尤其是在偏远地区）在未满 19 岁前就离开了校园而流动到大中城市寻找工作。这些青少年，常被称作"国内移民"，可能面临较差的工作环境，失去教育机会，遭受剥削、贫困和安全威胁[11-13]。据估计，2005 年我国共有大约 146 860 000 流动人口，其中约 35.7%（n=52 490 000）是 14～29 岁，约 52%（n=76 390 000 人）是

14～35 岁，而 14～29 岁人口中约有 17.9% 为流动人口，比全国人口的总体流动率（即 11.5%）高出 6.4 个百分点，男、女流动人口分别各占同年龄组总人口的 16.5% 和 19.2%[11]。但遗憾的是，并没有相关统计真正显示青少年人口的流动情况，说明需要改变我国的国家统计方案，以促进全球性的比较。

另有资料揭示，青少年国内移民在出生或居住地以外的城市中生活时有适应不良的倾向，导致出现行为不良问题，包括性生殖问题、青少年犯罪、情绪障碍、学习困难和道德问题[13-17]。与国外移民相比，青少年国内移民可能需要更多性生殖健康、心理健康、安全防卫与支持方面的教育。

此外，更大外部环境因素对青少年也会产生更强烈的影响，这些因素包括大众传媒、工矿企业、社区机构、宗教团体、政治社会体系和经济机会，但不局限于此[3]。城市比农村有更多的机会和更好的环境，据估计，2008 年流出的农村户籍人口大约为 1.49 亿，2009 年增加至 1.6 亿，而全国流动人口总数也不过才 1.8 亿[16]。与当地社区人群相比，流动规模可能造成青少年移民的相对贫困[11]，而贫困则可能使青少年失去获得发展的基本要素，尤其是在入学、职业培训及卫生服务方面，还有可能使青少年接触到更多的暴力、被重新安置和福利受限[3]。

因此，卫生工作者和学校教师应对人口、社会和经济状况保持敏感，采用与当地社会文化期望相兼容的方式，根据执业范围匹配服务。

青少年健康发展的重要性

与儿童和成人相比，青少年患病率和死亡率较低，因此看上去就相对比较健康，但这并非没有危险。事实上，在获取一系列相关知识和技能从而能过上幸福多姿生活的过程中，青少年可能面临着严峻的健康挑战，而这些技能对于青少年保持健康、完成学业、谋取工作或营生以及充分融入社会至关重要。

就全球范围而言，10～24 岁的年轻人约占全球疾病和伤害负担的 15%，每年约有一百多万人死去，大部分死因都可预防、可治疗，例如，意外、自杀、暴力、妊娠并发症、营养缺乏，而成人中大约 70% 的早亡（即 65 岁之前去世）与青少年阶段开始形成的行为有关，如吸烟、营养习惯不良和危险性行为[3, 5, 18]。

有很多理由要求我们必须重视青少年的健康发展，最主要的就是为了青少年自身、他们今后的生活以及他们的下一代[18]。健康是青少年发展的关键要素，他们有权拥有最佳的健康状态，因此必须努力减少青少年的死亡、患病以及健康危险行为。青少年阶段的健康和不健康生活方式影响可持续一生，例如，不良饮食习惯可以导致营养不良，引发终身健康问题；忽视普遍存在的青春期性行为、怀孕、流产及分娩则可能导致不孕、性传播疾病、弃婴、早婚、婚姻生活不良或离婚[18]。

此外，今天的青少年在将来可能成为教师、家长、社区领导者、政策制定者或是其他承担社会责任的人，对青少年健康发展进行投资就是为美好的前景奠定基础，这种投资可以打破贫困造成的恶性循环，还可以保护人力资本，如此一来，除了自我实现，青少年也能按照期望履行角色，并为经济和社会发展作出贡献[5, 18]。必须强调，一定要致力于超越简单的生存之道，从而使青少年走向潜能的充分实现，青少年及其家长以及周围更大的社会支持网络就必须要提供机会促进其健康发展，这样才有助于形成健康高产的社会群体[19]。

健康问题

人们越来越认识到，某些青少年确实存在影响健康的问题和很多不健康行为[20, 21]，WHO 对这些可能影响青少年健康的问题和行为进行分类（表2-1）[4, 18]。

表 2-1　发展中国家年轻人患病与健康相关行为分类

年轻人特有疾病	尤其影响青少年的疾病与不健康行为	主要见于年轻人但始于儿童期的疾病	年轻人患有的疾病和不健康行为，主要影响其未来健康	对年轻人影响低于对儿童影响但高于对成人影响的疾病
疾病： ● 第二性征发育障碍 ● 社会心理发展困难 ● 青少年生长发育突增不理想	疾病： ● 孕产疾病与死亡 ● 性传播感染 ● 结核病 ● 血吸虫病 ● 肠蠕虫 ● 心理障碍	疾病： ● 美洲锥虫病 ● 风湿性心脏病 ● 脊髓灰质炎	疾病： ● 性传播感染 ● 麻风 ● 牙科疾病	疾病： ● 营养失调 ● 疟疾 ● 肠胃炎 ● 急性呼吸道感染
行为：	行为： ● 酗酒 ● 其他物质滥用 ● 伤害	行为：	行为： ● 烟草滥用 ● 酒精与药物滥用 ● 饮食不良 ● 缺乏锻炼 ● 不安全性行为	行为：

更进一步来说，WHO 通过分析世界各地的数据，提出了可能影响青少年的优先健康问题，即故意和非故意伤害、性生殖健康问题（包括艾滋病）、物质使用与滥用（包括烟草和酒精）、心理健康问题、营养问题、地方病和慢性病，这些将在第六、七、八章节中详述。

此外还发现，男女青少年在发病率和死亡率上存在显著不同。就全球而言，男性青少年伤害发生率和死亡率较高，主要由暴力、事故和自杀引起；女性青少年与性行为有关的患病率和死亡率较高。表 2-2 显示了男、女青少年的前十位的死因 [4]。

表 2-2　1999 年世界青少年前十位死因

男	女
1. 道路交通事故	1. 艾滋病
2. 疟疾	2. 孕产患病
3. 下呼吸道感染	3. 疟疾
4. 其他非故意伤害	4. 下呼吸道感染
5. 溺水	5. 结核病
6. 他杀	6. 自杀
7. 自杀	7. 腹泻
8. 艾滋病	8. 道路交通事故
9. 腹泻	9. 火灾
10. 结核病	10. 其他非故意伤害

根据我国 2008 年的统计数据，引起城乡青少年死亡的首要原因是伤害和中毒（城乡发生率分别约为 13×10^{-6}、32×10^{-6}）、大部分由道路交通和其他事故（城市 7×10^{-6}，农村 15×10^{-6}）、溺水（城市 5×10^{-6}，农村 10×10^{-6}）和自杀（城乡发生率分别约为 2×10^{-6}、3×10^{-6}）引起。排在第二位的青少年死因是癌症，城乡发生率均约为 8×10^{-6} [9]。这意味着，非常需要基于家庭和学校的教育和社会心理支持，以预防伤害、中毒、溺水的发生，促进提供姑息护理，这与WHO 在其促进 AHD 策略发展方向 [19] 中所建议的优先领域是交相呼应的。

青少年发展的关注点

在生物生态学理论中，"发展"被定义为人类个体和群体连续的生物心理特征变化现象，此现象呈现于个体生命全程，连续数代，贯穿历史，包括现在和过去。该理论辩称，人类的发展是在不断进行的、越来越复杂的互动过程中发生的，这种互动存在于不断进化的、积极主动的生物心理人类有机体和其他处于邻近社会和物理环境（即近端过程）中的人类个体、物体和符号之间 [22]。家长和教师与青少年的互动属于这种过程类型，青少年通过参与到此类动态过程中而发展能力、动机、知识和技能,从而能够与他人及内在的自己进行互动。由此可见,近端过程(尤其是养育),在青少年从儿童期向成年期过渡的过程中,对塑造发展青少年具有至关重要的作用。

特别需要指出的是,为全面了解青少年阶段,Simpson 进行了广泛的文献回顾以集成现有研究发现和相关行动基础,即抚养青少年,尤其是对家长而言[23]。他提出,青少年需要在此阶段完成十项发展任务,那就是:

1. 适应身体和感觉上的性成熟:面对身体的显著变化(如体格增长、性特征的获得),青少年需要作出调整,学会处理所伴随的生理和性体验,学习健康性行为(如接吻、触摸、爱抚、性交)。此任务还包括建立性别认同、发展恋爱关系的能力。

2. 发展应用抽象思维技能:通常情况下,此阶段的青少年会在思维方式上发生深刻的改变,这使得他们能够更加有效地理解和统筹抽象概念,对所有可能性进行思考,能尝试提出假设,能提前思考或规划,能对思维本身进行思考,并能构建哲学理念。

3. 发展应用更复杂层次的多角度思考:通常情况下,青少年会获得强大的新技能,从而懂得从他人的视角去理解人际关系,还会同时考虑自己和他人的思考角度,并能用这种新技能去解决人际关系问题与人际冲突。

4. 发展应用新的应对技能进行决策、解决问题与处理冲突:面对生理及心理的显著转变,青少年需要发展新的能力去思考和规划未来,需要在决策、解决问题、处理冲突时采取更有教养的策略,还需要对自己的冒险行为作出调整,从而促进而非危害目标的达成。

5. 识别有意义的道德标准、价值观和信仰体系:面对自身的改变和社会的多样化,青少年通常会对道德行为和深层次的正义与关怀原则产生更为复杂的理解。他们开始质疑最初的信仰,学会采用对个人来说更有意义的价值观、政治观、宗教观及信仰体系来指导自己的决策和行为。

6. 理解并表达更复杂的情感体验:随着社会互动和心理变化的增加,青少年或隐或显地会获得识别和传达更复杂情感的能力,能更加有教养地理解他人的情感,并能用抽象的方式思考各种情感。

7. 建立相互支持的、亲密的友谊:与童年期的同伴友谊相比,青少年的同伴友谊具有更强有力的作用。这种友谊一般是由共享兴趣和活动开始,逐步转向分享想法和感受,在此过程中伴随产生对相互的信任和理解。

8. 确立身份认同的关键层面:身份认同的形成是一个终身的过程,尽管如此,那些体现个性化以及与重要人物和团体关联性的关键身份认同都发生在青少年阶段。更重要的是,人们期望青少年建立积极的性别身份认同(即生物性别的社会建构形式)、身体特点、性别、民族等。

9. 满足日益成熟的角色和责任要求：通常是通过精心养育，青少年逐渐学会承担到成年期时被期望承担的角色（这包括为进入劳动力市场而学会获取知识和技能），并满足为家庭、社区及公民义务而恪尽职守的责任期待。

10. 与成人重新商定养育角色：对青少年及其父母而言，青少年阶段是一个在独立自治与亲子关联之间建立平衡的阶段。在平衡构建过程中，文化背景起着至关重要的作用，例如，东亚文化有助于形成集体主义，这种文化对家庭联系的重视超过对独立自主的重视[24]。

健康发展资产

从上述描述不难得出结论：家长、老师和卫生工作者充分认识到青少年的健康发展任务，是实现青少年从童年期向成年期最佳过渡的先决条件。如今已不再是简单地对青少年问题进行命名，或是努力去预防或减少青少年问题的发生，而是更重视对青少年生活中具有积极建设意义的板块进行命名和增量，亦即资产方案[25]。

在卫生相关文献中最早使用"资产"这一概念者可追溯至 Beiser[26]，所关注的是个性和个人资产是管理变革的基础。随着时间的推移，此概念倾向于在个体（尤其是儿童和青少年）、家庭和社区范畴内予以讨论。采用概念分析技术，健康资产被定义为潜力的集合，是个体所拥有的内外部优势特质，既可以是固有的，也可以是获得性的，这些优势特质能够驱动个体采取积极的健康行为，并产生最佳的健康结局[27]。Search Institute[28]（中译名"搜索研究院"）对发展资产方案进行研究，找出了如下建设性板块（即内部资产和外部资产），以帮助青少年健康成长、培养其具有爱心和责任心。**外部资产**包括四个亚类共计 20 项资产，即：

- **支持**
  1. **家庭支持**：家庭生活能提供高水平的爱与支持；
  2. **积极的家庭沟通**：青少年与父母之间积极沟通，青少年愿意听取父母的建议和劝告；
  3. **其他成人关系**：青少年能得到三个或更多的除父母之外的成年人的支持；
  4. **关爱的邻居**：青少年体验到给予关爱的邻里；
  5. **关爱的学校氛围**：学校提供关爱、鼓励的环境；
  6. **家长参与学校教育**：家长积极参与，帮助青少年获得学业成功。
- **授权**
  7. **社区重视青少年**：青少年感觉到在社区中被成年人重视；

8. **青少年被视为资源**：在社区中，青少年被给予有用的角色；

9. **服务他人**：青少年每周为社区服务一小时或更长时间。

- **界线与期望**

10. **安全**：青少年在家里、学校和社区中感觉安全；

11. **家庭界线**：家庭有明确的规范和违规处罚，并监督青少年的行踪；

12. **学校界线**：学校有明确的规范和违规处罚；

13. **邻里界线**：邻里承担监督青少年行为的责任；

14. **成人角色榜样**：父母和其他成人示范出积极负责的行为；

15. **积极的同伴影响**：青少年的好朋友示范出负责任的行为；

16. **高期望**：父母和教师鼓励青少年要做好。

- **建设性地利用时间**

17. **创造性活动**：每周花 3 小时或更多时间在音乐、戏剧及其他艺术课业或练习上；

18. **青年活动**：每周花 3 小时或更多时间在体育运动、俱乐部活动、校内和（或）社区内组织活动上；

19. **在家的时间**：在"没什么特别的事情去做"的情况下，每周与朋友外出不超过两个晚上。

另外四个亚类共计 20 项资产属于**内部资产**，也就是：

- **尽心学习**

20. **成就动机**：有在学校要做出成绩的动机；

21. **学业投入**：青少年积极参与学习；

22. **家庭作业**：每个上学日至少有 1 小时用于家庭作业；

23. **学校纽带**：关心她（他）的学校；

24. **乐于读书**：每周花 3 小时或更多时间读自己喜欢的读物。

- **积极价值观**

25. **关爱**：青少年高度重视帮助他人；

26. **平等与社会公正**：青少年高度重视促进平等、消除饥饿和贫困；

27. **正直**：青少年按照信条行动，积极捍卫自己的信仰；

28. **诚实**：青少年"即便不易也要讲真话"；

29. **责任感**：青少年接受并承担个人责任；

30. **自我约束**：青少年相信性活动不活跃、不饮酒或服用其他药物非常重要。

- **社交能力**

31. **规划与决策**：青少年懂得如何提前规划、做出选择；

32. **人际能力**：青少年具有同情心、敏感度和交友技能；

33.文化能力：青少年知晓并能与不同文化、种族、民族背景的人融洽相处；

34.抵抗力：青少年能抗拒负面同伴压力、应对危险情形；

35.和平消解冲突：青少年寻求非暴力手段解决冲突。

● **积极身份认同**

36.个人能力：青少年感到自己能控制"发生在自己身上的事"；

37.自尊：青少年说自己自尊心强；

38.目的感：青少年说"有自己的生活目的"；

39.积极未来观：青少年对自己的未来很乐观。

显然，结合各种方案（包括预防和减少健康危险行为[29]、增强健康发展资产[27,28]），将更有可能产生理想的 AHD 结局。有研究者[28]开发了具有良好心理测评属性的工具来评估青年资产，这可用于指导设计 AHD 资产建设干预措施。

简言之，没有什么简单的方法去应对各种健康发展问题。对政府而言，采用跨越式的、涉及所有常见 AHD 关注点的方案，可能是最经济有效的方式。WHO 在《阿拉木图宣言》[30]和《渥太华健康促进章程》[31]中分别阐明了相关立场，亦即初级卫生保健方案和健康促进策略，重点应对全球普遍存在的个体健康不平等现象、促进实现"人人享有卫生保健"这一目标，上述几点就构成了 AHD 和青少年友好卫生服务（亦即亲青卫生服务，AFHS）[18]的指导原则，具体内容将在第三章详解。

（蒲林哲，唐永云，臧渝梨）

参 考 文 献

[1] WHO. Strengthening the health sector response to adolescent health and development [EB/OL]. World Health Organization，2010 [2011-6-12]：http：//www.who.int/child_adolescent_health/documents/cah_adh_flyer_2010_12_en.pdf.

[2] Steinberg L. Adolescence[M]. 8th ed. New York：McGraw-Hill，2008.

[3] WHO. The Second decade：improving adolescent health and development[EB/OL]. Department of Child and Adolescent Health and Development，World Health Organization，[2011-06-12]：http：//whqlibdoc.who.int/hq/1998/WHO_FRH_ADH_98.18_Rev.1.pdf.

[4] WHO. Orientation programme on adolescent health for health-care providers[M/OL]. Geneva，Switzerland：World Health Organization，2006[2011-6-14]：http：//whqlibdoc.who.int/publications/2006/9241591269_Handout_eng.pdf.

[5] Rosen JE. Adolescent Health and Development（AHD）：A Resource Guide for

World Bank Operations Staff and Government Counterparts[M/OL]. Washington, Ameica: World Bank, 2004[2011-6-12]: http: //siteresources.worldbank.org/ HEALTHNUTRITIONANDPOPULATION/Resources/281627-1095698140167/Rosen-AHDFinal.pdf.

[6] 吴烨宇. 青年年龄界定研究 [EB/OL]. 中国青年网, 2007-8-27[2009-12-1]: http: //xinli. youth.cn/xygs/phb/200912/t20091201_1095645.htm.

[7] 共产主义青年团. 中国共产主义青年团 [EB/OL]. 中国共产主义青年团, 2005-3-31 [2011-6-17]: http: //en.youth.cn/youth/200911/t20091102_1066307.htm.

[8] 中国共青团. 中国共产主义青年团章程 [EB/OL]. 中国共产主义青年团, 2008-6-13 [2011-6-17]: http: //www.gqt.org.cn/ccylmaterial/regulation/.

[9] 中华人民共和国卫生部. 2010 中国卫生统计年鉴 [EB/OL]. 中华人民共和国卫生部, 2011[2011-5-25]: http: //www.moh.gov.cn/publicfiles/business/htmlfiles/zwgkzt/ptjnj/ year2010/index2010.html.

[10] 中华人民共和国国家统计局. 2010 年第六次全国人口普查主要数据公报（第 1 号） [EB/OL]. 中华人民共和国国家统计局, 2011[2011-5-25]: http: //www.stats.gov.cn/tjgb/ rkpcgb/qgrkpcgb/t20110428_402722232.htm.

[11] 中国青少年研究中心. 当代中国青年人口发展状况研究报告 [EB/OL]. 中国青少年研究中心, 2008[2011-5-19]: http: //www.cycs.org/Article.asp?Category=1&Column=389& ID=7869.

[12] Wikipedia. Migration in the People's Republic of China [EB/OL]. Wikipedia.com, 2011-5-9 [2011-6-19]: http: //en.wikipedia.org/wiki/Migration_in_the_People%27s_Republic_of_China.

[13] 杨丽. 社区流动青少年心理行为健康服务模式研究进展 [J]. 护理研究, 2009, 23 （23）: 2076-2078.

[14] 邓远平, 林赞歌. 流动人口家庭环境特点及其对子女心理健康的影响 [J]. 江西农业大学学报（社会科学版）, 2010, 9（3）: 147-151.

[15] 王志强. 流动人口中青少年犯罪问题的分析 [J]. 青少年犯罪问题, 2003, 5: 33-37.

[16] 武俊青. 中国流动人口的性与生殖健康现况 [J]. 国际生殖健康 / 计划生育杂志, 2010, 29（6）: 414-417, 421.

[17] 张京晶, 李宁秀, 邓奎, 等. 城市流动儿童、青少年健康综合评定及其影响因素分析 [J]. 现代预防医学, 2009, 36: 1689-1691, 1694.

[18] WHO. Adolescent Friendly Health Services: An Agenda for Change [EB/OL]. Geneva, Switzerland: World Health Organization, 2002[2011-7-8]. http: //whqlibdoc.who.int/ hq/2003/WHO_FCH_CAH_02.14.pdf.

[19] WHO. Strategic directions for improving the health and development of children and

adolescents [EB/OL]. World Health Organization，2003 [2011-6-25]：http：//whqlibdoc. who.int/hq/2002/WHO_FCH_CAH_02.21_chi.pdf.

[20] Jones R，Bradley E. Health issues for adolescents [J]. Paediatrics and Child Health，2007，17（11）：433-438

[21] Nicol MJ，Manoharan H，Marfell-Jones MJ，et al. Issues in adolescent health：A challenge for nursing [J]. Contemporary nurse：a journal for the Australian nursing profession，2002，12（2）：155-163.

[22] Bronfenbrenner U. Making human beings human：bioecological perspectives on human development [M]. Thousand Oaks，California：Sage，2005.

[23] Simpson AR. Raising teens：a synthesis of research and foundation for action [M/OL]. Boston，Massachusetts：Harvard School of Public Health，2001[2011-5-11]：http：//www. hsph.harvard.edu/chc/parenting/report.pdf.

[24] Singelis TM，Triandis HC，Bhawuk DPS，et al. Horizontal and vertical dimensions of individualism and collectivism：a theoretical and measurement refinement [J]. Cross-cultural Research，1995，29（3）：240-275.

[25] Scales PC. Reducing risks and building developmental assets：essential Actions for promoting adolescent health [J]. Journal of School Health，1999，69（3）：113-119.

[26] Beiser M. A study of personality assets in a rural community [J]. Archives of General Psychiatry，1971，24（3）：244-254.

[27] Rotegård AK，Moore SM，Fagermoen MS，et al. Health assets：a concept analysis [J]. International Journal of Nursing Studies，2010，47（4）：513-525.

[28] Oman RF，Vesely SK，McLeroy KR，et al. Reliability and validity of the youth asset survey（YAS）[J]. Journal of Adolescent Health，2002，31（3）：247-255.

[29] Rew L，Horner SD. Youth resilience framework for reducing health-risk behaviors in adolescents [J]. Journal of pediatric Nursing，2003，18（6）：379-387.

[30] WHO. Declaration of Alma-Ata [EB/OL]. World Health Organization，1978 [2011-6-21]：http：//www.who.int/hpr/NPH/docs/declaration_almaata.pdf.

[31] WHO. Ottawa Charter for Health Promotion [EB/OL]. World Health Organization，1986 [2011-6-21]：http：//www.who.int/hpr/NPH/docs/ottawa_charter_hp.pdf.

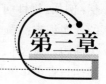

青少年友好卫生服务

10～19岁的青少年在全球总人口中占有很大比例。据估计，该群体在全球的数量已达12亿，是有史以来年轻人最多的一代，其中绝大部分（85%）居住在发展中国家，在某些地区能占到当地人口的1/3还多[1]。在过去几十年里，青少年健康发展谱系发生了巨大的变化，传统的卫生服务供给模式已不能满足青少年对健康和发展的需求，这驱动WHO领导和倡议实施青少年友好卫生服务（adolescent friendly health service，AFHS），或称"亲青卫生服务"[2]。

本章主要介绍亲青卫生服务的背景及其深层次的指导原则，再阐述其具体特征，之后引出优化青少年卫生服务的策略与做法。本章最后是要点检查，您可用此来评估自己对亲青卫生服务的理解。

第1节　亲青卫生服务的背景

在相当长的时间里，人们都想当然地认为青少年一般都很健康，之所以这样说，是因为青少年比儿童和老年人患急慢性疾病较少，而这一年龄段（10～19岁）人群的死亡率也较低[2, 3]。但实际上，如今的青少年面临着他们的父母不曾面对过的更多风险和更复杂挑战，他们的青春期有所提前，但结婚又相对较晚，造成婚前性成熟时间的延长[1]。

青少年的脆弱性

在青少年中期（大约14～17岁），大脑仍然处在发育阶段，也就是说，出现与青春期激素（如雌激素和雄激素）水平以及社会和物理环境相适应的精细功能重建，主要表现在对情感、思想和行为的控制能力增强[4-6]。在不成熟阶段，青少年更容易被危险的诱惑或短暂的快感所影响，在没有认真考虑眼前和远期后果时就做出是否参与的判断，导致健康危险行为的发生[6, 7]。

特别需要指出的是，慢性病与青少年生长发育存在交互作用，加剧患病青少年的脆弱性。这些慢性病包括非传染性疾病，例如哮喘、癫痫、囊性纤维化、儿童型糖尿病和血红蛋白疾病（如镰刀细胞病）[3,8,9]。这种交互作用包括：例如，慢性病可能引起青春期发育延迟，而生长激素可以影响糖尿病患者的代谢调控；另一方面，青少年的心理社会发展状况可能引起遵医不良或行为问题。表 3-1 所显示的是 Suris 等 [9] 在广泛文献回顾基础上总结出来的慢性病与青少年生长发育交互作用效应。

表 3-1　青少年生长发育与慢性病的交互效应

慢性病对青少年生长发育的影响	青少年生长发育对慢性病的影响
生物效应	**生物效应**
青春期发育延迟或受损	生长发育需要的能量增加，可能会对患病状况造成负面影响
体格矮小	青春期激素可能影响患病状况（如，生长激素影响糖尿病的代谢调控）
骨量增加程度下降	
心理社会效应	**遵医不良，疾病控制不佳，原因有：**
幼化现象	抽象思维和规划能力不良（运用抽象概念进行规划和做准备的能力下降）
采纳病态角色身份认同	展望未来存在困难，自我概念是"防弹型"
自我中心持续至晚期青少年阶段	拒绝接受专业卫生人员，把这作为脱离父母的一部分内容
性感觉与自我吸引力的发展受损	探索性（冒险）行为
认知功能和信息加工能力受损	
社交性	**伴随健康危险行为**
在该独立的时候独立性下降	混乱的饮食习惯可能导致营养不良
同伴关系和亲密（伴侣）关系失败	吸烟，饮酒和药物使用往往高于正常人群发生率
社会疏离	危险性行为，可能是预见到有限的生命周期临近
教育、就业、独立生活能力的发展失败	

发育心理学家常用"居住环境"这一术语，它是指包括家庭、社区和更广泛社会环境在内的生态体系。这种居住环境对塑造青少年的发展、缓冲外部负面影响、强化青少年应对健康威胁（如危险行为、急慢性或致死性疾病）的能力具有至关重要的作用。如果卫生服务不能帮助青少年克服前述的那些脆弱性，青少年就更可能出现更多健康问题，尤其是与性活动相关的健康问题诸如怀孕、流产和性传播性感染（sexually transmitted infections, STIs）[10-13]。

如图 3-1 所示的青年弹力概念框架，既强调了降低健康风险的方案，也强调了增加保护性资产的方案 [14]，该概念框架是在生物生态人类发展论 [15]、发展资产论 [16,17] 和积极青年发展论 [18] 基础上发展起来的，这些理论均强调内外部因素对健康的影响，还强调青少年可以获得的资源（或资产）以应对健康威胁,同时完成身体、心理和性方面的发展任务。然而,传统教育和卫生服务体系习惯于强调降低风险或预防问题发生这一方案,对加强适应性培养、促进积极发展(或被称作强项方案)不够重视[19]。

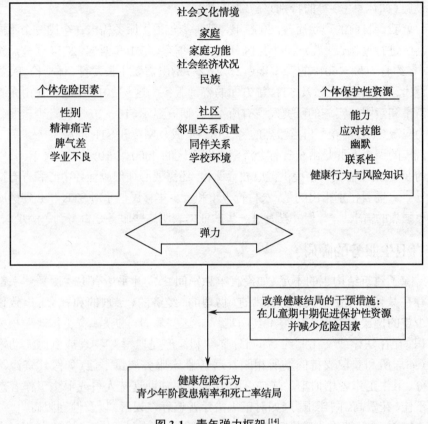

图 3-1　青年弹力框架[14]

　　一般来说,一切关键需求(包括诸如居所、食物、饮水)都必须得到满足,这是实现从儿童期向成年期全方位过渡的先决条件[8, 9],对于患有慢性病的青少年(包括残障青少年)来说更是如此[20, 21]。对于挣扎在生存线上的青少年而言,要想茁壮成长非常困难。青少年需要发展各种才干和技能(包括学术、社交、情商、职业能力和文化能力等),从而为就业和成年生活做好准备。更重要的是,青少年要有机会参加有意义的活动,要有发言权,要对自己的行为负责,还要积极参与公民活动,在此过程中达到对家庭、社区、国家和文化的归属感,实现茁壮成长[22]。前述这些迥异的宽泛需求激发了人们对积极青年发展项目的倡议,尤其是面向患有慢性病青少年的积极青年发展项目[19]。

　　积极青年发展方案受到的关注日益增多,这主要是因为该方案强调强项或实力建设,包括住院和慢性病管理对青少年各方面生活影响的敏感反应,最新的临床改革和研究发现也支持这种强项方案,反映了临床青少年护理的根本性演化 [19-23]。对于住院青少年,过去通常是被安置在儿科或成人病房,他们实际上需要单独的青少年病区,以满足他们对物理环境、员工态度和条件设施(如休息室)等的特别兴趣需求 [24]。

就我国目前的现状而言,2006 年曾就青少年卫生服务需求在全国三个不同的县区进行过调查 [25],这三个县区分别代表华东、华中和西部,2734 名被调查者中,约有 50%～60% 的青少年(12～22 岁)指出需要生长发育、体格检查、生殖健康、性器官卫生以及 STIs 等方面的咨询服务。这与 2010 年 8 月在山东省临沂市和蒙阴县实施的研究发现有所不同,研究显示,10～20 岁的青少年面临压力应激(主要由竞争日益激烈的考试体系造成)、网瘾和 STIs 的威胁 [26]。另一大规模的调查人群是山东省省会济南市四个区的 4000 名 10～24 岁青年,其中大约 80% 指出需要学校提供健康教育课程,还需要心理健康辅导中心和青春期指导 [27]。需要特别指出的是,农村青少年和青少年移民似乎对 STIs 和心理健康有更强烈的需求 [28-30],但并没有进一步的证据表明这些服务是否得到了满足。

亲青卫生服务的障碍

除了建筑结构上的不足(如没有单独空间)[31],几乎所有卫生服务体系都还存在其他诸多阻碍因素,法律的、物理的、经济的、心理的和社会的,致使青少年的健康与发展需求得不到满足 [24]。这些障碍可能是:青少年缺乏相关知识、存在法律或文化制约(如婚外怀孕和流产是耻辱)、物理或资源流动限制(如居所和获取支持的场所相距甚远)、临床服务质量不佳(如医疗资源不充分、卫生工作者培训不足或缺乏动力)、医院辅助支持人员或卫生工作者态度不佳、花费高、同伴压力(如对正规治疗普遍存在误解)以及性别阻碍 [3]。

WHO 在认清上述形势后启动了一系列活动,其中包括论证有必要加强对青少年健康与发展的关注,这些活动促成了对亲青卫生服务的倡议。这种服务理念的提出是基于:为了青少年个体今后和后代的福祉;降低青少年的患病和死亡是政府和家庭不可或缺的责任;就不断改善青少年的健康和发展进行投资肯定有助于保护人力资本、降低晚年疾病负担,这是因为,大多数老年慢性疾病都与青少年阶段发展起来的行为和生活方式有关 [2]。一如惯例,WHO 坚决拥护联合国儿童权利公约中的儿童权利立场声明,公约第 24 条明确指出,生存、发展、达到最高健康水准、获得疾病治疗和康复设施是儿童和青少年的基本权利 [32]。

自 1989 年哥斯达黎加实施全国青少年健康项目以来,许多发展中国家都成功实施了亲青卫生服务。自 2000 年起,WHO 开始加强倡导亲青卫生服务,重要标志之一就是 2001 年 3 月在日内瓦组织召开的亲青卫生服务全球咨询会议 [2, 33]。已经认清的是,提供亲青卫生服务并非是要设立单独的服务机构，而是要在当地社区综合卫生服务场所内予以实施，通过提高卫生工作者的能力，促进有效应对青少年需求，这才是最大的亲青卫生服务受益之道。

自建国以来我国就非常重视青少年，青少年总是被视为最积极的社会力量，代表着社会的未来。20 世纪 80 年代改革开放以来，青少年所面临的健康与发展风险、压力和其他威胁等日趋增加，远远超过起前几代人所经历的[28]。尽管如此，几乎没有什么资料表明亲青卫生服务已经在我国开展，而"亲青卫生服务"这一术语（包括其英文缩略语 AFHS）对卫生工作者包括护士来说都显陌生。以该术语的全名及其英文缩略语为关键词在各类中文数据库（如 CNKI）检索，未见相关文献，说明迫切需要将亲青卫生服务融入医学、护理及其他卫生专业课程体系或培训项目中，以加强我国的青少年卫生服务。

优先健康与发展领域

青少年和卫生规划者对青少年健康的关注优先顺序有所不同：对卫生规划者来说，他们比较关心 STIs、意外伤害、心理问题、青少年过早怀孕和血吸虫病；与此不同，青少年更关心人际关系、外貌、有无打架斗殴、学业和考试压力、可否获得避孕和孕期服务[3]。适宜的政策对青少年的健康和未来大有裨益，但这种不一致性可能会影响适宜政策的制定和政策的完善。

WHO[34] 针对青少年和卫生规划者所有可能的关注点，提出如下优先领域，促进开展一致性的干预：

a）促进健康发展和健康生活方式，包括适当饮食、规律锻炼、保持良好口腔卫生、推迟初次性交；

b）预防健康危险行为，如吸烟、饮酒和其他物质滥用、无保护性行为；

c）推迟结婚和生育年龄；

d）获取适宜 AFHS，涉及计划生育、妊娠、生育、预防和治疗 STIs（包括 HIV/AIDS）和其他传染病、营养缺乏、伤害和心理问题；

e）获取健康辅导服务，包括 HIV 检测和咨询；

f）提高成年人的实力，包括家庭中的成人，从而能够关爱青少年，建立负责任的关系；

g）促进健康校园环境建设，使之有利于青少年的生理和心理健康；

h）使青少年有机会与同伴发展健康关系；

i）使青少年有机会参与或帮助社区实施亲社会活动；

j）使青少年有机会在健康校园环境中继续接受教育或职业培训；

k）保护青少年使之免于经受有危险的分娩；

l）保护青少年使之免受有害文化传统的伤害，如女性生殖器毁损、未达到生理和社会成熟之前结婚。

上述这些策略方向反映了严重影响青少年生活、需要优先考虑解决的健康问题，也留意到青少年所处的情景，以有利于创设满意的支持性社会环境。为鼓励和引导社会变革，WHO 特别提出如下需优先考虑的健康问题：故意和非故意伤害、性生殖健康问题（包括 HIV/AIDS）、物质使用和滥用（包括吸烟、饮酒）、心理问题、营养问题、地方病与慢性疾病[3]。亲青卫生服务不仅要解决这些问题，还要更关注发展适合青少年的整套基本服务，并且要行之有效、能够获得、能够支付得起，还能被当地社会所接受[2, 3]。

第 2 节　亲青卫生服务的特征

亲青卫生服务代表了一种服务方案，它将青少年对质量的需求与最佳公共卫生服务体系必须达到的最高服务标准结合在一起[3]。若要被视作亲青，服务必须具有 EAAAE 特征，EAAAE 是如下五个英文关键词的首字母缩写[1]：

- **平等**（equitable），意思是，所有青少年（而非仅有某特定群体）都能获得所需要的卫生服务；
- **可及**（accessible），意思是，青少年能够获得所提供的卫生服务；
- **可接受**（acceptable），意思是，提供的卫生服务方式能够满足青少年的需求；
- **适宜**（appropriate），意思是，提供青少年所需要的各种卫生服务；
- **有效**（effective），意思是，采用正确的方式提供正确的卫生服务，有助于青少年健康与发展[1]。

亲青卫生服务的特征

亲青卫生服务有三个指导原则：第一、关注到不平等，促进对人权的尊重、保护和实现；第二、采取生命全程观，认识到人从出生到儿童期、从青少年阶段到成年期是一个连续变化体；第三、实施公共卫生服务方案，关注那些威胁人群整体的主要健康问题，运用系统发展模式以确保获得有效的、相关的干预措施去解决这些问题[34]。

在 WHO 领导下，2000 年 10 月在非洲首次对 AFHS 进行了公开讨论，随后于 2001 年 3 月在日内瓦进行 AFHS 全球咨询会。在此期间达成了一致共识，亦即青少年有权获得卫生服务，这些卫生服务可使其免受健康威胁，同时，这些服务要具有亲青性，要与当地需求相适应，需要考虑花费、流行病学因素以及青少年的优先发展领域[2, 3]。

首个完全版的 AFHS 特征涉及政策、服务程序、卫生工作者、卫生辅助支持人员、服务设施设备、青少年参与性以及社区导向的服务发展和服务有效性[3]。随着时间推移，AFHS 各项特征得到进一步讨论，才形成了上述五个宽泛的质量维度，即 EAAAE（见表 3-2）。

表 3-2　亲青卫生服务特征[1]

特征	内涵界定
（一）平等：所有青少年（不止是某些特定群体）均能获得所需要的卫生服务	
政策和程序到位，无条件提供卫生服务	没有因年龄、性别、社会地位、文化背景、民族、残障或其他差别而限制向青少年提供卫生服务的政策或程序
卫生工作者平等对待、关心和尊重所有青少年	卫生工作者对所有青少年给予同样的关心和考虑，不因年龄、性别、社会地位、文化背景、民族、残障或其他因素而区别对待
卫生辅助支持人员平等对待、关心和尊重所有青少年，不论地位如何	卫生辅助支持人员对所有青少年给予同样的关心和考虑，不因年龄、性别、社会地位、文化背景、民族、残障或其他因素而区别对待
（二）可及：青少年能够获得所提供的卫生服务	
政策和程序到位，确保青少年卫生服务是免费或是可以支付得起的	所有青少年都能得到免费卫生服务，或能支付得起必须支付的费用
提供服务的场所在便利时间运行	卫生服务能够在便利的时间段提供
青少年知悉可以获得的生殖健康服务范围以及如何获取这些服务	青少年能够意识到所提供的卫生服务以及在哪里提供、如何获得
社区成员理解青少年获得所需卫生服务的益处，并支持提供这些服务	社区成员（包括家长）知悉卫生服务怎样供给后将有助于帮助青少年，他们会支持供给这些服务，并支持青少年使用这些服务
所选社区成员、延伸服务人员以及青少年自己在社区提供某些卫生服务和卫生相关用品	根据所处情形、延伸服务人员情况、所选社区成员（如体育教练）以及青少年自己的情况，通过各种努力在距离青少年近便的地方提供卫生服务
（三）可接受：卫生服务的提供方式能满足青少年服务对象的需求	
政策和程序到位，确保服务对象保密性	政策和程序到位，在任何时候为青少年保密（除非员工有法律义务向有关权威机构汇报服务对象情况，例如性侵犯、道路交通意外、枪击事件）。这涉及： ● 登记：保密状态下采集青少年身份信息、就诊问题； ● 就诊：在青少年就诊卫生服务场所全程（就诊之前、之中和之后）都要保密； ● 记录：在安全的地方保存个案记录，仅授权接触； ● 信息披露：未经青少年个人允许，工作人员不得向第三方（如家庭成员、学校老师或员工）泄露他所得到的信息

续表

特征	内涵界定
卫生服务供给场所确保私密	卫生服务供给场所建立在能确保青少年可私密使用的地方，要有指定的设计标识确保青少年就诊全程的私密性，这包括入口处、接待区、等候区、检查区和患者记录保存区
卫生工作者要具有非评判性、考虑周全、容易接近	卫生工作者不要批评青少年患者，即使他们不赞成这些患者所说所做，他们也要为青少年考虑周全，并能以友好的态度靠近他们
卫生服务场所要确保就诊等候时间短暂，不论有无预约，并且要在需要时快速转诊	青少年能在通知后短时间内见到卫生工作者就诊，不论是否正式预约，如果因健康情况需要转诊他处，转诊预约也要在短时间内进行
卫生服务场所清洁、吸引人	卫生服务场所要友好、清洁，有吸引力
卫生服务场所要运用多种手段提供信息和健康教育	要以不同的方式（如海报、手册、单页）提供青少年健康相关信息，要用青少年所熟悉的语言准备资料，要易于理解，要能吸引其注意力
青少年积极参与到卫生服务的设计、评估与供给中	向青少年提供机会使其能分享获取卫生服务的体验，表达需求和喜好，要将其纳入某些适宜的卫生服务供给层面

（四）适宜：提供青少年所需的卫生服务

在卫生服务场所或转诊机构提供所需的整套卫生服务，以满足所有青少年的需要	卫生服务场所或转诊机构所提供的服务要涵盖所有青少年的健康问题和需求，所提供的服务能够满足主流和边缘青少年群体的特殊需要

（五）有效：正确提供正确的卫生服务，对健康产生积极影响

卫生工作者要具备为青少年工作的能力，提供他们所需要的卫生服务	卫生工作者具备为青少年工作、为青少年提供卫生服务所需要的知识和技能
卫生工作者利用有科学依据的处置方案和指南提供卫生服务	卫生服务供给要依据技术科学、证明有效的处置方案和指南，较为理想的是，这些方案和指南还要根据临床状况作出调整，并得到相关权威机构的批准
卫生工作者能够尽职尽责，确保有足够的时间为青少年服务对象有效地工作	卫生工作者能够尽职尽责，确保有足够的时间为青少年服务对象有效地工作
卫生服务场所有相应仪器设施设备以提供所需要的服务	每个卫生服务场所都要有必要的仪器设施设备（包括药品和基础服务如水、清洁设备）以提供所需的卫生服务

这些 AFHS 特征清晰地反映了 WHO 在加强卫生服务体系上所做的努力，涉及卫生服务体系的六大基本元素，亦即卫生供给、卫生人力、信息、医用品以及疫苗和技术、财务、领导力与管理或公务，强调初级卫生保健方针

方案[35, 36]。初级卫生保健指的是在人们工作或生活的地方提供基本医疗服务[36, 37]。以上述 AFHS 特征为基础,已经开发了一系列质量评估工具,以帮助评价青少年卫生质量,促进识别需要改进的弱项,这些工具可分别供青少年服务对象、卫生工作者、卫生辅助支持人员、管理者、延伸服务人员和社区成员使用[1],标志着 AFHS 已经由关注理论和政策转向关注实践变革和质量保障。

我国地域辽阔,人口众多,再虑及 AFHS 的宽泛性,改变我国现有的卫生服务体系还需要相当长的时间。2010 年 3 月,国家五部门(亦即国家人口计划生育委员会、教育部、中国扶贫开发协会、中国科学技术协会,中国计划生育协会)在全国选了八个试点地区联合展开行动,促进青少年健全人格发展,包括生理和社会心理[38]。尽管在我国尚没有整套的青少年基本卫生服务,这五部门的行动反映了我国在促进青少年发展上所作的跨部门努力,而这还需要卫生部的参与才能使服务具有亲青性。

AFHS 基本服务

最初提议包括以下基本临床服务[2],后来出现争议,指出这些基本服务不应该是固定不变的,需要与当地的需求相适应。

- 一般卫生服务涵盖结核病、疟疾、地方病、伤害、事故及牙齿保健;
- 生殖健康服务包括避孕、治疗 STI、孕期保健和流产后管理;
- 提供 HIV 检测和咨询,采取保密和自愿原则;
- 性暴力的管理;
- 心理卫生服务,包括吸烟、饮酒和滥用药物;
- 提供信息和辅导,涉及青少年阶段的发展、生殖健康、营养、卫生、性与物质滥用。

通过区域性咨询,WHO 泛美地区办公室提出如下促进青少年健康与发展的整套核心服务,具体包括[3]:

- 监测生长发育;
- 识别和评估问题行为,如果可能就要进行管理,不能管理时要转诊;
- 提供信息和辅导,涉及青少年阶段的发展变化、个人保健以及寻求帮助的方式;
- 提供免疫,如,接种风疹疫苗、流脑疫苗、肝炎疫苗和破伤风疫苗。

很显然,没有什么简单的答案可以回答整套的青少年核心卫生服务究竟包括哪些服务内容,尽管如此,为青少年提供的服务必须能满足该特殊年龄群体的需要和希望。卫生服务只有在具备如下特征时才会有助于青少年的发展:①治疗可能致病的健康问题或青少年所关注的健康问题;②防治或对那些可能致残、引起死亡或发展为慢性病的健康问题做出反应；③进行生长发育监测，重视青少年所关注的问题，为那些追求良好健康的青少年提供支持；④当青少年为寻求摆脱健康问题而有所关注时，或在危机时刻与其互动；⑤与其他可能为青少年提供支持服务（如咨询服务）的机构建立联系[3]。在发展整套的青少年卫生服务时，上述这些都需要考虑到。

第3节　优化青少年卫生服务

亲青卫生服务，包括预防性、促进性的治疗和康复服务，都可以在医院或卫生服务中心、学校或社区场所中提供。亲青卫生服务可以从顶层开始规划，或是由一群敬业的卫生专业人员来启动，这些卫生专业人员能洞察到青少年的需求还没有得到满足，并且坚信所提供的服务还可以更加切实有效。下面提供一些示例，主要是来自 WHO 的青少年导向项目（Orientation Program）中的亲青卫生服务模块[3]，为在我国各种可能的场所（包括诸如青少年中心、青苹果之家）采取有关行动提供借鉴。

在卫生服务中心或医院的服务

最基本的卫生服务在当地社区普通的卫生服务中心即可提供，没什么理由不满足许多青少年的需求。很重要的一项任务就是培训和支持这些机构中的员工，改善其技能，促进其发展同理心，从而使青少年更愿意前往就诊。可在员工取得资质后继续进行常规培训，或是通过运用系统化的临床方案和指南，辅以同行专家评估和质量监督与管理，使这些技能得以持久发展。可在正常营业时间之外提供特别时段服务，或辟出单独的青少年入口、抑或在机构内加强保密，从而促进改善私密性。很多医院都有专门的青少年服务，在门诊部或主楼某个区域开辟青少年门诊。基于医院的服务通常都有专科人员在现场服务，能够提供全面的医疗服务，但这些服务可能仅限于处于中心位置的人群，也可能因经费不足而使发展受到限制。

也有一些专门的卫生服务中心可以提供全方位的服务，尤其是针对青少年的服务。这些中心可能分布在城市或较大的乡镇，那里的成本效益相对较好，或是由非政府组织（non-governmental organizations，NGOs）运营作为"导航服务"以展示他们能做什么。这样的服务中心可以提供培训，对卫生工作人员也有启发作用，只不过，这些工作通常只是在某个地区产生作用，并且由于经费限制，这些服务不可能在主流服务体系中被复制再现。

其他各类中心的服务

有些青少年不愿去卫生机构，那么，他们所需要的服务可以在那些青少年原本就要去的地方予以提供。我国有很多青少年活动中心，在过去是非常受青少年欢迎的去处，假期或业余时间可以参加课外活动。自去年开始，为帮助青少年发展健全人格，我国政府开始建设青苹果之家，开展文化欣赏、同伴指导、养育培训、健康辅导或是象棋、唱歌、书法、陶艺等艺术活动[39]。与青少年活动中心相比，青苹果之家的服务更多地将青少年作为完整的人类个体来关注其行为、社会、心理和性的发展，这提示，如果这些服务能够朝着亲青方向发展，在不久的将来可能会更加吸引青少年。

在青少年活动中心或社区卫生服务中心，可专门开设门诊，由护士或医生坐诊，同伴教育者可帮助青少年与有关卫生机构或社会支持机构取得联系。这些中心的优势在于，他们原本就已经为青少年所用，青少年并不需要特别费力非要去什么地方接受卫生服务，但缺点可能在于，某个特定的中心可能只吸引一部分青少年去使用，可能主要是男孩、女孩或是某特定年龄段的人群。

延伸服务

无论在城市还是在农村，都需要在医院和卫生中心之外的地方提供服务，将服务延伸到那些不可能来医院或卫生中心就诊的青少年，由购物中心、社区或青少年活动中心所提供的城乡服务在不断增加。

有些国家在互联网上推广服务来吸引那些有机会使用电脑的青少年。偏远乡村的青少年经常被排除在常规卫生服务之外，当地卫生服务机构的卫生工作人员可以通过流动设施送服务到乡村，大面积覆盖所及区域的青少年。可以在村民聚会的地方提供服务，包括进行疾病筛查和免疫接种，对于那些需要更进一步治疗或指导的村民，可以单独提供随访服务。出诊的卫生工作人员也可与青少年进行健康教育式的对话或提供面向青少年的健康教育资料。

有些"漏网"的青少年也需要延伸服务，尽管从地理位置上看，他们附近已有卫生服务机构。街头青少年（或称流浪青少年）可能会发现获取主流服务很有难度，但他们会对针对这一脆弱群体的服务做出反应。这些延伸服务可在诊所里运行，或是由非政府组织提供，一旦与那些游离于体系之外的青少年建立联系，更重要的就是找到某种办法在延伸服务和主流服务之间建立联系。

校园卫生服务

学校是青少年接受健康教育和卫生服务的自然入口，而校园则是进行健康教育、卫生指导、疾病筛查、常见病诊疗以及常规之外的更多免疫接种（如，我国 2009 年推出的 15 岁及以下儿童青少年的乙肝疫苗接种）的理想场所。但在现实生活中，很少有人认识到校园的这种潜力。学校通常是缺乏资源的，而教师既没有接受过相关健康教育培训，也未把提供健康教育作为重要的工作内容,要转变这种局面就需要对学校员工进行有效的培训,培养其积极性和相关技能,可能还需要外界支持以便提供性教育课程。也有些成功的做法是培训青少年成为校园同伴教育者,就像在延伸服务部分所提到的,一定要在校园卫生服务与当地的主流卫生服务之间建立联系,只有这样,那些需要随访服务的学生才能得到所需要的服务,但并不需要重复劳动。

同样重要的是,要确保校园服务得到社区的支持。许多学校负责人担心自己会因向青少年提供服务受到抨击,因此,学校和社区都需要做出努力,确保这种由学校提供卫生服务的转变能够得到支持。有证据表明,学生家长欢迎负责任的成年人就某些敏感的话题跟自己的子女交流对话,因为他们觉得自己在家里解决不了这些问题。

工作场所卫生服务

单位负责人和工会组织通常都会对有助于使劳动力保持健康的服务感兴趣,而很多工厂或作坊中许多员工都是青少年。有些国家在工作场所已经成功实施过艾滋病同伴教育,而在另外一些国家,国家劳工部通常会在上班聚会的场所提供延伸服务项目,也在工厂内为年轻女员工提供健康教育项目以满足其生殖健康需求,当然,这些国家的劳工部也为占有相当比例的女员工提供一般技能培训课程。

需要特别指出的是,护士因其所受的教育、数量规模和实践场所的多样化,对于促进青少年达到最高限度的健康和发展水平肯定会有所贡献。因此,为真正实施亲青卫生服务,非常有必要将青少年健康发展相关内容整合到护理课程中,已有许多国家(包括我国在内)就这种内容整合活动进行过探索[40-44]。尽管如此,要使护士真正承担起在任何工作场所都能为青少年提供卫生服务的角色责任,还有很长一段路要走,这主要是因为,在传统观念里,人们对护士和护理工作的理解仍然比较狭隘。

第4节 练 习

您可利用以下各要点检查图(图3-2～图3-4)来进行自我评估,以了解您对 AFHS 的知晓程度[3]。

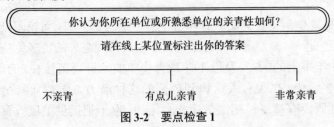

你认为你所在单位或所熟悉单位的亲青性如何?

请在线上某位置标注出你的答案

不亲青   有点儿亲青   非常亲青

图 3-2 要点检查 1

青少年经常不能很好地利用可以获得的卫生服务
是因为……

请勾选最主要的原因

……他们期望员工告知家长

……他们不喜欢等候或填表

……他们不感兴趣

……他们不了解疾病

……他们想把钱用在别的地方

……他们不喜欢卫生工作者对待他们的方式

……他们不想引起他人的注意

……他们觉得与朋友交谈比与卫生保健工作人员交谈容易

……他们不知道到哪里去

图 3-3 要点检查 2

亲青卫生服务最重要的特征是什么?

请填写如下空格

图 3-4 要点检查 3

（李云峰，刘晓燕，臧渝梨）

参 考 文 献

[1] WHO. Quality assessment guidebook: a guide to assessing health services for adolescent [M/OL]. Geneva, Switzerland: World Health Organization, 2009[2011-7-8]: http://whqlibdoc.who.int/publications/2009/9789241598859_eng.pdf.

[2] WHO. Adolescent friendly health services: an agenda for change [EB/OL]. World Health Organization, 2002[2011-7-8]: http://whqlibdoc.who.int/hq/2003/WHO_FCH_CAH_02.14.pdf.

[3] WHO. Orientation programme on adolescent health for health-care providers [M/OL]. Geneva, Switzerland: World Health Organization, 2006[2011-6-14]: http://whqlibdoc.who.int/publications/2006/9241591269_Handout_eng.pdf.

[4] Nelson EE, Leibenluft E, Mcclure EB, et al. The social re-orientation of adolescence: a neuroscience perspective on the process and its relation to psychopathology [J]. Psychological Medicine, 2005, 35(2): 163-174.

[5] Steinberg L. Cognitive and affective development in adolescence [J]. Trends in Cognitive Sciences, 2005, 9(2): 69-74.

[6] Steinberg L. Adolescence [M]. 8th ed. New York: McGraw-Hill, 2008.

[7] Keeler HJ, Kaiser MM. An integrative model of adolescent health risk behavior [J]. Journal of Pediatric Nursing, 2010, 25(2): 126-137.

[8] Michaud P, Suris J, Viner R. The adolescent with a chronic condition. Part II: healthcare provision [J]. Arch Dis Child, 2004, 89(10): 943-949.

[9] Suris J-C, Michaud P-A, Viner R. The adolescent with a chronic condition. Part I: developmental issues [J]. Archives of Disease in Childhood, 2004, 89(10): 938-942.

[10] Gavin LE, Catalano RF, David-Ferdon C, et al. A review of positive youth development programs that promote adolescent sexual and reproductive health [J]. Journal of Adolescent Health, 2010, 46(3, Suppl1): S75-S91.

[11] Jones R, Bradley E. Health issues for adolescents [J]. Pediatrics and Child Health, 2007, 17(11): 433-438.

[12] Nicol MJ, Manoharan H, Marfell-Jones MJ, et al. Issues in adolescent health: a challenge for nursing [J]. Contemporary Nurse: a journal for the Australian nursing profession, 2002, 12(2): 155-163.

[13] Surís J-C, Resnick MD, Cassuto N, et al. Sexual behavior of adolescents with chronic disease and disability [J]. Journal of Adolescent Health, 1996, 19(2): 124-131.

[14] Rew L, Horner SD. Youth resilience framework for reducing health-risk behaviors in adolescents [J]. Journal of pediatric Nursing, 2003, 18(6): 379-387.

[15] Bronfenbrenner U. Making human beings human: bioecological perspectives on human development [M]. Thousand Oaks, California: Sage, 2005.

[16] Oman RF, Vesely SK, McLeroy KR, et al. Reliability and validity of the youth asset survey(YAS)[J]. Journal of Adolescent Health, 2002, 31(3): 247-255.

[17] Scales PC. Reducing risks and building developmental assets: essential actions for promoting adolescent health [J]. Journal of School Health, 1999, 69(3): 113-119.

[18] Guerra NG, Bradshaw CP. Linking the prevention of problem behaviors and positive youth development: Core competencies for positive youth development and risk prevention [J]. New Directions for Child and Adolescent Development, 2008, 2008(122): 1-17.

[19] Chung RJ, Burke PJ, Goodman E. Firm foundations: strength-based approaches to adolescent chronic disease [J]. Current Opinion in Pediatrics, 2010, 22(4): 389-397 10.1097 /MOP.0b013e32833a468e.

[20] SAM. Transition to adult health care for adolescents and young adults with chronic conditions [J]. Journal of Adolescent Health, 2003, 33(4): 309-311.

[21] Wang G, McGrath BB, Watts C. Health care transitions among youth with disabilities or special healthcare needs: an ecological approach [J]. Journal of Pediatric Nursing, 2010, 25(6): 505-550.

[22] Dotterweich J. Positive Youth Development Resource Manual [M/OL]. New York: Cornell University, Family Life Development Center, 2006[2011-7-5]: http://ecommons.cornell. edu/bitstream/1813/21946/2/PYD_ResourceManual.pdf.

[23] CPS. Issues of care for hospitalized youth [J]. Pediatric Child Health, 2008, 13(1): 61-64.

[24] Smith S. Adolescent units--an evidence-based approach to quality nursing in adolescent care [J]. European Journal of Oncology Nursing, 2004, 8(1): 20-29.

[25] 狄江丽, 巫琦, 王林虹, 等. 青少年对青少年保健门诊服务内容的需求调查 [J]. 中国妇幼健康研究, 2008, 19(4): 319-321.

[26] Hutton A, Grant J. Expanding the role of nurses for a rapidly urbanising China [J/OL]. RCNAreport: nursing news, views & attitudes, 2011: http://www.apnedmedia.com.au/ email/rcna-report-feb-11-web-ready.pdf.

[27] 许俐, 宫露霞, 张淑平, 等. 青少年对生殖健康服务的需求和相关因素调查分析 [J]. 中国妇女和儿童健康研究杂志 2006, 21(1): 93-95.

[28] CYCRC. China Youth Development Report [EB/OL]. China Youth and Children Studies, 2008[2011-5-19]: http://www.cycs.org/Article.asp?Category=1&Column=389& ID=7869.

[29] 胡晓江, Cook S, Salazar MA. 中国流动人口的健康问题 [EB/OL]. 2008[2011-7-9]: http://www.old.bjmu.edu.cn/extra/col19/1225161485.pdf.

[30] 巫琦, 狄江丽, 吴久玲, 等. 农村青少年身心健康卫生保健服务需求调查 [J]. 中国公共卫生 2007, 23（11）: 1334-1336.

[31] Smith S. Adolescent units--an evidence-based approach to quality nursing in adolescent care[J]. European Journal of Oncology Nursing，2004，8（1）: 20-29.

[32] UN. Convention on the Rights of the Child [EB/OL]. Office of the United Nations High Commissioner for Human Rights, 1990[2011-7-8]: http: //www2.ohchr.org/english/law/crc.htm.

[33] WHO. Global Consultant on Adolescent Friendly Health Services: A Consensus Statement [EB/OL]. World Health Organization，2001[2011-7-8]: http: //www.who.int/child_adolescent_health/documents/pdfs/who_fch_cah_02.18.pdf.

[34] WHO. Strategic Directions for Improving the Health and Development of Children and Adolescents [EB/OL]. World Health Organization，2003[2011-7-25]: http: //whqlibdoc.who.int/publications/2003/9241591064.pdf.

[35] WHO. Strengthening Health Systems to Improve Health Outcomes: WHO's Framework for Action [EB/OL]. World Health Organization，2007[2011-7-8]: http: //www.who.int/healthsystems/strategy/everybodys_business.pdf.

[36] WHO. The World Health Report 2008 - Primary Health Care（Now More Than Ever）[M/OL]. Geneva，Switzerland: World Health Organization，2008[2011-7-25]: http: //www.who.int/whr/2008/en/index.html.

[37] WHO. Declaration of Alma-Ata [EB/OL]. World Health Organization，1978[2011-6-21]: http: //www.who.int/hpr/NPH/docs/declaration_almaata.pdf.

[38] NPFPC，MoE，CAPAD，CAST & CFPA. Notice to Implement Healthy Personality Program [EB/OL]. 2010[2011-7-25]: http: //www.hxshdy.com/gwgg/518.html.

[39] Shan J. Press conference for 2010 Survey Report of Adolescent healthy pesonality program[EB/OL]. China Daily，2011[2011-7-8]: http: //www.chinadaily.com.cn/dfpd/shehui/2011-03/14/content_12168478.htm.

[40] 鞠小莉, 臧渝梨, 娄凤兰, 等. 开设青少年健康与发展课程必要性的探讨 [J]. 中华护理教育, 2009a, 6（9）: 401-403.

[41] 鞠小莉, 臧渝梨, 娄凤兰. 中国应用青少年健康和发展课程的实用性研究 [J]. 护理学杂志, 2009b, 24（2, 外科版）: 8-10.

[42] 刘婷, 潘尧云, 臧渝梨. 护士对青少年健康和发展能力的认知调查 [J]. 护理学杂志, 2011, 26（3, 综合版）: 53-56.

[43] 潘尧云, 刘婷, 臧渝梨. 将青少年健康和发展融入本科生教育的研究 [J]. 护理学杂志, 2010, 25（9, 综合版）: 64-66.

[44] 潘尧云, 刘婷, 臧渝梨. 本科护士对青少年健康和发展的认知测量工具构建和应用 [J]. 护理学杂志, 2011, 26（2, 外科版）: 65-68.

青少年身体生长和发育

第四章

青春期以生长发育变化为特点,在该时期青少年经历身体上和性成熟的变化,伴随着生殖功能形成和第二性征的出现。青春期发育是指激素和身体的一系列变化,包括性成熟和身体发育。本章针对青少年生长发育,介绍青春期男孩女孩的身体变化、第二性征及 Tanner 性成熟分期,帮助青少年及其父母、教师等评估青少年的性成熟度;同时详细介绍男女生殖系统的结构,并选择一些常见问题,如月经、青春期发育延迟等给予回答。然而,要达到对青少年更好的理解,必须始终谨记身体变化不可避免地与心理变化互相交织[1]。

第 1 节 概 述

青春期是儿童期到早期成年期的一个过渡时期,同时,它被描述为个体不再是儿童,但也不是成人的时期。此时期个体经历巨大的身体变化。青春期生长发育的峰值仅次于胎儿期及婴儿期,但是与婴儿期及幼童时期相比,在发展里程碑时间以及在生长速率变化的程度上,青春期有更大的个体差异[2]。这些身体变化伴随性成熟出现,常导致亲密关系的形成、抽象思维的发展、自我认同及越来越强的独立性[3]。

因此,青春期被定义为从第二性征出现到性与生殖成熟的进程;心智过程及成人认同的发展以及从完全的社会 - 经济依赖性转变到相对独立的过渡[4]。尽管从 10～19 岁这十年是一个对青少年时期的时间界定,但重要的是要认识到,由于个体间青春期起始及变化持续时间的差异[5,6],这一时期发生的变化,可能与确切的年龄不能完全一致。

并且,该过渡时期会因文化不同而有所差异。对这个时期的认识明显受社会、经济、文化因素的影响。因此,青春期的经历不同个体之间存在差异,在任何一个社会,不同性别,不同条件,如残疾、疾病、社会经济状况及贫穷也有影响[7]。

　　WHO 明确认识到"青春期"在个体的生命中是一个阶段,而非一个固定时间,可以分为三个时期,即早期、中期和晚期,年龄组上大致相当于 10 到 14 岁,15 到 17 岁,18 到 21 岁。尽管该年龄 - 分组方法没有被广泛接受,但是在实践中,它给理解青少年发展提供了一个基本的框架。在早、中、晚青春期,伴随生长变化的其他方面的身体改变见表4-1。

表 4-1　青少年不同阶段的变化 [8]

特征	青少年早期	青少年中期	青少年晚期
年龄范围	11~13 到 14~15 岁	14~15 到 17 岁	17~21 岁(可变)[*]
认知	● 具体思维占主导 ● 以存在为导向 ● 不能感知当前决定和行动的远期影响	● 迅速获得抽象思维能力 ● 能够感知当前行为和决定的远期影响,但稳定性差 ● 在压力下转向具体操作	● 建立抽象思维过程 ● 以未来为导向 ● 能够感知和实践远期选择
心理自我和自我认知	● 沉浸于身体的快速改变 ● 先前身体形象被打乱 ● 关注隐私 ● 频繁的情绪波动、心境不稳 ● 强烈的自我为中心	● 随着生长减速和趋于平稳重建身体形象 ● 极度关注外貌和身体 ● 在探究扩大认知及未来选择时,充满幻想和理想主义 ● 冒险举动增加 ● 形成一种全能及无敌感	● 获得解放 ● 建立智力和功能身份 ● 当面对社会自治需求时会经历"21岁危机" ● 身体形象与性别角色定义基本固定
家庭	● 定义独立 - 依赖界限 ● 发生冲突,但多源于小问题	● 冲突的频率减少,但强度增加 ● 争取解放	● 由儿童 - 父母依赖关系向成人 -成人模式转变
同龄群体	● 寻求同龄人依附感以对抗快速变化产生的不稳定 ● 与同性别 / 年龄的人比较自己的常态和接受能力 ● 同性别朋友及小组活动	● 强烈的认同需要,以证明自我形象 ● 在解放过程中,向同龄群体看齐,以定义行动方式 ● 异性间友谊更加普遍	● 在个人友谊与亲密关系上,群体重要性降低

*上限年龄依赖于文化、经济,以及教育因素。

实际上，在这些阶段发生的变化与发展并不一定是连续的；它们会交叉且不同，与性别、文化、社会经济及其他因素有关[9]。重要的是要注意到青少年并非一个同质群体；他们的需求会因性别、成长阶段、生活条件及社会经济情况的不同而不同[6]。然而，我们希望每一个青少年完成以下所有发展任务：适应身体和感觉的性成熟；发展并应用抽象思维技巧；发展并应用更复杂层次的多角度思维；在某些领域，如决策、解决问题及处理冲突，发展并应用新的应对技能；识别有意义的道德标准、价值观和信仰体系；理解并表达更复杂的情感经历；建立紧密、相互支持的友谊；确立身份的重要层面；满足不断成熟的角色和责任要求；与成人重新商定父母-子女关系[5, 8]。

第2节　青春期身体变化

当一个儿童成长到青春期时，其身体开始为成为父母做准备。青少年身体变化的主要阶段，通常被认为是青春期，包含乳房、身高、体毛及生殖器改变，表示从胎儿到达到完全性成熟及具备生育力[3, 10]，下丘脑-垂体-性腺（HPG）反馈系统（或称作HPG轴，图4-1）发展连续体的一个阶段。

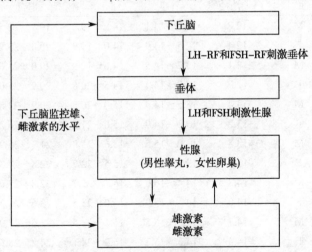

图4-1　下丘脑-垂体-性腺反馈系统 [3]
LH-RF：黄体生成素-释放因子；FSH-RF：卵泡刺激素-释放因子；
LH：黄体生成素；FSH：卵泡刺激素

HPG轴在胎儿及新生儿发育阶段经历一个活跃期，在之后的儿童期进入静止期，然后进入青春期。同时，HPG轴在激素的影响下被激活，如黄体生成素-释放因子（LH-RF）、卵泡刺激素-释放因子（FSH-RF）、黄体生成素（LH）、卵泡刺激素（FSH）以及性甾体（如雌二醇，睾酮），引起青春期的表现：乳腺发育缩写为 B,生殖器增大缩写为 G,阴毛缩写为 PH,子宫,卵巢,睾丸 [3, 11]。

以上过程持续 2～5 年。同时,身高、体重和肌肉系统显著增长 [12]。身体部分的比例随时间改变,而且这些变化在不同性别之间明显不同,如在身高、体重、第二性征等方面。

一般而言,从青春期的起始到结束,女孩的突增比男孩早两年。男孩平均可以增高 28cm,在雄性激素的作用下,他们的体重明显增加,肌肉组织发达。青春期之后,男孩的平均肌肉组织质量比女孩更高,且可以持续到成年期。然而平均来说,男孩的身体脂肪的百分比仍然一样,而女孩身体脂肪的百分比明显增加 [7, 11, 13, 14]。

体重指数(BMI),指一个人的千克体重除以他的身高的平方(kg/m^2),是最常用来分类严重消瘦、消瘦、正常,尤其是超重及肥胖 [15, 16] 的指标。表 4-2 列出了 10～18 岁青少年基于 BMI 分类的全球标准,以促进对青少年营养状况的了解。对那些 19 岁的青少年来说,应参考成人的分类标准:超重:$BMI>25kg/m^2$;肥胖:$BMI>30kg/m^{2[16]}$。

表 4-2 青少年 BMI 筛查分类标准(kg/m^2)[16]

年龄(岁)	性别	严重消瘦	消瘦	正常	超重	肥胖
10	M	≤12.8	12.9～14.1	14.2～19.2	19.3～22.5	≥22.6
	F	≤12.4	12.5～13.9	14.0～19.9	20.0～23.7	≥23.8
11	M	≤13.1	13.2～14.5	14.6～19.9	20.0～23.6	≥23.7
	F	≤12.7	12.8～14.4	14.5～20.8	20.9～25.0	≥25.1
12	M	≤13.4	13.5～14.9	15.0～20.8	20.9～24.8	≥24.9
	F	≤13.2	13.3～14.9	15.0～21.8	21.9～26.2	≥26.3
13	M	≤13.8	13.9～15.5	15.6～21.8	21.9～25.9	≥26.0
	F	≤13.6	13.7～15.4	15.5～22.7	22.8～27.3	≥27.4
14	M	≤14.3	14.4～16.0	16.1～22.7	22.8～27.0	≥27.1
	F	≤14.0	14.1～15.9	16.0～23.5	23.6～28.2	≥28.3
15	M	≤14.7	14.8～16.5	16.6～23.5	23.6～27.9	≥28.0
	F	≤14.4	14.5～16.2	16.3～24.1	24.2～28.9	≥29.0
16	M	≤15.1	15.2～16.9	17.0～24.3	24.4～28.6	≥28.7
	F	≤14.6	14.7～16.4	16.5～24.5	24.6～29.3	≥29.4
17	M	≤15.4	15.5～17.3	17.4～24.9	25.0～29.2	≥29.3
	F	≤14.7	14.8～16.4	16.5～24.8	24.9～29.5	≥29.6
18	M	≤15.7	15.8～17.6	17.7～25.4	25.5～29.7	≥29.8
	F	≤14.7	14.8～16.5	16.6～25.0	25.1～29.7	≥29.8

M= 男;F= 女。

青少年时期更重要的变化与第二性征的发展有关,它突出了主要由激素变化引起的生殖生长潜力。

第二性征

性分化在孕期性腺形成时即开始。在青春期前,男孩女孩在一般体质、体型、面貌以及性激素水平方面是相似的。随着青春期进展及性激素水平提高,尽管男孩和女孩身体变化相似,但性别差异变得明显。

对于男性来说,睾酮水平的增加直接诱导睾丸和阴茎的增长,并间接(通过双氢睾酮,DHT)影响前列腺。它也直接增加肌肉、声带及骨骼的大小和质量,使声音变得低沉,改变面孔及骨骼的形状。睾酮在皮肤中转化成双氢睾酮(DHT),它加速对雄激素敏感的面部及身体毛发的生长,但是也减慢并最终使头发的生长停止。

对于女性,乳房是更高水平雌激素(如雌二醇)的表现。雌激素水平的增加增宽骨盆,并增加髋部、大腿、臀部及乳房脂肪的数量,另外,诱导子宫的生长、子宫内膜的增殖,以及月经。关于青春期性别差异的典型改变,详见表4-3。

表4-3 青少年男孩和女孩第二性征 [7]

	青少年男孩	青少年女孩
体毛	体毛生长,包括面部、腋下、腹部、胸部及阴毛;	体毛生长,多数以腋毛及阴毛为主。
皮肤	油脂及汗腺分泌增加,常引起痤疮和身体异味; 由于皮下脂肪较少,皮肤质地粗糙或硬化;	
声音与乳房	喉增大(喉结)及声音变低;	乳房增大,乳头直立;
身体构成	体型增大,成年男性比女性高; 肌肉质量及力量增加,股骨前面大腿肌更大; 颅骨及骨结构更重; 肩部变宽,较髋部更宽; 腰部与髋部比例较青春期前或成年女性或青春期前男性平均较高。	股骨后大腿肌肉较前面肌肉迅速增长; 髋部变宽,腰部与髋部比例比成年男性平均较低; 体重、脂肪的分布改变,皮下脂肪更多,脂肪主要沉积在臀部、大腿和髋部。
生殖体征	遗精	月经

性成熟 Tanner 分期

第二性征发育的不同阶段通常是指 Tanner 分期(图4-2,图4-3)或性成熟评定(SMR):B1 到 B5 为乳房发育,PH1 到 PH5 为阴毛生长,以及 G1 到 G5 为生殖器官生长 [4, 11, 17]。

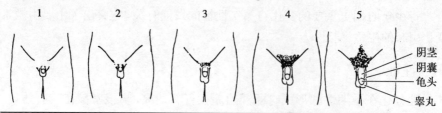

阶段	阴毛（PH）	生殖器官（G）	
		阴茎	睾丸
1	无	青春期前	青春期前
2	少，色浅	略大	阴囊增大，不再呈粉红色
3	略黑，开始卷曲，量少	更长	更大
4	类似成人类型，但量少，卷曲	更大，阴茎体变大变粗	更大，阴囊变黑
5	成人分布，至大腿根部表面	成人大小	成人大小

图 4-2 Tanner 男性性成熟评定[17]

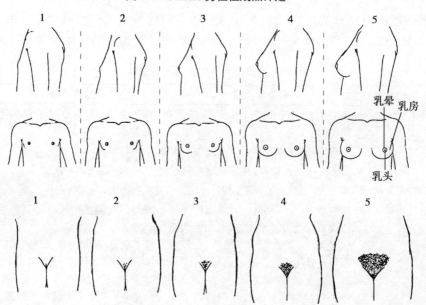

阶段	阴毛（PH）	乳腺（B）
1	青春期前	青春期前
2	稀疏，色浅，阴唇内侧缘平直	乳腺和乳头隆起如小丘，乳晕增大
3	变暗，开始卷曲，数量增加	乳腺及乳晕增大，无轮廓分离
4	变粗、卷曲、浓密，但较成人量少	乳晕及乳头形成第二个小丘
5	呈成年女性三角形，分布至大腿根部表面	成熟，乳头突出，一般乳房乳晕轮廓形成

图 4-3 Tanner 女性性成熟评定[17]

第二性征的开始

男性性发育平均开始于 11.2 岁（8.2～14.2 岁），在性成熟第二阶段（SMR2）持续大约 2～5 年 [3, 11]。男性典型青春期事件的顺序是：肾上腺功能初现；生长突增的开始；睾丸发育；阴毛开始及生长速度高峰（图 4-4）。特别指出的是，98% 男性青春期的第一个身体体征是睾丸的增大；射精通常发生在性成熟评定的第三阶段（SMR3），第一次遗精大约发生在 13.4 岁（范围 11.7～15.3 岁）。尽管 SMR4 常常与生育有关，但是可能会在 SMR3 发生。

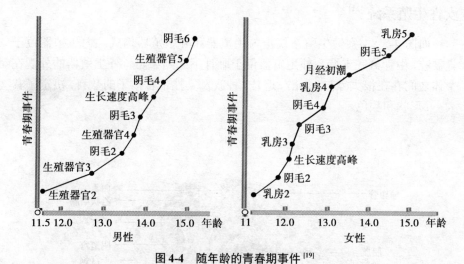

图 4-4 随年龄的青春期事件 [19]

女性性发育的平均年龄开始于 10.4 岁（范围 8.0～12.6 岁）[11]，青春期事件的典型顺序见图 4-4。通常乳房开始发育是青春期的第一个身体征象。研究发现，第二性征包括月经初潮，开始的年龄随着时间的推移而减小（即长期趋势），主要是由于营养改善、肥胖症增加、激素水平及其他环境或社会改变 [18] 造成。这种长期趋势可能会对健康产生影响，原因是由于性活动危险的增加、怀孕、流产或者乳腺癌 [18]。平均来说，女性生长速度高峰的到来要早，与男性在 SMR4 相比，会在 SMR2；半数以上女性初潮发生在 PH4，但是接近五分之一会发生在 PH3。

其他与青春期开始有关，需要进一步了解的方面是心理影响。一致认为，这种影响因性别而异：发育早的男性较其同龄人更加趋于自信，且更可能达到学业、社会及运动上的成功。相比而言，青春期较早的女孩会出现更多的情感、行为问题及较少的成就，与相对低自尊有关 [13, 14, 20]。发育晚的女孩和男孩之间的其他区别包括：与后者相比，前者没有表现出明显的自尊困难 [14]。

第3节 青少年生殖系统

为了更好地理解有关生殖功能的变化并促进对性成熟的评估，本节简要概括了典型的女性和男性生殖系统，以反映青春期的内在改变。生殖系统的器官与整个生殖过程有关，并且每一个器官适于完成特定任务。这些器官是独特的，因为它们的功能对每个个体的生存来说并不是必需的；相反，它们的功能对人类的延续是至关重要的。

女性生殖系统 [21]

如图 4-5[22]，女性生殖系统由内生殖器和外生殖器构成。内生殖器位于骨盆腔，由骨盆底支持。外生殖器位于耻骨下缘到会阴。外生殖器的外观在个体之间存在很大差异，年龄、遗传、种族及女性生育孩子的数目，决定了其大小、形状和颜色。

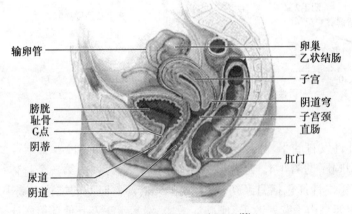

输卵管
卵巢
乙状结肠
子宫
膀胱
耻骨
G点
阴蒂
尿道
阴道
阴道穹
子宫颈
直肠
肛门

图 4-5　女性生殖系统图示 [22]

内生殖器包括子宫、阴道、输卵管及卵巢：子宫是一个中空器官，大小和形状如一个倒梨，位于膀胱与直肠之间，由阔韧带悬挂于骨盆。它是产生月经的器官（后面会具体讲述），在怀孕期间它接受受精卵，保持并给它提供营养，直至分娩时将胎儿娩出。阴道为壁薄的肌性管道，从子宫到外生殖器，长约15cm。它是胎儿娩出及经血排出的通道；是女性的性交器官。

每个输卵管大约10cm长，从每侧卵巢向内伸展到子宫底部。这两个管道将卵子从卵巢运输到子宫腔内。卵巢大小和形状如杏仁，位于骨盆外侧壁，左右各一，其功能是产生卵细胞（女性性细胞）和类固醇激素（雌激素和孕激素）。输卵管和卵巢之间没有直接接触。当卵母细胞从卵巢排出，输卵管伞产生液体流将卵母细胞运到输卵管。卵母细胞在输卵管蠕动和纤毛将其向前推动的联合作用下，被运送到子宫。受精最理想的地方是输卵管。

外生殖器包括阴阜、大阴唇、小阴唇、阴道前庭、会阴及前庭大腺。这些结构围绕在尿道和阴道的开口处。阴阜是位于耻骨联合前的隆起部，由皮肤及很厚的脂肪层所构成，被浓密阴毛覆盖；大阴唇为一对纵长隆起的、具有弹性的皮肤皱襞，覆盖有阴毛，它们围绕并保护其他外生殖器，而小阴唇是两个被大阴唇包绕的小的皮肤皱襞，它们保护阴道及尿道的开口。阴道前庭由阴蒂、尿道口及阴道口组成。阴蒂是一个小且能勃起的器官，位于阴道前庭的顶端，其功能是性兴奋。尿道口是尿道的开口；而尿道是将尿液从膀胱引流到尿道口的小管状结构。

阴道口为阴道的入口。会阴是阴道口与肛门之间的软组织，它有助于收缩尿道、阴道及肛门开口，也帮助支持骨盆内容物。前庭大腺位于阴道口的两侧，它们分泌的黏液在性交时具有滑润作用。

月经 [11, 13]

月经是周期性地血液、黏液及上皮细胞从子宫排出的现象。它通常以每月为周期，除了怀孕及哺乳时通常被抑制之外，贯穿整个生殖期。

月经周期由垂体前叶分泌的卵泡刺激素（FSH）及黄体生成素（LH），以及卵巢分泌的孕酮（progesterone）和雌激素（estrogen）的周期性活性所影响。在第3到第5天（称为月经期），缺乏受精卵信号引起雌激素及孕酮产量的下降，而孕酮的下降导致增厚子宫内膜崩溃脱落，称作月经。

大概从第6到第14天（称为增生阶段），孕酮及雌激素水平的下降刺激垂体前叶卵泡刺激素（FSH）的释放。卵泡刺激素（FSH）刺激成熟卵泡卵子的成熟。这一阶段接近结束时，黄体生成素（LH）的释放增加，引起类似卵子释放的突然暴发，称为排卵。

在月经的晚期（第15到第28天，称为分泌阶段），高水平的黄体生成素引起排空的成熟卵泡生成黄体。黄体释放孕酮，增加子宫内膜的血液供应。如果卵子受精，胚胎产生人绒毛膜促性腺激素（HCG）。人绒毛膜促性腺激素发出信号使黄体继续供应孕酮来维持子宫内膜。持续的孕酮水平防止卵泡刺激素的释放及排卵停止。

事实上，月经周期的长短非常不同，从21~39天不等。对所有女性来说，只有一个间歇是非常恒定的，从排卵（例如卵细胞从成熟卵泡的释放）到月经的开始,几乎总是 14 或 15 天。月经周期通常在女性达到 50 岁,或者 50 岁之前结束,称为绝经。

男性生殖系统 [23]

男性生殖道由外生殖器和内生殖器组成。这些器官位于盆腔(图 4-6)。男性生殖系统在胎儿早期对睾酮反应时即开始发育。基本上儿童期没有睾酮产生。青春期开始睾酮恢复产生,刺激男性生殖结构及第二性征的生长和成熟。睾酮是由睾丸间质细胞分泌的男性生殖激素。

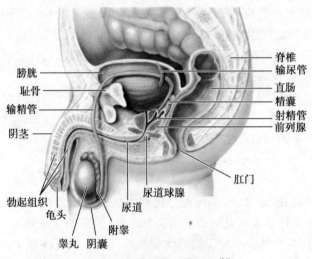

脊椎
输尿管
直肠
精囊
射精管
前列腺
膀胱
耻骨
输精管
阴茎
肛门
尿道球腺
勃起组织
尿道
龟头
附睾
睾丸　阴囊

图 4-6　男性生殖系统图示 [24]

男性生殖系统的主要功能是产生男性性细胞,即精子。男性生殖系统的主要器官是形成精细胞的两个睾丸,其他结构有管道系统及附属腺结构。睾丸是两个杏仁形的腺体,其功能是产生精子及睾酮。睾丸悬挂于盆腹腔外侧的阴囊。一般认为,睾丸位于体腔的外侧,由于对热非常敏感,因此身体较高的温度不利于精子的产生。每个睾丸由称作白膜的坚厚白色纤维膜包裹,纤维膜向内延伸将睾丸分成许多小叶,每个睾丸小叶含有四个紧密盘曲的生精小管(这是精子真正产生的位置)。生精小管将精子排空到睾丸网络,在此精子进入位于睾丸外面的附睾。

管道系统是精子排出身体的通道系统,包括附睾及输精管。附睾是卷曲导管,约 50cm 长,覆盖在睾丸的上部,并沿其后边下行。附睾构成了管道系统的第一部分,并提供了未成熟精子的临时储存位置。当男性性兴奋时,附睾壁收缩将精子排泄到管道系统的下一部分,并穿过输精管持续前行。输精管由附睾向上到腹股沟管进入盆腔，并呈弓形弯曲在膀胱上，它在一个结缔组织鞘内被血管和神经包围，该鞘被称为精索。由输精管到射精管，携带精子排空到尿道。

附属腺体结构包括精囊、前列腺、Cowper腺（尿道球腺）以及阴茎。两个精囊是储存精子的袋子。60%的精液由精囊产生。所分泌黏液富含糖（果糖），以营养并活化精子穿过通道。前列腺是单一腺体，大小与形状如栗子，它环绕尿道上段，恰好在膀胱下面。前列腺分泌一种乳白色碱性液体，其作用是保护精子免受阴道酸性环境的影响。Cowper腺是微小如豌豆大的腺体，功能次于前列腺。它们分泌一种黏稠透明黏液，并被引流到尿道。该分泌物主要作为性交时的润滑剂。阴茎是一个圆柱形状的器官，位于阴阜外表，阴囊之上。它由勃起组织组成，内有空洞样间隙。性冲动时，血液流入这些空间，使之由绵软状态转变成增大、坚硬、直立器官。阴茎光滑的帽被称作龟头，由一层松软皮肤覆盖，形成包皮。外科手术去除这层包皮，被称作包皮环切术，是常见手术。阴茎也是男性尿道系统的一部分。

第4节　常见青少年问题解答

青少年在青春期可能比较关注他（她）们身体的新变化。通过几年全球的努力，WHO[7]明确了青少年常见的一些问题（例如，青春期发育延迟、月经周期不规律），并为青少年及父母准备了相应的解答。本节的焦点是描述从最新WHO资料中选择的与青春期、包皮及月经相关的问题及解答[7]。

青春期

当一个孩子成为青少年时，身体便开始为做父母作准备。这一持续2～5年的阶段称为青春期。身体产生的化学物质称为激素，由其触发这些变化的出现。青春期过程中，身高、体重及肌肉组织都会增长，并以性器官的生长发育为标志，同时伴随出现一些变化如面部、体毛发育及青春痘。

个体间青春期开始的时间存在明显的差别，男孩一般约10岁开始，并持续至15或16岁；女孩一般约9岁开始，通常在14～16岁完成。

青春期发育延迟

在特定年龄身体尚未出现某些变化，我们称之为晚于正常或青春期延迟。例如，对男孩来说，到14或15岁性器官还没有开始发育；对女孩来说，14岁时乳房还没有增大，会阴部没有毛发，或16岁时还没有来月经。

青春期延迟最常见的原因为正常的变异。这些变异常存在于家庭且不需要治疗。然而,有时营养不良或慢性疾病可能导致青春期延迟。因此在采集病史及体检时询问、观察也是非常重要的。当青少年遭遇发育延迟时,他们可能感到焦虑和孤立。

不同的青少年以不同的速率度过青春期,这决定于他们的家庭特征和营养状况。几乎所有的青少年都将顺利度过青春期。健康工作人员应该有能力借助一些工具或体格检查做出评估,帮助青少年减轻发育延迟引起的焦虑。如果存在潜在的问题,建议转介给专业人员。

月经流血过多

月经过多常发生于月经出现的前 2 年内,且大多数情况下,与任何严重的潜在疾病无关。大多数情况下,严重月经出血并不影响个体目前或将来怀孕的能力。如何知道月经周期是正常的呢?青少年可以牢记三个方面:正常月经周期持续 2～7 天;正常月经量的"经验法则"是,每天浸透并更换 7 片或以下卫生棉;青少年时期正常的月经周期为 21～35 天。

月经周期不规律

自上次月经的第一天至下次月经的第一天之间的间隔,若少于 21 天或多于 35 天,则称之为月经周期不规律。最短月经周期和最长月经周期间隔时间超过 20 天,也称为月经周期不规律(例如,有些月经周期间隔 20 天,有些则 41 天)。月经周期不规律的最常见原因是身体还在发育。第一次来月经后,周期需要一段时间才能变得规律。有时月经周期不规律可能由于营养不良。比较少见的是身体状况,尤其是与激素不平衡有关的身体状况导致周期不规律。相应地,如果月经周期不规律与潜在病因无关,则没有不良影响。

如果由于营养不良导致月经周期不规律或停经,建议食用健康食物。如果不是由于营养不良引起,建议咨询专家以进行恰当的治疗。

痛经

痛经,一种非常普遍的现象,发生在月经期或之前。疼痛可能是持续性或反复性的,在月经期的前期疼痛最重,随着时间推移,疼痛程度有所减轻。一些青少年女孩可能担心身体出了问题,然而在大多数情况下,疼痛与潜在的疾病无关,而是月经期体内产生的化学物质导致子宫平滑肌收缩所致。如果疼痛非常严重,可能伴随头痛、腹泻、恶心和呕吐。有时会给个体的日常活动造成困难,也会影响心情。然而,此种疼痛或其他症状并没有长期的不良影响。

如果遇到痛经，青少年女孩可以采取一些措施来减轻疼痛，例如，应用热敷（在腹部或背部用热水袋或暖布垫），或服止痛药来减轻疼痛。如果疼痛不严重，继续日常活动将有助于将注意力转移到其他事情上而减轻疼痛。月经疼痛通常在分娩后会减轻，这是因为分娩过程中宫颈（子宫口）扩张或者宫颈部位某些神经纤维受到损伤。

包皮问题

与女孩月经相关的问题相比，男孩对增大的阴茎及其包皮表现出更多关心。男孩外生殖器最常见的担心可能是包茎或嵌顿包茎。包茎是指阴茎前端的皮肤不能从阴茎头部向后退/收回，可能由于包皮的发育过程，也可能是由于炎症或感染造成的瘢痕引起的。类固醇有助于将包皮拉回到阴茎头部后端。如果包茎常常复发或药物无效，建议转至外科进行手术做阴茎包皮环切。

相比而言，嵌顿包茎是指一旦包皮从阴茎头部推出或拉回，将不能回归到原有位置。这可能由于包皮被强烈地从阴茎头部后拉引起的。嵌顿包茎可能伴随疼痛和肿胀，药物和冷敷可以缓解疼痛和肿胀。如果包皮不能拉回到阴茎头部后则需要手术。及时治疗避免对阴茎头部造成永久伤害是非常重要的。肿胀消失后，建议做包皮环切术预防嵌顿包茎再次发生。

提醒青少年注意以下事项是非常重要的：清洗阴茎时，轻推包皮，尽可能多而舒适地暴露阴茎头部，用温和的肥皂和温水轻轻地清洗阴茎头部和包皮暴露的下面。清洗时可能会发现一些白色的物质，虽说正常，仍需清洗掉。否则，身体的分泌物及尿液可能堆积在包皮下面，引起刺激或引发感染。如果做了包皮环切术，冲澡或泡澡时用肥皂清洗阴茎有助于保持干净。清洗阴茎时不要使用刺激性强的化学物质，如清洗剂。清洗剂可能会损害脆弱的皮肤，造成疼痛和不适。

青少年时期外生殖器的发育还有很多其他的问题，例如，局部疼痛、溃疡或排尿问题、分泌物（阴道、尿道）问题，这些可能是性传播性感染的症状。关于这些问题的解答请参考性与生殖健康章节。

（孟庆慧，刘　茜，潘尧云，蒲林哲）

参 考 文 献

[1] Cobb NJ. Adolescence: continuity, change, and diversity [M]. 7th. California, America: Mayfield Publishing Company, 2010.

[2] Berer M. By and for young women and men [J]. Reproductive Health Matters, 2001, 9(17): 6-10.

[3] Steinberg L. Adolescence [M]. 8th. New York: McGraw-Hill, 2008.

[4] Tanner JM. Fetus into man: physical growth from conception to maturity [M/OL]. Revised Edition. Harvard, Colorado: Harvard University Press, 1990[2011-8-4]: http: //www. google.com/books?hl=zh-CN&lr=&id=YxpimctaWd4C&oi=f23nd&pg=PA1&dq=Foetus+ into+man: +Physical+growth+from+conception+to+maturity&ots=7tiQkdbK1T&sig= ygsOdw7OqkuMqmDBBXT4yZ8A-7k#v=onepage&q&f=false.

[5] Simpson AR. Raising teens: a synthesis of research and a foundation for action [M/OL]. Boston, Massachusetts: Harvard School of Public Health, 2001[2011-5-11]: http: //www. hsph.harvard.edu/chc/parenting/report.pdf.

[6] WHO. Orientation programme on adolescent health for health-care providers [M/OL]. Geneva, Switzerland: World Health Organization, 2006[2011-7-14]: http: //whqlibdoc. who.int/publications/2006/9241591269_Handout_eng.pdf

[7] WHO. Adolescent Job Aid: a handy desk reference for primary level health worker [M/ OL].Geneva, World Health Organization, 2008[2011-7-21]: http: //www.youthnet.org.hk/ adh/4_4Sframework/3_Services_n_commodities/2_ Services/Adolescent%20job%20aid/ Adolescent%20Job%20Aid%20-%20prototype%203.pdf.

[8] Fleming M, Towey K. Delivering culturally effective health care to adolescents [M/OL]. Chicago, IL: American Medical Association, 2001[2011-7-23]: http: //www.ama-assn. org/resources/doc/ad-hlth/culturallyeffective.pdf.

[9] WHO. The second decade: improving adolescent health and development [EB/ OL]. Department of Child and Adolescent Health and Development, World Health Organization, 2001. [2011-07-12]: http: //whqlibdoc.who.int/hq/1998/WHO_FRH_ ADH_98.18_Rev.1.pdf.

[10] Graber JA, Nichols TR, Brooks-Gunn J. Putting pubertal timing in developmental context: Implications for prevention [J]. Developmental Psychobiology, 2010, 52(3): 254-262.

[11] Brämswig J, Dübbers A. Disorders of Pubertal Development [J]. Deutsches Ärzteblatt International, 2009, 106(17): 295-304.

[12] Columbia University. Reproductive Anatomy and Physiology [EB/OL]. Columbia University Mailman School of Public Health, 2008-5-2[2011-7-18]: http: //www. columbia.edu/itc/hs/pubhealth/modules/reproductiveHealth/anatomy.html.

[13] Bordini B, Rosenfield RL. Normal pubertal development: Part I: The endocrine basis of puberty [J]. Pediatrics in Review, 2011b, 32(6): 223-229.

[14] Hazen E, Schlozman S, Beresin E. Adolescent psychological development: a review [J]. Pediatrics in Review, 2008, 29(5): 161-168.

[15] Reilly JJ. Assessment of obesity in children and adolescents: synthesis of recent systematic reviews and clinical guidelines [J]. Journal of Human Nutrition and Dietetics, 2010, 23 (3): 205-211.

[16] WHO. Growth Reference Data for 5~19 Years [EB/OL]. World Health Organization, 2011 [2011-7-27]: http://www.who.int/growthref/en/.

[17] Morris NM, Udry JR. Validation of a self-administered instrument to assess stage of adolescent development [J]. Journal of Youth and Adolescence, 1980, 9 (3): 271-280.

[18] Zembar MJ, Blume LB. Middle childhood development: a contextual approach [M]. Upper Saddle River, New Jersey: Pearson Education, 2007.

[19] Neinstein LS. Puberty-Normal Growth and Development (A1) [EB/OL]. 2002[2011-7-21]: http://www.usc.edu/student-affairs/Health_Center/adolhealth/content/a1.html.

[20] Bordini B, Rosenfield RL. Normal pubertal development: Part Ⅱ: clinical aspects of puberty [J]. Pediatrics in Review, 2011a, 32 (7): 281-292.

[21] NIH. Female Reproductive System [EB/OL]. U.S. Department of Health and Human Services National Institutes of Health, 2011-7-19[2011-7-23]: http://www.nlm.nih.gov/medlineplus/femalereproductivesystem.html.

[22] Wikipedia. File: Female reproductive system lateral nolabel.png [EB/OL]. 2005-10-26 [2011-7-21]: http://en.wikipedia.org/wiki/File: Female_reproductive_system_lateral_nolabel.png#file.

[23] NIH. Male Reproductive System [EB/OL]. U.S. Department of Health and Human Services National Institutes of Health, 2011-7-19[2011-7-23]: http://www.nlm.nih.gov/medlineplus/malereproductivesystem.html.

[24] Wikipedia. File: Male reproductive system lateral nolabel.png [EB/OL]. 2005-7-22[2011-7-11]: http://en.wikipedia.org/wiki/File: Male_reproductive_system_lateral_nolabel.png.

第五章

青少年精神心理健康

青少年时期的心理变化显著,此时期身体发育迅速,大脑发生细微的变化。面对这些发育和变化,青少年会出现一些心理困扰甚至心理障碍。本章将介绍正常的青少年心理发展,并简要介绍一些青少年心理疾病及精神心理亚健康状况的常见症状。

第1节　正常青少年心理发展

青春期是介于童年和成年之间的一个过渡阶段,此时期青少年从不成熟逐步发育至完全成熟。在这个阶段,青少年的心理和身体发展具有其独特的特征,例如,心理发展较身体发育的滞后性导致身心发育之间的失衡。

青少年的发展任务

由于个体和文化的差异,不同的地域对于青春期的发展任务界定不同(如身体、认知、心理、道德等各方面),而并非单纯依据年龄进行界定[1]。除了身体发展任务(如飞速发育和第二性征发育),青春期主要的社会、情感和认知发展任务包括:增强独立和自我调节能力(即自我约束能力)、认同感,如性别认同和社会认同、抽象推理能力、接受先进理论的能力、评估风险能力、语言技能的提高等方面[1,2]。虽然有关道德发展规范一直存在争议,但青少年阶段其心理发展具有一些共同特征,表现为采纳他人观点的能力有所增强,在抽象的基础上极力表现出好的行为、负责任的一面[1,3]。这些心理发展的任务似乎是不现实的和理想化的,但他们代表了正常的青少年心理发展,以下将更多地介绍这些任务。

正常的心理发展

在青春期,主要的心理发展包括认同感、自我约束和性,其中包括个人的情绪、动机和行为的改变。这些方面虽然不是青少年所独具的，但是在青少年时期会相继出现这些特定的问题。了解青少年出现这些心理发展的原因以及相关表现是卫生保健工作者的关注热点。

1. 自我意识的发展

自我意识是有关对自我、自尊感的发展以及对"我是谁"的心理深入发展过程的一种认识。自我意识的发展始于儿童期，进入青春期后，人开始自觉地认识和评价自己的精神世界、个性品质。在整个青春期，这些方面大概都匀速发展。它包括以下内容：他们的长处和弱点是什么；他们与社会的关系（也就是他们期望从别人身上或别人从他们本人身上可以得到什么）；开始意识到性别角色，并开始制定自己的人生计划（成年后所将从事的职业及个人身份等）。在这段时间，青少年开始疑惑他们的前方即将面临的是什么，这是一个试图发现真实的自我的过程[4]。青少年关于自我的描述会扩展到包括个性特征和对待自我的态度，如"我过时了，我不喜欢什么样的人"等想法[5, 6]。

针对自我认识的发展，埃里克森的心理理论认为人类发展按照预定计划有两个要素。首先，是个体要走向成人模式，其次是个体要经历社会的考验[7]。根据埃里克森的理论，个体从出生至死亡发育要经历八个阶段，当特定情形出现时，如果妥善处理，结果将是积极的；反之，结果将是消极的。

个体发育的4、5阶段将面临显著的冲突，这个阶段的冲突或早或晚都会影响青少年的发展。青少年发展阶段4指的是潜伏期（年龄6～11岁），阶段5指的是少年期和青年期（年龄12～18岁）。在此时期，青少年开始考虑自己的未来和将来将要从事的职业。在这个阶段，他们的身份与角色是相互冲突混乱的。如果青少年制定行动、计划未来的想法得到满足，其结果是积极的，则认同感确立。相反，青少年制定行动、计划未来的想法未得到满足，其结果是消极的，则出现认同危机、对于未来，青少年将漫无目的、没有任何行动计划或生活没有安全感。

通过其他相关报道，我们知道，随着认知的变化、智力的成熟，人可以通过更多的不同方式去认识自我。一些青少年能够很清醒地认识其内在的和外在的自我，有些人可能有较强的自尊，但有时他们的自信是不够的，因此很容易受外界影响产生自卑感。此外，青少年在自我意识形成过程中往往容易模仿某些人或有自己崇拜的偶像。

同时，青少年可能成为时尚的前沿或者喜欢获得同龄人的认可。有时他们甚至会放弃或改变他们先前的一些看法、行为和标准，以便与同龄人相似，比如说变得物质化、追求时尚品牌、崇拜偶像等[8]。

此外，青少年可能更注重未来的方向，他们希望能够预知自己的选择可能产生的后果。青少年已经出现的抽象推理能力允许他们为未来着想，去尝试不同的社会身份[8]。

2. 独立性的发展

青春期是从依赖性为主的儿童期到相对自立的成年期的一个过渡过程。对于大多数青少年，建立自主意识对于个体是重要的一部分，成为一个能够自我约束的成人、建立认同感、成为一个眼界开阔的人是青春期一个重要的发展任务，这个过程是渐进的和重要的[9]。

青春期的青少年开始质疑家长与教师的权威。但这种青春期自主性的发展经常被误解，经常与反叛等状况相混淆。在这一阶段，青少年开始变成独立的个体、脱离家庭并建立自己的风格[8]。

独立性特点包括：①情感自主，主要是改变与个人的亲密关系，尤其是与父母的关系；②行为自主，独立作出决定并执行这些决定的能力；③价值自主，不仅仅是为满足他人的要求而抵抗一定的压力；他们有着自己的一套有关正确与错误的、重要与不重要的原则。

3. 认知发展

根据皮亚杰的认知发展理论，儿童发展需要经过四个认知阶段，即初级阶段（出生至2岁），准行为阶段（2～7岁），完全行为阶段（7～11岁）和规范行为阶段（11～15岁）。每一个阶段孩子在问题解决能力和逻辑思维能力方面都展现出一个质的飞跃，随时可能发生僵化思维到逻辑思维的转变[7]。

这些思考过程的进展（也被称为形式逻辑运算）可以分为几个方面[5, 6, 10]：**抽象思维**意味着对于一些不能看到的听到的或者是触摸到的事情的推理，比如信任、信仰等；**逻辑推理**包括思考的能力，对于多个可能发生事情的选择性和可能性等。它包括多个逻辑思维过程的能力，也包括提出和回答这个问题的能力，例如"如果……，会……?"。**思考问题的能力**是一个过程，被称为"元认知"。元认知允许个人去思考他们在想什么，它涉及个体想到自己如何被他人感知的问题。它也可以被用来发展战略，也被称为记忆装置，用于改善学习。例如，音乐人通过（e, g, b, d 和 f）来记录"every good boy does fine"。

根据美国教育部和美国心理协会的报道，青少年在这期间经常**为了辩论而进行辩论**[11, 12]。更多细节如下：持续的争论和看似的智慧是青少年的一个特点。他们往往偏离主题，似乎无明显的原因就开始辩论；这些令许多成年人非常沮丧。但是，对于青少年，他们需要这样的机会去练习推理能力，这是令人愉快的。**跳跃式结论**，在青春期早期，即使他们具有一定的逻辑思维能力,有时他们会得出令人吃惊的跳跃式结论。随着认知的进一步发展,年长的青少年能够抑制冲动行为并能够处理日益复杂的社会情况。**以自我为中心**,青少年往往认为,每个人都像他们自己一样关心他们的思想和行为,这导致青少年一直相信他们有一个"假想的观众",总在关注着他们。另一方面,青少年非常以自我为中心,要他们学会从别人的角度去思考问题这需要一定的时间,事实上,这是一个可以学到的技能。**在成人的位置上不断发现错误**,青少年开始质疑成人(尤其是父母)的权威和社会标准。对于他们感到安全的成年人,有时他们会公开地质疑或批评。他们不再盲目地仰视那些有权威的人,而是去选择他们认为值得尊重的人去尊重。他们总是会反抗父母的影响和建议。**过于戏剧化**,对于十几岁的青少年一切似乎是一个"大事件"。但是,对于一些青少年来说,过于戏剧性或夸大自己的意见和行为是自然而然的[13]。

青少年在三个发展阶段中的主要心理变化和简单对比见表 5-1。

表 5-1　青少年在三个发展阶段中的主要心理变化和简单对比[13]

青少年的 发展阶段	青春期早期 (10~14岁)	青春期中期 (15~16岁)	青春期后期 (17~21岁)
独立性和自我意识的发展	自我意识的形成受内部或外部因素的影响;喜怒无常;具有更强的表达能力;更倾向于用行动表达情感(男性更为明显);渴望更亲密的友谊;较少注意父母,偶尔粗鲁;意识到父母不完美;认识自己的缺点;寻找除了父母之外的爱;面临压力表现出幼稚的一面;兴趣、爱好、服装款式受同龄人的影响等	自我参与;在不切实际的高期望和失败忧虑之间变换;抱怨父母干涉他们的独立;尤其关注自己的外表和身体;对自我和身体存在陌生感;忽略父母的意见;努力结交新朋友;对同龄人的追随;体验内心感受,包含写日记等	更牢固的自我意识;通过意识思考问题的能力;用言语表达意识的能力;幽默感的发展;情感和爱好更稳定;独立做决定的能力;折衷的能力;对于工作的骄傲;更加关注他人等
未来的兴趣和认知的发展	越来越浓厚的职业兴趣;对目前和不久的将来更加感兴趣;工作能力日益突出	更加注重智力爱好;将性与争强好胜的精力逐渐转移到创作和职业兴趣当中;更加关心学习成绩	更明确的工作习惯;更关注未来;思考自己的人生角色
伦理与自我导向	极力摆脱规则的限制;尝试香烟、大麻和酒精;抽象思考问题的能力	理想的发展和角色模型的选择;具有更明确的良知;更大的目标设置能力;道德推理的兴趣	有益的见解;关注个人尊严;设定和实现目标的能力;接受社会规范和传统文化;自尊的自我调整

青春期发展的冲突

在机体内部或外部失调或发生分歧的时候,冲突就会出现。显著的身体或心理的变化给青少年带来了巨大挑战,这些都可能会影响青少年的发展。倪建明[14]总结了发生在青春期的各类冲突类型如下:

(1)心理上的成人感与半成熟现状之间的矛盾:身体的快速成长,性机能的快速成熟使青少年产生自己已经发育成熟的体验,认为自己生理上已经是成人,思想和行为就属于成人水平,应该被社会平等对待,但实际上由于心理发展速度的相对缓慢,尚处于从幼稚向成熟发展的过渡阶段。

(2)独立性与依赖性的矛盾:青少年的个体独立意识开始迅速发展,他们反抗儿童时代同成人形成的依附关系,要求在精神上摆脱成人的束缚,但实际上,青少年的心理尚未成熟,考虑问题不够全面,遇事比较冲动,因此在面对许多复杂的矛盾和困惑时,他们依然希望得到成人的理解、支持和保护。

(3)闭锁性与开放性的矛盾:进入青春期后,第二性征的出现,给青少年带来神秘感,他们不再像儿时那样外露与直爽,他们开始有了自己的秘密。但与此同时,他们又感到非常孤独寂寞,希望有人来关心和理解他们,希望与他人交流、沟通,正如斯普兰格指出的:"没有任何人会像青年那样深深地陷入孤独之中,渴望被人接近和理解,没有任何人像青年那样站在遥远的地方,向人们呼唤着",他们不断地寻找能推心置腹的知己,渴望向他们敞开心扉。

(4)自傲与自卑的矛盾:由于青少年自我评价与自我认识能力水平的局限,还不能对自己作出全面客观的评价。他们常凭借一时的感觉来评价自己,他们的情绪经常波动。偶然的成功会使其沾沾自喜,自以为是;相反,偶尔的失败又会令其对自己产生怀疑,感到极度的自卑。

(5)青少年期萌动与社会规范的矛盾:性生理成熟为青少年带来了一定的困扰。青少年产生了对异性的好感、爱慕及追求的要求。但是,传统与现代的性规范或惯例往往互相冲突,甚至截然对立,他们不能很好地协调性冲动和社会规范之间的关系,由此产生萌动与社会规范的矛盾。

第2节 青少年常见心理问题

青少年在成长过程中面临着学习、生活和社会各方面的困难与挫折,由于缺乏必要的心理卫生知识和充分的心理准备,难免会出现这样或那样的心理问题，如抑郁、焦虑、严重者甚至出现自杀倾向。据统计，青少年心理疾病发病率约为 10%，14 岁左右的青少年为高发人群[15]，而中国 4～16 岁的人群心理疾病发病率竟高达 12.97%[16]。因此了解青少年心理发展特点、青少年心理问题的早发现早治疗对维护促进青少年健康尤为重要[17]。

抑郁症

抑郁症是一种以持久（2 周以上）的情绪低落状态为特征的神经症性障碍，常伴有沮丧、无助、兴趣衰退，严重者甚至有自杀倾向。研究表明，15%～20% 的人群在青少年阶段曾有抑郁表现[18]，严重者有自杀倾向，其中男性较女性患者更易出现自杀行为。据统计，自杀是导致 5～24 岁人群死亡的第三大原因[18]，因此及早发现青少年抑郁症，并进行恰当治疗干预意义重大。

抑郁症的临床表现主要有：悲观失望、焦虑无助、缺乏兴趣、精力衰退、食欲不振、睡眠障碍、自杀倾向[18, 19]。有自杀倾向的患者对生活的兴趣明显减退，他们会向曾经有自杀行为的朋友倾诉自己的自杀想法。

当青少年出现抑郁症表现时，可给予以下应对措施：

1. 增进家庭交流：家庭因素在青少年成长中扮演着重要角色。家庭成员间有效的情感沟通与交流可以减轻青少年的孤独感，从而避免抑郁的不良后果[20]。

2. 增强自尊与自信：自尊是个体的自我价值判断，自信是个体对自身能力自我肯定的信念，良好的自尊与自信可以帮助个体正确认识自我[21]。青少年抑郁症患者通常缺乏自尊与自信，因此应积极鼓励他们认识自我、接受自我、肯定自我，不要与他人攀比，不要惧怕失败，并且帮助他们发掘潜能，弥补不足。

3. 适当控制情绪：青少年在生理上进入青春期发育的同时，其心理发展也表现出许多特殊的变化，情绪波动显著[22]，因此应该鼓励青少年正确表达及控制情感，告诉他们表达情绪时要分析原因，例如"我很生气是因为我的同学取笑我的缺点"，"我很开心是因为我学习进步了"。

自杀与抑郁存在潜在关联，自杀在全球人群死亡原因中排名前二十，目前已成为全球健康隐患。每年有一百万人死于自杀，一到两千万人有自杀倾向，五千万至一亿两千万因亲人自杀而遭受精神重创[23]。据调查，中国城市人口 70% 至 80% 的自杀源于压力与抑郁[24]，自杀的危险因素主要包括心理疾病、抑郁、酒精滥用、吸毒、暴力、文化与社会等因素。

当青少年患者出现自杀倾向时，应马上为其进行专业心理干预。不要认为有自杀想法的青少年只是口头说说而不会付诸行动；不要认为对有自杀倾向的青少年无能为力，80% 的人在自杀前会向他人传达自杀信息，早发现早干预可有效降低自杀率；不要惧怕在青少年面前谈及自杀话题，谈及它未必会导致青少年自杀行为，相反正向、积极的引导与讨论能使有自杀倾向的青少年感到被重视与理解。如果自杀行为在所难免，应速将患者送至最近的急救中心进行抢救。

焦虑症

焦虑症是一种无法自控的以情绪过度焦虑和紧张为主要临床表现的神经性障碍 [25]。轻度焦虑对促进青少年成长发育具有一定的积极作用，但重度焦虑将危及青少年健康。

焦虑症是儿童和青少年期最常见的心理问题，近 13% 的 9 岁至 17 岁儿童和青少年曾有不同程度的焦虑症状，且女性比男性高发 [18]。

焦虑症的主要临床表现为对现实生活杞人忧天，紧张恐惧，迫切要求消除恐惧或疑虑，或伴有身体不适感如胃疼、心悸、出汗、晕厥、恶心、濒死感等 [18]。

青少年焦虑症患者应适当控制情绪、掌握避免、减少压力的技巧方法。

1. 常见的控制情绪的方法包括 [21]：

1）焦虑情绪的产生有时是注意力太集中于问题的负性方面，因此，学习把注意力转移到积极的或愉快的事情上，就可以从焦虑情绪中解脱出来。青少年可以通过做一些其他的事情如洗脸、喝水等转移注意力，或者采取听音乐、做运动的方式进行情绪放松，暂时不去理会导致焦虑的人或事。

2）当遭遇挫折时首先要保持镇静，客观理智分析受挫原因，积极寻求补偿的途径，使用积极的心理防卫方式和心理调控方法，减轻挫折感，提高耐受力。

3）学会向老师、家长、同学、朋友倾诉心事以宣泄负性情绪。

4）引导青少年树立正确的人生观与价值观，使其认识到人生起伏跌宕，在竞争激烈、生活节奏加快的社会中，只有迅速地调整自己，改变自己的生活方式、行为方式、思维方式，才能实现自我价值。

5）保持乐观外向的性格，不要因为一次失败而对未来丧失信心与希望。

2. 青春期的压力与焦虑难以避免，青少年常用的减少压力的技巧与方法包括：

1）有条不紊地进行时间管理，按部就班地安排学习与生活。

2）调整心态，尽量避免不必要的担心顾虑。

3）为保证身心健康，保持平衡膳食、充足睡眠、合理作息、适量运动、培养健康的兴趣爱好及乐观开朗的性格。

4）开阔眼界，关注时事，用知识武装头脑，善于借鉴他人的经验与教训。

5）和谐的人际关系会使人得到更多的心理支持，保持良好的人际关系，学会向人倾诉。

6）通过音乐、运动绘画等方式转移注意力以暂时缓解压力。

7）找到压力源，学会乐观面对难题，并积极寻求解决方法[26]。

精神疾病

精神疾病是指严重的心理障碍，精神疾病患者的思维及认知出现异常，不能正常学习、工作和生活。妄想、幻觉及思维障碍是精神疾病的主要特征[27]。

研究发现，全球精神疾病的发生率在2%～16%之间[28]，发病年龄通常为12～18岁[29]。由于精神疾病对患者个人、家庭及社会均有显著的影响，因此必须及早注意识别其早期症状。其早期症状主要包括妄想、幻觉及思维障碍。

1. 妄想

妄想是指错误的信念，如认为有人正在对他指指点点或者电视正在发送秘密消息。在精神病学中，妄想是指在精神病态中产生的错误信念（疾病本身或者是疾病进展引起）[30]。

妄想一般发生在精神病状态下或心理疾病中，其不局限于某一特殊疾病，在许多疾病中都会出现（包括生理疾病及心理疾病）[31]。然而，妄想在神经分裂症、妄想痴呆及抑郁症等精神疾病中具有重要的诊断意义。

2. 幻觉

幻觉是指在缺乏外部刺激的作用下产生的感官知觉，幻觉与妄想或知觉歪曲不同，后者是指外部刺激导致的错误知觉[32]。幻觉可发生在五种感官中的任何一种中，并表现为多种形式，其中包括单纯的感觉幻觉（如光、颜色、味道及气味），也包括更有意义的经验，如看到并与动物和人交流、听到声音、拥有复杂的触觉。

幻听，尤其是听到声音，是一种常见的、精神症的常见特征。幻音可能是与人交谈，也可包括几个不同的谈话者。当幻听内容具有贬损、命令或指控的特征时，是极其令人烦恼的。然而，听到声音不一定都是消极的。一项研究指出，大多数幻听患者不需要精神治疗[33]。因此，幻听运动应运而生，无论听到声音的人是否被认为患有精神疾病。

3. 思维障碍

思维障碍是指意识思维的潜在异常，多根据思维障碍对言语及写作的影响进行分类[34]。受影响者表现为关联的松弛，即言语和写作的语义内容断开或无序。严重情况下，言语不能被理解。例如，如果话题转换太快，语句太长，过于啰嗦，主旨不明，或者词语组合有误导致不易理解，均会导致言语理解障碍[35]。

言语体现思维，思维形式的观察自然涉及个体言语的观察。思维障碍的可能症状和体征包括：①思维中断，这是指语句在完成前，讲话者不能想起正在讲的主题。②思维奔逸，这是指在谈话过程中刺激导致的话题转化。③模仿言语，这是指重复自己或他人的言语，可只重复一次、也可能不断重复，重复的内容可能仅仅是几个词语，也可能是讲话者句子的最后几个词语。④持续言语，这是指不断重复语句或思想[35]。

4. 精神分裂症

精神分裂症是常见的精神疾病之一，通常表现为妄想、幻觉及思维障碍。精神分裂常首发于年轻人，全球终生患病率为 0.3%～0.7%[36]。一项于 1982～1985 年在 12 个地区开展的研究结果显示，15 岁以上的精神分裂患者时点患病率为 4.75‰[37]。下列案例用于早期识别精神分裂症的典型症状。

案例 5-1　精神分裂症

患者 LM，女，17 岁，未婚，因自我偏激行为、偶发攻击行为持续十余天经急诊收入女性精神病房。其病史显示，患者对日常活动缺乏兴趣，自尊极强，思想变化快速，社会交往及个人生活均受到一定的影响，同时伴有奇怪的行为，如将垃圾分类，朝特定方向发呆，工作消极，说一些奇怪的话，如"她无所不能，所有人都应该按照她说的做"或者"她能利用上帝赋予她的力量毁灭宇宙"。她的生理功能（尤其是睡眠及食欲）也有改变。

需强调的是，精神分裂症的症状在人群中表现为一个连续体，在做出精神分裂症的诊断之前，其症状的严重性需达到一定的程度，且诊断只能由专业心理专家做出。由于疾病进展没有可靠的标准，精神分裂症的预防有一定的困难。一旦被确诊为精神分裂症的患者，应接受家庭疗法、社区疗法、支持性就业、认知矫正、技能培训、认知行为疗法、安定药、住院等治疗[38]。

第 3 节　青少年身心社会亚健康

概述

继世界卫生组织公布的健康概念得到广泛应用后，20 世纪 80 年代中期，前苏联学者 N·布赫曼教授发现，在健康和疾病之外，人体还有一种非健康非患病的中间状态，称为"灰色状态"或"第三状态"[39]。中国学者将其称为"亚健康"（sub-health）。它是介于健康疾病之间的边缘阶段，具有向健康方面或向疾病方面转化的双向性。早期发现，及时调理，能够有效预防疾病，提高生命质量。

1. 概念演变

1995 年在北京召开了"首届亚健康学术研讨会"，确定了"亚健康状态"这一名称，并给出了广义的亚健康概念：疾病与健康之间的过渡状态称为亚健康状态。其后很多学者对其概念进行了具体描述和定义，引用较多者为：亚健康是指人的机体虽然没有明显的疾病，但已有程度不同的发生某种疾病的高危倾向，甚至已经处于某种疾病的边缘或早期状态，是人们处于健康与疾病之间的健康低质量状态。叶芳在其博士学位论文中这样描述亚健康："亚健康是一种动态的状态，可导致个体可自我感受到的生理功能、心理功能或社会适应功能不同程度的下降，但未达到任何可诊断疾病的标准。"[40] 但至今没有被广泛公认的定义。西方国家及日本未用"亚健康"这一名词，但存在与此相关的研究，如慢性疲劳综合征（chronic fatigue syndrome，CFS）、阈下精神障碍（subthreshold psychiatric disorders）。

2. 发生率

国外研究发现，青少年 CFS 发病率逐步上升，11 岁后发病率和成年人基本相当[41]。阈下精神障碍在任何年龄都存在，国内学者调查表明，抑郁症状在儿童青少年群体中具有很高的流行率，湖南城乡高中女生的抑郁症状显著高于男生[42]。合肥市小学生抑郁症状检出率为 11.9%，深圳市小学生抑郁症状检出率 8.2%[43]。中国优生优育协会在 2008 年对全国 22 个省市青少年调查显示我国有三千万青少年处于亚健康状态。国内另一项对青少年亚健康全国常模制定的研究中，显示青少年亚健康检出率为 9.5%[44]。

3. 危害

对青少年来讲，亚健康带来的食欲不振和代谢紊乱会造成营养不良，影响骨骼和神经发育；同时伴随而来的悲观、没耐心、兴趣不高等负面情绪会造成不自信、多疑、偏执等不良性格；另外，亚健康令人感到学习动力不足，缺乏效率甚至产生厌学情绪。据文献报道，CFS 现已成为影响青少年不能维持日常生活和在校学习的主要因素，并给家庭、社会产生诸多消极影响，增加社会的医疗负担[45]。有研究[46]表明，阈下精神障碍可能是发展为精神障碍的前奏，会引起更多的阈下精神障碍的综合疾病。总之，亚健康状态对青少年有生理、心理、精神及社会适应方面的诸多危害。

评估

1. 亚健康的识别

（1）典型表现：亚健康状态下，虽然没有器质性的疾病，但机体功能上已出现改变，如机体活力、耐力、反应能力、适应能力及免疫能力的降低，生理功能的减弱等[47]。通俗地说，可见身体上的失眠、乏力、疲倦、性机能减退等；心理上的情绪低落、精神萎靡、记忆力下降等；社交情感上的冷淡、无助、孤独感、空虚等。

（2）评估标准、分类和分型：目前国内外尚无统一的评估标准及分类分型依据。在生理亚健康方面，美国、澳大利亚、英国、日本等国，针对亚健康状态中最普遍的慢性疲劳综合征，先后制定了诊断标准，但各国在诊断标准上各有差别：美国诊断标准认为只要日常活动减少一半以上即可确诊为疲劳，而英国和澳大利亚的诊断标准则强调疲劳必须很严重，在其他诊断方面也存在许多分歧。在心理亚健康方面，国际学者有少量研究，1994年 Judd [48,49] 等提出"亚综合抑郁"的概念，它属阈下抑郁的多形性表现之一，是指在普通人群中有大约 20%～30% 存在抑郁症状，虽未达到抑郁症的诊断标准，但同样会造成严重的职业功能下降、社会功能损害等危害。David 等也提出"阈下强迫障碍"一词，是指有强迫症状，但在症状持续时间和程度上不符合诊断标准的一种状态。这些"精神疲劳"、"亚综合征抑郁"、"阈下强迫障碍"等都与所谓的心理亚健康状态密切相关。国内学者多采用自评健康的方法进行。但尚无公认评估标准，各研究采用不同的定义和标准，结果差异显著，难以进行横向比较，不利于研究成果的运用与推广。

纵观国内外亚健康研究现状，评估标准、分类和分型缺乏统一，有必要达成世界范围的统一标准，有利于更好地开展研究和治疗。

2. 常用评估工具

当前国内比较认可和得以推广的青少年亚健康评定量表是《青少年亚健康多维评定问卷》（Multidimensional Sub Health Questionnaire of Adolescents，MSQA)[50]，MSQA 由安徽医科大学陶芳标教授领导的课题组编创，并证实信度、效度良好[51][量表的重测相关系数、Cronbaeh α 系数、分半信度系数分别为 0.868、0.957、0.942；以 SCL-90、康奈尔医学指数（CMI）问卷作为效标，效标关联效度分别为 0.636、0.649 和反应度良好[52]]。他进一步描述全国青少年身心亚健康症状的分布特征，制定了全国常模[44]：他在全国 9 个省份的 9个城市选取城乡初中、高中以及大学共 22 325 名学生，运用《青少年亚健康多维评定问卷》进行评定，计算青少年学生在身心亚健康及其躯体、心理亚健康

2个领域，以及躯体活力不足、生理功能减退、抵抗力下降、情绪问题、品行问题、社会适应困难6个维度的亚健康症状数的 P_{85}、P_{90} 和 P_{95}。结果证实男、女生躯体、心理及总体亚健康症状检出率的差异无统计学意义；躯体、心理及身心亚健康症状检出率年级间差异有统计学意义；城乡学生躯体亚健康和身心亚健康症状的检出率差异无统计学意义。他同时提出 P_{90} 作为青少年不同维度亚健康状态划界值的流行病学判定标准，公布了青少年亚健康状态评价划界值（躯体亚健康症状数3，心理亚健康症状数8，总症状数11），便于统一和简便使用；同时，也分别提出初中生（躯体亚健康症状数3，心理亚健康症状数7，总症状数10）、高中生（躯体亚健康症状数4，心理亚健康症状数11，总症状数15）和大学生（躯体亚健康症状数2，心理亚健康症状数6，总症状数8）人群亚健康状态划界值。并且通过后续研究证实，青少年亚健康状态与自杀、自伤等多种健康危险行为以及生活满意度有关，还能预测因病缺课率、烟酒使用、自杀意念、自杀计划、自杀未遂和多种自伤行为[53]。

MSQA 量表发布后，得到广泛应用。徐长恩[54]等用其对温州市高校学生进行调查，发现身心亚健康检出率为 9.4%；廖学舟[55]等用其对鄂州市中学和高校学生进行调查，结果表明，有 42.7% 的青少年处于不同程度的亚健康状态；屠春雨[56]等用其对绍兴市高校、高中、初中青少年进行调查，发现躯体、心理、身心亚健康症状数略低于全国常模平均水平。邵际晓[57]等用其对重庆市高校、高中、初中青少年进行调查，发现躯体亚健康、心理亚健康和身心亚健康的状态检出率分别为 13.8%、13.8%、12.6%。总之，多维亚健康评定在青少年群体中应用广泛，但仍处于起步阶段，调查结果分歧较大，还需要大范围、大规模地进一步对划界值作出实证研究，获得更多的效度资料。

干预

及时干预有助于早期发现损害健康的问题，可及时扭转青少年亚健康状态，也可以降低由亚健康过渡为疾病所负担的医疗费用，促进青少年身心的健康成长。国外对于亚健康范畴临床状态的处理多为对症处理[58]。国内，陶芳标[59]建议将青少年亚健康的早期发现和干预纳入学校卫生服务领域，做好日常监督和教育工作，对青少年亚健康状态进行早期识别。陈金彪[60]发现上海大学生亚健康状况与体育运动模式、睡眠模式、饮食模式和休闲模式有显著的相关性，提示可以从坚持适当运动、合理安排膳食、建立良好的作息习惯等方面，提高青少年的健康水平。另外，梁兴华[61]研究发现采用传统医学中的中草药调理可以从身体、心理和社会各方面提高亚健康人群的健康水平，提示中医中药在亚健康干预和预防方面可发挥重要作用。

小结

亚健康是较新的医学概念,逐步得到公众与学术界的广泛重视。但是现阶段,其概念不统一、范畴宏观模糊、分类标准不一、分类研究结论缺乏一致性等,与相关疾病的关系认识尚存在分歧,这些问题都妨碍亚健康评估、干预体系的形成。而青少年亚健康作为亚健康分支,研究进展更为迟缓,应加强研究、评估和早期干预,促进青少年健康的发展。

(霍　苗,关持循,陈　林,唐永云,李云峰)

参 考 文 献

[1] Hazen E, Schlozman S, Beresin E. Adolescent psychological development: a review [J]. Pediatrics in Review, 2008, 29(5): 161-168.

[2] Steinberg L. Adolescence [M]. 8th ed. New York: McGraw-Hill, 2008.

[3] Hart D, Carlo G. Moral development in adolescence [J]. Journal of Research on Adolescence, 2005, 15(3): 223-233.

[4] Meeus W, Iedema J, Helsen M, et al. Patterns of adolescent identity development: review of literature and longitudinal analysis [J]. Developmental Review, 1999, 19(4): 419-461.

[5] Ruffin N. Adolescent growth and development [EB/OL]. Virginia Cooperative Extension, 2009-5-1[2011-6-25]: http://pubs.ext.vt.edu/350/350-850/350-850.html.

[6] Perkins DF. Adolescence: developmental tasks [EB/OL]. University of Florida IFAS Extension, 2008[2011-6-24]: http://www.education.com/reference/article/Ref_Developmental_Tasks/.

[7] Lewis J. The physiological and psychological development of the adolescent [EB/OL]. Yale-New Haven Teachers Institute, 1991[2011-7-7]: http://www.yale.edu/ynhti/curriculum/units/1991/5/91.05.07.x.html.

[8] Student Health Service. Psychological Health of Adolescents [EB/OL]. Department of Health, the Government of the Hong Kong Special Administrative Region, 2011-7-5[2011-7-7]: http://www.studenthealth.gov.hk/english/health/health_ph/health_ph_young.html.

[9] Zimberoff D, Hartman D. The ego in heart-centered therapies: ego strengthening and ego surrender [J]. Journal of Heart Centered Therapies, 2000, 3(2): 3-66.

[10] Lucile Salter, Packard Children's Hospital. Cognitive development [EB/OL]. Lucile Salter Packard Children's Hospital, [2011-6-24]: http://www.lpch.org/DiseaseHealthInfo/HealthLibrary/adolescent/cogdev.html.

[11] U.S. Department of Education. My Child's Academic Success: How can I help my child to become more confident [EB/OL]. U.S. Department of Education, 2003-9-11[2011-6-

24]: http://www.ed.gov/parents/academic/help/adolescence/part8.html.

[12] American Psychological Association. Developing adolescents: a reference for professionals [EB/OL]. American Psychological Association, 2002[2011-6-24]: http://www.apa.org/pi/pii/develop.pdf.

[13] Spano S. Stages of adolescent development [J/OL]. 2004[2011-7-3]: http://ecommons.cornell.edu/bitstream/1813/19311/2/StagesAdol_chart.pdf.

[14] 倪建明. 青春期的心理冲突 [EB/OL]. 桐庐叶浅予中学, 2010-9-13[2011-6-24]: http://www.yqyzx.com/Moral/ShowArticle.asp?ArticleID=209.

[15] Warren BJ, Broome B. The culture of mental illness in adolescents with urologic problems [J]. Urologic Nursing, 2011, 31(2): 95-103.

[16] 静进. 我国儿童青少年面临的主要心理卫生问题及对策 [J]. 中国心理卫生杂志, 2010, 24(5): 321-324.

[17] Whitlock J, Schantz K. Mental illness and mental health in adolescence [EB/OL]. ACT for Youth Center of Excellence, 2008-12[2011-6-20]: http://www.actforyouth.net/resources/rf/rf_mentalhealth_1208.pdf.

[18] Martin L, Milot A. Assessing the mental health of adolescents: a guide for out-of-school time program practitioners [EB/OL]. Child Trends, 2007-3[2011-6-18]: http://www.childtrends.org/files/mentalhealth.pdf.

[19] 刘新民. 变态心理学 [M]. 北京: 中国医药科技出版社, 2005.

[20] WHO. Caring for Children and Adolescents with Mental Disorders [EB/OL]. World Health Organization, 2003 [2011-6-25]: http://www.who.int/mental_health/media/en/785.pdf.

[21] 王颖, 张银玲. 护理心理学 [M]. 北京: 中国医药科技出版社, 2005.

[22] 严红. 青少年心理特点及教育策略 [EB/OL]. 上海浦东教育发展研究院, 2009[2011-6-25]: http://wenku.baidu.com/view/fba40237ee06eff9aef80767.html.

[23] Hendin H, Phillips MR, Vijayakumar L, et al. Introduction: suicide and suicide prevention in Asia [M/OL]. 2008[2011-6-26]: http://www.who.int/mental_health/resources/suicide_prevention_asia/en/.

[24] Centerstone. The international crisis intervention symposium [EB/OL]. 2008-6-30[2011-6-26]: http://wenku.baidu.com/view/8a7ee1649b6648d7c1c746ab.html.

[25] 陈彦芳. 精神科护理学 [M]. 北京: 人民卫生出版社, 2005.

[26] 古茂盛. 人格心理学 [M]. 北京: 中国医药科技出版社, 2006.

[27] Gelder M, Mayou R, Geddes J. Psychiatry[M]. New York: Oxford University Press Inc. 2005.

[28] 张雯菲. 辽宁省 6～17 岁儿童青少年精神障碍流行病学调查 [D]. 大连: 大连医科大学, 2010.

[29] 王莉莉. 青少年神经症与精神障碍发病的现状分析 [J]. 现代中西医结合杂志, 2005, 14(18): 2447.

[30] Ellis HD. Delusions: a suitable case for imaging [J]. International Journal of Psychophysiology, 2007, 63: 146-151.

[31] Matthew RB, Lisa B. Mental Illness as Mental: In Defense of Psychological Realism [J/OL]. Humana Mente, 2009, 11: 25-43 [2011-6-25]: http://www.humanamente.eu/PDF/Issue11_Paper_Bortolotti_Broome.pdf.

[32] Harper D. Hallucinate. Online Etymology Dictionary [EB/OL].[2011-6-24]: http://www.etymonline.com/index.php?search=hallucinate&searchmode=none.

[33] Honig A, Romme MA, Ensink BJ, et al. Auditory hallucinations: a comparison between patients and nonpatients [J]. Journal of Nervous and Mental Disease, 1998, 186(10): 646–651.

[34] Metsanen M, Wahlberg K-E, Saarento O, et al. Early presence of thought disorder as a prospective sign of mental disorder [J]. Psychiatry Research, 2004, 125: 193-203.

[35] Wikipedia. Thought disorder [EB/OL].Wikipedia, 2011-7-28 [2011-7-31]: http://en.wikipedia.org/wiki/Thought_disorder.

[36] van Os J, Kapur S. Schizophrenia[J]. The Lancet, 2009, 374(9690): 635–645.

[37] dingding. 什么是精神分裂症 [EB/OL]. 山东红十字会医院, 2010-3-4[2011-6-25]: http://www.sdsmyy.com/jingshenfenlie/leixing/201003041200.shtml.

[38] Wikipedia. Schizophrenia [EB/OL]. Wikipedia, 2011-6-24[2011-6-27]: http://en.wikipedia.org/wiki/Schizophrenia.

[39] 马京华. 21 世纪健康自助手册 [M]. 北京: 中国轻工业出版社, 2001.

[40] 叶芳. 改进德尔菲(Delphi)法研究亚健康的描述性定义及评价标准 [D]. 北京: 中国协和医科大学, 2008.

[41] Chalder T, Goodman R, Wessely S, et al. Epidemiology of chronic fatigue syndrome and self reported myalgic encephalomyelitis in 5～15 year olds: cross sectional study [J]. BMJ, 2003, 327(7416): 654–655.

[42] 罗英姿, 王湘, 朱熊兆, 等. 高中生抑郁水平调查及其影响因素研究 [J]. 中国临床心理学杂志, 2008, 16(3): 274 - 277.

[43] 许娟, 林德南, 王坚杰, 等. 合肥市和深圳市小学生抑郁症状及其影响因素比较 [J]. 中国心理卫生杂志, 2008, 22(4): 246 – 252.

[44] 陶芳标, 邢超, 袁长江, 等. 青少年亚健康多维评定问卷的全国常模制定 [J]. 中国学校卫生, 2009, 30(4): 292-295.

[45] Richards J, Turk J, White S. Children and adolescents with chronic fatigue syndrome in non-specialist settings: beliefs, functional impairment and psychiatric disturbance [J]. Eur Child Adolesc Psychiatry, 2005, 14(6): 310-318.

[46] Cuijpers P，Smit F. Subthreshold depression as a risk indicator for major depressive disorder: a systematic review of prospective studies [J]. Acta Psychiatr Scand，2004，109 (5)：325-331.

[47] Briggs NC，Levine PH. A comparative review of systemic and neurological symptomatology in 12 outbreaks collectively described as chronic fatigue syndrome，epidemic neuromyasthenia and my-ologic encephaomyelitis [J]. Clinical Infectious Diseases，1994，18(Suppl 1)：S32-S42.

[48] Judd LL，Rapaport MH，Paulus MP，et al. Subsyndromal symptomatic depression：A new mood disorder[J]. Jclin Psychiatry，1994，55(suppl 4)：18-28.

[49] Judd LL，Akiskal HS，Paulus MP. The role and clinical significance of subsyndromal depressive symptoms in unipolar major depressive disorder [J]. J Affect Disorders，1997，45(1)：5-18.

[50] 齐秀玉，陶芳标，胡传来，等. 中国青少年亚健康多维问卷编制 [J]. 中国公共卫生，2008，24(9)：1025-1028.

[51] 邢超，陶芳标，袁长江，等. 青少年亚健康多维评定问卷信度和效度评价 [J]. 中国公共卫生，2008，24(9)：1031-1033.

[52] 万宇辉，胡传来，陶芳标，等. 青少年亚健康多维评定问卷反应度分析 [J]. 中国公共卫生，2008，24(9)：1035-1036.

[53] 万宇辉. 青少年亚健康与多种身心健康问题的相关性研究 [D]. 安徽：安徽医科大学，2009.

[54] 徐长恩，王若蛟，郝加虎，等. 大学生亚健康状态新划界标准的应用 [J]. 中国学校卫生，2010，31(12)：1423-1425.

[55] 廖学舟，张娟，张隆明，等. 鄂州市青少年亚健康现状及影响因素 [J]. 中国社会医学杂志，2010，27(1)：8-10.

[56] 屠春雨，邢超，傅利军，等. 绍兴市青少年亚健康状态划界标准 [J]. 中国学校卫生，2010，31(12)：1415-1419.

[57] 邵际晓，王宏，李雷雷，等. 重庆市青少年亚健康状况调查 [J]. 现代预防医学，2011，38(9)：1667-1669.

[58] Fulcher KY，White PD. Randomised controlled trial of graded exercise in patients with the chronic fatigue syndrome [J]. BMJ，1997，314(7095)：1647-1652.

[59] 陶芳标. 青少年亚健康早期发现与干预：学校卫生服务新领域 [J]. 中国学校卫生，2009，30(4)：290–291.

[60] 陈金彪. 上海大学生亚健康状态的自评方法及生活方式多因素交互作用的研究 [D]. 上海：华东师范大学，2008.

[61] 梁兴华. 香港地区亚健康现状的初步研究 [D]. 南京：南京中医药大学，2009.

第六章

青少年健康行为

很多儿科专家和其他的卫生专业人员都认为青少年是健康的，因为与儿童和成年人相比，他们表现出较低的死亡率和发病率，大多数青少年也认为自身是健康的。但是，人们正不断接受这样一个事实，即青少年也存在健康问题，并且许多青少年存在严重影响他们健康或导致成年期健康问题的健康危险行为。

2005年，在卫生部的领导下，北京大学儿童青少年卫生研究所进行了一项全国范围内的青少年健康危险行为调查[1]，结果显示，我国城市青少年人群各类健康危险行为发生率呈现上升趋势，主要归纳为五个方面，分别是不健康饮食行为、非故意伤害事故、自杀、物质滥用和过早性行为。因此，卫生工作者应该帮助青少年避免健康危险行为，并建立正确健康的行为方式，促进青少年健康成长。

内布拉斯加框架[又称"青少年健康危险行为整合模型（IMAHRB）"]是通过各学科文献综述的方法建立起来的，用来回答"什么过程影响并鼓励青少年来参与或避免危险因素？"内布拉斯加框架包括：保护或提高因素、危险刺激、判断、危险避免或冒险行为、结果。应用内布拉斯加框架，能识别并调动青少年现在的保护和提高因素，同时对青少年的危险过程有一个更加全面的看法[2]。

这一章将主要讨论青少年健康行为的三个方面，分别是健康饮食、体育锻炼和物质滥用。非故意伤害将在本书的其他章节进行讨论。学校老师和专业健康教育者可应用下面的小组作业（表6-1）来鼓励学生进行有关健康行为的自我思考。

表 6-1　小组作业

小组作业：
把学生分成两组并且让两组来讨论我们日常生活中的健康和不健康行为。
第一组：讨论健康行为和由它们带来的益处。
第二组：讨论不健康行为和由它们导致的后果。
问题：
1. 你认为该如何形成健康行为？
2. 关于健康和不健康行为，你还想知道哪些？

第1节 健康饮食

青春期是生长发育的第二个高峰期,对营养的需求量比生命周期的其他时段要高一些。充足的营养和能量摄入对于健康发展是很关键的[3]。健康的饮食可以使身体最优化,同时可以减少诸如肥胖、心脏疾病、糖尿病等慢性病的风险。

健康饮食

健康饮食被定义为多吃蔬菜和水果,低脂,高纤维,饮食平衡而全面[3]。青少年需要用健康的饮食来维持生长发育以及保持功能的最优化[4]。一份健康的饮食,应该包括满足青少年能量所需的足量食物,并且食物种类齐全,各种类之间保持均衡。如图6-1所示,有五种基本的食物种类:含淀粉的食物(例如面包、米饭、马铃薯等);牛奶和奶制品;蛋白质(例如肉、鱼、蛋、豆类);脂肪类食物;水果和蔬菜。

图6-1 五种食物种类[4]

青少年应该吃由上述五种食物构成的均衡饮食。一天应该进食多次面包、米饭和马铃薯,全麦类更好。通常,一天需要量为250~400g,这是中国居民膳食宝塔的基础(图6-2)。

不饱和植物油和软黄油类	25~30g
盐	6g
牛奶和奶制品	300g
豆类和坚果	30~50g
家禽类	50~75g
鱼	50~100g
蛋	25~50g
蔬菜	300~500g
水果	200~400g
所有谷类、面包、大米和马铃薯	250~400g
水	1200ml

图6-2　中国居民膳食金字塔(中国营养学会2007)

　　因此,青少年每天应该多吃几次各种新鲜的、当地的水果和蔬菜。水果和蔬菜中含有对人体有益的多种维生素。每天推荐吃蔬菜300~500g,水果200~400g。肉类特别是瘦肉在我们日常生活中是必不可少的。可以用鱼、家禽和蛋类来替代油腻的肉类和肉制品。对于青少年来说,使用牛奶和奶制品300g(纯奶和酸奶)是很好的,它们的脂肪和盐含量都很低。豆类和坚果类因含有高质量的蛋白也被推荐使用。脂肪类的摄入应当控制(不超过每天能量的30%),大多数的饱和脂肪酸应当被不饱和的植物油和软人造黄油所替代。除此以外,低盐饮食是健康的,每天全部盐的摄入应当不超过6g,包括面包中的盐和加工的食物中的盐[5]。

　　除了平衡饮食外,还有一些需要知道的原则。食物的加工应该安全和卫生。对于青少年来说,选择低糖食物,限食精制糖、糖类饮料和甜点,都将保护他们的牙齿。最好能够通过每天中等强度的体育运动将体重控制在推荐范围内[BMI指数是18.5~25,BMI是体重(千克)除以身高(米)的平方]。

　　青少年的健康饮食需要与这些原则相符,他们可以选择他们喜欢的每组中的不同食物。对于青少年来说,最重要的事情是他们能把每天健康的饮食习惯和自身的生活方式融为一体。这样,他们就能从健康的饮食中大大受益。

不健康的饮食

根据 2005 年全国青少年健康危险行为的调查结果 [1]，19.5% 的青少年从来不喝牛奶或者豆奶，3.6% 从来不吃早餐，27.2% 通常吃甜点，12.8% 频繁饮用软饮料，4.3% 一周吃快餐 4～5 次。这些不健康的饮食习惯将伤害青少年。

不健康的饮食是慢性疾病的一个危险因素 [6]，它包括不平衡的膳食、过多的食物摄入、不充足的食物摄入等。不平衡的膳食将导致血压升高、血糖升高、异常的血脂等，同时，过多的食物摄入或者不充足的摄入可能导致发育问题。不健康的饮食包括不吃早餐、喜食快餐、喝碳酸饮料、节食、偏食。这些习惯将从不同方面影响青少年的健康和生长发育。

早餐非常重要，对一些疾病能起到预防作用 [7]。不吃早餐将引起早晨饥饿的感觉，并将诱使人吃零食，尤其是那些含糖和脂肪高的零食 [8]。进食太多的快餐和饮用碳酸饮料将导致营养失调，同时零食能降低食欲并影响营养的吸收。快餐能导致肥胖，这将影响健康和自我形象。一些节食的青少年不吃肉不喝牛奶来减肥，蛋白质和钙质的缺乏可能导致营养失调和骨质疏松。一些青少年挑食严重，通常吃他们最喜欢的食物。因此，他们的饮食不平衡，一些营养过剩而另一些营养则不足。

健康指导

青少年的营养问题或者不健康的饮食习惯，起源于青少年的早期生活。遵循下列健康指南，有可能得以纠正。树立健康饮食的正确观念，养成良好的饮食习惯，会预防饮食相关疾病。整个家庭，乃至整个社会都应该倡导健康饮食。

家庭环境是影响青少年饮食行为的重要因素 [9]。父母应该按照青少年自身的偏好以及他们的营养和健康需求，为其准备平衡的饮食，并在饮食上起主导作用，为他们树立健康饮食的好榜样。尽量选择全营养食品，如吃全麦面包而不是其他面包，不要把食物作为一种奖励或惩罚的手段。鼓励一家人一起吃饭。另外家人、照顾者、朋友、学校、媒体等，应该一起为青少年建立一个良好的饮食环境，因为这些外在因素会影响青少年的饮食习惯和食物选择 [10]。

青少年应该每天吃早餐，并确保他们摄入足够的碳水化合物和牛奶或豆奶 [11]。饮食要有规律，并尽量少吃零食。每天吃足够的新鲜蔬菜和水果。指南建议每天至少摄入 5 份水果和蔬菜，减少饱和脂肪和盐的摄入，增加复合碳水化合物的摄入 [9]。青少年也应该少吃糖或甜食，以保护牙齿并维持正常的血糖水平。

学校老师可以用下面的案例（表6-2）来帮助青少年自觉杜绝某些不健康的饮食行为。

表6-2　关于软饮料的案例

案例研究

　　有些中学生喜欢在运动后立即喝冷饮或在放学后吃零食，这是很不健康的。他们没意识到这种生活方式对他们的身体是有害的。

　　作为老师，我认为我们可以在实验课上做一个实验，检测饮料中维生素C含量。通过这种学生自己做实验的方式，他们会认识到饮料中的维生素C含量非常少，并非像广告中描述的那样。这是一种好方法，可以让学生自己自然而然地减少饮用饮料。

第2节　体育锻炼

体育锻炼包括体育活动（如足球）和运动锻炼（如慢跑），也包括有规律的日常活动，例如步行去学校和在家做家务（如打水）或工作（如粉刷房间）。

体育锻炼的益处

规律的体育锻炼对青春期及以后的生活有重要的生理、心理及社会益处。生理上，体育锻炼不仅有助于骨骼和肌肉的生长发育，还有助于保持身材匀称；心理上，体育锻炼有助于青少年建立自信和自尊，还有助于更好地学习和工作，而且当青少年焦虑、忧伤或生气时，体育锻炼能帮助平静心情；社会上，参与体育锻炼能帮助青少年结识一些人并建立友情。此外，青少年可以学习怎样按规则玩，怎样与团队其他成员合作，怎样处理成功与失败等[4]。

体育锻炼不足

体育锻炼不足可导致青少年体质健康下降。青少年体质下降问题是一个全球性难题，美、日、韩等国都先后出现过类似情况。从1985年开始，我国进行了五次"全国青少年体质健康监测"，调查结果显示，中国青少年体质在总体上呈下降趋势[12]。之所以造成这样的情况，归根结底是因为生活环境急剧变化的同时，生活方式却没及时跟进。与此同时，广大中小学生课业负担过重导致学生学习时间过长，从体育锻炼中挤占时间成了必然。另外，随着快速城市化的发展，进行体育锻炼的场地变得越来越小。所有这些因素导致了青少年体育锻炼不足。

体育锻炼运动量

每天大约60分钟的体育锻炼是比较合适的，但是每个人需要根据自身的健康状况调整适合自己的活动强度和活动量。中央关于加强青少年体育增强青少年体质的意见中也指出,要确保学生每天锻炼 1 小时 [13]。

有氧运动

体育锻炼比较有效的方式是有氧运动。有氧运动是指,人体在氧气充分供应的情况下进行的体育锻炼。也就是说,在运动过程中,人体吸入的氧气与需求相等,达到生理上的平衡状态。简单来说,是指任何富有韵律性的运动,其运动时间较长(约 15 分钟或以上),运动强度在中等或中上的程度(最大心率之 75%~85%)[14]。衡量的标准是心率,心率保持在 150 次 / 分钟的运动量为有氧运动。要求每次锻炼的时间不少于 1 小时,每周坚持 3~5 次 [15]。常见的有氧运动项目有:步行、慢跑、滑冰、游泳、骑自行车、打太极拳、跳健身舞、做韵律操等。

第 3 节　物 质 滥 用

青少年经常会尝试吸烟、饮酒等物质滥用行为,促使他们滥用这些精神活性物质的原因有很多,比如想要模仿成年人、迎合朋友、表达个人独立、反抗家长或者仅仅是为了释放压力。但是长期物质滥用会给青少年及其成年后带来不利影响 [4, 6]。

现在,青少年物质滥用已经逐渐演变成一个全球范围内的重大公共卫生问题。在美国,青少年预防犯罪办公室指出,有 65% 年龄在 15~17 岁的青少年在过去的一个月中有酗酒行为 [16]。在中国,青少年饮酒的男、女性别比例分别为 36.4% 和 23.8%[17]。2005 年全国青少年健康危险行为调查结果显示[1],青少年吸烟率为 14.9%(男性占 22.4%,女性占 3.9%)。中国青少年网络协会调查结果显示,14.1% 青少年有网络成瘾现象 [18]。

什么是物质?

精神活性物质(如酒精、烟草、海洛因等易成瘾的物质),是指主要作用于中枢神经系统,从而影响人的视觉、听觉、味觉、嗅觉、思考、感觉或行为的化学物质 [19]。精神活性物质通常可以分为镇静剂、兴奋剂以及阿片类迷幻剂,其中有些是非违禁物品,比如酒精、烟草等,有些是违禁物品,比如海洛因、阿片等。

学校教师和专业健康教育者可以通过以下小组活动(表 6-3),增强青少年对物质滥用的自律性及自我防范意识。

表 6-3　小组活动

小组活动	
把学生分成 2 组，要求每组学生列出并分类他们曾经听过、见过以及使用过的精神活性物质，把答案写在纸上。	
1组	2组
种类 I	种类 I
种类 II	种类 II
种类 III	种类 III
……	……

青少年物质滥用的预测与诊断

美国精神病学协会出版的《精神疾病诊断与统计手册》(DSM-IV)[20] 中对物质滥用的诊断作了如下规定：反复使用酒精等精神活性物质，尚未成瘾的，以及停用精神活性物质不会出现明显戒断症状的情况。当个体持续使用精神活性物质，即使没有出现相应症状，也可诊断为物质依赖。强迫性反复使用可导致物质耐受，同时减量或停用会出现戒断症状。

物质依赖是对某种物质的使用导致适应不良的情况出现，从而导致临床显著的功能损伤或痛苦，且临床形式多样。该诊断见于《精神疾病诊断与统计手册》(DSM-IV)。护理人员或健康教育者可以根据青少年的临床表现或咨询精神科医生来做出预测诊断。

物质滥用对青少年的不良影响

由于精神活性物质从某些程度上能够影响人们的视听感觉、行为及思考，所以物质滥用可能会直接或间接地影响青少年生理及心理发展[21]。这些不利因素可能会以急性或慢性的健康问题影响青少年时期甚至成人期。

生理危害包括创伤、急性中毒、器官功能损伤、感染等。物质滥用会出现精神问题，导致创伤性事故发生率增加，比如跌倒、交通意外、溺水等问题。大约 45% 的交通事故死亡是由饮酒所引起的。物质滥用最常见并且危害最大的是急性中毒，甚至可以直接引起死亡。物质滥用可能导致心、肝、肺等重要脏器发生病变，并可导致多种恶性肿瘤的发生，还可导致不孕不育。比如饮酒可以导致肝硬化，吸烟可以导致肺癌、肺气肿和其他慢性疾病。如果多人共同使用不经消毒的注射器注射成瘾药物，就可能会感染艾滋病、乙肝等感染性疾病，同时还可导致局部感染，如脓肿、静脉炎等。除此之外，过量使用精神活性物质会为今后患肿瘤、心血管疾病、呼吸系统疾病埋下隐患[22]。

使用精神活性物质后很多青少年在心理上发生改变，表现为焦虑、记忆力及理解力下降以及精神病发作（固定虚假的想法）等，长期使用会导致焦虑或者抑郁等心理障碍，这也是青少年自杀的重要原因。物质滥用会导致青少年发生失职行为，比如离家出走、社会功能退缩、学习困难、失业及丧失经济来源、暴力事件等，甚至有些青少年为了获得金钱购买毒品，做出盗窃、抢劫等犯罪行为。

健康干预

如果物质滥用导致机能失调，那么青少年需要得到一些健康干预来康复。康复需要护士、父母、青少年、指导老师或精神科医生的合作。途径包括心理疗法和行为矫正 [23] 及 GAPS 途径 [24, 25]。

认知疗法是心理治疗的一种方法，它的目标是纠正不正常的思维，帮助病人改变不正确的假设。教师和家长应该纠正青少年关于物质滥用的态度，同时让他们认识到其危害。因此，青少年可能增强他们的意识，逐渐控制物质滥用行为。

厌恶疗法，另一种类型的心理治疗，把物质滥用和不愉快的、处罚性的经历相连接，例如把催吐药的应用和喝酒的经历相配对 [26]。

在另一种心理治疗方法——系统脱敏疗法和奖励方法中，教师和家长应该要求青少年每天逐渐减少物质滥用的量，同时，如果他们达到了今天的目标，教师、父母或者青少年自身应该给他们一定的奖励，这将巩固和加强他们的成绩。

在行为矫正中，根据青少年的个人情况，他们应当参加适当的运动。最初阶段，他们可以参加低强度的运动，例如在公园里散步、做室内的运动等。当情况好转时，可以提高运动的强度。

GAPS 方法包括一定的步骤。首先，健康专家应该收集包括年龄、性别、物质滥用的时间、频率、量等信息。其次，健康专家应该评估物质滥用的程度、环境、文化程度、身体状况以及和家族成员和同事的关系。第三，确定损害的程度。对于中度影响者，讨论并请教如何戒掉物质滥用是必需的。对于严重影响者，重点是对他们追踪和提供全面的治疗。上述过程后，健康专家应当与青少年讨论戒除物质滥用的障碍同时制定个体化的详细方案。

除此以外，应该仔细治疗并发症（比如戒断症状、失眠、坐立不安、腹泻等），因为这样可以减少身体的不适，带来勇气并能预测治疗的结果。在照顾戒断症状的病人时，给青少年提供适当的安慰、减轻对戒断症状的焦虑是非常重要的 [27, 28]。

对于有失眠症状的青少年，教给他们睡觉前放松和沉思的技巧。告诉青少年营养充足的饮食和适当的锻炼有助于睡眠。对于坐立不安的青少年要有耐心。鼓励青少年与他们的父母或者同伴交谈。对于他们来说，出去走走或者洗个热水澡会减轻焦躁。

有腹泻症状的青少年应该进食营养、易消化、低脂的食物。鼓励青少年喝低浓度盐水和果汁来预防脱水。除此以外，好好休息和保持会阴的清洁将有助于康复。

学校老师和专业健康教育者可以运用角色扮演活动（表 6-4）[19]，让学生知道物质滥用的危害及应对方式，以下仅以吸烟为例。

表 6-4　青少年吸烟的角色扮演

角色扮演
假如你是一个 12 岁的年轻人（男孩或女孩），因最近三周咳嗽，并且因晚上呼吸困难来健康中心。 　　面对健康中心人员的询问，你坦言最近一年一直在吸烟，因为父母都吸烟，大部分烟能从家里得到，吸烟能使自己看起来酷，感觉像个成年人，而且也有吸烟的朋友。你没有男（女）朋友，以前善于运动（可以任选一个）并希望自己能够保持。现在，发现自己呼吸困难。 开动脑筋，尽力找出答案： 1. 吸烟能引起什么后果？ 2. 另外，健康工作者能给这个年轻人什么建议？

健康促进

健康促进从不同层次（比如个人、学校和社区）阻止青少年物质滥用。它需要学校、家长和社会的共同支持。学校需要加强教育；父母需要与青少年沟通并且树立良好的榜样；同时社会应该创造一个健康的环境，通过媒体的力量宣传某类物质的危害。以下从三个方面分别就这些预防策略进行描述。

学校可以教青少年哪些物质是有害的以及如何对其加以辨别，从而加强教育、避免物质滥用，并通过同龄人教育巩固教学效果。比如，可以先教授班级或团队领导者物质滥用的危害，他们一旦知道了这些危害，就可以把这些知识告诉其他伙伴和同学。教师应帮助青少年树立正确的人生观并培养乐观的心态。因此，学校需要为所有学生创造一个健康的环境。

家庭预防也同样重要。家长应为青春期的孩子创造一个自由轻松的家庭环境，和他们进行有效的沟通，以便及早发现问题。家长应通过自己的行为为孩子们树立良好的榜样。如果青少年能在一个没有烟酒的健康环境中长大，那么他们接触到这些物质的可能性就会降低。对青少年来说，他们也应不断提高自身各方面的素质，学会物质滥用的知识，懂得其中的危害。在日常生活中，他们需加强自我控制，树立正确的人生观、价值观，并具有良好的道德。

社会也可以通过媒体增加影响。媒体是影响青少年行为的一条重要途径。比如，在中国我们可以利用国际禁毒日组织一些活动，通过卡片、宣传册、视频等方式，呼吁青少年远离毒品。同时，食品药品监管部门也需努力确保青少年健康成长。所有这些的目的都是为了创造一个健康和谐的环境。

反对物质滥用在行动

《中华人民共和国未成年人保护法》规定：向未成年人出售烟酒是违法行为。家长和其他监护人有义务告知青少年远离烟酒。在山东省，由山东省政府法律办公室制定的《山东省未成年人保护条例》[29]规定：家长和老师有义务引导孩子或学生养成良好的习惯；一旦发现青少年吸烟或喝酒，他们应及早对这些坏习惯加以纠正。

随着互联网的普及，越来越多的青少年接触到电脑，成为容易上网成瘾的人群，而这种成瘾也是心理依赖的一种形式。我国政府通过各种途径努力为青少年创造健康的上网环境，保障青少年的健康和发展。另外，国家应鼓励发展对青少年有益的研究性网络，并开发新的网络技术来防止青少年网络成瘾。比如，禁止在中小学周边设立网吧，营业性上网场所不应允许青少年进入。教会青少年合理使用互联网是整个社会的共同职责。

为更好地理解当地青少年中存在的健康危险行为，表6-5就此给出了一个社会实践的示例。

表6-5　社会实践

社会实践
选择一个青少年为主体的中学，就不健康行为和危险因素进行调查。 目标：理论联系实际，即运用所学知识辨明不健康行为，探究危险因素，为学生健康促进策略提供支持。 形式：为本次实践活动制定计划并征得校方的同意。在与学生接触开展工作时注意沟通技巧，并努力了解他们的真实想法。进行数据分析，帮助他们增进健康行为。实践活动结束后，作出总结并说明主要的经历。

小结

本章讨论了青少年的健康行为，目的是帮助青少年认识到健康行为的重要性，并培养他们接受健康行为、拒绝不健康行为的能力。青少年健康和发展是一个社会问题，需要全社会的关注。现在越来越多的国家已经开始关注这一课题，所以，在卫生专业人员、教师、家长和健康机构的共同影响下，青少年健康状况在未来必将发生变化。

（张　雯，江　宁，王笑蕾，杨　黎，王丽媛）

参 考 文 献

[1] 季成叶. 青少年健康危险行为 [J]. 中国学校卫生, 2007, 28 (4): 289-291.

[2] Keeler HJ, Kaiser MM. An integrative model of adolescent health risk behavior [J]. Journal of Pediatric Nursing, 2010, 25 (2): 126-137.

[3] Croll JK, Neumark-Sztainer D, Story M. Healthy eating: what does it mean to adolescent? [J]. Journal of Nutrition Education, 2001, 33 (4): 193-198.

[4] WHO. Adolescent Job Aid Part 3: Information to be provided to adolescents and their parents [EB/OL]. World Health Organization, 2010[2011-8-3]: http://www.advancefamilyplanning.org/system/files/Adol%20Job%20Aid%20Part%203.pdf.

[5] WHO/Europe. A healthy lifestyle [EB/OL]. Copenhagen, World Health Organization Regional Office for Europe, 2011[2011-7-6]: http://www.euro.who.int/en/what-we-do/health-topics/disease-prevention/nutrition/a-healthy-lifestyle.

[6] WHO. Diet and physical activity: a public health priority [EB/OL]. Geneva, World Health Organization, 2011[2011-7-12]: http://www.who.int/dietphysicalactivity/en/.

[7] Giovannini M, Agostoni C, Shamir R. The relevance of breakfast: concluding remarks [J]. Critical Reviews in Food Science and Nutrition, 2010, 50 (2): 129.

[8] Billon S, Lluch A, Gueguen R, et al. Family resemblance in breakfast energy intake: the Stanislas Family Study [J]. European Journal of Clinical Nutrition, 2002, 56 (10): 1011-1019.

[9] Shepherd J, Harden A, Rees R, et al. Young people and healthy eating: a systematic review of research on barriers and facilitators [J]. Health Education Research, 2006, 21 (2): 239-257.

[10] Roblin L. Childhood obesity: food, nutrient, and eating-habit trends and influences [J]. Applied Physiology, Nutrition, and Metabolism, 2007, 32 (4): 635-645.

[11] Schlundt DG, Hill JO, Sbrocco T, et al. The role of breakfast in the treatment of obesity: a randomized clinical trial [J]. American Society for Clinical Nutrition, 1992, 55 (6): 45-51.

[12] 张勇, 张岩. 学校健康促进与增强青少年体质的研究 [J]. 阜阳师范学院学报（自然科学版）, 2008 (12): 74-75.

[13] 中共中央. 中共中央国务院关于加强青少年体育增强青少年体质的意见 [J]. 时政文献辑览, 2008, 3 (00): 847-851.

[14] 刘源. 浅析有氧运动的锻炼价值 [J]. 网络财富, 2010, 13 (7): 148-149.

[15] 曲绵域, 于长隆. 实用运动医学 [M]. 第 4 版. 北京: 北京大学医学出版社, 2003: 155.

[16] Pacific Institute for Research and Evaluation. Drinking in America: myths, realities, and

prevention policy [EB/OL]. Office of Juvenile Justice and Delinquency Prevention, U.S. Department of Justice, 2002[2011-7-12]: http://www.udetc.org/documents/Drinking_in_America.pdf.

[17] 季成叶. 我国中学生饮酒行为流行现状 [J]. 中国学校卫生, 2010, 31(10): 1153-1156.

[18] 中国青少年网络协会. 中国青少年网瘾报告(2009)[EB/OL]. 腾讯教育, 2009[2011-7-12]: http://edu.qq.com/edunew/diaocha/2009wybg.htm.

[19] WHO. Orientation Programme on Adolescent Health for Health-care Providers [M/OL]. Geneva, Switzerland: World Health Organization, 2006[2011-6-14]: http://whqlibdoc. who.int/publications/2006/9241591269_Handout_eng.pdf.

[20] APA. Diagnostic and Statistical Manual of Mental Disorders DSM-IV-TR [M]. 4th ed. Virginia: American Psychiatric Publishing, 2000.

[21] athealth.com. Getting the fact about adolescent substance abuse and treatment[EB/OL]. athealth.com, 2007-1-15[2011-7-12]: http://www.athealth.com/Consumer/adolescentsufacts.html.

[22] WHO. The World Health Report 1995: Bridging the Gaps [EB/OL]. Geneva, World Health Organization, 1995[2011-7-15]: http://www.who.int/whr/1995/en/whr95_en.pdf.

[23] 杨茂彬, 冯煜, 张官柏, 等. 中美戴托普戒毒治疗康复模式简介 [J]. 卫生软科学, 2002, 16(5): 23-25.

[24] Arnett JJ. The myth of peer influence in adolescent smoking initiation [J]. Health Education Behavior, 2007, 34(4): 594-607.

[25] American Medical Association. Guidelines for Adolescent Preventive Services(GAPS) [EB/OL]. Department of Adolescent Health, American Medical Association, 1997[2011-8-3]: http://www.ama-assn.org//resources/doc/ad-hlth/gapsmono.pdf.

[26] Wikipedia. Aversion therapy [EB/OL]. Wikipedia, 2011-7-2[2011-7-26]: http://en.wikipedia.org/wiki/Aversion_therapy.

[27] Collins RL, Ellickson PL. Integrating four theories of adolescent smoking [J]. Substance Use & Misuse, 2004, 39(2): 179-209.

[28] 唐奕. 护理人员在实施戒烟干预中的作用 [J]. 当代护士, 2006, 10(10): 4-6.

[29] 山东省政府法律办公室. 山东省未成年人保护条例 [EB/OL]. 2010-10-6[2011-7-15]: http://www.sd-law.gov.cn/Section/InfoDisplay.aspx?InfoId=fe58007d-eb35-4828-a4be-946bb6e6a9a0.

第七章

性与生殖健康

性与生殖发展是青少年成熟过程中不可缺少的重要组成部分。由于青少年有更多的途径获得正确系统的教育,不同的工作机会,更多地接触来自媒体、无线电通讯和互联网的新思想,不安全食物等[1],这些环境正在快速发生变化,影响了青少年作出性与生殖健康的相关决策。

今天的青少年在未来数十年将决定社会组织、经济生产力以及人类社会的生殖健康和幸福[2]。因此,促进青少年性与生殖健康对青少年及其家庭和社会具有重要意义,在全球生存环境变化的情况下,应该引起相应的适当反应[3]。

据报道,在很多国家青少年性的开始及参与婚前性行为的发生率在上升[4,5],而性传播感染(STIs),尤其是艾滋病(HIV/AIDS)的流行也加剧了性活动对健康的负面影响[6]。青少年性活动,尤其是婚内或婚外的无保护性活动,都可能对生殖健康产生不良影响,增加意外妊娠、非意愿分娩及流产以及包括艾滋病在内的性传播感染的风险。

第1节 概 述

对性健康的理解受到政治、社会以及历史事件的影响(例如,20世纪60年代的性解放运动)。此外,为流产和生殖权利而进行的不断斗争、同性恋权利运动、人口增长、疾病模式的改变(例如包括艾滋病在内的性传播感染不断增加)都影响对性健康的理解[7]。

目前,性健康的定义为与性活动相关的生理、情感、精神及社会功能的完好状态;而不仅是没有疾病、功能障碍或虚弱状态[8]。性健康需要以一种积极、尊重的方式来对待性活动及性关系,以及拥有愉悦而安全的性体验的可能性,并且免受胁迫、歧视和暴力。为了获得并维持性健康,所有人的性权利都应该得到尊重、保护和满足[8]。

性健康和生殖健康在概念和实际中有所重叠。生殖健康强调生命全阶段的生殖过程、功能和生殖系统。生殖健康意味着人们能拥有负责、满意和安全的性生活，并且具有生殖的能力和决定是否、何时及多久进行生殖的自由[9]。需指出，支持正常的生殖功能（例如，妊娠、分娩）还意味着减少性活动和生殖所带来的不良后果[10]。

常见的性与生殖健康问题

青少年时期是一个性探索和性表达的时期，很多青少年在此时期发展婚前、婚内或婚外的性关系。缺乏知识和技能、获取避孕方法（包括安全套）途经有限、易受到胁迫性活动，都使青少年处于发生艾滋病在内的性传播感染的高风险中。世界卫生组织指出，性与生殖健康是全球需要优先紧急干预的领域之一，青少年常见的性与生殖健康问题包括过早和无保护性行为、妊娠、不安全流产和性传播感染[11]。

性活动、妊娠和流产的发生率

据报道，在20世纪70年代，15~19岁美国女孩中大约有四分之一自述其有过性行为的经历，但是到80年代末期，这一比例上升到五分之三。有关发生初次性行为的年龄也有报道，例如，在加拿大、英国和美国，女孩首次发生性行为的平均年龄大约为17岁，美国女孩在13岁前发生性行为的比例相对较高[12]。

另外，在美国每年大约有74.5万年龄不足20岁的年轻人怀孕，从2005~2006年，拥有孩子的15~19岁青少年比例增长了3%[13]。根据世界卫生组织的数据，全世界每年大约有两千万年龄不足20岁的女孩怀孕，其中约有二百万到四百万进行不安全流产[11, 14]。据估计，每年大约有八万妇女死于不安全流产，而有幸生存下来的人也可能在以后生活中面临急性或慢性健康问题（例如，出血、盆腔感染、不孕、后续妊娠时自然流产、心理悲痛）[15, 16]。

危险性行为的促成因素

与前几代人相比，青春期发育和首次性行为的年龄提前、结婚延迟以及营养和健康状况改善，由此导致过早性行为和其他健康风险性行为增加[17]。同时，存在很多体验性感觉的方式，这也可能诱发性行为。

许多因素，如生物的、社会的、文化的和对性愉悦感的信仰，会影响青少年的性行为。事实上，青少年时期的性关系经常是无计划的和突发的，有时可能是由于压力或强迫而发生的[18]。青少年的很多性活动是非常危险的，例如，完全无保护的性行为、间断使用安全套或其他避孕方式，导致意外妊娠及不安全流产。很多原因导致这些危险行为的发生，例如，知识有限或获取避孕措施有限，担心性愉悦感或性关系的负面影响，或误解从同龄人、媒体或互联网所获得的有关妊娠或性传播感染的信息[19-21]。

保守的性文化具有双重作用：一方面，保守性文化可以保护青少年不介入婚前、婚内或婚外的危险性行为；另一方面，也可能限制青少年学习安全性行为和恰当性观念的机会，导致意外妊娠以及为避免羞耻和社会排斥而私自或不安全流产的发生[22,23]。

青少年性活动的不良后果

鉴于青少年尚未达到生理、心理和性方面的成熟，青少年时期早期、频繁和多样的性关系（例如，无保护性行为、滥交、不安全或多次流产）对青少年有很多不良影响，如，学校表现不佳、情感障碍、分娩和妊娠并发症、经济和社会地位低下、行为不良、物质使用甚至过早死亡[24]。有文献记录，15岁以下青少年分娩和妊娠出现并发症的危险比那些大于25岁的人高25倍[12,25]。

因此，如果已发生无保护性行为，教育青少年对妊娠征象保持警觉是非常必要的。妊娠常见的征象包括：停经、恶心或呕吐（也称为早孕反应）、乳房胀大或疼痛等，有时也会发生腹部疼痛和阴道流血。如果青少年未能给予安全流产，可能发生感染而出现发热、脱水的症状，或在子宫内发现一些避孕产品[11]。

妊娠

妊娠是指胚胎和胎儿在子宫内生长发育的过程，始于受精，止于胎儿娩出。一般来说，妊娠是一个正常的生理过程，但每个步骤都伴随着体内平衡的扰乱。妊娠过程中，受胎盘激素和神经-内分泌系统的影响，母体需要做出一系列改变，以适应胎儿生长发育的需求。胎儿从母体血液中获得营养，因此母亲必须提供两个人的营养。除了供给营养，母体排泄器官包括肾，也必须排出胎儿的分泌物。因此，妊娠女性处于一个人为的不健康生活状态，可能面临很多问题和失衡。妊娠所伴随的各类症状包括早孕反应、剧吐、食欲反复无常、便秘、静脉曲张等[26]。

然而，对于发生妊娠的青少年来说，这可能是人生中需要面临的最为艰难的经历之一，因为妊娠可致使学业或其他规划中断。妊娠还可引起情感危机，导致羞愧感和恐惧感。同时，青少年所承担的如何将妊娠告知父母的压力更为巨大，寻求帮助似乎不可能，这使青少年可能在压力下崩溃[27]。此外，妊娠青少年可能不会寻求恰当的医疗服务，且他们自身生理上尚未完全成熟来应对妊娠和分娩的压力，进而导致发生医疗并发症的危险增加[28]。

相比而言,青少年妊娠引起母亲和孩子出现并发症的风险更大。然而,这种风险通常是那些生理发育不完全的青少年所经历的,这些青少年常遭受最严重的并发症,如妊娠重度贫血、高血压。同时,孩子也会面临很多问题,如早产、低体重、死胎、智力缺陷或脑损伤,出生后体重不升等[27]。

流产

流产是指在妊娠 22 周前,胎儿自发或者通过人工诱导死亡并从子宫内排出。流产可分为多种类型,如自然流产和人工流产。当流产自然发生,没有任何外界帮助时,称之为自然流产;人工流产是通过干预,如药物、手术或者使用中草药及其他传统方式,引起子宫排出或部分排出其内容物[29]。

通常流产是个很安全的过程,但对青少年来说是有风险的。与年长的女性相比,青少年因担心父母发现,很可能求助于技能不熟练的医务工作者,或者推迟寻求妊娠终止的时间[28]。当流产由具有经验的医生操作,并遵守无菌操作时,通常没有危险或者危险很小;然而,若由不合格、不认真的医生和助产士粗心操作时,流产则会对病人的健康甚至生命带来很大危险。同时,流产是女性过早死亡和慢性病的一个重大原因[30]。

流产后的症状可包括大量出血、下腹部或背部疼痛、呕吐、恶心、腹部绞痛、发烧、恶臭分泌物、腹胀、寒战或流感症状[26]。最常见的并发症是不完全流产、败血症、出血和腹内损伤(例如,子宫穿孔和破裂),不安全流产所导致的常见长期健康问题包括慢性疼痛、盆腔炎症、输卵管堵塞和继发不孕[29]。

第 2 节　性传播性感染(STIs)

性传播性感染(sexually transmitted infections,STIs)是指一系列由病原体引起的临床综合征,这些病原体可以通过性活动、接触污染血液或妊娠及分娩时的母婴传播而获得并感染[11,31]。这类疾病包括:艾滋病(HIV/AIDS)、衣原体感染、淋病、生殖器疱疹、人乳头瘤病毒(human papilloma virus,HPV)感染、盆腔炎、梅毒、滴虫病、软下疳。表明发生 STIs 的症状包括但不仅限于以下方面:尿道分泌物、排尿疼痛、生殖器疼痛、生殖器溃疡、下腹部疼痛或压痛、异常阴道分泌物及瘙痒、局部皮肤感染及发热[32,33]。在所有的 STIs 中,艾滋病因目前尚无法治愈,可能最具威胁性。全世界艾滋病患者持续增长,据估计,2009 年大约有 3330 万人感染艾滋病,其中包括 260 万新感染者及 180 万艾滋病相关的死亡病例[34]。

其中有些 STIs 是威胁生命的(如 HIV、梅毒),另外一些(如乙肝、HPV、

HIV）可能导致恶性肿瘤或破坏生育功能（如淋病、衣原体感染）[35]。STIs 不仅给青少年带来生理上的损害，而且引起心理悲痛，给伴侣、孩子和家庭带来不幸，也类似一种社会疾病给人类社会带来巨大损失。更严重的是，患有 STIs 的青少年可能会面临慢性疾病，如，永久不孕、慢性疼痛、宫颈癌、心脏或脑损伤。与男孩相比，患有 STIs 的女孩可能会面临更多的挑战，因为妊娠及分娩时会有母婴传播，从而给下一代带来严重后果。

大多数青少年可能认为他们太年轻或太缺乏性经验而不会感染 STIs，或者错误地认为 STIs 只发生于那些性滥交或进行异常性行为的人。必须强调的是，青少年尤其容易感染 STIs，因为他们缺少 STIs 预防和治疗相关的信息和资源，并因担心、忽视、害羞或没有经验而拒绝寻求支持[36]。在需要时为青少年提供与 STIs 预防、保护和治疗相关的信息和支持，将包含在青少年基本的服务项目中[11]。

艾滋病 / 获得性免疫缺陷综合征（HIV/AIDS）

人类免疫缺陷病毒（HIV）又称艾滋病毒，引起获得性免疫缺陷综合征（AIDS）。AIDS 是一种人类免疫系统进行性衰竭，进而引发机会性感染和癌症，威胁生命的疾病。艾滋病毒可通过输血、精液、阴道分泌物、射精前的分泌物或乳汁传播[37]。

艾滋病毒感染可分为三个阶段，即急性感染期（原发感染期）、潜伏期、艾滋病期。当人暴露于艾滋病毒后的第 2～4 周（直到 3 个月后），可出现一种急性病，通常被描述为"最严重的流感"，此时称为急性感染期，可持续数周，症状可有发烧、寒战、皮疹、淋巴结肿大、咽喉痛、肌肉疼痛、心神不安以及口腔和食管溃疡。这些症状没有特异性，诊断时需特别留意[35]。在潜伏期阶段，症状很少或者没有，持续时间因人而异，可从 2 周到 20 年或更长时间不等。当病毒感染进展到艾滋病期时，很多病人开始出现疲劳、腹泻、恶心、呕吐、发热、寒战、盗汗，甚至晚期消耗综合征。艾滋病期的很多体征和症状来自于病人免疫系统损伤所引起的机会性感染、癌症和其他状况[38]。

衣原体感染

衣原体感染由沙眼衣原体引起，是报道最多的细菌感染，每年大约有 280 万新发病例，此种感染可损害女性的生殖器官。青少年和年轻人是最容易感染沙眼衣原体的人群[35]。性伴侣数目越多，感染的几率越大。青少年女孩和年轻女性是感染的高危人群，因其子宫颈尚未完全发育成熟，更易于感染。因衣原体可通过口交、肛交传播，与男性发生性关系的男性也有衣原体感染的危险。

因大部分感染者没有症状，衣原体被认为是一种"沉默"的疾病。即使有症状，一般出现在暴露后 1～3 周内。子宫颈是女性感染的最常见部位，患有衣原体子宫颈炎的女性，一般无症状，或者仅有非特异性症状，如阴道分泌物、性交后出血、排尿时烧灼感。三分之二的女性感染者没有任何体征或症状[35]。此外，如果感染从子宫颈扩散到输卵管，一些女性仍没有体征或症状；其他人可能出现下腹部疼痛、腰背痛、恶心、发烧、性交痛或月经间期出血。男性感染者可能会出现排尿困难、尿频、排尿时烧灼感和尿道分泌物（在早晨最严重）。发生肛交的男性或女性可能会发生直肠衣原体感染，导致直肠疼痛、分泌物或出血。衣原体感染还可见于与感染者发生口交的女性和男性的咽喉部位[35, 39]。

然而，若不经治疗，衣原体感染可以进展至严重的生殖与其他健康问题，带来短期和长期的影响。可引起盆腔炎和输卵管感染，而没有任何症状。上生殖道的盆腔炎和"沉默"感染可对输卵管、子宫及周围组织造成永久损伤，进而导致慢性盆腔疼痛、不孕和潜在致命性的异位妊娠。衣原体感染还可能增加 HIV 感染的机会[39]。

淋病

淋病由淋病奈瑟菌引起，该细菌容易在温暖、湿润的生殖系统部位生长和繁殖，包括女性的子宫颈、子宫和输卵管、男性和女性的尿道，还可在口腔、喉部、眼睛和肛门处生长，任何性活跃的人都可以感染淋病。淋病通过与阴茎、阴道、口腔或肛门接触传播，也可在分娩时通过母亲传染给胎儿。

感染的范围因性别而异，但总体而言，可从孤立的、自限性感染到严重、甚至威胁生命的全身性感染。对男性而言，有些感染者可能毫无症状，其他人则可能在感染后 1～14 天出现体征或症状，包括排尿时烧灼感，或者白色、黄色或绿色阴茎分泌物，睾丸疼痛或肿胀。此外，淋病若不治疗可导致附睾炎，引起不育[35]。

对女性而言，淋病的症状通常较为轻微，但大多数女性感染者没有症状。最初的症状和体征包括排尿时疼痛或烧灼感，阴道分泌物增加，或者月经间期阴道出血。无论有无症状或者症状的严重程度如何，女性淋病患者均有发展严重并发症的危险，例如盆腔炎。此外，淋病可传播至血液或关节，引起生命危险。淋病患者还容易感染艾滋病毒[39]。

生殖器疱疹

生殖期疱疹由 I 型或 II 型单纯性疱疹病毒（HSV）引起，大部分 HSV 感染者没有或者仅有很少的体征或症状。若出现体征，典型表现为在生殖器或直肠周围出现一个或者更多水疱。水疱破溃后，留下柔软的溃疡，首次可在 2～4 周后痊愈。但是患者一年内可出现多次（一般 4～5 次）水疱破溃。初期的其他体征和症状包括溃疡的再次出现，流感样症状包括发烧、腺体肿大。然而，很多 II 型 HSV 感染者从不出现溃疡，或者仅有轻微的症状而不被注意或者误认为昆虫叮咬或其他状况 [39]。

疱疹为一种慢性、终身感染的疾病，患者可以在暴发期和无症状期排出病毒。生殖器疱疹可引起生殖器反复出现疼痛性溃疡，免疫系统受抑制的人感染疱疹则更为严重。不论症状轻重，确诊为生殖器疱疹的患者在处理感染所带来的心理影响时，比应对生理不适存在更多的困难。另外，疱疹使人们更易于感染 HIV，并使 HIV 感染者更具传染性 [35, 39]。

人乳头瘤病毒感染

人乳头瘤病毒（HPV）感染是最常见的性传播性感染之一，有 40 多种 HPV 可引起生殖器部位、口腔和咽喉部感染，产生不同的症状和健康问题。至少有 13 种 HPV 基因型可导致癌症。HPV 通过生殖器官接触如阴交、肛交或口交、生殖器 - 生殖器接触传播。HPV 感染具有高传染性，大部分男性和女性在一生中的某个时间都会获得 HPV 感染。然而，仅有小部分人将继续发展为癌症 [40, 41]。

HPV 感染最主要的临床转归是宫颈癌。全球每年大约有 25 万女性宫颈癌患者死亡，是女性中癌症相关死亡的首要原因之一 [42]。HPV 也可在男性和女性中引起其他类型的非生殖器癌症，如头颈部癌症、生殖器疣。据估计，HPV 每年引起约 50 万例新发癌症，其中大部分影响发展中国家的女性 [41, 43]。生殖器疣通常以一个小肿块或成群肿块出现在生殖器部位。它们可小可大，突起或扁平，或者形似一个菜花。疣可在与受感染伴侣性接触后数周或数月内出现，即使受感染伴侣没有生殖器疣的体征。若不经治疗，生殖器疣可能消失、保持不变或者在大小或数目上增多，但不会转变成癌症。然而，宫颈癌通常只有发展到晚期时才会出现症状 [39]。

盆腔炎

盆腔炎（PID）指子宫、输卵管和其他生殖器官的感染，是某些性传播感染（尤其是衣原体感染和淋病）的一种严重并发症。性活跃女性在生育年龄最容易处于感染风险，与年龄大于 25 岁者相比，小于 25 岁者更容易发生盆腔炎。部分原因为青少年女孩和年轻女性的宫颈尚未完全成熟，增加了她们对盆腔炎相关的性传播感染的易感性。此外，使用灌洗器或宫内避孕器的女性在植入时患盆腔炎的风险更大。

盆腔炎的症状从轻微到严重程度不等,当盆腔炎由衣原体感染引起时,女性很可能只有轻微的症状。患有盆腔炎的女性最常见症状为下腹部疼痛,其他体征和症状包括发烧、异常阴道分泌物(可有臭味)、性交痛、排尿疼痛、不规则月经出血和右上腹部疼痛。严重的是,感染细菌可悄悄侵入输卵管及子宫和卵巢周围的组织,引起严重后果,如不孕、异位妊娠、脓肿形成和慢性盆腔疼痛[39]。

梅毒

梅毒由梅毒螺旋体引起,可通过直接接触梅毒溃疡而在人与人之间传播。梅毒溃疡主要出现在外生殖器、阴道、肛门或者直肠,也可出现在嘴唇和口腔中。梅毒螺旋体可通过阴交、肛交或口交传播,妊娠女性患者可将感染传给其婴儿[37]。

很多梅毒感染者可以数年没有症状,但若不治疗,仍有发展晚期并发症的危险。梅毒三个阶段的体征和症状有所不同,早期梅毒的典型特征为硬下疳,是一个在原发部位的坚硬、非化脓的无痛溃疡;二期梅毒典型特征是一个弥散的、鳞状的丘疹样突起,典型损伤处有个质地坚韧的突起边界,出现于感染后 3 周[44]。从感染梅毒到首次出现症状的时间可为 10～90 天(平均 21天),硬下疳通常坚硬、圆形、小、无痛,持续 3～6 周。

在二期,皮疹和黏膜损伤是典型特征。二期梅毒的皮疹可能是出现在手掌和脚底的圆形、红色或红棕色斑点,通常不痒。然而,不同外观的皮疹可出现在身体的其他部位,有时像其他疾病所引起的皮疹。除皮疹之外,症状还可有发烧、淋巴结肿大、咽喉痛、斑片状脱发、头痛、体重减轻、肌肉痛和疲劳。

梅毒潜伏期和晚期出现于早期和二期症状消失后,如果不进行治疗,梅毒将继续潜伏在体内,甚至没有体征或症状,此潜伏期可持续数年。在晚期,梅毒可继发损伤内部器官,包括大脑、神经、眼睛、心脏、血管、肝脏、骨骼和关节。后果可包括肌肉协调运动障碍、瘫痪、麻木、渐进性失明、痴呆甚至死亡[39]。

阴道滴虫病

阴道滴虫病由单细胞原生动物寄生虫——阴道毛滴虫引起,阴道和尿道分别是女性和男性最常见的感染部位。毛滴虫通过阴茎 - 阴道性交、外阴 -外阴接触而进行传播,女性可从被感染的男性或女性被传染而患滴虫病,但男性一般仅通过被感染的女性被传染。

大部分患滴虫病的男性一般不表现任何体征或症状,然而,有些人可能暂时出现阴茎内刺激、轻微分泌物、排尿或射精时轻微烧灼感。有些女性感染者出现泡沫、黄绿色、带有恶臭味的阴道分泌物。感染还可引起性交和排尿时不适，以及女性生殖器部位的刺激和瘙痒。女性一般感染 5～28 天后出现症状，患有滴虫病可增加女性对艾滋病毒的易感性，并增加艾滋病毒女性患者将艾滋病毒传染给其性伴侣的几率 [39]。

软下疳

软下疳是一种由杜克雷嗜血杆菌引起，具有高传染性但可治愈的性传播感染，包括在生殖器溃疡的鉴别诊断中。表现为一个边界清晰、无硬结、疼痛的表浅性溃疡，通过性交传播。潜伏期一般是接触后 3～5 天，溃疡可伴随单侧、局部淋巴结病 [44]。软下疳通过两种方式传播，即皮肤接触开放性溃疡的直接性传播，以及溃疡处的脓液转移到身体的其他部位或其他人的非性传播方式。

软下疳的症状一般出现于感染后 4～10 天。软下疳引起溃疡，通常出现在生殖器部位。溃疡最初是柔软、突起的肿块或丘疹，以后变为充满脓液、具有侵蚀样或锯齿状边缘的开放性溃疡。男性患者的溃疡可疼痛，但是女性通常觉察不到。腹股沟部位肿大、疼痛的淋巴结，或腹股沟淋巴结炎常提示软下疳。若不治疗，软下疳可促进艾滋病毒的传播 [45]。

第 3 节　应对青少年性与生殖健康问题

青少年可以从很多渠道获取关于性生活的信息和提示，例如教师、父母、兄弟姐妹、同龄人、杂志、书籍、大众媒体、互联网。但是，很难说从这些渠道收集的信息是恰当或完整的。还发现，许多青少年忽视青春期阶段的生理、心理社会变化以及青少年时期的发展任务，尤其那些与性活动相关的变化。

青少年服务要求是友好性的 [11]，健康服务应该帮助青少年保护和改善他们目前的健康状况，理解他们的性与生殖健康需求，学会采用积极负责任的态度对待他们的生殖健康问题，预防意外妊娠，预防由于过早妊娠或不安全流产而带来的严重健康问题和过早死亡，避免 STIs 以及关于生殖健康作出知情选择。

青少年尝试危险性行为对其自身的发展和成功构成了威胁，对其家庭、教育和健康服务的应对能力也提出了挑战。所有相关人员可以采取促进青少年性与生殖健康的不同策略和行动，但无论采用何种方案，强调控制青少年性活动的意义都是非常必要的。

青少年

对大部分没有开始性活动的青少年来说，非常有必要教给他们学会评估自己的生理和心理社会成熟度来参与性活动、承担相应责任或负担，并考虑性活动可能带来的近期和远期影响。对于那些已经发生性活动的青少年来说，应把注意力集中在安全性行为（如使用安全套）和不安全性行为的不良后果上（尤其是意外妊娠、不安全流产和包括艾滋病在内的STIs）。只要可能，青少年就应该尽量远离有性行为企图的人或避免到可能发生违背意愿的胁迫性行为的地方。青少年可以采取一些措施来降低不良后果的风险，如体外射精、安全套、紧急避孕、安全期、口服避孕药等。不论如何，须牢记不同方法的有效性有所不同。一旦发生性行为，青少年最好对身体的异常变化保持警觉，如异常的生殖器或尿道分泌物、生殖器疼痛、阴道或尿道流血、瘙痒[33]。

父母和教师

家庭和学校是青少年成长和学习的主要场所和最接近的生态环境。支持性的环境对青少年寻求信息和其他资源至关重要，有助于青少年应对困难和挑战，并调整负性情绪或行为反应。只要可能，教师和家长都应当具备必需的能力来帮助青少年解决青春期变化、性别身份发展、安全性行为及危险性活动的预防与保护。应当鼓励青少年、父母和教师之间开放式讨论"性"这一话题，这有助于青少年采取与其生活环境相适应的恰当的价值观、信念和行为态度等。

在有关性的讨论中父母和教师可能会感觉不舒服。可以采用多种方法开启与青少年关于性的交谈，有很多不同的方法值得去尝试：父母和教师可以与青少年分享他们所了解的内容，如有关性的最新信息、他们的价值观；也可利用"可教学时刻"（如媒体信息、当前事件、学校里发生在朋友身上的故事）；或者父母和教师可以询问青少年对具体的性行为或不良后果的看法[46]。理想的父母和教师有能力处理好个人性问题（包括歧视和缺点），并以真诚和科学的方式表达，尊重人类在性观念和性实践方面所表现出的多样性，有能力帮助青少年识别不同观点[47]。

大多数情况下，父母和教师能力欠缺使得他们不能为青少年提供自由谈论兴趣、感受和性与生殖健康问题的机会，也不能倾听青少年的心声以更好地理解他们。有时，父母和教师可与青少年一起找出有用的资源，或鼓励青少年向其他相关人寻求帮助（如学校卫生工作人员）。无论如何，并没有一种确切的方法可用来帮助促进青少年的健康与发展，真正需要的是采用照护的方式去关注青少年的健康与发展。此外，父母和教师总可以从专业卫生人员（如校园医生／护士、社区卫生人员）处获得支持，也可以阅读关于青春期发育及心理变化方面的相关书籍，了解青少年的身心变化，帮助其顺利度过青春期。

专业卫生人员

世界卫生组织指出，青少年专业卫生人员应具备为青少年服务的能力，并投入足够的时间，运用循证协议和指南、以非评判性和考虑周全的方式，为青少年提供所需要的健康服务[11,48]。这些能力包括：具备正常性发展的知识；能够评估与青少年性活动相关的常见的价值观和实践；能够评估青少年性活动的风险和责任；具备常见 STIs 的知识，包括后遗症和相关的预防策略；能够评估 STIs 预防和治疗措施资源的可获得性，能够评估青少年的怀孕意图和接受性[49]。

专业卫生人员是满足青少年性与生殖健康需求的重要资源，尤其对那些得不到充分服务的人群或边缘人群[50]。然而，令人失望的是，在中国大陆，尽管父母、教师和卫生保健人员认为这些性与生殖健康的能力很重要，但很少有人愿意去发展这些能力，也就是说他们在这些能力方面相当薄弱。

然而，一些研究证实了由专业卫生人员与学校和家庭合作开展基于学校的性与生殖健康促进活动的有效性[5,51,52]。同时也发现，并没有开展性与生殖健康促进活动的通用方法，单一的干预措施也无法起作用，综合的行为干预方案尤其与课程相联系的方案，可能是适当的[5]。

研究发现，其他较为成功的青少年性与生殖健康促进项目，是以媒体、社区、工作场所或健康设施为基础开展的[53]。更有趣的是，随着互联网的广泛普及，网络逐渐成为解决敏感话题包括性与生殖健康问题有前景的平台。已有证据表明，青少年更愿意从网上获取信息，因为他们认为网络是一个安全的场所，可以询问或收集关于个人健康问题的信息[54]。

总之，对青少年及其重要的知情人来说，性与生殖健康是一个敏感、较难解决但又非常重要的话题。中国大陆关于青少年合理干预的证据较为有限，还需要付出长期和更大的努力。

（潘尧云，刘　婷，王丽媛，杨　黎）

参 考 文 献

[1] Laski L, Schellekens S, Khatib-Maleh M. Generation of change: young people and culture [M/OL]. United National Foundation of Population Fund, 2008[2011-7-18]: http://www.unfpa.org/webdav/site/global/shared/documents/publications/2008/swp_

youth_08_eng.pdf.

[2] Dixon-Mueller R. How young is "too young"? Comparative perspectives on adolescent sexual, marital, and reproductive transitions [J]. Studies in Family Planning, 2008, 39(4): 247-262.

[3] Hindin MJ, Fatusi AO. Adolescent sexual and reproductive health in developing countries: an overview of trends and interventions [J]. International Perspectives on Sexual and Reproductive Health, 2009, 35(2): 58-62.

[4] Ali MM, Cleland J. Sexual and reproductive behavior among single women aged 15~24 in eight Latin American countries: a comparative analysis [J]. Social Science &Medicine, 2005, 60(6): 1175-1185.

[5] Wellings K, Collumbien M, Slaymaker E, et al. Sexual behavior in context: a global perspective[J]. Lancet, 2006, 368(9548): 1706-1728.

[6] Dixon-Mueller R. Starting young: sexual initiation and HIV prevention in early adolescence [J]. AIDS and Behavior, 2009, 13(1): 100-109.

[7] Edwards WM, Coleman E. Defining sexual health: a descriptive overview [J]. Archives of Sexual Behavior, 2004, 33(3): 189-195.

[8] WHO. Gender and human rights-sexual health [EB/OL]. Geneva, Switzerland: World Health Organization, 2002[2011-7-11]: http://www.who.int/reproductivehealth/topics/gender_rights/sexual_health/en/.

[9] WHO. World Health Statistics 2011[M/OL]. Geneva, Switzerland: World Health Organization, 2011b[2011-7-18]: http://www.who.int/whosis/whostat/EN_WHS2011_Full.pdf.

[10] Glasier A, Gulmezoglu M, Schmid GP, et al. Sexual and reproductive health: a matter of life and death [J]. Lancet, 2006, 368(9547): 1595-1607.

[11] WHO. Promoting and safeguarding the sexual and reproductive health of adolescents [M/OL]. Geneva, Switzerland: World Health Organization, 2006a [2011-7-18]: http://whqlibdoc.who.int/hq/2006/RHR_policybrief4_eng.pdf.

[12] 吴静, 熊光练, 石淑华. 青少年性健康行为研究概况 [J]. 中国社会医学杂志, 2006, 23(2): 97-101.

[13] 王凤秋, 李玉, 崔洪弟, 等. 高中生性与生殖健康知识、态度、行为调查 [J]. 中国心理卫生杂志, 2007, 21(1): 42-45.

[14] 高尔生, 楼超华, 涂晓雯, 等. 青少年及未婚青年生殖健康现状、展望及策略 [M]. 上海: 第二军医大学出版社, 2002.

[15] 霍金芝. 我国青少年性健康和性健康教育存在的问题及思考 [J]. 中国校医, 2004, 18(4): 379-380.

[16] Olukoya AA, Kaya A, Ferguson BJ, et al. Unsafe abortion in adolescents [J]. International

Journal of Gynecology & Obstetrics, 2001, 75(2): 137-147.

[17] WHO. Orientation programme on adolescent health for health-care providers [M/OL]. Geneva, Switzerland: World Health Organization, 2006b [2011-7-18]: http://whqlibdoc. who.int/publications/2006/9241591269_Handout_eng.pdf.

[18] Ochieng MA, Kakai R, Abok K. The influence of peers and other significant persons on sexuality among secondary school students in Kisumu District, Kenya [J]. Asian Journal of Medical Sciences, 2011, 3(1): 26-31.

[19] Abiodun OM, Balogun O. Sexual activity and contraceptive use among young female students of tertiary educational institutions in Ilorin, Nigeria [J]. Contraception, 2009, 79 (2): 146-149.

[20] Adedimeji AA, Omololu FO, Odutolu O. HIV risk perception and constraints to protective behavior among young slum dwellers in Ibadan, Nigeria [J]. Journal of Health, Population and Nutrition, 2007, 25(2): 146-157.

[21] Gomes KR, Speizer IS, Oliveira DD, et al. Contraceptive method use by adolescents in Brazilian state capital [J]. Journal of Pediatric and Adolescent Gynecology, 2008, 21(4): 213-219.

[22] 俞颖, 高晶蓉. 试述青少年性行为现状及影响因素 [J]. 健康教育与健康促进, 2008, 3(4): 53-56.

[23] 郑立新, 朱嘉铭, 田佩玲, 等. 广州外来未婚年轻女工性行为状况及影响因素 [J]. 中国计划生育学杂志, 2000, 8(4): 162-192.

[24] 陶芳标, 孙莹, 郝加虎. 青春发动时相提前与青少年性及生殖健康服务 [J]. 国际生殖健康/计划生育杂志, 2010, 29(6): 406-409.

[25] 赵倩. 青少年性健康状况国内外研究现状 [J]. 公共卫生与预防医学, 2005, 16(5): 40-42.

[26] Banerjee SK, Clark KA. Exploring the pathways of unsafe abortion: a prospective study of abortion clients in selected hospitals of Madhya Pradesh, India [M/OL]. New Delhi, India: Ipas India, 2009[2011-7-30]: http://www.ipas.org/Publications/asset_upload_file573_4424.pdf.

[27] Adoption .com. Teen Pregnancy [EB/OL]. Adoption.com, 2011[2011-7-22]: http://www.teenpregnancy.com/teenage/are-there-any-complications-that-could-arise-during-or-after-pregnancy.html.

[28] Xu JS, Shtarkshall R. Determinants, outcomes and interventions of teenage pregnancy-an international perspective [J]. Reproductive & Contraception, 2004, 15(1): 9-18.

[29] WHO. Adolescent Job Aid: a handy desk reference for primary level health worker [M/OL]. Geneva, Switzerland: World Health Organization, 2008b [2011-7-18]:

http：//www.youthnet.org.hk/adh/4_4Sframework/3_Services_n_commodities/2_Services/Adolescent%20job%20aid/Adolescent%20Job%20Aid%20-%20prototype%203.pdf.

[30] Robinson WJ. Woman-Her Sex and Love Life [M/OL]. The Project Gutenberg，1929[2011-7-22]：http：//www.gutenberg.org/files/21840/21840-h/21840-h.htm#Chapter_Sixteen.

[31] Workowski KA，Berman S. Sexually transmitted disease treatment guidelines，2010：recommendations and reports[J/OL].Morbidity and Mortality Weekly Report（MMWR），2010，59（RR-12）：1-116[2011-7-30]：http：//www.cdc.gov/mmwr/preview/mmwrhtml/rr5912a1.htm.

[32] Altini L，Coetzee D. Syndromic management of sexually transmitted infections [J/OL]. Continuing Medical Education，2005，23（2）：62-66[2011-7-30]：http：//www.cmej.org.za/index.php/cmej/article/viewFile/599/573.

[33] WHO. Managing Incomplete Abortion [M/OL]. Geneva，Switzerland：World Health Organization，2008a [2011-7-24]：http：//whqlibdoc.who.int/publications/2008/9789241546669_3_eng.pdf.

[34] WHO. Reproductive health [EB/OL]. World Health Organization，2011a [2011-7-7]：http：//www.who.int/topics/reproductive_health/en/.

[35] Nelson AL，Woodward J. Sexually transmitted diseases-a practical guide for primary care [M/OL]. Totowa，New Jersery：Humana Press，2006[2011-7-30]：http：//springerlink.lib.tsinghua.edu.cn/content/978-1-58829-570-5/#section=293351&page=1&locus=73.

[36] Barnett B，Schueller J. Meeting the needs of young clients：a guide to providing reproductive health services to adolescents [EB/OL]. Family Health International，2002-1-26[2011-7-12]：http：//aidsdatahub.org/dmdocuments/A_Guide_to_Providing_Reproductive_Health_Services_to_Adolescents.pdf.

[37] Zenilman JM，Shahmanesh M. Sexually transmitted infections：diagnosis，management，and treatment [M]. 1st. Sudbury，Maryland：Jones & Bartlett Learning，2011.

[38] AIDS.gov. Signs & Symptoms [EB/OL].U.S. Department of Health & Human Services，2011-6-20[2011-7-22]：http：//www.aids.gov/hiv-aids-basics/hiv-aids-101/overview/signs-and-symptoms/index.html.

[39] CDC. Sexually Transmitted Diseases（STDs）[EB/OL]. Center for Diseases Control and Prevention，2010-8-4[2011-7-23]：http：//www.cdc.gov/std/general/default.htm.

[40] Myers ER，McCrory DC，Nanda K，et al. Mathematical model for the natural history of human papillomavirus infection and cervical carcinogenesis[J]. American Journal of Epidemiology，2000，151（12）：1158-1171.

[41] WHO. Human Papillomavirus and HPV vaccines [M/OL]. Geneva，Switzerland：World

Health Organization，2007[2011-7-24]：http：//whqlibdoc.who.int/hq/2007/WHO_
IVB_07.05_eng.pdf.

[42] Palefsky JM. Human palliomavirus-related disease in men：not just a women's issue [J].
Journal of Adolescent Health，2010，46（4 Suppl.）：S12-S19.

[43] Hobbs CGL，Sterne JAC，Bailey M，et al. Human papillomavirus and head and neck cancer：
a systematic review and meta-analysis[J]. Clinical Otolaryngology，2006，31（4）：259-266.

[44] Allen HB. Dermatology Terminology [M]. 1st. London：Springer，2009.

[45] Illinois Department of Public Health. Chancroid [EB/OL]. Illinois Department of Public
Health，2008-1[2011-7-22]：http：//www.idph.state.il.us/public/hb/hbchancroid.htm.

[46] Baber KM. Adolescent sexuality[EB/OL]. Center on Adolescence，University of New
Hampshire，2005-6[2011-7-18]：http：//chhs.unh.edu/sites/chhs.unh.edu/files/docs/fs/
adolescent_resources/Adolescent_Sexuality.pdf.

[47] 过保录. 以学校为基础的青少年性与生殖健康教育解读 [J]. 中国性科学，2008，17
（3）：23-29.

[48] WHO. Quality Assessment Guidebook：a guide to assessing health services for adolescent [EB/
OL]. 2009[2011-7-8]：http：//whqlibdoc.who.int/publications/2009/9789241598859_eng.pdf.

[49] Keeney BG，Cassata L，McElmurry JB. Adolescent health and development in
nursing and midwifery education [M/OL]. Geneva，Switzerland：World Health
Organization，2004 [2011-7-18]：http：//whqlibdoc.who.int/hq/2004/WHO_EIP_HRH_
NUR_2004.1.pdf.

[50] Braeken D，Otoo-Oyortey N，Serour G. Access to sexual and reproductive health care：
adolescents and young people [J]. International Journal of Gynecology & Obstetrics：the official
organ of the International Federation of Gynaecology and Obstetrics，2007，98（2）：172-174.

[51] Gavin LE，Catalano RF，David FC，et al. A review of positive youth development
programs that promote adolescent sexual and reproductive health [J]. Journal of Adolescent
Health，2010，46（3，Suppl.1）：S75-S91.

[52] Zang YL，Zhao Y，Yang Q，et al. A randomised trial on pubertal development and health
in China. Journal of Clinical Nursing [J]，2011，20（21-22）：3081-3091.

[53] Speizer IS，Magnani RJ，Colvin C. The effectiveness of adolescent reproductive health
interventions in developing countries：a review of the evidence [J]. Journal of Adolescent
Health：official publication of the Society for Adolescent Medicine，2003，33（5）：324-348.

[54] de Nooijer J，Veling ML，Ton A，et al. Electronic monitoring and health promotion：an
evaluation of the E-MOVO website by adolescents [J]. Health Education Research，2008，
23（3）：382-391.

第八章

青少年常见伤害

伤害是全球青少年的主要杀手。根据 2004 年世界卫生组织全球疾病负担（WHO Global Burden of Disease，WGBD）估计，平均每年有 950 000 名 18 岁以下的青少年死于各种伤害。2010 年中国卫生统计年鉴 [1]（China's Health Statistical Yearbook，CHSY）显示，因伤害致死的青少年中，10～19 岁占 32.58/100 000，有成千上万的青少年因非致命性伤害住院，还有许多青少年伴随终身残疾，如截肢。青少年伤害已成为公共卫生问题，需要迫切关注。

随着社会发展，全球化、城市化、机动化及环境变化增加了青少年暴露于伤害的风险，成为青少年伤害的主要影响因素。伤害不是必然的，而是可以预防或控制的。本章主要介绍几种青少年常见伤害（如淹溺、道路交通伤害、中毒、烧伤及其他伤害，如跌落、暴力）的流行病学、危险因素及基本的干预措施。

第1节 淹 溺

2002 年世界各地的专家提出，淹溺（又称溺水）是人淹没或浸泡于水或其他液体中引起呼吸障碍的过程，淹溺的预后分为死亡、发病和不发病 [2]。在大多数国家，淹溺位居意外伤害前三位死亡原因之首 [3]。根据 WGBD 统计，2004 年世界各地大约 175 000 名 20 岁以下的青少年死于淹溺 [4]。淹溺也是中国青少年意外伤害的主要原因之一 [5]。

流行病学

2010 CHSY 数据显示，城市 10～14 岁青少年的淹溺死亡率为 3.23/100 000，15～19 岁青少年为 1.70/100 000。与城市居民相比，农村 10～14 岁青少年的淹溺死亡率为 5.35/100 000，15～19 岁青少年为 3.38/100 000 [1]。从以上数据可以看出，无论在城市还是农村，10～14 岁青少年的淹溺死亡率均高于15～19岁青少年。

中国浙江省的研究数据显示，儿童中所有淹溺死亡的 66.7% 发生在 6～14 岁年龄段 [6]，男孩的淹溺死亡率比女孩高。淹溺主要发生在池塘、水库和河流，而缺乏院前急救极易致青少年溺水死亡。因此，必须高度重视淹溺的危险因素、初级预防、及时抢救及现场复苏。

危险因素

掌握淹溺的危险因素是有效预防青少年淹溺的前提。淹溺的主要危险因素简述如下：

社会和人口学因素

研究表明，农村青少年的溺水率比城市高得多 [7]，尤其是人口稠密、有很多开放水域的低收入国家或地区的青少年更容易存在溺水的危险 [8]。

淹溺的死亡率随年龄组的不同而不同。在中国，淹溺是 1～14 岁儿童伤害致死的首位原因 [9]。随着年龄的增长，青少年的独立性增强，冒险行为增加，接近开放水域机会增多，常使青少年面临更多的溺水危险。

研究 [3] 还表明，男性淹溺死亡率高于女性，可能与男性接触水的机会多，易采取一些危险行为，如独自游泳、沉迷于水上娱乐活动等有关。

环境因素

青少年的淹溺常发生在自然淡水区域，尤其是在低收入国家，开放的水体或者水井的存在与溺水的风险紧密相关。这些水体包括池塘、沟渠、湖泊、河流、水井和蓄水池等。一项关于农村地区青少年淹溺的研究发现 [10]，多数的溺水死亡发生在日常活动中，如娱乐、工作、清洗、取水及过河等。

监管不力

监管不力是导致淹溺的最常见因素。在不熟悉的地点、非指定的地点或者没有救生员的地点游泳导致很多青少年淹溺 [11, 12]。恶劣的天气条件（如洪水或海流），即使是在一次事件中也可导致青少年发生淹溺 [6]。

其他因素

水上运输船只缺乏安全装备可能增加溺水的风险。吹塑玩具、充气筏和空气垫均属于不安全的游泳装备 [13]。在发达国家，大约 25%～50% 的青少年和成人的溺水与酒精有关。酒精能够损害人体的平衡、协调和判断能力，增加溺水风险，但在中国，少有学者研究酒精对青少年溺水的影响 [4]，这可能与中国青少年饮酒行为较少有关。

癫痫、自闭症和某些心律失常可能增加溺水的风险[11]。同没有癫痫的人相比，有癫痫发作的儿童和青少年发生淹溺的风险更大。一项小规模淹溺死亡的研究表明[14]，自闭症有增加溺水风险的可能。

干预措施

游泳指导

很多研究表明游泳指导可以提高游泳能力[13,15]。游泳技能和生存技能的提高可以减少青少年发生淹溺的危险。游泳指导的内容包括：游泳前做好充分的准备，在开放的安全水域游泳，学会识别危险的岩石、海浪以及恶劣的天气条件，掌握溺水自救常识等。

改善环境

消除危险因素是预防淹溺最有效的方法。在发展中国家，架设安全的桥梁或安装自来水系统能够显著减少溺水事件的发生[4]。在水体前设立障碍物也是非常有效的预防措施，如在水井上加盖，在池塘和河堤附近建立防护屏障，以及建造防洪堤坝等[12]。

有效监管

有效的监管有助于减少青少年淹溺的发生。在泳池旁和海边配备训练有素的救生员，不但可以实施现场救援和复苏，控制游泳者的危险行为，还可以监控水面状况和限制在海中危险区域游泳，进而最大限度地减少淹溺的不良后果，如死亡或脑损伤[2,6]。教给父母和照顾者一些基本的救生和急救技能，并培训一般的心肺复苏术也是非常有效的办法[15]。无论如何，溺水的专业救援举足轻重。帮助青少年认识溺水的危险因素，认识自身的游泳能力，增强淹溺的急救和复苏技能，有利于提高青少年对淹溺的认知[7]。

处理淹溺

现场救援可以帮助淹溺患者赢得抢救生命的最佳时机[16]。水中的急救措施包括自救和他救。不会游泳者，自救时要采取仰面体位，头顶向后，口鼻露出水面，设法呼吸，等待他救；会游泳者，当腓肠肌痉挛时，将痉挛下肢的踇趾用力向上方拉，将踇趾跷起，持续用力，直至疼痛消失；若手腕肌肉痉挛，自己将手指上下屈伸，并采取仰卧位，用两脚划游。他救时，救护者应从背后接近淹溺者，用一只手从背后抱住淹溺者头颈，另一手抓住淹溺者手臂，游向岸边,以防被淹溺者紧紧抱住。地面抢救措施包括:清除口咽部的污泥、杂草、呕吐物及分泌物,保持呼吸道通畅;用膝顶法、肩顶法或抱腹法倒出呼吸道和消化道的水分,以有效减轻由于缺氧造成的脑损伤。如果青少年出现呼吸和脉搏丧失,即刻的心肺复苏对于减轻神经系统的损伤至关重要[13]。口对口人工呼吸和胸外按压是现场目击者首先应该采取的措施[15]。胸外心脏按压的部位位于胸骨下切迹上移两横指,按压的力度使胸骨下陷胸廓前后径的1/3(大约5cm),按压的频率至少为100次/分。8岁以上淹溺者,单、双人按压与通气比均为30:2,1~8岁儿童按压与通气比单人为30:2,双人为15:2。

综上所述,淹溺是一个值得全世界关注的公共卫生问题,本节简述了青少年淹溺的有效干预措施。关于淹溺的危险因素和保护因素需要做进一步的科学探讨。

第2节　道路交通伤害

道路交通伤害是指发生在公路上的由碰撞引发、终止或涉及部分或全部交通车辆而导致的任何伤害,也可以定义为由于道路交通事故引起的致命或非致命的伤害[2, 17]。据报道,大多数国家道路交通伤害是意外伤害死亡的两大原因之一,尤其是15~19岁的青少年最容易发生道路交通伤害。在全球范围内,道路交通伤害是10~19岁青少年死亡的首位原因[4]。据预测,到2020年,中国大陆发生的道路交通事故死亡人数将猛增到97%左右[18]。

流行病学

2004年,19岁以下青少年死于道路交通事故的人数超过262 000[4]。2010 CHSY的数据显示,城市10~14岁青少年道路交通伤害发生率为1.17/100 000,15~19岁青少年为3.78/100 000。与城市居民相比,农村10~14岁青少年道路交通伤害发生率为1.73/100 000,15~19岁青少年为7.74/100 000[1]。

来自中国疾病预防控制中心(Chinese Center for Disease Control and Prevention, CDC China)的调查显示:超过3/4的道路交通伤害发生在路上。其主要原因是不良的骑车习惯和违反交通规则[19]。全球的道路交通伤害死亡率随年龄增加呈上升趋势,反映出不同年龄段青少年使用道路的方式不同:起初是作为行人,然后是作为骑自行车者、骑摩托车者,最后是作为机动车驾驶员。亚洲国家的调查表明,道路交通伤害是导致儿童和青少年死亡的两大首位原因之一[4]。

危险因素

目前,作为公共卫生问题,道路交通伤害日趋增加。许多因素增加了青少年发生道路交通伤害的风险,如身体和认知能力发育不足,监管不力,超速,酒后驾驶,未使用交通安全装备和其他涉及车辆安全、道路环境的因素。

青少年自身因素

年龄

有证据表明[20],10～12岁的青少年把视觉信号全面整合成有意义联系的能力尚未发育完善。一项研究表明[21],青少年大脑的认知发展过程可能会增加他们作为驾驶员发生道路交通事故的风险。在全球范围内,15～19岁的青少年倾向于寻求冒险行为,因而,他们发生道路交通伤害的危险最大。同时,在低、中及高等收入国家,道路交通事故的死亡率均随着年龄增加出现上升趋势[22]。

性别

研究发现,性别与道路交通伤害密切相关,男、女交通伤害发生率的比例从3∶1到5∶1不等[4]。调查表明,中国城市10～14岁男性青少年道路交通伤害发生率几乎是女性的两倍,15～19岁男性道路交通伤害的发生率是5.28/100 000,而女性是2.20/100 000。此外,农村10～14岁青少年道路交通伤害的发生率高于城市同年龄段青少年[1]。

不同的道路使用者

在许多中、低等收入国家,道路是玩耍、工作、步行、骑车和驾驶的共享空间[23],因此,青少年存在发生道路交通伤害的高风险。作为行人,个人的冒险行为和同伴的压力可能增加青少年发生道路交通伤害的危险。作为骑自行车者,道路交通伤害的发生与缺乏防护装备、能见度低、在人行道和混合车道骑车有关。北京一项研究表明[24],近三分之一的交通死亡发生在骑自行车者。作为年轻驾驶者,一些相互关联的因素可能增加发生道路交通伤害的风险,如酒后驾驶、超速、未系安全带、驾驶时注意力分散、疲劳驾驶和违反交通规则[25]。

监管不力

缺乏监督是青少年发生道路交通事故的危险因素[4]。有力的监管可以显著降低他们发生道路交通事故的可能性。特殊家庭的家长或照顾者往往不能很好承担对青少年的监管职责,这些家庭可能存在家庭离异、家长工作繁忙或至少一位家长生病或抑郁[26]等问题。

环境和与车辆有关的因素

有缺陷的车辆设计是青少年道路交通伤害的重要危险因素。有安全保险杠、倒车传感器的标准设计车辆有利于保障青少年的道路交通安全[27]。一些环境因素会导致青少年在路面活动时发生危险,如交通流量大,土地利用和道路网络规划不合理,缺乏操场、人行道和自行车道,缺乏安全和高效的公共交通系统,或车速过快等[22, 28]。因此,创建安全的道路环境对减少青少年发生道路交通伤害至关重要。

治疗不及时

创伤护理服务的有效性、可及性和质量对发生道路交通伤害的青少年非常关键。许多青少年发生道路交通伤害时没有得到及时的治疗。在北京,接受治疗的受伤者比例是 1∶254[29]。在道路交通伤害的院前急救和急救护理方面存在的严重问题包括:缺乏训练有素的卫生保健和救援人员,缺乏充分高效的院前急救和急救护理,发生伤害和到达医院的过程存在延误,或不适当的转介服务[4]。

干预

整体干预对保障青少年道路安全尤为重要,如训练道路使用者遵守交通规则,设计合适的车辆以保护车辆内外的青少年,改善道路环境,严格执行道路安全法规,加强紧急医疗服务[4, 25]等。

开展交通安全教育,遵守交通安全条例

安全教育在道路交通伤害的预防中起着重要的作用。目前关于交通安全教育的研究提示,培训青少年的实践技能可能更有效[30]。这些重要的技能包括处理问题能力和决策能力。在学校和家庭范围都可以开展道路安全教育。但青春期是一个很难通过采取教育方式取得成效的年龄阶段,电视节目、角色扮演、同伴教育或许是较好的方法[31]。

建立并严格执行道路安全法规可以防止近一半的道路交通伤亡发生[32]。适当提高饮酒的法定年龄,严格限定新手司机血液中的最低乙醇浓度,使用适当的儿童约束装置和安全带等,这些策略均可以预防青少年发生道路交通伤害[33]。加强道路安全的立法和执法,提高公众的交通安全意识,提供公众能买得起的头盔,对减少道路交通事故的发生有协同作用[4]。

改良车辆设计,配备安全装置

良好的车辆设计和符合标准的车辆可以保障车辆内、外青少年的安全,

如设计吸能区域、改良车辆前身、运用倒车报警和影像、使用酒精监测连锁系统等。多数证据表明,适当使用防护设备对保障青少年道路安全非常有效[34, 35]。系安全带、戴自行车头盔和摩托车头盔均能够降低从车辆中弹出、遭受严重甚至致命交通意外伤害的风险。

改善道路环境

为机动车辆设计道路时,应充分考虑道路环境安全问题,确保青少年的行走和骑车空间。在居民区、玩耍区和学校附近,为保障行人和骑车者的安全,车速应限制在 30km/h 以下[4]。为此,应采取各种措施加强必要的基础设施设计,如设计小型回弯处、改善道路照明和设立单向街道等[36]。同时,要确保青少年的上学路上安全,还可以提供专门巴士运送学生去学校,鼓励学生步行去上学,有可能的话,穿着醒目背心的成年志愿者可以引导学生沿着安全路线行走。通过基础设施建设分开不同类型的道路使用者是预防道路交通伤害的另一项措施,如分别隔离自行车道、机动车道和人行道[2]。

处理道路交通伤害

及时、有效、高效的院前急救可以减少由交通事故导致的伤亡人数[37]。救护车辆需要为青少年配备专门的医疗设备,工作人员需要训练如何评估和管理受伤的青少年,志愿者、青少年或紧急救援人员应掌握急症识别、寻求帮助和现场急救等技能[38]。道路交通伤害所致的伤害多为撞击伤、摔伤、挤压伤,甚至被玻璃刺伤等。现场救援时,首先要帮助伤者脱离危险环境,同时拨打“120”求救;对出血的伤员一般采取加压包扎止血;对心搏骤停者立即行心肺复苏;对昏迷伤员,使其头偏向一侧,保持呼吸道通畅;对骨折、关节损伤者,用夹板临时固定。高效的医院内急救是拯救伤者生命的关键,提供足够的人力资源(包括适当的技能、培训和人员)和物力资源(包括仪器设备和物品供应),可以确保优质的医疗服务,取得满意的急救效果[4]。

第3节 中 毒

中毒是指外来物质侵入人体造成伤害,导致细胞损伤,甚至死亡。毒物可以通过呼吸道、消化道、皮肤或黏膜进入人体[4]。中毒分为急性中毒和慢性中毒,临床表现也因此不同。

2004 年 WGBD 数据表明,约 45 000 例与中毒有关的死亡患者年龄在 20 岁以下[4]。在 15~19 岁的青少年中,中毒排在死亡主要原因的第 13 位。一般情况下，婴儿期的中毒死亡率最高，随着年龄递增到 14 岁时死亡率下降，此后，随着年龄递增到 15 岁或 15 岁以上时死亡率再次升高，可能与此年龄段的青少年更容易接触有中毒风险的工作场所有关[4]。

中毒的种类很多，主要取决于当地的工业和农业活动。在中、高等收入国家，药物是 5 岁以下儿童非致命性中毒的首位原因[39]。中国哈尔滨一家医院的调查显示，随着青少年发生故意自我伤害行为的增加，青少年安眠药中毒有逐年增加的趋势[40]。江苏省 1994~1995 年 0~14 岁儿童意外死亡的前瞻性调查显示，农村 5 岁以下儿童以灭鼠药中毒为主，5~14 岁以农药中毒为主[9]。一氧化碳吸入或酒精滥用也可以造成青少年中毒，但国外的一项研究[41]发现一氧化碳中毒更容易发生在老年人群。

中国徐州的调查数据显示[42]，0~9 岁儿童因中毒导致的意外死亡为 6.38%。研究[43]发现，20~29 岁年龄组发生中毒死亡的人数最多。不过，另有研究[44]发现中毒发生的高峰年龄段在 30~39 岁，69.7% 的中毒死亡患者年龄在 20~49 岁之间。大多数情况下，5 岁以下儿童的中毒属于意外中毒，但青少年的中毒可能是故意的，且可能属于有意的自我伤害[4]。

作为公共卫生问题，青少年中毒需要引起高度关注。可以根据中毒的原因不同采取相应的干预措施。加强药品市场管理是防止青少年发生催眠药物中毒的有效干预措施，使用低毒或安全农药可以防止急性农药中毒。为树立中毒意识和提高中毒预防的知识和技能，应教育家长和照顾者如何预防中毒[45]。此外，全社会应该关注青少年的心理健康，尤其是家长应该增加与孩子的交流机会，减轻他们的心理压力[40]。

发生中毒后，首要的现场急救措施是快速终止接触毒物，特别是液态或气态毒物溢漏时，应及时切断毒源，迅速将中毒者移至通风良好、空气新鲜处，同时做好自身安全防护，必要时戴防毒面具；其次是解开衣领，去除口腔异物，保持呼吸道通畅，有条件者给予氧气吸入；体表接触毒物者，可以给予微温清水冲洗体表；口服中毒者，如患者清醒，可用手指、棉棒、筷子等刺激软腭、咽后壁及舌根部催吐；密切观察患者神志、体温、脉搏、呼吸及血压的变化，必要时送医院急救处理。

第 4 节 烧　伤

烧伤可能伴随剧痛和长期疾病，甚至痛苦终生。通常，青少年出于好奇去探索周围未知的世界，如玩火或触摸热的物体，进而导致烧伤。据估计，2004 年全世界有超过 96 000 名 20 岁以下的青少年由于烧伤而导致致命的伤害[4]。在中国，烧伤也是造成青少年伤害的主要原因之一，占 28.6%[46]。

定义与分类

烧伤是指皮肤或其他器官因热创伤导致的伤害,包括烫伤(热液体)、接触伤(热固体)以及蒸汽伤(蒸汽)。辐射、放射、电、摩擦或接触化学物质导致的烧伤也包括在内[47]。

根据致伤机制或病因,烧伤可以分为蒸汽伤或吸入伤。根据烧伤的深度可以分为Ⅰ°(表皮浅层)、Ⅱ°(真皮层)、Ⅲ°(皮肤全层)烧伤[48]。医学上,成人用"九分法"估计烧伤面积(图8-1)。九分法是指头颈部占体表面积的9%,每侧上肢9%(包括手),每侧下肢18%(包括脚),以及躯干18%(背、胸以及腹部)[47]。幼儿和婴儿用"五分法"。

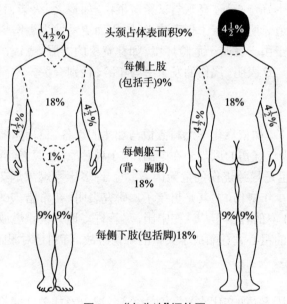

图 8-1 "九分法"评估图

流行病学

据 WHO 统计,因意外伤害死亡的病例中,大约有 10% 死于与火有关的烧伤,还有更多的病例是死于烫伤、电伤、化学物质伤及其他形式的烧伤[49]。总而言之,1~9 岁的儿童死于烧伤的风险较大,从全球来看,这个比例达到3.9/100 000[4]。在山东省农村地区进行的一项包含 511 名高中生伤害的调查显示[50],66.7% 曾被烧伤过胳膊(其中 53.8% 是因为沸水和熟食)。

厨房是存放开水、热油及火炉的地方,因此烧伤多发生于室内的厨房[51]。需要注意的是,烧伤是唯一一种女孩发生率高于男孩的意外伤害。在与火相关的死亡中,女孩发生率为 4.9/100 000,而男孩发生率为 3.0/100 000[4],郭宁晓等人[52]也曾有类似的报道。

烧伤不仅导致死亡,而且会造成终生残疾或毁容,给患者、家庭及卫生保健机构带来巨大的压力。因此,采取措施减少烧伤的发生非常重要。

危险因素

烧伤的分类方法及损伤机制不同,这与烧伤多种多样的危险因素(如化学烧伤、沸腾液体烫伤)有关。

青少年自身因素

青少年天生好奇心强,喜欢尝试新奇事物,如篝火、火柴、打火机或烟花。香港的一篇报道表明,男孩子更喜欢尝试,因而更易发生烧伤[53]。相比而言,一些国家女孩子由于暴露于危险环境,如穿宽松的衣服、煮饭,其烧伤的发生率高于男孩子。这表明,烧伤的发生率与年龄、性别有关。

环境因素

危险的设备,如依靠化学燃料煮饭与加热的设备、日用电器、插头及电线等,增加了青少年烧伤的风险。在中国,由于种种原因,易燃物品(如煤油)储存在家里,这也是导致烧伤的危险因素[54]。许多国家燃放烟花来庆祝节日,这极易导致青少年烧伤,尤其是男孩子。研究表明,在希腊,70% 的烟火烧伤发生于 10～14 岁的青少年[4]。在中国,尽管许多地方禁止燃放烟火,但烟火储存及燃放时的粗心大意酿成了大量的烧伤事故,特别是对眼睛的损伤[55]。

其他因素

社会经济因素(如文化水平、家庭经济状况以及相关法律规定)可能增加烧伤的风险[56]。WHO[49] 报道,烧伤的死亡率及致病率与贫穷有关,低、中等收入国家以及高等收入国家中的贫困家庭,20 岁以下的青少年烧伤发生率更高。

除此之外,监管不力也是青少年烧伤的主要因素。缺少充足的水来阻止火势蔓延以及非正常运行的烟雾探测器是青少年烧伤的更大危险[4]。

干预措施

以下措施可能会避免或减少烧伤的发生。

加强教育与监管

研究[57] 表明,许多烧伤的发生与粗心或缺乏烧伤知识有关。提高青少年及其照顾者对烧伤发生原因、危险因素、机制以及初级卫生保健的意识与知识，可能是阻止烧伤、降低烧伤程度的有效措施[58]。青少年天生好奇心强，喜欢体验新事物，造成他们更易遭受烧伤的伤害[53]。通过教育父母，可以加强父母对青少年的监管（如烟火的使用）[4]。教给父母识别孩子可能的烧伤、辨别烧伤的状况[59]，采取积极的、简单的院前急救等措施，可以挽救青少年生命，预防感染发生[60]。

改善环境

改善环境能够降低青少年烧伤的发生率，可以采取以下措施：使用更好的电子设备（如安全的灯具、炉灶）；建造符合建筑标准的安全厨房；移除地面及房间里危险的烹煮设备等[4]；使用烟雾报警器与住宅洒水装置，可以及时检测火灾发生的苗头，迅速阻止火焰蔓延，有效降低青少年烧伤[60]。

处理烧伤

青少年烧伤后以及被送往医院前，家庭成员首先应该让青少年保持稳定，采取冷水浸泡患肢等措施，以冷却烧伤部位，防止进一步的烧伤或感染[47]。

一旦烧伤青少年转送到急救中心，首先，应检查其气道、呼吸及循环状况[4]。其次，从头到脚仔细、全面地检查烧伤的任何其他征象。然后根据烧伤的程度与深度，采取不同的治疗与康复措施。如果发生休克，补液至关重要。卫生保健人员必须明确前 24 小时是抢救生命的黄金时期[47]。如果烧伤青少年在前 48 小时幸存，但由于缺乏阻碍细菌入侵的屏障而存在感染并发症并由此面临死亡的危险时，应采用适当的抗生素治疗[51]。

需要强调的是，并不是每一位烧伤的青少年都需送到医院接受治疗。一些国家成立了社区卫生部门及康复中心，其医疗花费相对低廉，许多贫困家庭可以承受得起[61]。

烧伤发生率与地区的医疗及经济状况有关。许多干预措施在实施前需要进行严格、系统的评估，而广泛的实施有待更多的证据支持。

第5节　其他伤害

除了上述伤害，青少年还存在其他的伤害的危险，如跌落与暴力，这也是青少年致病与致残的主要原因，由此给社会及经济带来沉重负担[29]。在中国江西省，跌落是青少年死亡的第四位原因（0～17 岁中占 3.1/100 000）[4]。调查[62]发现，一百多万人由于暴力而丧命，其中主要是年轻人。这些伤害也成为现存的公共卫生问题。

根据 WHO [63]，跌落是指"导致人们非故意地躺在地面、地板或其他较低平面的事件"。疾病控制中心 [64] 将青年暴力定义为"因个体威胁使用或在事实上运用权力或武力，导致或极大可能导致他人身体或心理伤害或死亡"。

研究 [65] 表明，人口、社会以及文化特征与跌落及暴力行为有关。通常，男孩子比女孩子更易发生跌落，男孩子跌落发生率比女孩子多 3.5 倍，而农村地区比城市发生率高 [4]。据估计，接触过暴力的青少年比未接触者更易做出暴力行为 [66]。

不同的伤害类型应采取不同的干预措施。概括地说，跌落和暴力都应采取一级、二级和三级预防策略。一级预防是以整个人群为对象，而不仅仅是针对那些处于风险的人 [67]，目的是降低问题或疾病的发生率。通过教育所有青少年进行一级预防，有望降低未来青少年的伤害行为。二级预防是以处于风险的青少年为目标，如为防止青少年骑马或滑冰时发生跌落伤害，配戴头盔和腕带可能是有用的策略 [4]。对于暴力而言，识别早期的攻击行为、社交技巧的匮乏、邻里关系的恶化、枪械或毒品的来源途径和扭曲的同伴关系是非常重要的 [68]。伤害发生后，对青少年采取的治疗措施被认为是三级预防 [67]。一旦伤害发生，青少年应尽可能在医院或社区得到治疗。需要强调的是，伤害的后期效果，如致残、心理状况等不可忽视。

（侯晓红，宋　洁，王春美）

参 考 文 献

[1] 中华人民共和国卫生部. 2010 中国卫生统计年鉴 [EB/OL]. [2011-5-25]: http://www. moh.gov.cn/publicfiles/business/htmlfiles/zwgkzt/ptjnj/year2010/index2010.html

[2] Peden M，McGee K，Sharma G. The Injury Chart Book：a Graphical Overview of the Global Burden of Injuries [EB/OL]. World Health Organization，2002[2011-7-2]： http://whqlibdoc.who.int/publications/924156220X.pdf.

[3] Madrid C，Maldonado MH，Parra AR，et al. Epidemiology of drowning deaths in Venezuela, 1996-2007[J]. International Journal of Infectious Diseases，2010，14（Suppl. 1）: e138.

[4] Peden M，Oyegbite K，Ozanne-Smith J，et al. World Report on Child Injury Prevention [EB/OL]. World Health Organization，2008[2011-6-22]: http：//whqlibdoc.who.int/ publications/2008/9789241563574_eng.pdf.

[5] 农全兴，杨莉. 儿童溺水流行病学研究进展 [J]. 中国公共卫生，2006，22（3）: 363-365.

[6] 钟政武，周招美，王月武. 溺水儿童死亡危险因素与干预措施的探讨 [J]. 浙江临床医

学，2008，10（2）：199.

[7] Barss P，Subait OM，Ali MHA，et al. Drowning in a high-income developing country in the Middle East: newspapers as an essential resource for injury surveillance [J]. Journal of Science and Medicine Sport，2009，12（1）：164-170.

[8] Hyder AA，Borse NN，Blum L，et al. Childhood drowning in low- and middle-income countries: urgent need for intervention trials [J]. Journal of Paediatrics and Child Health，2008，44（4）：221-227.

[9] 张佩斌，陈荣华，邓静云，等. 江苏省 1994～1995 年 0～14 岁儿童意外死亡前瞻性调查 [J]. 中华流行病学杂志，1998，19（5）：290-293.

[10] 万勇. 对农村青少年溺水事故的思考 [J]. 游泳季刊，2008，3：14-16.

[11] Morgan D，Ozanne-Smith J，Triggs T. Descriptive epidemiology of drowning deaths in a surf beach swimmer and surfer population [J]. Injury Prevention，2008，14（1）：62-65.

[12] Webber JB. Drowning，the New Zealand way: prevention，rescue，resuscitation [J]. Resuscitation，2010，81（2，Suppl. 1）：S27.

[13] McIntosh G. Swimming lessons may reduce risk of drowning in young children [J]. The Journal of Pediatrics，2009，155（3）：447.

[14] Sibert JR，Lyons RA，Smith BA，et al. Preventing deaths by drowning in children in the United Kingdom: have we made progress in 10 years? Population based incidence study [J]. British Medical Journal，2002，324（7345）：1070-1071.

[15] Moran K. Child drowning prevention and parental understanding of CPR [J]. Journal of Science and Medicine in Sport，2010，12（Suppl. 2）：e30.

[16] Minto G，Woodward W. Drowning and immersion injury [J]. Anaesthesia and Intensive Care Medicine，2008，9（9）：409-412.

[17] Peden M，Scurfield R，Sleet D，et al. World report on road traffic injury prevention [EB/OL]. World Health Organization，2004[2011-7-2]: http: //whqlibdoc.who.int/publications/2004/9241562609.pdf.

[18] Kopits E，Cropper M. Traffic fatalities and economic growth [J]. Accident Analysis and Prevention，2005，37（1）：169-178.

[19] 新华网. 道路交通伤害成我国儿童意外伤害第二大死因 [EB/OL]. 2007-4-26[2011-7-2]: http: //news.xinhuanet.com/fortune//2007-04/26/content_6032438.htm.

[20] Káldy Z，Kovács I. Visual context integration is not fully developed in 4-year-old children [J]. Perception，2003，32（6）：657-666.

[21] Giedd JN. Structural magnetic resonance imaging of the adolescent brain [J]. Annals of the New York Academy of Sciences，2004，1021（1）：77-85.

[22] Sauerzapf V，Jones AP，Haynes R. The problems in determining international road

mortality [J]. Accident Analysis and Prevention, 2010, 42(2): 492-499.

[23] Morgan A, Mannering FL. The effects of road-surface conditions, age, and gender on driver-injury severities [J]. Accident Analysis and Prevention, 2011, 43(5): 1852-1863.

[24] Li GH, Baker SP. Injuries to bicyclists in Wuhan, People's Republic of China [J]. American Journal of Public Health, 1997, 87(6): 1049-1052.

[25] Ghorbanali M. Road traffic fatalities among pedestrians, bicyclists and motor vehicle occupants in Sirjan, Kerman, Iran [J]. Chinese Journal of Traumatology(English Edition), 2009, 12(4): 200-202.

[26] Towner E, Dowswell T, Errington G, et al. Injuries in children aged 0~14 years and inequalities [EB/OL]. Health Development Agency, London, 2005[2011-7-2]: http://www.nice.org.uk/niceMedia/pdf/injuries_in_children_inequalities.pdf.

[27] Yeung JHH, Leung CSM, Poon WS, et al. Bicycle 29 related injuries presenting to a trauma centre in Hong Kong [J]. Injury, 2009, 40(5): 555-559.

[28] Spoerri A, Egger M, von Elm E. Mortality from road traffic accidents in Switzerland: Longitudinal and spatial analyses [J]. Accident Analysis & Prevention, 2011, 43(1): 40-48.

[29] Linnan M, Giersing M, Cox R, et al. Child mortality and injury in Asia: An Overview[EB/OL]. UNICEF & Innocenti Research Centre, Oct. 2007[2011-7-2]: http://www.unicef-irc.org/publications/pdf/iwp_2007_04.pdf.

[30] Bina M, Graziano F, Bonino S. Risky driving and lifestyles in adolescence [J]. Accident Analysis and Prevention, 2006, 38(3): 472-481.

[31] Shope JT. Influences on youthful driving behavior and their potential for guiding interventions to reduce crashes [J]. Injury prevention, 2006, 12(Suppl. 1): i9-i14.

[32] Stevenson M. Childhood pedestrian injuries: what can changes to the road environment achieve? [J]. Australia New Zealand Journal of Public Health, 1997, 21(1): 33-37.

[33] Hingson RW, Assailly J-P, Allan WF. Underage drinking: frequency, consequences, and interventions [J]. Traffic Injury Prevention, 2004, 5(3): 228-236.

[34] Hung DV, Stevenson MR, Ivers RQ. Barriers to, and factors associated, with observed motorcycle helmet use in Vietnam [J]. Accident Analysis and Prevention, 2008, 40(4): 1627-1633.

[35] Thompson DC, Rivara FP, Thompson R. Helmets for preventing head and facial 28 injuries in bicyclists [J/OL]. Cochrane Database of Systematic Reviews, 2009, 1): http://www.thecochranelibrary.com/userfiles/ccoch/file/Safety_on_the_road/CD001855.pdf.

[36] Lin M-R, Kraus JF. A review of risk factors and patterns of motorcycle injuries [J]. Accident Analysis & Prevention, 2009, 41(4): 710-722.

[37] Nguyen TLH, Nguyen THT, Morita S, et al. Injury and pre-hospital trauma care in

Hanoi, Vietnam [J]. Injury, 2008, 39 (9): 1026-1033.

[38] Sharma BR. Development of pre-hospital trauma-care system——an overview [J]. Injury, 2005, 36 (5): 579-587.

[39] Andiran N, Sarikayalar F. Pattern of acute poisonings in childhood in Ankara: what has changed in twenty years? [J]. The Turkish Journal of Pediatrics, 2004, 46 (2): 147-152.

[40] 王青, 葛蕾, 车淑华. 103 例青少年过量服用催眠药引发中毒的原因调查及分析 [J]. 哈尔滨医药, 1999, 19 (1): 10-11.

[41] Nazari J, Dianat I, Stedmon A. Unintentional carbon monoxide poisoning in Northwest Iran: a 5-year study [J]. Journal of Forensic and Legal Medicine, 2010, 17 (7): 388-391.

[42] 李虎, 胡鹏展. 徐州市 10 岁以下儿童意外死亡动态分析 [J]. 中国校医, 1999, 20 (3): 230.

[43] 刘良, 刘艳, 黄光照. 389 例不同年份的中毒尸检资料对比分析 [J]. 刑事技术, 1999, 6): 16-18.

[44] Liu Q, Zhou L, Zheng N, et al. Poisoning deaths in China: type and prevalence detected at the Tongji Forensic Medical Center in Hubei [J]. Forensic Science International, 2009, 193 (1-3): 88-94.

[45] Nixon J, Spinks A, Turner C, et al. Community based programs to prevent poisoning in children 0-15 years[J]. Injury Prevention, 2004, 10 (1): 43-46.

[46] Wang HJ, Xiao J, Zhang J, et al. Comparable results of epidemiology of children with burns among different decades in a burn unit in Jinzhou, China [J]. Burns, 2011, 37 (3): 513-520.

[47] 吴孟超, 吴在德, 黄家驷. 外科学. 第 7 版. [M]. 人民卫生出版社: 北京, 2008.

[48] Bartlett SN. The problem of children's injuries in low income countries: a review [J]. Health Policy and Planning, 2002, 17 (1): 1-13.

[49] Mock C, Peck M, Peden M, et al. A WHO plan for burn prevention and care [EB/OL]. World Health Organization, 2008-6-22: http://whqlibdoc.who.int/publications/2008/9789241596299_eng.pdf.

[50] 贾存贵, 张京云, 薄其贵, 等. 山东农村 511 名高中生伤害的现况调查 [J]. 中国慢性病预防与控制, 2003, 11 (6): 263-265.

[51] WHO. Facts about injuries: burns [EB/OL]. World Health Organization & International Society for Burn Injuries, 2006[2011-6-22]: http://www.who.int/entity/violence_injury_prevention/publications/other_injury/en/burns_factsheet.pdf.

[52] 郭宁晓, 李集宇, 丘春萍, 等. 3677 名 6～19 岁中小学生伤害流行病学特征分析 [J]. 中国校医, 2008, 22 (3): 256-258.

[53] Ying SY, Ho WS. Playing with fire -- a significant cause of burn injury in children [J].

Burns，2001，27（1）：39-41.

[54] 张学智. 现代家庭火灾事故发生的原因及预防对策 [J]. 消防科学与技术，2010，29（9）：841-843.

[55] 史爱国，赵亮. 鞭炮爆炸烧伤的临床特点 [J]. 吉林医学，2010，31（22）：3648-3649.

[56] Edelman LS. Social and economic factors associated with the risk of burn injury [J]. Burns，2007，33（8）：958-965.

[57] Sarma BP. Prevention of burns：13 years' experience in Northeastern India [J]. Burns，2011，37（2）：265-272.

[58] 张翠萍，丁桂兰. 烧伤的预防 [J]. 社区医学杂志，2006，4（11）：72-73.

[59] Forjuoh SN. Burns in low- and middle-income countries：a review of available literature on descriptive epidemiology，risk factors，treatment，and prevention [J]. Burns，2006，32（5）：529-537.

[60] Parbhoo A，Louw QA，Grimmer-Somers K. Burn prevention programs for children in developing countries require urgent attention：a targeted literature review [J]. Burns，2010，36（2）：164-175.

[61] Mistry RM，Pasisi L，Chong S，et al. Socioeconomic deprivation and burns [J]. Burns，2010，36（3）：403-408.

[62] Sousa S，Correia T，Ramos E，et al. Violence in adolescents：social and behavioural factors [J]. Gaceta sanitaria，2010，24（1）：47-52.

[63] WHO. Violence and Injury Prevention and Disability（VIP）：Falls [EB/OL]. World Health Organization，2011-5-24[2011-7-2]：http：//www.who.int/violence_injury_prevention/other_injury/falls/en/index.html.

[64] Centers for Disease Control and Prevention. Centers for Disease Control and Prevention，America，2010-7-26[2011-7-2]：http：//www.cdc.gov/ViolencePrevention/youthviolence/definitions.html.

[65] Rappaport N，Thomas C. Recent research findings on aggressive and violent behavior in youth：implications for clinical assessment and intervention [J]. Journal of Adolescent Health，2004，35（4）：260-377.

[66] Kennedy AC，Bybee D，Sullivan CM，et al. The effects of community and family violence exposure on anxiety trajectories during middle childhood：the role of family social support as a moderator [J]. Journal of Clinical Child and Adolescent Psychology，2009，38（3）：365-379.

[67] Fields SA，McNamara JR. The prevention of child and adolescent violence：a review [J]. Aggression and Violent Behavior，2003，8（1）：61-91.

[68] Assis SG，Avanci JQ，Santos NCd，et al. Violence and social representation in teenagers in Brazil [J]. Rev Panam Salud Publica，2004，16（1）：43-51.

残障青少年

    残障是人类社会中的正常现象，几乎所有人都可能在生命历程的某个时刻遭受残疾的威胁，可能是暂时性的，也可能是永久性的。残障人士（person with disability, PWD）特别是青少年是社会弱势群体之一，很多残障人士并没有平等享受医疗服务[1, 2]。本章主要是简单讲述残障有关议题，对残障青少年会有所倾斜。

残障的定义

    采用积极的生理心理社会方法，WHO 将功能和残障视作健康连续体中的部分内容，现已发展形成国际功能、残疾与健康分类（International Classification of Function, Disability and Health, 习惯简称 ICF）这一概念框架，用于解释因健康问题而使个体与环境在进行动态互动时所表现出来的功能与残障情况[2, 3]。

    根据上述 ICF[2, 4]框架，人体功能问题可归为三个相互联系的方面：残损、活动局限、参与受限。残损是指身体结构发生改变，或是身体某些机能出现问题或衰退，例如，瘫痪或失明；活动局限是指动作完成存在困难，例如，行走或进食；参与受限则是指不能充分参与到生活的各个方面，例如，在就业和交通方面受到不平等对待或歧视。残障是总括性概念，涵盖残损、活动局限和参与受限三种情况，所反映的是存在有健康问题的个体与周围情景因素（包括环境因素和个人因素）进行交互作用时的消极层面。在此框架下，健康问题是指患有疾病、存在损伤或是有功能障碍（图 9-1）。

贫困、残障与健康

    人们日益领会到，残障不仅仅是人权问题，也是重要的发展问题。越来越多的证据表明，残障人士的社会经济状况明显不如非残障人士，贫困程度也更严重。已有细述[1, 5]，贫困（尤其是持续时间较长的重度、多维度的贫困）

与残障可交相恶化,致使残障人士陷入恶性循环之中,由贫困和残障造成的双重劣势日益严重,这其中也包括所感觉到的社会排斥和所觉察到的耻辱(图 9-2)。尤其需要指出的是,已经发现,罹患慢性病(如癌症)的青少年患者,疾病本身与青少年阶段的发展成长之间存在交互的恶性影响,涉及发展成长的各个方面,亦即生理的、心理的和社会的[6, 7]。

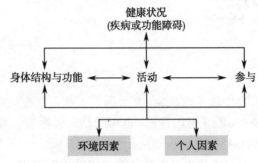

图 9-1　国际功能、残疾与健康分类示意图[2]

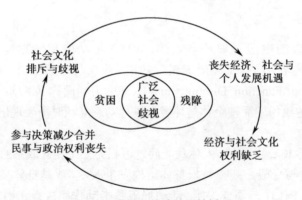

图 9-2　贫困与残障的恶性循环

除了保障就业和充足的社会保障收入之外,接受教育、上学可能是打破甚至扭转由贫困、残障、健康和总体脆弱性构成的恶性循环的最佳手段。从初级保健原则(不止限于平等、可及、支付得起、可获得、最基本)出发,WHO[8] 提出残障社区康复模式(community based rehabilitation, CBR,图 9-3),强调在社区开展涵盖卫生、教育、生计、赋权和社会等方面的复杂行动。实际上,WHO 一贯强调上述原则,始终敦促各国改革卫生体系,促进人人享有卫生保健[9, 10]。

群体特征

全国乃至国际调查研究都不太重视青少年的健康与发展,与此相似,残障青少年得到的关注也非常有限，例如，没有多少资料可用于估算残障青少年的人口规模。有资料预测，10～19 岁的残障青少年约占残障总人口的5%[2, 11]，若以 2010 年全国普查初步分析结果和第二次全国残疾人抽样调查资料进行估计[12, 13]，我国大约有 2 亿残障人士，其中约 800 万（4.13%）为残障青少年。

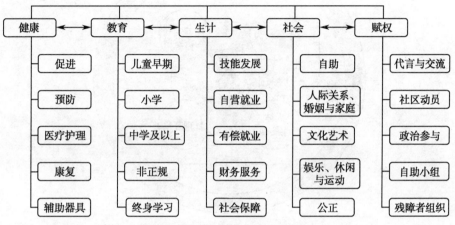

图 9-3　社区康复模式矩阵图[8]

与非残障青少年相比，残障青少年在生理及社会心理方面都面临着更多挑战。根据生物生态理论（图 9-4），整体健康与发展包括身体、心理和精神层面（亦即生理、心理与信仰），最内层的生物圈包括同伴、父母及其他成人角色榜样，它在促进残障青少年的健康与发展、促进向成年期的过渡方面具有非常重要的作用[14-16]。

需要特别指出的是，性是人类不可或缺的部分，但现在仍然有人把残障人士当作是无性的[17-19]，这样一来，人们就很容易忽视残障青少年的青春期性成熟，导致可能发生更多不良性行为后果，如意外怀孕、流产、性虐待、性传播性感染等[19-21]。经常有报道指出，与非残障青少年相比，残障青少年往往人际关系较差、情绪相对更不稳定、学业较差、教育水平及就业程度相对较低，但却有更多暴力、虐待与自杀企图，这提示，需要进行多方面的干预[20, 22-24]。尽管经常有报道称，生活技能培训是有所裨益的，然而，由于资源限制，所产生的阳性结果并非那么显著，干预方案又那么复杂，这些都会限制生活技能培训项目的拓展实施。不论开展什么项目，至关重要的就是，一定要吸纳残障青少年参与其中，尤其是在通过科研寻找有效的策略和措施时，吸纳残障青少年参与其中更是效用匪浅[25]。为残障人士发展项目时，大家都必须牢记这句名言,"不纳入我们残障人士,就不可能是关于我们残障人士的"[1, 2]。

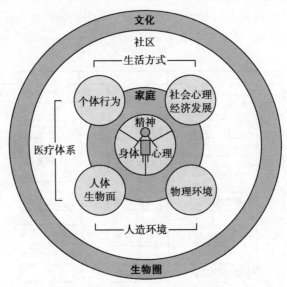

图 9-4　生物生态理论下的残障青少年健康与发展

卫生工作者对待残障的态度

我国虽有大约 5% 的人口是残障青少年[2, 11],但却会惊诧地发现,有关残障青少年发展成长的数据却极为有限,表明对这一群体的关注程度真的是微乎其微。就专业卫生人员而言,卫生专业的教育及临床工作普遍存在对残障相关事宜的不敏感,重视程度也很有限[18, 26-28]。有研究显示,护生和护士对待残障人士的态度较差,虽说比没有接受过医学培训的同龄人的态度要好,但却比医科生和医生的态度要差[26-28]。

实际上,十年前就已有所揭示,残障患者觉得护士和护生的态度是带有贬低意味的,是让人自感无能的[29]。鉴于有论证指出,授权残障人士是护士的重要责任,社会学层面的内容因此需要整合到护理教育与护理临床工作中,以缓冲对人类生物属性或疾病层面的过分强调[30]。过去十年里已经出现过一些教学改革报道,虽然较为有限,例如,新西兰对本科护理课程进行了修订,专门加入了残障单元,然而,在随后对学生进行的便利取样调查却显示,在学习该单元后,护生对待残障的态度并未发生具有显著统计学意义的变化[31]。因此,势在必行的就是,需要作出更多努力改变现有的卫生专业课程体系,提升卫生专业学生和卫生工作者的残障服务能力,这是提供优质残障卫生服务、消除健康差异的先决条件[32, 33]。

促进向成年期过渡

残障青少年在向成年期过渡的过程中需要得到更多的支持,而护士也已在促进过渡的过程中显示出了至关重要的角色和作用[34]。一般情况下,过渡是指从一种状态、状况或位置转向另一种状态、状况或位置的过程或运动[35]。对卫生工作者来说,过渡性服务是指那些为残障青少年统筹提供的、具有结果导向的系列活动,重点是学业和功能上的进步与改善。设计这些活动是为了促进青少年从学校走向学校外,包括中等教育后教育、职业培训、综合就业、继续教育和成人教育、成年期服务、独立生存或社区参与等。完整的过渡应涵盖卫生服务、教育、社交网路、社区生活、就业或职业生涯选择等层面[34, 36]。

当具有如下基本特征时,就可以认为已达到最佳过渡性服务实践模式,亦即家庭参与、跨机构跨学科合作、自我决策技能和过渡规划,在此过渡规划中,必须包含在包容性机构的工作经验,这样的机构通常是残障人士首先考虑的工作地点,典型场所是庇护工厂[34]。尽管如此,有调查显示,残障青少年的家长(n=573)对所提供的过渡活动并不满意,但卫生工作者(n=141,主要是儿科医生)认为他们所提供的服务多于家长认为他们所提供的服务[37]。而在被调查的13项过渡服务活动中,家长认为大多数(n=7)是重要或非常重要的,说明这些过渡服务活动非常有必要,具体包括:一般健康与残障照顾、统筹卫生专业人员的连续卫生服务供给、帮助获取医疗保险、帮助寻找成年期的卫生工作人员、教会残障者进行自我健康管理、与学校统筹实施健康照顾[37]。

为引导卫生工作者更好地为残障青少年提供过渡服务,青少年医学研究会(Society of Adolescent Medicine)发布如下立场声明:①要确保有医疗场所提供初级卫生保健服务;②要找出卫生工作者所需要的知识和技能,如果适用,也要找出残障青少年及其家庭所需要的核心知识与技能;③准备并维护便携式残障青少年医疗状况摘要;④制订过渡性卫生服务规划;⑤提供初级卫生保健和预防保健;⑥确保有医疗保险[36, 38]。美国卫生和公共服务部下属的卫生资源与服务管理局(Health Resources and Services Administration)提出了相应的核心结果指标,以评估针对残障青少年的过渡性服务活动,最终结局是残障青少年接受了所有必要的过渡性服务,涉及生活各方面的过渡,包括成年期卫生服务、就业和独立生存[37, 39]。

与发达社会所作出的巨大努力相比,我国在残障青少年过渡性服务方面所做的工作相对较少。卫生工作者可以充分借鉴其他国家或社会的经验,不断发展自己在促进残障青少年从儿童期向成年期过渡中的角色和作用。

（刘　茜，臧渝梨，刘　静）

参 考 文 献

[1] Schranz B, Shrivastava A, Mohapatra B, et al. Mainstreaming disability in community based disaster risk reduction—a training manual for trainers and field practitioners [M/OL]. New Delhi, India: Handicap International-India, 2008[2011-6-23]: http://www.disabilityindrr.org/TrainingManual_Normal.pdf.

[2] WHO & World Bank. World Report on Disability [M/OL]. Malta: World Health Organization, 2011[2011-6-26]: http://whqlibdoc.who.int/publications/2011/9789240685215_eng.pdf.

[3] WHO. Towards a Common Language for Functioning, Disabilty and Health ICF [EB/OL]. World Health Organization, 2002[2011-6-28]:http://www.who.int/classifications/icf/training/icfbeginnersguide.pdf.

[4] WHO. WHA58.23 Disability, including prevention, management and rehabilitation [EB/OL]. World Health Organization, 2005[2011-7-25]:http://www.who.int/disabilities/WHA5823_resolution_en.pdf.

[5] DFID. Disability, poverty and development [EB/OL]. UK Department for International Development, 2000[2011-6-26]:http://handicap-international.fr/bibliographie-handicap/4PolitiqueHandicap/hand_pauvrete/DFID_disability.pdf.

[6] Michaud P, Suris J, Viner R. The adolescent with a chronic condition. Part II: healthcare provision [J]. Archives of Disease in Childhood, 2004, 89（10）: 943-949.

[7] Suris J-C, Michaud P-A, Viner R. The adolescent with a chronic condition. Part I: developmental issues [J]. Archives of Disease in Childhood, 2004, 89（10）: 938-942.

[8] WHO. Community-based Rehabilitation（CBR）[EB/OL]. World Health Organization, 2010[25 Jul. 2011]: http://www.who.int/disabilities/cbr/en/.

[9] WHO. Declaration of Alma-Ata [EB/OL]. World Health Organization, 1978[2011-6-21]: http://www.who.int/hpr/NPH/docs/declaration_almaata.pdf.

[10] WHO. The World Health Report 2008 - Primary Healthcare（Now More Than Ever）[M/OL]. Geneva, Switzerland: World Health Organization, 2008[2011-7-25]: http://www.who.int/whr/2008/en/index.html.

[11] 中国青少年研究中心. 当代中国青年人口发展状况研究报告 [EB/OL]. 中国青少年研究, 2008[2011-5-19]: http://www.cycs.org/Article.asp?Category=1&Column=389&ID=7869.

[12] 中国残疾人联合会. 2006 全国残疾人分残疾类别和残疾等级的年龄构成 [EB/OL].

中国残疾人联合会 , 2008[2011-7-25]: http://www.cdpf.org.cn/sytj/content/2008-04/07/content_30336060.htm.

[13] 中华人民共和国国家统计局 . 全国人口普查主要数据公报 (第 1 号) [EB/OL]. 中国国家统计局 , 2011[2011-5-25]: http://www.stats.gov.cn/tjgb/rkpcgb/qgrkpcgb/t20110428_402722232.htm.

[14] Bronfenbrenner U. Making human beings human: bioecological perspectives on human development [M]. Thousand Oaks, California: Sage, 2005.

[15] St Leger L. Health promotion and health education in schools: trends, effectiveness and possibilities [M]. Noble Park North, Victoria: Royal Automobile Club of Victoria (RACV) Ltd. 2006.

[16] Wang G, McGrath BB, Watts C. Health care transitions among youth with disabilities or special health care needs: an ecological approach [J]. Journal of Pediatric Nursing, 2010, 25 (6): 505-550.

[17] Esmail S, Darry K, Walter A, et al. Attitudes and perceptions towards disability and sexuality [J]. Disability and Rehabilitation, 2010, 32 (14): 1148-1155.

[18] Shakespeare T, Lezzoni L, Groce-Kaplan N. The Art of Medicine: Disability and the training of health professionals [J]. The Lancet 2009, 374 (9704): 1815-1816.

[19] WHO, UNFPA. Promoting sexual and reproductive health for persons with disabilities [M/OL]. Geneva, Switzerland: World Health Organization, 2009[2011-6-28]. http://extranet.who.int/iris/bitstream/123456789/614/1/9789241598682_eng.pdf.

[20] Blum RW, Kelly A, Ireland M. Health-risk behaviors and protective factors among adolescents with mobility impairments and learning and emotional disabilities [J]. Journal of Adolescent Health, 2001, 28 (6): 481-490.

[21] Surís J-C, Resnick MD, Cassuto N, et al. Sexual behavior of adolescents with chronic disease and disability [J]. Journal of Adolescent Health, 1996, 19 (2):124-131.

[22] Lisa Skär RN. Peer and adult relationships of adolescents with disabilities [J]. Journal of Adolescence, 2003, 26 (6): 635-649.

[23] Stevens SE, Steele CA, Jutai JW, et al. Adolescents with physical disabilities: Some psychosocial aspects of health [J]. Journal of Adolescent Health, 1996, 19 (2): 157-164.

[24] Svetaz MV, Ireland M, Blum R. Adolescents with learning disabilities: risk and protective factors associated with emotional well-being: findings from the National Longitudinal Study of Adolescent Health[J]. Journal of Adolescent Health, 2000, 27 (5): 340-348.

[25] Kingsnorth S, Healy H, Macarthur C. Preparing for adulthood: a systematic review of life skill programs for youth with physical disabilities [J]. Journal of Adolescent Health, 2007, 41 (4): 323-332.

[26] Matziou V, Galanis P, Tsoumakas C, et al. Attitudes of nurse professionals and nursing students towards children with disabilities. Do nurses really overcome children's physical and mental handicaps? [J]. International nursing review, 2009, 56（4）: 456-460.

[27] Sahin H, Akyol AD. Evaluation of nursing and medical students' attitudes towards people with disabilities [J]. Journal of Clinical Nursing, 2010, 19（15-16）:2271-2279.

[28] Klooster-ten PM, Dannenberg J-W, Taal E, et al. Attitudes towards people with physical or intellectual disabilities: nursing students and non-nursing peers [J]. Journal of advanced nursing, 2009, 65（12）: 2562-2573.

[29] Scullion PA. Conceptualizing disability in nursing: some evidence from students and their teachers [J]. Journal of advanced nursing, 1999, 29（3）: 648-657.

[30] Scullion PA. Enabling disabled people: responsibilities of nurse education [J]. British Journal of Nursing, 2000, 9（15）: 1010-1014.

[31] Seccombe JA. Attitudes towards disability in an undergraduate nursing curriculum: The effects of a curriculum change [J]. Nurse education today, 2007, 27（5）: 445-451.

[32] Monsen RB. School nurses and health disparities [J]. Journal of Pediatric Nursing, 2006, 21（4）: 311-312.

[33] WHO. WHA62.14. Reducing health inequities through action on the social determinants of health [EB/OL]. World Health Organization, 2009[2011-6-28]:http://apps.who.int/gb/ebwha/pdf_files/EB124/B124_R6-en.pdf.

[34] Betz CL. Facilitating the transition of adolescents with developmental disabilities: nursing practice issues and care [J]. Journal of Pediatric Nursing, 2007, 22（2）: 103-115.

[35] Schumacher KL, Meleis AI. Transitions: a central concept in nursing [J]. Journal of Nursing Scholarship, 1994, 26（2）: 119-127.

[36] Park MJ, Adams SH, Irwin Jr CE. Health care services and the transition to young adulthood: Challenges and Opportunities [J]. Academic Pediatrics, 2011, 11（2）: 115-122.

[37] Geenen SJ, Powers LE, Sells W. Understanding the Role of Health Care Providers During the Transition of Adolescents With Disabilities and Special Health Care Needs[J]. Journal of Adolescent Health, 2003, 32（3）: 225-233.

[38] SAM. Transition to adult health care for adolescents and young adults with chronic conditions [J]. Journal of Adolescent Health, 2003, 33（4）: 309-311.

[39] HRSA. The national survey of children with special health care needs chartbook 2005-2006 [EB/OL]. U.S. Department of Health and Human Services Health Resources and Services Administration, 2008[2011-7-3]: http://www.uconnucedd.org/actearlyct/PDFs/National.pdf.

青少年健康与发展监测

前面几章从不同侧面阐述了青少年的健康与发展，涉及青春期生长发育、心理社会发展与健康、健康危险行为和残障。2006年，WHO泛美地区办公室[1]提出，青少年健康与发展监测是亲青卫生服务（adolescent friendly health service, AFHS）的核心组成部分，本章因此重点介绍青少年健康与发展相关测评工具。这些工具中的大多数都已在国际上被广泛使用，为进一步推广使用这些工具、同时也为促进跨文化的比较，我国已在10～19岁青少年群体中使用，结果显示其具有良好的测评属性。

以下将逐一介绍这些测评工具，分别涉及人口社会与经济特征、青春期发育、认知发展、家庭功能障碍，也涉及情绪、行为或社会方面的长处与困难，以及因健康问题而在生活各方面所感知到的困难程度。本章还会介绍青春期相关知识、态度与行为的测评，以具体评价青少年对青春期和青少年发展阶段的理解。

第1节　人口社会与经济特征

与人口社会与经济特征相关的题项大部分来自我国卫生部《国家基本公共卫生服务规范》（2009年版）[2]中的居民健康档案，涉及患病与残障情况、健康问题、医疗保险、健康危险因素、既往史（包括疾病、外伤、手术、输血）、家族史和遗传病史；其他还包括：是否独生子女、生长发育（即身高、体重）、父母教育背景、主要照顾者以及所感知到的家庭收入、学习成绩和父母婚姻状况等。科研工作者、教师和卫生工作者可根据需要选用其中某些题项有目的地去收集相关信息，具体参见表10-1。

对于离校但已有工作的青少年，可以用与工作有关的题项（如所在单位名称、职业类型）去替换与学校生活有关的题项（如学校名称、年级、学习成绩）。职业类型的答题选项包括：①国家机关、党群组织、企业、事业单位负责人；②专业技术人员；③办事人员和有关人员；④商业、服务业人员；⑤农、林、牧、渔、水利业生产人员；⑥生产、运输设备操作人员及有关人员；⑦军人；⑧不便分类的其他从业人员[2]。

表10-1　个人基本信息表

题项	内容
学校与年级	学校 _____ 年级 _____
出生年月（阳历）	_____ 年 _____ 月　　　　实足年龄：_____ 周岁
民族	①汉族　②少数民族（请注明）_____
性别	①女　　②男
是否独生子女	①否　　②是
生长发育情况	身高：_____ 厘米　　　体重：_____ 千克
家庭居住地	①城市　②城郊（城乡结合部）　③农村
户口所在地	①城市　②城郊（城乡结合部）　③农村
妈妈文化程度	①小学或没上过学　②小学毕业　　③初中 ④高中或中专　　　⑤大专及以上
爸爸文化程度	①小学或没上过学　②小学毕业　　③初中 ④高中或中专　　　⑤大专及以上
父母婚姻状况	①和睦　②一般　③不和睦　④分居　⑤离异　⑥其他
家庭类型	①核心家庭（仅由父母和子女组成） ②大家庭（不少于三代人共同组成）　③寄养家庭 ④单亲家庭　⑤重组家庭
主要照顾者	①父母　②（外）祖父母　③其他
家庭收入（与周围比）	①下等　②中下等　③中等　④中上等　⑤上等　⑥不知道
学习成绩（与周围比）	①下等　②中下等　③中等　④中上等　⑤上等
是否抽烟	①从来没有过　②几乎没有　③有时　④经常　⑤总是
是否喝酒	①从来没有过　②几乎没有　③有时　④经常　⑤总是
是否醉酒	①从来没有过　②几乎没有　③有时　④经常　⑤总是
是否使用成瘾药物	①否　②是 □镇静剂（如安眠药）　□兴奋剂（如尼古丁） □阿片类药物（如吗啡）□迷幻剂（如摇头丸、咳嗽水）
医疗费用支付方式	①全公费　②部分公费　③城镇职工医疗保险 ④城镇居民医疗保险　⑤商业医疗保险　⑥新型农村合作医疗 ⑦贫困救助　⑧全自费　⑨其他
药物过敏史	①无　②有　□青霉素　□磺胺　□链霉素　□其他
暴 露 史	①无　②有　□化学品　□毒物　□射线

续表

题项				内容
既往史	疾病	①无	②有	病名1_____确诊时间_____年; 病名2_____确诊时间_____年;
	手术	①无	②有	名称1_____时间_____年; 名称2_____时间_____年;
	外伤	①无	②有	名称1_____时间_____年; 名称2_____时间_____年;
	输血	①无	②有	原因1_____时间_____年; 原因2_____时间_____年;
家族史与遗传病史	父亲	①无 ②有		病名1_____病名2_____
	母亲	①无 ②有		病名1_____病名2_____
	兄弟姐妹	①无 ②有		病名1_____病名2_____
有无残疾		①无	②有	□听力残疾 □言语残疾 □肢体残疾 □智力残疾 □视力残疾 □精神残疾 □多重残疾 程度描述_____

此外,在卫生部最新颁布的《国家基本公共卫生服务规范》(2011年版)[3]中,增加了以下与生活环境有关的题项(包括答题选项):

- 厨房排风设施:①无　②油烟机　③换气扇　④烟囱
- 燃料类型:①液化气　②煤　③天然气　④沼气　⑤柴火　⑥其他____
- 饮水:①自来水　②经净化过滤的水　③井水　④河湖水　⑤塘水⑥其他_____
- 厕所:①卫生厕所　②一格或二格粪池式　③马桶　④露天粪坑　⑤简易棚厕
- 禽畜栏:①单设　②室内　③室外

上述这五个题项的增加反映了对生活环境影响健康状况的重视在不断增加。由于社会、政治与经济形势以及疾病谱的差异,不同乡镇或地域在不同时段对健康的关注点会有所不同,鉴于这部分题项相对较多,最好是仅从中选取的确有助于更好地了解所关注健康问题的方面进行资料收集,切实做到经济有效。

第2节　青春期发育量表

除了卫生专业人员进行直接视诊之外,最初的青春期发育状态评估可以追溯到 Tanner 标准图片法,所反映的是性成熟随时间的渐进变化 [4, 5]。这种图片法后被 Morris 和 Udry 的流线图法所取代[6]，以回应人们的某种心理需要，那就是，最好不要那么直接地联系到人的性征部位，如外生殖器、乳房[7]。为促进青少年与父母在接受评估时的舒适感，Petersen 及其同事推出了文本式青春期发育量表（Puberty Development Scale, PDS）[8]，后由 Carskadon 和 Acebo 进行了修订[9]。

鉴于华人的性保守文化，香港在上述文本式 PDS 基础上形成了中文版 PDS 量表（以下简称 C-PDS），采用的是修订后的评价标尺和计分方法，已有证据表明 C-PDS 具有良好的信效度[10]。简体中文版的 PDS 量表（以下简称 MC-PDS，见表 10-2）源自 C-PDS[11]，目前已在 234 名 12~14 岁的内地青少年中使用，用于辅助评价所实施的校园健康教育项目。研究发现，男孩版和女孩版的 MC-PDS 内部一致性信度系数（即 Cronbach's α）分别为 0.66 和 0.80，间隔 10 天的复测信度组内系数（即 intraclass correlation）分别为 0.89 和 0.71[12]。

MC-PDS 的计分方法[9, 11] 为：对于男孩版，前四个答题选项分别计为 1~4 分，第五个选项"不知道"计为 0 分；对于女孩版，前四题的评分方法与男孩版的评分法一致，对于第五题的第一小题（即 5a），回答"有"计 1 分，回答"没有"计 0 分。

青春期类别分（Pubertal Categorization Score, PCS）的计算方法为：对于男孩版，累计第 2 题（体毛）、第 4 题（变声）和第 5 题（面部毛发或胡须）的得分，再按照如下分值标准进行分类：前青春期 =3 分；青春期早期 =4 分或 5 分，且无任何一项得 3 分；青春期中期 =6 分、7 分或 8 分，且无任何一项得 4 分；青春期晚期 =9~11 分；青春期后 =12 分。对于女孩版，累计第 2 题（体毛）、第 4 题（乳房发育）和第 5a 题（月经）的得分，根据如下分值标准进行分类：前青春期 =2 分，且没有月经；青春期早期 =3 分，且没有月经；青春期中期 >3 分，且没有月经；青春期晚期≤7 分，且已有月经；青春期后 =8 分，且已有月经[11]（表 10-2）。

表 10-2　青春期发育量表（PDS）

以下问题是有关你身体的改变，这些都是青少年时期的正常变化，但发生的年龄可能因人而异，请你仔细阅读后回答下列问题。每个问题后面有 5 个选项，请在相应选项下打勾（√），如果遇到不明白的问题或不知道答案，请选择"不知道"。

以下问题仅限于男孩

1. 你有身高上的增长吗？

　　①还没有　　②开始　　③已经有　　④好像已完成　　⑤不知道

2. 你的体毛开始增长了吗？（体毛是指除头发以外，身体上其他地方的毛发，如阴毛、腋毛）

　　①还没有　　②开始　　③已经有　　④好像已完成　　⑤不知道

3. 你有皮肤上的改变吗？例如脸上长出暗疮、粉刺

续表

| ① 还没有 | ② 开始有 | ③ 已经有 | ④ 好像已完成 | ⑤ 不知道 |

4. 你的声调变低沉了吗？

    ① 还没有 　　② 开始有 　　③ 已经有 　　④ 好像已完成 　　⑤ 不知道

5. 你面部开始长出胡须了吗？

    ① 还没有 　　② 开始有 　　③ 已经有 　　④ 好像已完成 　　⑤ 不知道

以下问题仅限于女孩

1. 你有身高上的增长吗？

    ① 还没有 　　② 开始有 　　③ 已经有 　　④ 好像已完成 　　⑤ 不知道

2. 你的体毛开始增长了吗？（体毛是指除头发以外，身体上其他地方的毛发，如阴毛、腋毛）

    ① 还没有 　　② 开始有 　　③ 已经有 　　④ 好像已完成 　　⑤ 不知道

3. 你有皮肤上的改变吗？例如脸上长出暗疮、粉刺。

    ① 还没有 　　② 开始有 　　③ 已经有 　　④ 好像已完成 　　⑤ 不知道

4. 你的乳房开始发育及胀起了吗？

    ① 还没有 　　② 开始有 　　③ 已经有 　　④ 好像已完成 　　⑤ 不知道

5a. 你开始有月经了吗？ 　　　　　　　　①有 　　　　　②没有

5b. 如果有的话，你的月经在多少周岁开始的？＿＿＿＿＿＿

总体而言，在校园、社区或家中进行健康筛查时，可以选用文本式青春期发育测评法来取代传统图形测评法。尽管如此，在医院里最好还是采用图形法和彻底的体格检查，这有利于专业卫生人员做出更准确的临床判断[7, 13]。

第3节　认知发展量表

青少年阶段是大脑认知和道德观念发展至关重要的时期[14-17]。以皮亚杰的认知发展阶段理论为基础，Perry 提出了智力、道德或伦理发展理论，揭示了人们如何给个人经历赋予意义，该理论的主要观点是：个体的逻辑推理形式超越所推理的内容，也就是说，个体如何进行推理是始终一致的，不论所推理的具体内容究竟是什么；而随着时间推移，适应性的逻辑推理形式将会逐渐被更好的推理形式所取代，但在某个特定时期，占优势的只是一种认知状态；而个体的推理水平通常是由较低向更高发展[18, 19]。

张博士及其同事[18-22]认识到了 Perry 理论在解释大学生认知发展上的

价值，尤其是与学习、人际互动和生活意义有关的认知发展，于是据此研发了包含 75 个题项的测评工具，亦即张氏认知发展量表（Zhang's cognitive development inventory, ZCDI），以评价学生在如下五个方面的认知发展情况：教育两极性（education dualism, ED, 共 20 题）、教育相对性（education relativism, ER, 共 14 题）、人际两极性（interpersonal dualism, ID, 共 20 题）、人际相对性（interpersonal relativism, IR, 共 14 题）、生活尽责性（life commitment, LC, 共 7 题），这五个方面的题项分别构成 ZCDI 的五个子量表。有人争论，学生的认知发展顺序是从两极性、相对性发展至生活尽责性，处于较高认知发展水平的学生倾向于进行深入而非浅显的学习，更具有立法性、公正性、层级性、整体性和自由性，但较少具有执行性、局部性、霸权性和规范性[18, 19]。

这个有 75 题项的 ZCDI 量表（示例题项见表 10-3）曾在数千名美国、我国香港地区和内地大学生中使用，结果显示，该工具有较好的内部一致性，Cronbach's α 系数分别是：ED 子量表 0.70～0.84，ER 子量表 0.57～0.71，ID 子量表 0.65～0.78，IR 子量表 0.56～0.62，LC 子量表 0.62～0.69；与思维风格、学习方式以及自评分析、创造、实践能力的相关分析显示，ZCDI 具有良好的内容效度，符合 Perry 理论[18, 19]。

表 10-3　张氏认知发展量表（ZCDI）题项示例

维度	题项示例
教育两极性（ED）	2. 理解一门课程的关键在于学会遵循老师的思维方式。 ①完全不同意　②不太同意　③稍有一点同意　④有些同意 ⑤基本同意　⑥同意　⑦非常同意　⑧不适用
教育相对性（ER）	11. 在学术辩论中，论证观点既需要推理，又需要冒险。 ①完全不同意　②不太同意　③稍有一点同意　④有些同意 ⑤基本同意　⑥同意　⑦非常同意　⑧不适用
人际两极性（ID）	9. 我习惯在某一特定时期内只与一个好朋友交往。 ①完全不同意　②不太同意　③稍有一点同意　④有些同意 ⑤基本同意　⑥同意　⑦非常同意　⑧不适用
人际相对性（IR）	19. 我同那些持有与我信仰截然不同的人照样相处得很好。 ①完全不同意　②不太同意　③稍有一点同意　④有些同意 ⑤基本同意　⑥同意　⑦非常同意　⑧不适用
生活尽责性（LC）	1. 为了实现我的几个主要目标，我已经按照其重要性将要做的事情进行了排列。 ①完全不同意　②不太同意　③稍有一点同意　④有些同意 ⑤基本同意　⑥同意　⑦非常同意　⑧不适用

ZCDI 量表采用 7 点评分法，评价被试学生对题项内容的赞成程度：自"完全不同意"至"非常同意"分别计 1～7 分，第 54 题（即好朋友在多数情

况下应该持相同的意见)反向计分,子量表中各题项得分之和为该子量表得分。鉴于认知发展是一连续体,ZCDI 已在我国 10~19 岁的青少年中试用,但额外增加了答题选项"不适用",计为 0 分,本章作者将在别处报告相关研究发现。

第 4 节　长处与困难问卷

青少年精神障碍早期可能表现为情绪症状、行为问题、注意力缺陷或同伴交往障碍,亲社会行为可能折射出青少年内心所具有的克服这些问题、并阻止其演变为精神障碍的能力;然而,出现上述问题是否就能反映出可能患有精神障碍,要取决于这些问题所引起的社交损害以及这些问题给青少年自己及其家长、教师和他人造成的负担。这些思考奠定了 Goodman 等学者研发长处与困难问卷(strength and difficulties questionnaire, SDQ)及扩展版长处与困难问卷(以下简称 Ext-SDQ)的基础 [23-26]。SDQ 和 Ext-SDQ 都可以分别用于 11~16 岁的青少年及其父母和教师,但需要根据目标被测人群而稍微调整关键人物指称,例如,自评版 SDQ 和 Ext-SDQ 中都是采用"你"而不是"您的孩子"进行指称。

随着时间推移,SDQ 已被证明具有良好的信效度,这些指标包括诸如,内部一致性信度(即 Cronbach's α)、区分效度、预测效度、因子结构效度等 [23-25, 27, 28]。如表 10-4 所示,SDQ 共有 25 个题项,为五因子或五维结构,每个维度由 5 个题项组成,这五个维度分别是:情绪症状(包括第 3、8、13、16、24 题)、品行问题(包括第 5、7、12、18、22 题)、多动注意缺陷(第 2、10、15、21、25 题)、同伴交往问题(包括第 6、11、14、19、23 题)和亲社会行为(包括第 1、4、9、17、20 题)。

表 10-4　长处与困难问卷 [29]

请依据你过去六个月内的经验与事实,回答以下各题,请从题目右边的三个选项:「不符合」、「有点符合」或「完全符合」的空格中,勾选出你觉得合适的答案。请不要遗漏任何一题,即使你对某些题目并不是十分确定。

编号	题项内容	不符合	有点符合	完全符合
1	我尝试对别人友善,我关心别人的感受	☐	☐	☐
2	我不能安定,不能长时间保持安静	☐	☐	☐
3	我经常头痛、肚子痛或是身体不舒服	☐	☐	☐
4	我常与他人分享(食物、玩具、笔等)	☐	☐	☐
5	我觉得非常愤怒及常发脾气	☐	☐	☐
6	我经常独处,我通常独自玩耍	☐	☐	☐

续表

编号	题项内容	不符合	有点符合	完全符合
7	我通常依照吩咐做事	□	□	□
8	我经常担忧,心事重重	□	□	□
9	如有人受伤、难过或不适,我都乐意帮忙	□	□	□
10	我经常坐立不安或感到不耐烦	□	□	□
11	我有一个或几个好朋友	□	□	□
12	我经常与别人争执,我能使别人依我的想法行事	□	□	□
13	我经常不快乐、心情沉重或流泪	□	□	□
14	一般来说,其他与我年龄相近的人都喜欢我	□	□	□
15	我容易分心,我觉得难于集中精神	□	□	□
16	我在新的环境中会感到紧张,我很容易失去自信	□	□	□
17	我会友善地对待比我年少的孩子	□	□	□
18	我常被指撒谎或不老实	□	□	□
19	其他小孩或青少年常捉弄或欺负我	□	□	□
20	我常自愿帮助别人(父母、老师、同学)	□	□	□
21	我做事前会先想清楚	□	□	□
22	我会从家中、学校或别处拿取不属于我的物件	□	□	□
23	我与大人相处较与同辈相处融洽	□	□	□
24	我心中有许多恐惧,我很容易受惊吓	□	□	□
25	我总能把手头上的事情办妥,我的注意力良好	□	□	□

采用 3 分评分法评价 SDQ 的 20 个题项: 0= 不符合; 1= 有点符合; 2= 完全符合; 对其余 5 个题项采用反向评分, 亦即依照吩咐做事(第 7 题)、有一个或几个好朋友(第 11 题)、被同辈喜欢(第 14 题)、做事前思考(第 21 题)、集中注意力做事(第 25 题)。困难总分是四个维度(即情绪症状、品行问题、多动与注意缺陷、同伴交往问题)共 20 个题项的累计总分 [23, 24, 26]。此外, SDQ 最后还有一开放性问题, 即"你是否有其他的意见", 目的是获取更多有临床启示意义的信息 [29]。

除了 SDQ 中的上述 25 个题项, Ext-SDQ 还包括更多题项: ①首个问题询问在情绪、行为、注意力、与人相处方面**所感知到的困难**, 采用 4 分评分法：0= 否；1= 是，有少许困难；2= 是，有困难；3= 是，有很大困难。若回答"否"，就不需要继续回答其他关于困难慢性度、影响度与负担度的问题；②以"这些困难出现了多久"询问慢性度，采用 4 分评分法：1= 少于一个月；2=1～5 个月；3=6～11 月；4= 超过一年以上；③以"这些困难是否困扰着你"询问**痛苦度**，采用 4 分评分法：0= 没有；1= 轻微；2= 颇为；3= 非常；④以"这些困难是否对你在下列的日常生活造成干扰"评价在家庭生活、和朋友的关系、上课学习、课外休闲活动四个方面的**社交不能**，评分法同前 [24]。如果特别关注识别出阳性案例时，另一选择是，对**痛苦度**和**社交不能**的评价可以采用如下 3 分评分法：0= 没有；0= 轻微；1= 颇为；2= 很多；⑤最后一题以"你的这些困难是否成为在你身边其他人（家人、朋友、师长）的负担"询问**负担度**，也采用 4 分评分法：0= 没有；1= 轻微；2= 颇为；3= 非常 [24, 29]。

　　SDQ 和 Ext-SDQ 已被译成 40 多种语言，成为在国际上适用于校园、社区和精神卫生诊所的行为筛查工具 [29]。我国香港 [30] 和内地多个地区均有使用中文版 SDQ 及 Ext-SDQ，上海还推出了 3～17 岁儿童青少年的界值标准 [31]。尽管如此，鉴于原创者仅推出了繁体中文版，而繁体与简体中文在文化、语言和地域背景上又存在细腻的差别，有学者指出，在使用中文版 SDQ 和 Ext-SDQ 时必须注意其文化适用性和跨文化可比性问题 [32]。因此，在目前暂时没有中文版 SDQ 系统文献综述的情况下，对 SDQ 得分的解释、跨文化比较以及常模参照都要非常谨慎。

　　最后必须指出，SDQ 和 Ext-SDQ 的格式有特别的设计，例如，SDQ 的所有 25 个题项均放在纸的一面，而另外被纳入 Ext-SDQ 中的社交损害题项则列置于该纸的另外一面。更多相关信息可以参考 youthinmind 网站，该网站发布有 SDQ 和 Ext-SDQ 的研发历史、所有语言版本的标准问卷、评分方法、所发表的相关文献以及各国常模等 [29]。

第 5 节　世界卫生组织残障评定量表

　　理想的状况是，最好能有一个工具可用于评价人生命全程中、不同严重程度的各种健康问题所造成的负面影响或困难程度。经过十余年的努力，在国际功能、残疾与健康分类体系指导下，WHO 研发了具有此种潜能的残障测评工具 2.0（WHO Disability Assessment Schedule 2.0，以下简称 WHODAS Ⅱ）[33, 34]。已有证据显示，该测评工具具有良好的信效度，例如，因子结构、复测信度组内相关系数（图 10-1）。

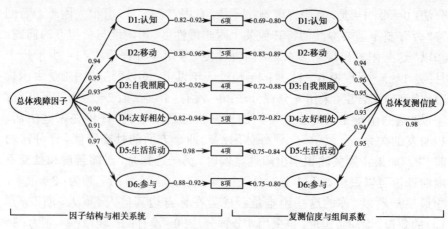

图 10-1　36 项自评版 WHODAS Ⅱ的因子结构与复测信度 [33,34]

WHODAS Ⅱ迄今形成共六个版本，分别是：包含 36 个题项的自评版、访谈版与代填版；包含 12 个题项的自评版和访谈版；以及 12 题项与 24 题项结合的访谈版 [33, 34]。必须强调的是，WHODAS Ⅱ的使用相对来说比较严格，需要获得 WHO 许可，并遵守用户协议，量表的结构化设计、转承语句的使用、字体的大小和颜色以及关键词下面的下划线，这些都有助于对题项内容的理解，确保所收集资料的质量，从而促进跨部门或跨国的数据比较。更多详尽的信息可自 WHO 网站获取 [34]，表 10-5 仅列出 36 项自评版 WHODAS Ⅱ供参考使用。

表 10-5　36 项自评版 WHODAS Ⅱ [34]

本问卷是询问你因健康状况而引起的困难。健康状况包括：疾病或疾患（即指那些持续时间或短或长的健康问题）、伤害、精神或情绪问题、以及酒药问题。

回想最近 30 天的情况，考虑你在从事如下活动时所遇到的困难有多大。困难包括吃力、不适或疼痛、迟缓、活动方式改变。对以下各题，每题仅圈选一个合适的答案。

最近 30 天，你在以下活动中存在多大困难：

理解与交流

D1.1　集中精力做事 10 分钟？

D1.2　记得要去做重要的事？

D1.3　在日常生活中分析并找到解决问题的办法？

D1.4　学习新任务（例如，学习如何到某个新地方）？

D1.5　大体上了解人们说什么？

D1.6　发起并维持一次对话？

四处走动

D2.1　长时间站立（比如，30 分钟）？

D2.2	从座位上站起？
D2.3	在家里来回移动？
D2.4	离开家？
D2.5	长距离行走（比如，1千米或相当于1千米）？

自我照顾

D3.1	全身洗浴？
D3.2	穿衣？
D3.3	进食？
D3.4	自己单独过几天？

与他人相处

D4.1	与不相识的人交往？
D4.2	维持一份友情？
D4.3	与跟你关系密切的人相处？
D4.4	结交新朋友？
D4.5	性生活？

生活活动

D5.1	承担家庭责任？
D5.2	很好地完成最重要的家务劳动？
D5.3	干完你需要做的所有家务劳动？
D5.4	根据需要，尽快干完家务劳动？

如果你有工作（有薪、无薪、自己经营）或上学，请完成如下D5.5~D5.8的问题，否则，跳至D6.1。

最近30天，由于你的健康原因，你在以下活动中存在多大困难：

D5.5	你的日常工作或学习？
D5.6	很好地完成你最重要的工作或学习任务？
D5.7	干完你需要做的所有事？
D5.8	根据需要，尽快做完事？

社会参与

最近30天：

D6.1	同其他人一样参加社区活动（例如，节日活动、宗教活动或其他活动）时，你遇到的困难有多大？
D6.2	因为你周围存在着的障碍或阻碍，你遇到的困难有多大？
D6.3	因为其他人的态度和行为，为了有尊严地生活，你遇到的困难有多大？
D6.4	你有多少时间花在自己的健康状况或其后果方面？
D6.5	你的健康状况对情绪的影响有多大？
D6.6	你的健康花费了你和家人多少资金？

D6.7	因为你的健康问题,你的<u>家庭</u>遇到了多大困难?	
D6.8	<u>你自己</u>在<u>放松</u>和娱乐上遇到了多大困难?	
H1	总体而言,最近 30 天,有<u>多少天</u>出现了这些困难?	记录天数_____
H2	在最近 30 天内,因为你的健康状况,有多少天你<u>无法做</u>通常所做的活动或工作?	记录天数_____
H3	在最近 30 天内,不算那些你完全不能做的日子,因为任何健康状况,有多少天你<u>不做或少做</u>通常所做的活动或工作?	记录天数_____

　　WHODAS Ⅱ的大多数题项可采用简易评分法:除了 H1、H2 和 H3 题,其余六个维度的 36 个题项均可采用 5 分评分法:1= 无;2= 轻度;3= 中度;4= 重度;5= 极重度 / 不能做;对各维度而言,维度得分就是该维度下所有题项的得分之和,而因健康问题所造成的困难总分则为各维度得分之和[33]。也有复杂算法,需要综合考虑各维度所占权重以及困难程度的实际得分,例如,答题选项"无"计为 0 分而非 1 分[33]。更多详情可从 WHO 网站或 WHO 有关官员那里获取。

　　随着时间推移,WHODAS Ⅱ已在大约 16 个国家试用,被试对象主要为18 岁及以上者[33, 34]。本书主编及其团队曾将中文 36 项自评版 WHODAS Ⅱ在 426 名 10～19 岁的城乡青少年中使用,以检验其可用性,相关验证性因子分析结果支持原有因子结构,比较拟合指数(CFI)为 0.95(应≥0.95),RMSEA为 0.08(约为 0.06),PCFI 为 0.62(应≥0.50),各项拟合指数均达到了括号内的参考标准[35]。还发现,WHODAS Ⅱ与 25 项 SDQ 的得分中度相关,而且,除了"与他人相处"维度(Cronbach's α=0.71),WHODAS Ⅱ总表以及其他维度的内部一致性信度系数(Cronbach's α)均达到了参考标准(即新发展测评工具的 α≥0.80)[36],分别为:总量表 α=0.96;理解与交流 α=0.91;四处走动 α=0.88;自我照顾 α=0.83;生活活动 α=0.93;社会参与 α=0.89。"与他人相处"维度的Cronbach's α 相对较低,可能与该维度中有关于性活动的题项(即 D4.5)有关,就我国而言,性活动一般是指性交而非也包括其他对性的表达(例如,拥抱、抚摸、接吻),且青少年并没有多少曾有性交经历,他们可能在回答此题时感觉不舒服或是不知如何回答。此外,D5.5～D5.8 题项之前的指导语相对较复杂,漏答率相对较高,说明在青少年中应用时,最好能在这些题项上给予提示。

第 6 节　家庭功能量表(APGAR)

　　家庭是儿童青少年的自然养育环境,在促进其发展成长中具有不可比拟的作用。家庭功能可从如下方面进行评价：适应度（adaptation）、合作度（partnership）、成熟度（growth）、情感度（affection）、亲密度（resolve），常用这五个方面英文关键词的首字母缩写 APGAR 指代家庭功能量表（详见表 10-6），包括 5 个题项，每个题项测评上述一个功能方面。20 世纪 40 年代开始强调患者的家庭治疗，自此以后，APGAR 开始被广泛应用[37]。

表 10-6　APGAR 量表

下面各题主要用来测评家庭功能，反映你对家庭功能的主观满意度，请在题目下面的选项中，勾选出你认为合适的答案。

当遇到问题时，可以从家人得到满意的帮助

　　①经常　　　　　　　　　②有时　　　　　　　　　③没有

很满意家人与我讨论各种事情以及分担问题的方式

　　①经常　　　　　　　　　②有时　　　　　　　　　③没有

当希望从事新的活动或发展时，家人都能接受且给予支持

　　①经常　　　　　　　　　②有时　　　　　　　　　③没有

很满意家人对我表达感情的方式及对我情绪的反应

　　①经常　　　　　　　　　②有时　　　　　　　　　③没有

很满意家人与我共享时光的方式

　　①经常　　　　　　　　　②有时　　　　　　　　　③没有

Smilkstein 认为，适应度是指家庭平衡遭受压力危机时，利用内外资源解决问题；合作度是指家庭成员共同决策、分担养育责任；成熟度是指家庭成员互相支持和指导，促进身心成熟和自我实现；情感度是指家庭成员之间的关爱关系；亲密度是指家庭成员奉献时间，促进身心健康，包括做出决策、分享金钱与空间[37]。

所设计的答题选项旨在反映对某方面家庭功能感到满意的频繁程度，采用 3 分评分法：0= 没有；1= 有时；2= 经常；家庭 APGAR 得分为 5 个题项得分之和：7～10 分表示家庭功能良好；4～6 分表示家庭功能中度障碍；0～3 分表示家庭功能严重障碍[37, 38]。某些情况下，可根据被询问成员在家庭中的身份而将各题项中的"家人"替换为配偶、重要他人、父母或子女[37, 38]。

有研究报道，APGAR 量表的 Cronbach's α 系数为 0.80～0.85，题项得分与量表总分的相关系数为 0.50～0.65，复测信度系数为 0.80～0.83；还发现，家庭 APGAR 与已有家庭功能测评工具（即 Pless-Satterwhile Index，$r=0.80$）和临床报告（$r=0.64$）均具有良好相关性[37-39]。

20 世纪 80 年代，中文版 APGAR 量表首先在我国台湾、香港使用，之后推广至内地[38, 40]。必须指出，APGAR 虽已得到广泛使用，最近一项对 401 名

儿科医生和家庭医生的调查似乎并不支持 APGAR 家庭功能评估上的有效性，相关资料来自 4～15 岁儿童青少年的 22 059 次连续诊疗服务 [41]。因此，在校园、家庭或社区等初级卫生保健场所使用 APGAR 量表应谨慎，遇到可疑案例时，最好结合使用其他家庭功能评估工具。

第 7 节　青春期知识、态度、行为调查表

青春期是指人类个体发展形成性生育能力的时期 [17]。相当长一段时间以来，西方国家就已从生物、生理和心理社会视角研究青春期，我国在这方面的科研积累却相对非常有限。根据 WHO 所提出的青少年健康与发展能力框架 [42, 43]，本书主编及其团队首先提出一系列陈述，用于评价青少年的青春期相关知识、态度与行为，通过小组讨论法和专家组法进行修改完善后形成了青春期相关知识、态度与行为量表（Puberty-related Knowledge, Attitudes and Behaviours Scale, 以下简称 Puberty-KAB, 表 10-7），采用 5- 分里克特评分法，其中 1= 非常不赞同；5= 非常赞同 [12]。

表 10-7　Puberty-KAB 的测评点

题号	陈述
1[a]	我了解喉结 / 乳房发育的知识
2[a]	我了解遗精现象 / 月经常识
3[a]	我了解外生殖器有关的知识 / 月经期的保健知识，如不能受凉
4[a]	我能接受遗精带来的生理变化 / 月经期的生理变化
5[a]	我能接受遗精带来的心理变化 / 月经期的心理变化
6	我经常清洗我的私密部位
7	我觉得自己在青春期的身体变化很自然，很正常
8	我期望改变我的形象
9	我总是积极参加学校安排的各种体育活动
10	业余时间我喜欢参加体育锻炼
11	我希望专门学习一项体育项目（如跆拳道、游泳、网球等）
12	现在我能控制吃麦当劳、肯德基等西式快餐的次数
13	我主动与父母沟通哪些饮食对我的健康最有利
14	父母平时非常注意我的饮食搭配
15	我的言行举止符合成年人对男孩 / 女孩的要求
16	我的行为非常容易受到周围同学、朋友的影响
17[a]	我觉得我喜欢上了某个女孩子 / 男孩子
18[a]	我渴望与喜欢的女孩子 / 男孩子一起玩

续表

题号	陈述
19[a]	我刻意接触过女孩的私密部位 / 有男孩刻意接触过我的私密部位
20	我感觉与父母的关系很融洽
21	我感觉与老师的关系很融洽
22	班主任老师对我的支持鼓励很多
23	我能处理好各种人际关系
24	我能与父母谈任何事情,包括学习、生活中遇到的问题
25	我能与老师谈任何事情,包括学习、生活中遇到的问题
26	我觉得在青春期阶段好好学习对我的生活很重要
27	我总是能够自觉主动地完成学习任务
28	我觉得周围所有人都在逼我学习
29	我对自己的发展很满意
30	我知道如何使自己避免受到伤害
31	我能够很好地调节自己的情绪

注:[a] 表示男孩版和女孩版有所不同。

此 31 项 Puberty-KAB 曾于一校园健康教育干预项目中,用以测评学生在参与活动前后的青春期相关知识、态度和行为[12],研究发现,男孩版和女孩版的 Cronbach's α 分别是 0.88 和 0.87,均已达到新研发工具需达到的较高内部一致性信度标准要求(即 α≥0.80)[36],间隔 10 天的复测信度分别是 0.91 和 0.84[12];因子分析还发现,男孩版和女孩版几乎所有题项均分别主要落于某个公因子上,各因子负荷均达到建议标准,除外女孩版第 20 题(即接触私密部位),这说明,尚需更多研究以进一步评估该量表的测评属性。

总之,本章描述了一系列精心挑选的测评工具,以供卫生工作者和学校教师评估青少年的发展水平、关键生活领域中所感知到的困难以及青春期相关知识、态度与行为。需要说明的是,这些测评工具更适于进行流行病学研究,有助于大体了解青少年的一般状况,并未涉及任何特定身心健康问题。对于任何可疑案例,在做出临床判断或疾病诊断前,都必须进行彻底的体检和心理社会学方面的检查。

(李　娜,扈丽萍,臧渝梨)

参 考 文 献

[1] WHO. Orientation programme on adolescent health for health-care providers [M/OL]. Geneva, Switzerland: World Health Organization, 2006[2011-6-14]: http://whqlibdoc.who. int/publications/2006/9241591269_Handout_eng.pdf.

[2] 卫生部妇幼保健与社区卫生司. 卫生部关于印发《国家基本公共卫生服务规范（2009 年版）》的通知 [EB/OL]. 2009-10-10[2011-8-4]：http://www.moh.gov.cn/publicfiles/ business/htmlfiles/mohfybjysqwss/s3577/200910/43183.htm.

[3] 卫生部妇幼保健与社区卫生司. 卫生部关于印发《国家基本公共卫生服务规范 （2011 年版）》的通知 [EB/OL]. 2011-5-24[2011-8-4]:http://www.moh.gov.cn/publicfiles/ business/htmlfiles/mohfybjysqwss/s3577/201105/51780.htm.

[4] Marshall WA, Tanner JM. Variations in pattern of pubertal changes in girls [J]. Archives of Disease in Childhood, 1969, 44（235）: 291-303.

[5] Marshall WA, Tanner JM. Variations in the pattern of pubertal changes in boys [J]. Archives of Disease in Childhood, 1970, 45（239）: 13-23.

[6] Morris NM, Udry JR. Validation of a self-administered instrument to assess stage of adolescent development [J]. Journal of Youth and Adolescence, 1980, 9（3）: 271-280.

[7] Coleman L, Coleman J. The measurement of puberty: a review [J]. Journal of Adolescence, 2002, 25（5）: 535-550.

[8] Petersen AC, Crockett L, Richards M, et al. A self-report measure of pubertal status: reliability, validity, and initial norms [J]. Journal of Youth and Adolescence, 1988, 17（2）: 117-133.

[9] Carskadon MA, Acebo C. A self-administered rating scale for pubertal development [J]. The Journal of Adolescent Health: Official Publication of the Society for Adolescent Medicine, 1993, 14（3）: 190-195.

[10] Chan NPT, Sung RYT, Kong APS, et al. Reliability of pubertal self-assessment in Hong Kong Chinese children [J]. Journal of Paediatrics and Child Health, 2008, 44（6）: 353-358.

[11] Chan NPT, Sung RYT, Nelson EAS, et al. Measurement of Pubertal Status with a Chinese Self-report Pubertal Development Scale [J]. Maternal and Child Health Journal, 2010, 14（3）: 466-473.

[12] Zang YL, Zhao Y, Yang Q, et al. A randomised trial on pubertal development and health in China [J]. Journal of Clinical Nursing, 2011, 20（21-22）: 3081-3091.

[13] Bond L, Clements J, Bertalli N, et al. A comparison of self-reported puberty using the Pubertal Development Scale and the Sexual Maturation Scale in a school-based epidemiologic survey [J]. Journal of Adolescence, 2006, 29（5）: 709-720.

[14] Enright RD, Lapsley DK, Harris DJ, et al. Moral development interventions in early adolescence [J]. Theory into Practice, 1983, 22（2）: 134-144.

[15] Hart D, Carlo G. Moral development in adolescence [J]. Journal of Research on Adolescence, 2005, 15（3）: 223-233.

[16] Steinberg L. Cognitive and affective development in adolescence[J]. Trends in Cognitive Sciences, 2005, 9(2): 69-74.

[17] Steinberg L. Adolescence [M]. 8th. New York, McGraw-Hill, 2008.

[18] Zhang LF. The Perry Scheme: across cultures, across approaches to the study of human psychology [J]. Journal of Adult Development, 2004, 11(2): 123-138.

[19] Zhang LF. Predicting cognitive development, intellectual styles, and personality traits from self-rated abilities [J]. Learning and Individual Differences, 2005, 15(1): 67-88.

[20] Zhang LF. A comparison of U.S. and Chinese university students' cognitive development: The cross-cultural applicability of Perry's theory [J]. The Journal of Psychology, 1999, 133(4): 425-439.

[21] Zhang LF. Thinking styles and cognitive development [J]. The Journal of Genetic Psychology, 2002, 163(2): 179-195.

[22] Zhang LF, Watkins D. Cognitive development and student approaches to learning: An investigation of Perry's theory with Chinese and U.S. university students [J]. Higher Education, 2001, 41(3): 239-261.

[23] Goodman R. The Strengths and Difficulties Questionnaire: a research note [J]. Journal Of Child Psychology And Psychiatry, And Allied Disciplines, 1997, 38(5): 581-586.

[24] Goodman R. The extended version of the Strengths and Difficulties Questionnaire as a guide to child psychiatric caseness and consequent burden [J]. Journal of Child Psychology and Psychiatry, 1999, 40(5): 791-799.

[25] Goodman R. Psychometric properties of the strengths and difficulties questionnaire [J]. Journal of the American Academy of Child & Adolescent Psychiatry, 2001, 40(11): 1337-1345.

[26] Goodman R, Meltzer H, Bailey V. The strengths and difficulties questionnaire: A pilot study on the validity of the self-report version [J]. European Child & Adolescent Psychiatry, 1998, 7(3): 125-130.

[27] Goodman R, Ford T, Simmons H, et al. Using the Strengths and Difficulties Questionnaire (SDQ) to screen for child psychiatric disorders in a community sample [J]. The British Journal of Psychiatry, 2000, 177(6): 534-539.

[28] Goodman A, Goodman R. Strengths and Difficulties Questionnaire as a dimensional measure of child mental health [J]. Journal of the American Academy of Child and Adolescent Psychiatry, 2009, 48(4): 400-403.

[29] youthinmind. SDQ: information for researchers and professionals about the Strengths and Difficulties Questionnaire [EB/OL]. 2009-9-12[2011-8-3]: http://www.sdqinfo.org/.

[30] Lai KYC, Luk ESL, Leung PWL, et al. Validation of the Chinese version of the strengths

and difficulties questionnaire in Hong Kong [J]. Social Psychiatry and Psychiatric Epidemiology, 2010, 45（12）: 1179-1186.

[31] Du Y, Kou J, Coghill D. The validity, reliability and normative scores of the parent, teacher and self report versions of the Strengths and Difficulties Questionnaire in China [J]. Child and Adolescent Psychiatry and Mental Health, 2008, 2（1）: 8.

[32] Toh TH, Chow SJ, Ting TH, et al. Chinese translation of strengths and difficulties questionnaire requires urgent review before field trials for validity and reliability [J]. Child and Adolescent Psychiatry and Mental Health, 2008, 2（1）: 23.

[33] Üstün TB, Kostanjsek N, Chatterji S, et al. Measuring health and disability: manual for WHO disability assessment schedule（WHODAS 2.0）[M]. Malta: World Health Organization, 2010.

[34] WHO. WHO Disability Assessment Schedule 2.0: WHODAS 2.0 [EB/OL]. World Health Organization, 2011[2011-7-17]: http://www.who.int/classifications/icf/whodasii/en/index. html.

[35] Zang YL. Chinese Female nurses' perceptions of and sensitivity towards male genitalia related care [D]. Hong Kong, Hong Kong Polytechnic University. 2007: 213-224.

[36] Davis LL. Instrument review: Getting the most from a panel of experts [J]. Applied Nursing Research, 1992, 5（4）: 194-197.

[37] Smilkstein G. The family APGAR: a proposal for a family function test and its use by physicians [J]. Journal of Family Practice, 1978, 6（6）: 1231-1239.

[38] Chan DH, Ho SC, Donnan SPB. A survey of family APGAR in Shatin private ownership homes [J]. The Hong Kong Practitioner, 1988, 10（7）: 3295-3299.

[39] Anonymous. Family APGAR [EB/OL]. 1978[2011-7-13]: http://www.iprc.unc.edu/ longscan/pages/measures/Baseline/Family%20APGAR.pdf.

[40] 吕繁, 顾湲. 家庭 APGAR 问卷及其临床应用 [J].《国外医学》医院管理分册, 1995（2）: 56-59.

[41] Gardner W, Nutting PA, Kelleher KJ, et al. Does the family APGAR effectively measure family functioning? [J]. Journal of Family Practice, 2001, 50（1）: 19-25.

[42] Keeney BG, Cassata L, McElmurry JB. Adolescent health and development in nursing and midwifery education [M/OL]. Geneva: World Health Organization, 2004[2011-7-25]: http://whqlibdoc.who.int/hq/2004/WHO_EIP_HRH_NUR_2004.1.pdf.

[43] WPRO. A framework for the integration of adolescent health and development concepts into pre-service Health Professional Educational Curricula WHO Western Pacific Region [EB/OL]. 2002[2011-7-25]:http://www.wpro.who.int/NR/rdonlyres/88E71899-5915-4932-AD47-A78EF3D8E7FB/0/ADHframework.pdf.

后　记

本双语著作运用生物生态学方法，强调了人类青少年阶段的生物、心理和社会性，标志着我国对青少年健康发展认识上的突破。

该著作向读者呈现了关于青少年发展和最佳服务的最新理念（尤其是亲青卫生服务，AFHS），这些理念秉承了初级卫生保健原理，涉及诸如健康危险行为、性生殖健康、残障青少年的特殊需要以及青少年健康发展状况筛查工具等重要议题。鉴于当前青少年健康发展相关教学、科研和实践的相对匮乏，期待本著作能为更好地从整体上理解青少年奠定基础，增进在各种环境（如学校、社区、工厂、司法场所、福利机构）下对儿童期向成年期过渡这一充满挑战的阶段的了解。

本著作历经近四年方以成稿，这其中包含着来自当地和国内外卫生及相关领域合作伙伴的共同努力。采用系统测评和实地观察法实施了一系列的活动，以获得对不同地域青少年健康发展状况差别的认识。所设计的调查研究，目的是获悉学校老师、医院、社区和校园卫生人员、护理专业学生以及家长对青少年健康发展能力的价值与需求的理解。

因此，我们有信心认为，本著作是有科学依据的，旨在促进改变现有的青少年教育和卫生服务，使今天的青少年在未来不久成长为更坚强的社会栋梁。为缩小东西方在该领域认识上的差距，我们又额外做了些语言上的努力，亦即本书采用汉语和英语同时撰写。可以相信，英语读者可从中国视角对青少年健康发展有更多了解，而汉语读者则可获得更多理念与参考文献，掌握提供更好服务的最新研究发现。

若没有世界卫生组织（即青少年职前课程改革项目、改善残障卫生服务质量项目）和山东大学（即山东大学资助创新基金项目、亚太区突发事件及灾害护理协作网平台学科建设项目）强有力的连续资助，也就没有过去四年所付出的编审上的巨大努力，相关工作也都不可能顺利完成。尽管一些作者和审稿者未直接参与本著作的撰写，但他们在其他相关活动中贡献很大，例如课程整合规划、青少年健康发展能力需求调查、青少年健康发展状况系统评估，都至少曾采用汉语和（或）英语参与过一次。

　　青少年健康发展在本质上属于边缘交叉学科领域，需要卫生、教育和法律等多部门的共同努力，本著作仅代表推进青少年健康发展的开端。很显然，没有任何捷径，也不可能逃避支持青少年追求更加美好未来的责任。

臧渝梨
博士　副教授
山东大学护理学院副院长

Advisor

Kathleen Fritsch
Regional Advisor for
Nursing,
WHO WPRO

Patanjali Dev Nayar
Technical Officer for Child &
Adolescent Heath,
WHO WPRO

Jeffrey Fuller
Professor,
Flinders University,
Australia

Chief Editors

Yuli Zang, PhD, Associate Professor,
Deputy Dean, Shandong University School of Nursing, #44
Wenhua West Road, Jinan, Shandong 250012

Yong Zhao, BEd, Associate Professor, Principal, The Middle
School Attached to Shandong University #5 Hongjialou Licheng
District, Jinan, Shandong Province, 250100

Roger Watson, PhD, Professor, University of Sheffield, UK;
Editor in Chief, *Journal of Clinical Nursing*, Samuel Fox House,
Northern General Hospital, Herries Road, Sheffield, S5 7AU, UK

Associate Editors

—— AHD ——

Huaxia Liu   MMed, Professor, Dean, Taishan Medical University School of Nursing

Middle of Changcheng Road, Taian, Shandong 271016

Guangjun Zhen   Director (Academic), The Middle School Attached to Shangdong University

#5 Hongjialou Licheng District, Jinan, Shandong Province 250100

Zhiming Wu   Professor, Deputy Dean, Dalian University School of Nursing

#10 Xuefu Street, Economy and Technology Development District, Dalian, Liaoning 116622

Yuling Hao   BMed, Associate Chief Nurse, Binzhou Medical University School of Nursing

#522 Yellow River Road Three, Binzhou, Shandong 256603

Bo Ban   MD, Professor, Dean, Jining Medical University School of Nursing
Deputy President, Affiliated Hospital of Jining Medical University

#79 Guhuai Road, Jining, Shandong 272019

Jie Song   BMed, DMed, Associate Professor, Shandong University of Traditional Chinese Medicine School of Nursing

Changqing District, Jinan, Shandong 250355

Qinghui Meng,   BMed, MMed, DMed Candidate, Associate Professor, Weifang Medical University School of Nursing

#7166 Baotong West Street, Weifang, Shandong 261053

Huaxia Liu
MMed, Professor, Dean,
Taishan Medical University
School of Nursing

Guangjun Zhen
BEd, Director (Academic),
The Middle School Attached to
Shandong

Zhiming Wu
Professor, Deputy Dean, Dalian
University School of Nursing

Yuling Hao
BMed, Associate Chief
Nurse, Binzhou Medical
University School of
Nursing

Bo Ban
MD, Professor, Dean, Jining
Medical University School of
Nursing, Deputy President,
Affiliated Hospital of Jining
Medical University

Jie Song
BMed, DMed, Associate
Professor, Shandong University
of Traditional Chinese
Medicine School of Nursing

Qinghui Meng
BMed, MMed, DMed Candidate, Associate Professor, Weifang Medical University
School of Nursing

Editorial and Review Committee
—— AHD ——

Advisor	
Kathleen Fritsch	Regional Advisor for Nursing, WHO WPRO
Patanjali Dev Nayar	Technical Officer for Child & Adolescent Heath, WHO WPRO
Jeffrey Fuller	Professor, Flinders University, Australia

Chairpersons	
Yuli Zang (Shandong University)	**Yong Zhao** (The Middle School Attached to Shandong University)

Co-Chairpersons（alphabetical）	
Bo Ban (The Middle School Attached to Shandong University)	**Huaxia Liu** (Taishan Medical University)
Guangjun Zhen (The Middle School Attached to Shandong University)	**Qinghui Meng** (Weifang Medical University)
Yuling Hao (Binzhou Medical University)	**Zhiming Wu** (Dalian University)
Jie Song (Shandong University of Traditional Chinese Medicine)	

Committee members （alphabetical）

Alison Hutton (Flinders University)	**Julian Grant** (Flinders University)
Liping Hu (Provincial Hospital Affiliated to Shandong University)	**Miao Huo** (Dalian University)
Ou Chen (Shandong University)	**Pengfei Liu** (Jining Medical University)
Qing Yang (The Middle School Attached to Shandong University)	**Wen Zhang** (Taishan Medical University)
Xiaoli Ju (Weihai Health School)	**Xiuyan Li** (Weifang Medical University)
Yongyun Tang (Binzhou Medical University)	

Committee members
—— AHD ——

Alison Hutton
PhD, Senior Lecturer, Flinders University School of Nursing and Midwifery

Julian Grant
PhD, Senior Lecturer, Flinders University School of Nursing and Midwifery

Alison Hutton, Julian Grant: GPO Box 2100, Adelaide 5001, South Australia

Liping Hu: #324 Jingwu Road, Jinan, Shandong 250021

Miao Huo: #10 Xuefu Street, Economy and Technology Development District, Dalian, Liaoning 116622

Liping Hu
BMed, MMed candidate, Attending Nurse, Provincial Hospital Affiliated to Shandong University

Miao Huo
BSN, MMed, Lecturer, Dalian University, School of Nursing

Ou Chen: #44 Wenhua West Road, Jinan, Shandong 250012

Pengfei Liu: #16 Hehua Road, Jining, Shandong 272067

Ou Chen
MMed, DMed candidate, Lecturer, Shandong University School of Nursing

Pengfei Liu
MMed, Lecturer, Jining Medical University School of Nursing

Qing Yang
BEd, MEd, Lecturer, The Middle School Attached to Shandong University

Wen Zhang
BMed, MMed, Lecturer, Taishan Medical University School of Nursing

Qing Yang: #5 Hongjialou Licheng District, Jinan, Shandong 250100

Wen Zhang: Middle of Changcheng Road, Taian, Shandong 271016

Xiaoli Ju: #1 West, Mishan East Road, Wendeng, Shandong 264400

Xiaoli Ju
BMed, MMed, Lectuer, Weihai Health School

Xiuyan Li: #7166 Baotong West Street, Weifang, Shandong 261053

Yongyun Tang: #522 Yellow River Road Three, Binzhou, Shandong 256603

Xiuyan Li
PhD, Professor, Weifang Medical University School of Nursing

Yongyun Tang
BMed, MMed candidate, Lecturer, Binzhou Medical University School of Nursing

Authors(alphabetical)
—— AHD ——

Chixun Guan	BMed, Lecturer, Dalian University School of Nursing
Chunmei Wang	BMed, MMed Candidate, Attending Nurse, Second Hospital of Shandong University
Hongxia Yang	BMed, MMed, Lecturer, Taishan Medical University School of Nursing
Jie Song	BMed, DMed, Associate Professor, Shandong University of Traditional Chinese Medicine School of Nursing
Jing Liu	BMed, MMed, RN, Staff Nurse, Provincial Hospital Affiliated to Shandong University
Liping Hu	BMed, MMed candidate, Attending Nurse, Provincial Hospital Affiliated to Shandong University
Lin Chen	BSN, MMed, RN, Staff Nurse, Provincial Hospital Affiliated to Shandong University
Linzhe Pu	BSN, MMed candidate, Shandong University School of Nursing
Li Yang	BMed, MMed, Lecturer, Taishan Medical University School of Nursing
Liyuan Wang	BMed, MMed candidate, Shandong University School of Nursing
Miao Huo	BSN, MMed, Lecturer, Dalian University School of Nursing
Na Li	BMed, MMed candidate, Shandong University School of Nursing
Ning Jiang	BMed, MMed, Assistant Teacher, Taishan Medical University School of Nursing
Qian Liu	BMed Candidate, Shandong University School of Nursing
Qinghui Meng	BMed, MMed, DMed Candidate, Associate Professor, Weifang Medical University School of Nursing
Ting Liu	BMed, MMed, PhD Candidate, Flinders University School of Nursing and Midwifery
Xiaohong Hou	BMed, MMed, RN, Staff Nurse, Provincial Hospital Affiliated to Shandong University
Xiaoyan Liu	BMed, MMed, Public Servant, Tianqiao District Health Bureau
Yaoyun Pan	BMed, MMed Candidate, Shandong University School of Nursing
Yongyun Tang	BMed, MMed candidate, Lecturer, Binzhou Medical University School of Nursing

Yuli Zang	PhD, Associate Professor, Deputy Dean, Shandong University School of Nursing
Yunfeng Li	BMed, MMed Candidate, Attending Nurse, Shandong Qianfoshan Hosptial
Wen Zhang	BMed, MMed, Lecturer, Taishan Medical University School of Nursing

Authors' Addresses (alphabetical)
—— AHD ——

Chixun Guan	#10 Xuefu Street, Economy and Technology Development District, Dalian, Liaoning Province 116622
Chunmei Wang	#247 Beiyuan Road, Jinan, Shandong 250033
Hongxia Yang	Middle Changcheng Road, Taian, Shandong 271010
Jie Song	Changqing District, Jinan, Shandong 250355
Jing Liu	#324 Jingwu Road, Jinan, Shandong 250021
Liping Hu	#324 Jingwu Road, Jinan, Shandong 250021
Lin Chen	#324 Jingwu Road, Jinan, Shandong 250021
Linzhe Pu	#44 Wenhua West Road, Jinan, Shandong 250012
Li Yang	Middle of Changcheng Road, Taian, Shandong 271016
Liyuan Wang	#44 Wenhua West Road, Jinan, Shandong 250012
Miao Huo	#10 Xuefu Street, Economy and Technology Development District, Dalian, Liaoning 116622
Na Li	#44 Wenhua West Road, Jinan, Shandong 250012
Ning Jiang	Middle of Changcheng Road, Taian, Shandong 271016
Qian Liu	#44 Wenhua West Road, Jinan, Shandong 250012
Qinghui Meng	#7166 Baotong West Street, Weifang, Shandong 261053
Ting Liu	GPO Box 2100, Adelaide 5001, South Australia
Xiaohong Hou	#324 Jingwu Road, Jinan, Shandong 250021
Xiaoyan Liu	#90 Wuyingshan Middle Road, Jinan, Shandong 250031
Yaoyun Pan	#44 Wenhua West Road, Jinan, Shandong 250012
Yongyun Tang	#522 Yellow River Road Three, Binzhou, Shandong 256603
Yuli Zang	#44 Wenhua West Road, Jinan, Shandong 250012
Yunfeng Li	#16766 Jingshi Road, Jinan, Shandong 250014
Wen Zhang	Middle Changcheng Road, Taian, Shandong 271016

Authors(alphabetical)
— AHD —

Chixun Guan

Chunmei Wang

Hongxia Yang

Jing Liu

Lin Chen

Linzhe Pu

| Li Yang | Liyuan Wang | Na Li |

| Ning Jiang | Qian Liu | Ting Liu |

| Xiaohong Hou | Xiaoyan Liu | Yaoyun Pan |

Yunfeng Li

Editorial and Review Committee
—— AHD ——

Previous Writing Contributors (alphabetical)

Lei Li	BMed, MMed, Lecturer, Taishan Medical University School of Nursing, Middle Changcheng Road, Taian, Shandong 271016
Lili Zhong	BSN, MMed, Lecturer, Dalian University School of Nursing, #10 Xuefu Street, Economy and Technology Development District, Dalian, Liaoning 116622
Pengfei Liu	MMed, Lecturer, Jining Medical University School of Nursing, #16 Hehua Road, Jining, Shandong 272067
Xiaolei Wang	BMed, MMed, Lecturer, Taishan Medical University School of Nursing, Middle of Changcheng Road, Taian, Shandong 271016
Xueqin Zhang	BMed, MMed, Lecturer, Taishan Medical University School of Nursing, Middle of Changcheng Road, Taian, Shandong 271016
Yangyang Han	BMed, MMed, Assistant Teacher, Taishan Medical University School of Nursing, Middle of Changcheng Road, Taian, Shandong 271016
Yanzhao She	BSN, Lecturer, Dalian University School of Nursing, #10 Xuefu Street, Economy and Technology Development District, Dalian, Liaoning 116622
Weixue Wang	BMed, MMed, Lecturer, Taishan Medical University School of Nursing, Middle of Changcheng Road, Taian, Shandong 271016

Lei Li

Lili Zhong

Xiaolei Wang

Xueqin Zhang

Yangyang Han

Yanchao She

Weixue Wang

Foreword

It's a great pleasure to introduce *Adolescent Health and Development Studies*, which is to be published in English and Chinese in the People's Republic of China. I recall the initial meeting between Shandong University and the Hong Kong Polytechnic University regarding translating the three modules for adolescent health and development (AHD) into Chinese during the 14th Biennial School Nurses International Conference in Singapore in August 2007. From then on, Dr. Yuli Zang took the leadership in mainland of China in analyzing curricular weakness related to AHD and piloting selective courses in Shandong University. Eventually additional schools of nursing of six universities, i.e., Dalian Medical University, Taishan Medical College, Weifang Medical University, Jining Medical University, Binzhou Medical University and Qingdao University, participated in relevant activities, including but not limited to, developing teaching materials, exploring appropriate teaching modalities to nurture undergraduates and postgraduates in health science and beyond, and training school teachers and healthcare providers in hospital, in community health centers and schools for better AHD competency. Meanwhile, Flinders University became a partner with a particular focus on the impact of urbanization on AHD.

As the Regional Advisor for Nursing, World Health Organization Western Pacific Regional Office (WHO WPRO), I witnessed the strategic efforts made by Dr. Zang and her team over the past few years. They demonstrate the determination to bring sustainable positive changes to university nursing education including continuous education and beyond by integrating available evidence and best practice experiences in other areas into local settings. School and community-based AHD interventions—mainly educational—have been designed and successfully implemented. A total of eight masters in nursing continue working on relevant projects, leading to the publication of one master's dissertation, six peer-reviewed papers in Chinese, one peer-reviewed paper in English and many media news reports. Shandong Health Bureau and The Middle School Attached to Shandong University facilitated the field implementation of interventions in addition to logistic and administrative support. All of these efforts make me believe that the book has been written based on a clear understanding about AHD and local Chinese society.

This ten-chapter book presents the fundamental knowledge, beliefs, and attitudes towards AHD, which is necessary for all healthcare providers who may encounter adolescent clients and for all school teachers who may need to answer adolescents' concern over puberty and other matters of interest. It is also useful for healthcare undergraduates and adolescents to reach a better understanding about AHD and to improve their own AHD competency.

I hope that you will enjoy reading this book, and I am sure that Dr. Zang and her team are looking forward to hearing your feedback which will be incorporated into future editions.

Kathleen Fritsch

Regional Advisor for
Nursing, WHO WPRO

Preface

It is a great pleasure to have produced the book *Adolescent Health and Development Studies* in English and Chinese in mainland of China. This represents a terrific leap in our professional life as educators across the boundary of language, discipline and territory.

During the last three years we have closely partnered with Dr. Yuli Zang, Associate Professor, and Deputy Dean of Shandong University School of Nursing, in the area of adolescent health promotion and positive youth development particularly targeting those in early adolescence. What inspired and encouraged us is the strong desire to improve the educational approaches to adolescent health and development as a whole, by involving school managers, teachers, parents or principal guardians, healthcare professionals and researchers. We are fully aware of the paucity of evidence for a better understanding about adolescents and their families in mainland of China in face of significant pubertal changes and associated psychosocial challenges. This leads to the limitation in delivering effective interventions.

A primary stress for adolescents and their families are their serious concern about academic achievements to ensure a bright future for the youth in mainland of China. We have to take the responsibility to support these adolescents and their family to deal with such challenges. We are also obliged to develop the skills and capacity of those who work with adolescents and their families as they help them to live towards the highest standard in all crucial life aspects as human beings. With this hope and enthusiasm, we formulate the international team involving Shandong University School of Nursing, The Middle School Attached to Shandong University, Flinders University School of Nursing and Midwifery, and other nursing schools to investigate competencies in adolescent health and development and ways to strengthen the capacity to serve adolescents to the optimum at home or in schools.

No success comes without efforts. The publication of the bilingual book *Adolescent Health and Development Studies* landmarks our cross-disciplinary, cross-sector and cross-country collaboration. Publishing this book is our contribution to bridge the gap between international and Chinese society (especially in mainland) and between the educational sector and health sector. These knowledge fundamentals will pave the way for broader and deeper collaboration in the area of adolescent health and development.

Adolescents are the future of human society with the most powerful potential towards a promising life. We humbly request support or collaboration from all of those who are committed to improving educational and health services to adolescents. With our concerted action and efforts, adolescents could overcome the difficulties and posed by academic stressors and pubertal changes to prepare themselves to face future challenges for a better life.

Jeffrey Fuller
Professor of Nursing
School of Nursing and Midwifery
Flinders University

Yong Zhao
Associate Professor, Principal
the Middle School Attached
Shandong University

Acknowledgement

In the long process of producing this bilingual book, we owe a great deal to many people.

First we extend our sincere thanks to Ms. Kathleen Fritsch, Regional Nursing Advisor of World Health Organization Western Pacific Regional Office (WPRO), without whom we would never have had the idea of investigating adolescent health and development in depth; neither would we overcome those unexpected difficulties and challenges to complete the work. She encouraged positive exploration and collaboration beyond nursing, which made the international collaboration possible over the last few years.

Also we would like to thank Dr. Patanjali Dev Nayar, Technical Officer, Child & Adolescent Health/WPRO, who guided and supported the organization and strengthening of nursing curricular review as well as other activities related to the needs of adolescent health and development competencies.

We are indebted to all these participating people and organisations. We will remember all of those who support us whenever in need and would like to take this opportunity to express our genuine gratitude for their contribution. Without them we would neither successfully develop those educational materials nor implement any interventions involving schools and families.

We can never forget the wonderful work done by postgraduate students in Shandong University School of Nursing. Some of them have graduated, some have moved to other countries to continue their academic journey overseas, while the others are still working closely with us in the area of adolescent health and development and beyond. All of them excel themselves because of their intelligence, diligence, commitment and strong interest in supporting the education and positive development of healthy adolescents.

Last but not least, we express our deepest love to our families, friends and leaders in the institutions where they work. They constitute the strongest supporting network, within which we get the freedom to investigate our interests scientifically with energy and happiness.

The way towards our goals is still far, challenging and unpredictable, but we are confident that with all of the support we get, we will make it in the end.

Adolescent Health & Development Team

Contents

Chapter 1   Introduction

Yuli Zang, Liyuan Wang

Adolescents of 10 to 19 years old are at the stage of growing up to adults, facing significant changes and challenges—physical and psychosocial—towards fulfilling their potential and meeting expectations in performing the different roles as prescribed as an adult member of society.

In the bioecological approach to health and human development, it is argued that the immediate social environment—particularly the family and the school—play a crucial role in shaping adolescents' health and development (Bronfenbrenner 2005, Kickbusch 1989, Simpson 2001). Highly competent health care workers, thereby, are needed to provide satisfactory services at home, in school or in community to facilitate the transition from childhood to adulthood, to strengthen the development of healthy lifestyle (e.g., balanced diet, adequate physical exercises), to prevent and reduce health-risks (e.g., poor diet, smoking, drinking, early sex, immunization), and to support the management of chronic conditions (e.g., asthma, diabetes, cancer) (Keeney et al. 2004, Michaud et al. 2004, Suris et al. 2004, WHO 2010).

Nurses are considered to be the main force in hospital and in community settings to achieve the above goals through the provision of comprehensive services (including health and development assessment and management, health promotion, preventive services, counseling, referral, services coordination, teaching and training relevant personnel, ect.) in any setting where adolescents may be present (Fritsch & Heckert 2007, Keeney et al. 2004, Levenberg 1998, Smith 2004). Many efforts have been made internationally to strengthen nurses' capacity in this regard through pre-service and continuing education committed to nurturing the life-long learning among health care providers (Council of School Health/CSH 2008, Reuterswärd & Lagerström 2010, St Leger 2006, Yoo et al. 2004). Nevertheless, a general weakness in the provision of appropriate services for adolescent health and development (particularly for those with disabilities) persists in current health systems and in the preparation of school nurses (McConkey & Kelly 2001, Moore et al. 2003, Park et al. 2011, WPRO 2002, WHO 2010).

A series of studies in hospital, educational institutions and community settings in mainland of China reveals a similar deficit in current health and educational systems, particularly in mainland of China (Hutton & Grant 2011, Ju et al. 2009a, b, Liu et al. 2011, Pan et al. 2010, 2011, Zang et al. 2011). Nevertheless, these studies reflect the continuous joint efforts in mainland of China and beyond involving partners from Hong Kong (e.g., The Hong Kong Polytechnic University) and Australia (i.e., Flinders University) under the guidance of WHO technical officers (e.g., Ms. Kathleen Fritsch, Dr. Patanjali Dev Nayar, WHO Western Pacific Regional Office or WPRO). It was consistently found that parents, teachers, school healthcare workers and nurses considered the majority of competencies for adolescent health and development recommended by WHO as important (Ju et al. 2009a, Liu et al. 2011, Pan et al. 2010, 2011). The competencies cover the areas of professional development (six items), physical self (18 items), psychosocial self (five items), healthy behaviors (13 items) and gender development (18 items) (Keeney et al. 2004, Pan et al. 2011, WPRO 2002). However, the competencies related to professional development and gender development are not as strongly considered to be required for development in comparison with those in the other three dimensions, i.e., physical self, psychosocial self and health behaviors (Zang et al. 2011), suggesting the cultural particularity in this regard in mainland of China.

This book, thereby, is devised in anticipation of the overall competency improvement at the basic level among health care workers— particulary nurses— to tackle the above mentioned general needs by addressing the major issues for adolescent health and development and to achieve the provision of adolescent friendly health services in accordance with developmental status. It will present an overview about the meaning of adolescent health and development in Chapter 2 and describe the characteristics of adolescent friendly health services (AFHS) in harmony with the guiding framework proposed by the WHO in Chapter 3. From Chapter 4 to 7, major concerns and issues surrounding adolescent health and development will be presented respectively as follows: physiological development (Chapter 4); psychosocial development (Chapter 5); healthy-risky behaviours

(Chapter 6); sexual and reproductive health (Chapter 7); and injuries (Chapter 8). The book will then move to an independent Chapter 9 for adolescents with disabilities and with the concluding Chapter 10 about useful tools to monitor adolescent health and development with the hope of encouragaing the use of this book. The contents related to the communication with key personnel inlcuding adolescents, their parents and teachers are integrated into relevant chapters (e.g., Chapter 5).

References

Bronfenbrenner U. Making human beings human: bioecological perspectives on human development[M]. Thousand Oaks, California: Sage, 2005.

CSH. Role of the school nurse in providing school health services[J]. Pediatrics, 2008, 121(5): 1052-1056.

Fritsch K, Heckert KA. Working together: health promoting schools and school nurses[J]. Asian Nursing Research, 2007, 1(3): 147-152.

Hutton A , Grant J. Expanding the role of nurses for a rapidly urbanising China [J/OL]. RCNA report: nursing news, views & attitudes, 2011, (2): 6[6 Aug. 2011]: http://www. apnedmedia.com.au/email/rcna-report-feb-11-web-ready.pdf.

Ju XL, Zang YL, Lou FL. A study on the applicability of the adolescent health and development course in China[J]. Journal of Nursing Science, 2009a, 24(2, Surgery Edition): 8-10.

Ju XL, Zang YL, Lou FL. Necessity of setting up Adolescent Health and Development course in nursing colleges[J]. Chinese Journal of Nursing Education, 2009b, 6(9): 401-403.

Keeney BG, Cassata L, McElmurry JB. Adolescent health and development in nursing and midwifery education[M/OL]. Geneva, Switzerland: World Health Organization, 2004[25 Jul. 2011]: http://whqlibdoc.who.int/hq/2004/WHO_EIP_HRH_ NUR_2004.1.pdf.

Kickbusch I. Approaches to an ecological base for public health[J]. Health Promotion International, 1989, 4(4): 265-268.

Levenberg PB. GAPS: An opportunity for nurse practitioners to promote the health of adolescents through clinical preventive services[J]. Journal of Pediatric Health Care, 1998, 12(1): 2-9.

Liu T, Pan YY, Zang YL. Investigation on nurses' cognition of competency of adolescent health and development[J]. Journal of Nursing Science, 2011, 26(3, General): 53-56.

McConkey R, Kelly M. Nursing inputs to special schools in N. Ireland[J]. International Journal of Nursing Studies, 2001, 38(4): 395-403.

Michaud P, Suris J, Viner R. The adolescent with a chronic condition. Part II: healthcare provision[J]. Arch Dis Child, 2004, 89(10): 943-949.

Moore G, McConkey R, Duffy M. The role of the school nurse in special schools for pupils with severe learning difficulties[J]. International Journal of Nursing Studies, 2003, 40(7): 771-779.

Pan YY, Liu T, Zang YL. The integration of adolescent health and development curriculum into undergraduate nursing education[J]. Journal of Nursing Science, 2010, 25(9, General): 64-66.

Pan YY, Liu T, Zang YL. Construction of a tool for measuring undergraduate nursing students' cognition and needs for adolescent health and development and its application[J]. Journal of Nursing Science, 2011, 26(2, Surgery): 65-68.

Park IS, Yoo CS, Joo YH, et al. Evaluation of the completeness of the nursing process for patients having gastrectomy using electronic nursing records[J]. Studies in health technology and informatics, 2009, 146: 739-740.

Park MJ, Adams SH, Irwin Jr CE. Health care services and the transition to young adulthood: challenges and opportunities[J]. Academic Pediatrics, 2011, 11(2): 115-122.

Reuterswärd M, Lagerström M. The aspects school health nurses find important for successful health promotion[J]. Scandinavian journal of caring sciences, 2010, 24(1): 156-163.

Simpson AR. Raising teens: a synthesis of research and foundation for action[M/OL]. Boston, Massachusetts: Harvard School of Public Health, 2001[11 May 2011]: http://www.hsph. harvard.edu/chc/parenting/report.pdf.

Smith S. Adolescent units—an evidence-based approach to quality nursing in adolescent care[J]. European Journal of Oncology Nursing, 2004, 8(1): 20-29.

St Leger L. Health promotion and health education in schools : trends, effectiveness and possibilities[M]. Noble Park North, Victoria: Royal Automobile Club of Victoria (RACV), 2006.

Suris J-C, Michaud P-A, Viner R. The adolescent with a chronic condition. Part I: developmental issues[J]. Archives of Disease in Childhood, 2004, 89(10): 938-942.

WHO. Strengthening the health sector response to adolescent health and development_[EB/OL]. World Health Organization, 2010_[12 Jun. 2011]: http://www.who.int/child_adolescent_ health/documents/cah_adh_flyer_2010_12_en.pdf.

WPRO. A framework for the integration of adolescent health and development concepts into pre-service health professional educational curricula WHO western pacific region[EB/OL]. 2002_[25 Jul. 2011]: http://www.wpro.who.int/NR/rdonlyres/88E71899-5915-4932-AD47-A78EF3D8E7FB/0/ADHframework.pdf.

Yoo IY, Yoo MS, Lee GY. Self-evaluated competencies of school nurses in Korea[J]. Journal of School Health, 2004, 74(4): 144-146.

Zang YL, Zhao Y, Yang Q, et al. A randomised trial on pubertal development and health in China[J]. Journal of Clinical Nursing, 2011, 20(21-22): 3081-3091.

Chapter 2   Overview of Adolescent Health and Development

—— Yuli Zang, Linzhe Pu, Yongyun Tang ——

There is a growing emphasis on the competencies among healthcare workers, especially school nurses, for adolescent health and development (AHD). The WHO promotes the '4-S framework' for strengthening health sector responses to AHD: S1, Gathering and using strategic information; S2, Developing supportive evidence-informed policies; S3, Scaling up the provision of health services and commodities; S4, Strengthening other sectors, particularly education and youth (WHO 2010). Through a series of provincial and national-wide activities, in compliance with the guiding principles for AHD (i.e., primary health care principles), the noticeable weakness in health and educational sectors is revealed in preparing healthcare workers and educators with necessary AHD competencies. This chapter aims to provide the knowledge necessary for a better understanding about AHD including those activities and studies which were carried out in mainland of China.

When the term 'adolescence' is used, it often means a great deal for health care professionals. This section focuses on the definition, developmental characteristics or tasks at this stage, and important issues to be aware of to promote adolescent health and development (AHD).

Defining adolescence

The word 'adolescence' originates from the Latin *adolescere*, meaning 'growing up into adulthood' (Steinberg 2008). In any society, adolescence is a period of transitions from the immaturity and dependency of childhood to the relatively maturity and independence of adulthood, involving significant physiological, psychosocial and economic changes, in accordance with social expectations and perceptions. Physical growth and development are often accompanied by sexual maturation and intimate relationships development, particularly romantic relationships (Steinberg 2008, WHO 2001, 2006, 2010). The health condition and developmental status at this stage should pave the way for the fulfillment of one's full potential for optimum living. Investing in adolescent health and development will benefit the next generation, improve later life and contribute to societal productivity and prosperity (WHO 2010). Strengthening adolescents' social responsibility, including filial obligation, is one of essential way—particularly in mainland of China—to tackle the aging of society and the growth of chronic diseases.

Given the ambiguous boundary of adolescence, most societies define 'adolescent' in terms of both age and life circumstances, leading to the use of different terms (e.g., adolescent, youth, young person) to describe the same period of the human life course (Rosen 2004). Taking mainland of China as an example, there is no consistent definition but only a proposed age range from 14 to 28 years to maintain alignment with the political eligibility for being a Youth League member under the leadership of the Chinese Communist Party (Wu 2003). For the comparability and mutual understanding across countries and disciplines, the age definition by WHO is preferred, therefore, 'young people' refers to the combined age group from 10 to 19 years and 'adolescents' as that from 15 to 24 years as 'youth' (Rosen 2004, WHO 2006).

In the case of mainland of China, the political concern plays an important role in defining 'adolescent' by age group, particularly the lower age limit in national statistics and academic areas. China Communist Youth League (CCYL), an organization for advanced youth under the leadership of the Communist Party of China, set the age eligibility criteria for being a CCYL member as 14 to 28 years old (CYL 2005, CCYL 2008). The age of 14 years is consistently taken as the lower limit for youth, whereas those younger than 14 years are called child and adolescent (Wu 2003). There is neither age definition for *adolescent* nor articulation about *adolescence*. Nevertheless, the Chinese government is used to report the definition, recommendation and position statements from United Nations (UN) including WHO. Therefore, in this book 'adolescent' refers to those from 10 to 19 years old inclusively to reflect the variance regarding the early beginning and the late completion of secondary sex characteristics development (e.g., face acne, body hair, breast and menstruation for girls, testes and penis for boys).

Sociodemographic and economic characteristics

Using the above age-group definition, it was estimated in 2000 that there are more than 1.1 billion adolescents worldwide, i.e., about one in every five people is aged between 10 and 19 years (WHO 2006). According to the World Bank (WB) in 2002, most (86%) of the world's 1.7 billion young people are living in developing countries where they often make up 30% or more of the population (Rosen 2004).

According to the 2008 survey by Ministry of Health of China (MoH), there are approximately 194 millions adolescents from 10 to 19 years, accounting for 14.6% of the population (1 178 521) with the sampling rate of 0.887‰ and the male-female ratio of 115:100 (MoH 2010). It is, thereby, estimated using the 2010 census data with the total population of 1 339 724 852 by the Chinese National Bureau of Statistics (CNBS) that there were approximately 195 599 828 adolescents in early November 2010 (CNBS 2011).

The primary determinants of AHD are education, employment and poverty. Education is vital to the achievement of desired socio-economic development through improved economic opportunities available to those who are educated. In particular, formal education is of more importance for the development of adolescents. Schools are not only the environment for adolescents to acquire knowledge and build literacy, numeracy, and thinking skills, but the major source of education and guidance on health issues and can offer safe and convenient settings for the provision of health screening and health services.

Though the 9-year compulsory education scheme was implemented nationally in mainland of China, a great many adolescents in mainland of China, particularly those in far and remote areas, leave school and migrate to cities and towns to find jobs before 19 years old. These adolescents, often called 'internal migrants', may face poor working conditions, deprivation of education, exploration, poverty, and safety threats (CYCRC 2008, Wikipedia 2011, Yang 2009). It was estimated that there are approximately 146 860 000 internal migrants in 2005, of whom about 35.7% (52 490 000) are aged from 14 to 29 years old, and approximately 52% (76 390 000) are aged from 14 to 35 years old (CYCRC 2008). Of those aged from 14 to 29 years old, approximately 17.9% migrated and is 6.4% higher than the overall migration rate among national population (i.e., 11.5%), while the male and female migrants accounts for 16.5% and 19.2% of those in the same age group. Unfortunately no statistics are available about adolescent internal migrants, suggesting the need to revise the national statistical scheme to facilitate global comparison.

It is also revealed that internal adolescent migrants tend to be poorly adjusted to their life in cities which were different from their birth or residency places, leading to misconduct, including sexual and reproductive problems, discrepancy, emotional disorders, learning difficulties and moral problems (Deng & Lin 2010, Wang 2003, Wu 2010, Yang 2009, Zang et al. 2009). Compared with immigrants, internal adolescent migrants may need more education on sexual and reproductive health, mental health, safety, protection and support.

Additionally, factors within the wider environment exert stronger influences over adolescents, including but not limited to mass media, industries, community institutions, religious bodies and the political and social system and economic opportunities (WHO 2001). There are more chances and better environments in urban areas than in rural areas. It is estimated that migrants from rural areas with countryside residency increased from 149 millions in 2008 to 160 millions (vs. a total of 180 millions) in 2009 (Wu 2010). The magnitude of migration may contribute to the relative poverty among adolescent migrants compared with the local community (CYCRC 2008), whereas poverty may deprive adolescents from the basic elements of development, particularly the access to schooling, vocational training and health services, and could increase the probability of exposing adolescents to physical violence, displacement and welfare (WHO 2001).

Therefore, heath care workers and school teachers should be sensitive to the demographic, social and economic status and match their services within the scope of their practice in ways that are compatible with local societal and cultural expectations.

Importance of adolescent health and development

Adolescents appear to be relatively healthy, meaning they show lower levels of morbidity and mortality compared with children and adults, but they are not hazard-free. In fact adolescents face serious health challenges during the acquirement of a range of interrelated knowledge and skills, allowing them to lead fulfilled and productive later lives. These skills are critical for adolescents to stay healthy, learn, obtain a job or livelihood and fully participate in society.

Globally young people (10~24 years old) account for 15% of the disease and injury burden, and more than 1 million die each year, mainly from preventable or treatable conditions (e.g., accidents, suicide, violence, pregnancy related complications, nutrition deficiency), and approximately 70% of premature deaths (i.e., die before 65 years old) among adults can be linked to behaviors (e.g., tobacco use, poor eating habits, risky sex) that are initiated during adolescence (Rosen 2004, WHO 2001, 2002).

There are many reasons to pay attention to adolescents' health and development: for this age group, for their later life and for the next generation (WHO 2002). Health is a key element of overall adolescent development, while adolescents have the right to optimal health (Rosen 2004). Efforts have to be taken to reduce death, disease and risky health behaviors in adolescents. Healthy and unhealthy practices adopted today can last for a lifetime (WHO 2002). For instance, poor eating habits can lead to malnutrition, causing lifelong health problems; ignoring the prevalence of sexual behaviors, pregnancy, abortion or delivery during adolescence could result in infertility, sexually transmitted infections, abandoned babies, early marriage, poor marital life or divorce. Besides, adolescents today will grow to be teachers, parents, community leaders, policy makers or any other incumbent required in human society. Investing in adolescents' health and development will lay the foundation for a promising future by breaking the vicious circle of poverty and by protecting human capital so that they are able to fulfill their roles as expected and contribute to the economic and societal development in addition to personal fulfillment (Rosen 2004, WHO 2002). A commitment to go beyond mere survival to the development of the full potential of adolescents is emphasized so that adolescents, their parents and their broader social networks must have opportunities for healthy growth and development, contributing to the healthy and productive communities (WHO 2003).

Health issues

There is a growing recognition that some adolescents do develop health problems and many adopt unhealthy behaviors (Jones & Bradley 2007, Nicol et al. 2002). The WHO classified those health problems and problem behaviors which may affect adolescent health as shown in Table 2-1 (WHO 2002, 2006).

Table 2-1   Classification of diseases and health-related behaviours of young people in developing countries

Diseases which are particular to young people	Diseases and unhealthy behaviours which affect young people disproportionately	Diseases which manifest themselves primarily in young people but originate in childhood	Diseases and unhealthy behaviours of young people whose major implications are on the young person's future health	Diseases which affect fewer young people than children but more of them than adults
Diseases:	**Diseases:**	**Diseases:**	**Diseases:**	**Diseases:**
● Disorders of secondary sexual development	● Maternal mortality and morbidity	● Chagas diseases	● STIs	● Malnutrition
● Difficulties with psychosocial development	● STIs	● Rheumatic heart diseases	● Leprosy	● Malaria
● Suboptimal adolescent growth spurt	● Tuberculosis	● Polio	● Dental disease	● Gastroenteritis
	● Schistosomiasis			● Acute respiratory infections
	● Intestinal helminths			
	● Mental disorders			
Behaviours:	**Behaviours:**	**Behaviours:**	**Behaviours:**	**Behaviours:**
	● Alcohol use		● Tobacco use	
	● Other substance abuse		● Alcohol and drug use	
	● Injuries		● Poor diet	
			● Lack of exercise	
			● Unsafe sexual practice	

To go further, drawing on data from around the world, the WHO generated a list of 'priority' health problems affecting adolescents, i.e., intentional and unintentional injuries, sexual and reproductive health problems including HIV/AIDS, substance use and abuse (e.g., tobacco, alcohol), mental health problems, nutritional problems, endemic and chronic diseases. More details are provided in Chapter 6, 7 and 8.

In addition, a significant difference was found between female and male adolescents with regard to morbidity and mortality rate. Globally, the male has higher rates of morbidity and mortality from injuries due to interpersonal violence, accidents and suicide, while the female has higher rates of morbidity and mortality related to sexual behaviors. The leading ten causes of death among male and female adolescents are shown in Table 2-2 (WHO 2006).

Table 2-2　Top ten causes of death in adolescents worldwide in 1999

Male	Female
1. Road traffic accidents	1. HIV
2. Malaria	2. Maternal conditions
3. Lower respiratory tract infection	3. Malaria
4. Other unintentional injury	4. Lower respiratory tract infection
5. Drowning	5. Tuberculosis
6. Homicide	6. Suicide
7. Suicide	7. Diarrhoea
8. HIV	8. Road traffic accidents
9. Diarrhea	9. Fires
10. Tuberculosis	10. Other unintentional injury

According to 2008 statistics in mainland of China, the leading cause of death for adolescents in urban and rural areas is injuries and poisoning (approximately 13×10^{-6} vs. 32×10^{-6}) mainly resulting from road traffic accidents and other accidents (approximately 7×10^{-6} vs. 15×10^{-6}), drown (approximately 5×10^{-6} vs. 10×10^{-6}) and suicide (approximately 2×10^{-6} vs. 3×10^{-6}) in urban vs. rural areas respectively (MoH 2010). The second leading cause of death for adolescent is cancer, approximately 8×10^{-6} for both urban and rural areas respectively (MoH 2010). This means that the family-and school-based educational and psychosocial support is greatly needed to prevent the occurrence of injuries, poisoning, drown and to deliver palliative care, which echoes the priority areas recommended by

WHO (2003) in its strategic directions for improving AHD.

Adolescent development concerns

Within the bioecological theory, 'development is defined as the phenomenon of continuity and change in the biopsychological characteristics of human beings both as individuals and as groups, while the phenomenon extends over the life course successive generations and through historical time, both past and present' (Bronfenbrenner 2005, p.3). It was argued that human development takes place through processes of progressively more complex reciprocal interaction between the active, evolving biopsychological human organism and other human beings, objects and symbols in the immediate social and physical environment (i.e., proximal process) (Bronfenbrenner 2005). Parent- and teacher-adolescent interactions are type of these processes. Adolescents develop the ability, motivation, knowledge and skills through participating in such dynamic processes that they are able to engage in the interaction with others and with themselves inside. The proximal processes (particularly the parenting) thereby play a crucial role in shaping adolescents' development during the transitional stage from childhood to adulthood.

In particular, to reach a complete understanding of adolescence, Simpson (2001) conducted a comprehensive literature review to synthesize the research and foundation for action, i.e., raising adolescents particularly for parents. He proposed the ten tasks requiring adolescent to accomplish during the stage of adolescence, that is:

1) **Adjust to sexually maturing bodies and feelings**: Adolescents are faced with adjusting to significant body changes (i.e., the size and the acquirement of sexual characteristics) and learning to manage the accompanying biological changes and sexual feelings and to engage in healthy sexual behaviors (e.g., kiss, touch, fondle, sex). This task includes establishing a sexual identity and developing the skills for romantic relationships.

2) **Develop and apply abstract thinking skills**: Adolescents typically undergo profound changes in their way of thinking during adolescence. This allows them to be more effective at understanding and coordinating abstract ideas, thinking about possibilities, trying out hypotheses, thinking ahead or planning, thinking about thinking, and constructing philosophies.

3) **Develop and apply a more complex level of perspective taking**:

Adolescents typically acquire the powerful new ability to understand human relationships for others' perspective. They learn to take into account both their own perspective and other persons' at the same time, and to use this new ability to resolve problems and conflicts in relationships.

4) **Develop and apply new coping skills in areas such as decision making, problem solving, and conflict resolution**: Being involved in dramatic shifts (biological, psychosocial), adolescents are required to develop new abilities to think about and plan for the future, to engage in more sophisticated strategies for decision-making, problem solving, and conflict resolution, and to moderate their risk-taking to serve goals rather than jeopardize them.

5) **Identify meaningful moral standards, values, and belief systems**: In face of their own changes and diversified social situations, adolescents typically develop a more complex understanding of moral behaviors and underlying principles of justice and care. They start questioning initial beliefs and adopt more personally meaningful values, political or religious views, and belief systems to guide their decisions and behaviors.

6) **Understand and express more complex emotional experiences**: With the growing of social interaction and mental dynamics, adolescents implicitly or explicitly acquire the ability to identify and communicate more complex emotions, to understand the emotions of others in more sophisticated ways, and to think about emotions in abstract ways.

7) **Form friendships that are mutually close and supportive**: Peer friendship plays a more powerful role for adolescents compared with that in childhood. The relationship tends to shift the sharing of interests and activities to the sharing of ideas and feelings in accompany with the development of mutual trust and understanding.

8) **Establish key aspects of identity**: Crucial aspects of identity, to reflect both the individuality and the connectedness to important people and groups, are typically forged during adolescence, though identity formation is a lifelong process. Of more importance, adolescents are expected to develop a positive identity around gender (i.e., social construction of biological sex), physical attributes, sexuality, ethnicity and so forth.

9) **Meet the demands of increasingly mature roles and responsibilities:** Usually adolescents are nurtured, gradually, to take on the roles being expected of them in adulthood, including learning to acquire knowledge and skills for moving

into the labor market, and to meet expectations for the commitment to family, community and citizenship.

10)**Renegotiate relationships with adults in parenting roles**: For adolescents and their parents, adolescence is a stage to build a balance between autonomy and continuing parent-child connection. Cultural background plays a crucial role in shaping the balance, e.g., the culture in Eastern Asian used to contribute to the collectivism, giving more weight to the connection with family than to autonomy (Singelis et al. 1995).

Health and developmental assets

It is not difficult to conclude from the above description: being fully aware of the developmental tasks for parents, teachers and healthcare workers is a prerequisite to the optimum transition for adolescents from childhood to adulthood. Currently this goes beyond simply naming problems and trying to prevent or reduce them; instead it places more emphasis on naming and increasing the positive building blocks in adolescents' life, i.e., assets approach (Scales 1999).

The first use of 'asset' in the health-related literature could be traced back to Beiser (1971), focusing on personality and personal assets as a foundation for managing change. Over time the concept tends to be discussed within the context of individuals (particularly children and youth), family and community. Through the technique of conceptual analysis, health assets are defined as the repertoire of potentials—internal and external strengthen qualities in the individual's possession, both innate and acquired—that mobilize positive health behaviors and optimal health/wellness outcomes (Rotegard et al. 2009). In the developmental assets approach, Search Institute identified the following internal and external building blocks (i.e., internal assets and external assets) of healthy development that help adolescents grow up healthy, caring and responsible. Four subcategories including 20 assets are classified as **External Assets**, that is:

● **Support**

1) **Family support**—Family life provides high levels of love and support;

2) **Positive family communication**—Young person and her or his parent(s) communicate positively, and young person is willing to seek advice and counsel from parents;

3) **Other adult relationships**—Young person receives support from three or

more non-parent adults;

4) **Caring neighborhood**—Young person experiences caring neighbors;

5) **Caring school climate**—School provides a caring, encouraging environment;

6) **Parent involvement in schooling**—Parent(s) are actively involved in helping young person succeed in school.

- **Empowerment**

7) **Community values youth as youth**—Young person perceives that adults in the community value youth;

8) **Youth as resources**—Young people are given useful roles in the community;

9) **Service to others**—Young person serves in the community one hour or more per week.

- **Boundaries & expectations**

10) **Safety**—Young person feels safe at home, school, and in the neighborhood;

11) **Family boundaries**—Family has clear rules and consequences and monitors the young person's whereabouts;

12) **School boundaries**—School provides clear rules and consequences;

13) **Neighborhood boundaries**—Neighbors take responsibility for monitoring young people's behavior;

14) **Adult role models**—Parent(s) and other adults model positive, responsible behavior;

15) **Positive peer influence**—Young person's best friends model responsible behavior;

16) **High expectations**—Both parent(s) and teachers encourage the young person to do well.

- **Constructive use of time**

17) **Creative activities**—Young person spends three or more hours per week in lessons or practices in music, theater, or other arts;

18) **Youth programs**—Young person spends three or more hours per week in sports, clubs, or organizations at school and(or) in the community;

19) **Time at home**—Young person is out with friends "with nothing special to do" two or fewer nights per week.

Additional four subcategories including the other 20 assets are classified to

Internal Assets, that is:

- **Commitment to learning**

20) **Achievement motivation**—Young person is motivated to do well in school;

21) **School engagement**—Young person is actively engaged in learning;

22) **Homework**—Young person reports doing at least one hour of homework every school day;

23) **Bonding to school**—Young person cares about her or his school;

24) **Reading for pleasure**—Young person reads for pleasure three or more hours per week.

- **Positive values**

25) **Caring**—Young person places high value on helping other people;

26) **Equality and social justice**—Young person places high value on promoting equality and reducing hunger and poverty;

27) **Integrity**—Young person acts on convictions and stands up for her or his beliefs;

28) **Honesty**—Young person 'tells the truth even when it is not easy';

29) **Responsibility**—Young person accepts and takes personal responsibility;

30) **Restraint**—Young person believes it is important not to be sexually active or to use alcohol or other drugs.

- **Social competencies**

31) **Planning and decision making**—Young person knows how to plan ahead and make choices;

32) **Interpersonal competence**—Young person has empathy, sensitivity, and friendship skills;

33) **Cultural competence**—Young person has knowledge of and comfort with people of different cultural/racial/ethnic backgrounds;

34) **Resistance skills**—Young person can resist negative peer pressure and dangerous situations;

35) **Peaceful conflict resolution**—Young person seeks to resolve conflict nonviolently.

- **Positive identify**

36) **Personal power**—Young person feels he or she has control over 'things that happen to me'.

37) **Self-esteem**—Young person reports having a high self-esteem.

38) **Sense of purpose**—Young person reports that 'my life has a purpose'.

39) **Positive view of personal future**—Young person is optimistic about her or his personal future.

Apparently using the combined approach, i.e., both health-risky behaviors prevention and reduction (e.g., resilience building) (Rew & Horner 2003) and assets approach, is more likely to generate desirable AHD outcomes. A group of researcher developed an instrument with satisfactory psychometric properties to measure youth assets (Oman et al. 2002), which could be used to guide the design of AHD assets building interventions.

In brief, there is no simple way to tackle health and developmental issues and concerns. To target at the most prevalent AHD concerns using an overarching approach might be the most cost-effective way for any government. WHO announced the general position in the Declaration of Alma Ata (WHO 1978) and Ottawa Charter for Health Promotion (WHO 1986) to address the global inequities of individual health and to achieve the goal of Health For All respectively, i.e., primary health care approach and health promotion strategy. These constitute the guiding principles for AHD and adolescent friendly health services (AFHS) (WHO 2002), which will be explained further in Chapter 2.

References

Beiser M. A study of personality assets in a rural community[J]. Archives of General Psychiatry, 1971, 24(3): 244-254.

Bronfenbrenner U. Making human beings human: bioecological perspectives on human development[M]. Thousand Oaks, California: Sage, 2005.

CCYL. Bylaw of China Communist Youth League[EB/OL]. China Commuist Youth League, 13 Jun. 2008 [17 Jun. 2011]: http://www.gqt.org.cn/ccylmaterial/regulation/.

CNBS. #1 Statistics Announcement about the six national population census [EB/OL]. China National Bureau of Statistics, [25 May. 2011]: http://www.stats.gov.cn/tjgb/rkpcgb/qgrkpcgb/t20110428_402722232.htm.

CYCRC. China Youth Development Report[EB/OL]. China Youth and Children Studies, 2008 [19 May. 2011]: http://www.cycs.org/Article.asp?Category=1&Column=389&ID=7869.

CYL. The Communist Youth League of China[EB/OL]. China Communist Youth League, 31 Mar. 2005 [17 Jun. 2011]: http://en.youth.cn/youth/200911/t20091102_1066307.htm.

Deng YP, Lin ZG. Family environment of mobile families and its effect on their children's psychological health[J]. Journal of Jiangxi Agricultural University, 2010, 9(3): 147-151.

Jones R, Bradley E. Health issues for adolescents[J]. Paediatrics and Child Health, 2007, 17(11): 433-438

MoH. 2010 China Health Statistics Yearbook[EB/OL]. Ministry of Health, China, [25 May. 2011]: http://www.moh.gov.cn/publicfiles/business/htmlfiles/zwgkzt/ptjnj/year2010/ index2010.html.

Nicol MJ, Manoharan H, Marfell-Jones MJ, et al. Issues in adolescent health: A challenge for nursing[J]. Contemporary nurse: a journal for the Australian nursing profession, 2002, 12(2): 155 - 163.

Oman RF, Vesely SK, McLeroy KR, et al. Reliability and validity of the youth asset survey (YAS) [J]. Journal of Adolescent Health, 2002, 31(3): 247-255.

Rew L , Horner SD. Youth resilience framework for reducing health-risk behaviors in adolescents[J]. Journal of pediatric Nursing, 2003, 18(6): 379-387.

Rosen JE. Adolescent Health and Development (AHD): A Resource Guide for World Bank Operations Staff and Government Counterparts[M/OL]. Washington, America: World Bank, 2004[12 Jun. 2011]: http://siteresources.worldbank.org/ HEALTHNUTRITIONANDPOPULATION/Resources/281627-1095698140167/Rosen-AHDFinal.pdf.

Rotegård AK, Moore SM, Fagermoen MS, et al. Health assets: a concept analysis[J]. International journal of nursing studies, 2010, 47(4): 513-525.

Scales PC. Reducing risks and building developmental assets: essential actions for promoting adolescent health[J]. Journal of School Health, 1999, 69(3): 113-119.

Simpson AR. Raising teeens: a synthesis of research and foundation for action[M/OL]. Boston, Massachusetts: Harvard School of Public Health, 2001[11 May. 2011]: http://www.hsph. harvard.edu/chc/parenting/report.pdf.

Singelis TM, Triandis HC, Bhawuk DPS, et al. Horizontal and vertical dimensions of individualism and collectivism: a theorectical and measurement refinement[J]. Cross-cultural Research, 1995, 29(3): 240-275.

Steinberg L. Adolescence[M]. 8th ed. New York: McGraw-Hill, 2008.

Wang ZQ. Analyais of juvenile crimes among migrant popuation[J]. Issues on Juvenile Crimes and Delinquency, 2003, (5): 33-37.

WHO. Declaration of Alma-Ata[EB/OL]. World Health Organization, 1978 [21 Jun. 2011]: http://www.who.int/hpr/NPH/docs/declaration_almaata.pdf.

WHO. Ottawa Charter for Health Promotion[EB/OL]. World Health Organization, 1986 [21 Jun. 2011]: http://www.who.int/hpr/NPH/docs/ottawa_charter_hp.pdf.

WHO. The Second Decade: improving adolescent health and development[EB/OL]. Department of Child and Adolescent Health and Development, World Health Organization, [12 Jun. 2011]: http://whqlibdoc.who.int/hq/1998/WHO_FRH_ADH_98.18_Rev.1.pdf.

WHO. Adolescent Friendly Health Services: an agenda for change[EB/OL]. World Health Organization, 2002 [8 Jul. 2011]: http://whqlibdoc.who.int/hq/2003/WHO_FCH_CAH_02.14.pdf.

WHO. Strategic directions for improving the health and development of children and adolescents[EB/OL]. World Health Organization, 2003 [25 Jul. 2011]: http://whttp://whqlibdoc.who.int/publications/2003/9241591064.pdf.

WHO. Orientation programme on adolescent health for health-care providers[M/OL]. Geneva, Switzerland: World Health Organization, 2006[14 Jun. 2011]: http://whqlibdoc.who.int/publications/2006/9241591269_Handout_eng.pdf.

WHO. Strengthening the health sector response to adolescent health and development [EB/OL]. World Health Organization, 2010 [12 Jun. 2011]: http://www.who.int/child_adolescent_health/documents/cah_adh_flyer_2010_12_en.pdf.

Wikipedia. Migration in the People's Republic of China[EB/OL]. Wikipedia.com, 9 May. 2011 [19 Jun. 2011]: http://en.wikipedia.org/wiki/Migration_in_the_People%27s_Republic_of_China.

Wu JQ. Current status of sexual and reproductive health among migrants in China[J]. J Int Reprod Health/Fam Plan, 2010, 29(6): 414-417, 421.

Wu YY. Age definition of youth[EB/OL]. China Youth, [1 Dec. 2009]: http://xinli.youth.cn/xygs/phb/200912/t20091201_1095645.htm.

Yang L. Research progress on psychological behavior health service model for floating youths in community[J]. Chinese Nursing Research, 2009, 23(8B): 2076-2078.

Zang JJ, Li NX, Deng K, et al. Assessment of general health of migrant children and adolescents in rural and health effective factors[J]. Model Preventive Medicine, 2009, 36(9): 1689-1691, 1694.

Chapter 3   Adolescent Friendly Health Services

—— Yuli Zang, Xiaoyan Liu, Yunfeng Li ——

Adolescents between 10 and 19 constitute a large proportion of the global population. It is estimated that the total of this subpopulation reaches 1.2 billion, the largest generation of young people in history. The vast majority of them (i.e., 85%) live in developing countries where they make up more than one third of local population in some areas (WHO 2009). During the past few decades, the spectrum of adolescent health and development has been altered dramatically, so that the traditional way to deliver services were found to be inadequate to meet adolescents' needs for health and development, which has motivated the world-wide advocacy for adolescent friendly health services (AFHS) under the leadership of the WHO (2002).

This chapter will present background information for the proposition of AFHS and then explain underpinning principles and characteristics, leading to the session on 'optimize adolescent health services'. You may use the three-spot checks in the end of the chapter to assess your understanding about AFHS.

Section 1   Background for AFHS

It has been taken for granted for a long time that adolescents are generally healthy in the sense that, compared with children and older people, much fewer adolescents suffer from acute or chronic health conditions, and death rates for this age range (i.e., 10~19 years) are low (WHO 2002, 2006). In reality, adolescents nowadays confront heightened risks and complex challenges which their parents did not face, and more are reaching puberty earlier but marrying later that a prolonged period of sexual maturity maybe present before marriage (WHO 2009).

Adolescent vulnerability

During middle adolescence (from around 14 to 17 years old), the brain is

177

still developing, i.e., delicate functional reconstruction occurs in harmony with puberty hormones (e.g., estrogen, testosterone) within the body and the social as well as physical surroundings, as reflected by the increasing capability in taking control over emotion, thoughts and behaviors (Nelson et al. 2005, Steinberg 2005, 2008). Before reaching maturity, adolescents are more susceptible to dangerous attractions or transient joyful moments without serious consideration over immediate or life-long impact before making judgments regarding involvement and engagement, leading to health-risk taking behaviors (Keeler & Kaiser 2010, Steinberg 2008).

In particular, there are revealed reciprocal effects between chronic conditions and adolescent development, intensifying the vulnerability of adolescents with chronic conditions. Chronic conditions for adolescents include non-communicable diseases such as asthma, epilepsy, cystic fibrosis, juvenile diabetes and hemoglobinopathics (e.g., sickle-cell disease) (Michaud et al. 2004, Suris et al. 2004, WHO 2006). For example, chronic conditions may cause the delay of puberty, while growth hormones may impair metabolic control in diabetes; psychosocial development status could cause poor medical compliance or problematic behaviors. Table 3-1 presents these effects which are summarized by Suris et al. (2004, p. 939) on the basis of a comprehensive literature review.

Table 3-1　Reciprocal effects of chronic conditions and adolescent development

Effects of chronic conditions on development	Effects of developmental issues on chronic conditions
Biological	**Biological**
Delayed or impaired puberty	Increased caloric requirement for growth may negatively impact on disease parameters
Short stature	Pubertal hormones may impact on disease parameters (e.g., growth hormone impairs metabolic control in diabetes)
Reduced bone mass accretion	
Psychological	**Poor adherence and poor disease control due to:**
Infantilisation	Poorly developed abstract thinking and planning (reduced ability to plan and prepare using abstract concepts)
Adoption of sick role as personal identifier	Difficulty in imagining the future; self-concept as being "bullet proof"

Continue

Effects of chronic conditions on development	Effects of developmental issues on chronic conditions
Egocentricity persists into late adolescence	Rejection of medical professionals as part of separation from parents
Impaired development of sense of sexual or attractive self	Exploratory (risk taking) behaviors
Impaired development of cognitive functions and information processing	
Social	**Associated health risk behaviors**
Reduced independence at a time of when independence is normally developing	Chaotic eating habits may result in poor nutrition
Failure of peer relationships then intimate (couple) relationships	Smoking, alcohol and drug use often in excess of normal population rates
Social isolation	Sexual risk taking, possibly in view of realisation of limited life span
Educational failure and then vocational failure; failure of development of independent living ability	

The living context (often refer to by developmental psychologists as ecological systems including the family, communities and wider society) plays a crucial role in shaping adolescent development, buffering adverse outside influences and reinforcing adolescent capability to cope with health threats (e.g., risk behaviors, lethal, acute or chronic health problems). If health services fail to help adolescents conquer the above vulnerability, it would be more likely for adolescents to develop a wider variety of health problems, particularly those in association with sexual activities like pregnancy, abortion and sexually transmitted infections (STIs) (Gavin et al. 2010, Jones & Bradley 2007, Nicol et al. 2002, Surís et al. 1996, WHO 2009).

Within the youth resilience framework (see Fig. 3-1 above), both the health-risk reduction approach and the strength-building approach are addressed (Rew & Horner 2003). This framework is underpinned by bioecological human development theory (Bronfenbrenner 2005), developmental assets theory (Oman et al. 2002, Scales 1999) and positive youth development theory (Guerra & Bradshaw 2008). All of these theories place emphasis on internal and external health determinants and available resources or assets for adolescents to tackle health threats and to accomplish developmental tasks, physically, psychosocially and sexually. Whereas, the traditional health and education systems used to stress the risks reduction or problem prevention without paying sufficient attention to the resilience building for positive development (or called as strength-based approach) (Chung et al. 2010).

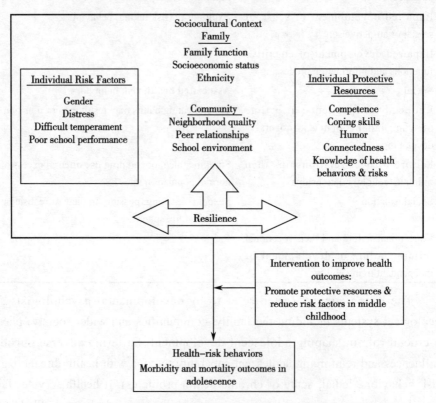

Fig 3-1   A youth resilience framework (Rew & Horner 2003)

Generally speaking, all critical needs (e.g., shelter, food, water) should be met, which preconditions the successful full-around transition from childhood to adulthood (Michaud et al. 2004, Suris et al. 2004). This is the case particularly for adolescents with chronic conditions including disabilities (SAM 2003, Wang et al. 2010). It is very difficult for adolescents in the survival status to thrive; adolescents need to develop competencies (ranging from academic, social, emotional to vocational, cultural) and skills to prepare them for work and adult life. Of more importance, adolescents need opportunities to engage in meaningful activities, have a voice, take responsibility for their own action and actively participate in civic discourse. Meanwhile they could actualize the belongingness to the family, communities and the county or culture to thrive (Dotterweich 2006). These widely different needs trigger the advocacy for positive youth development programs especially for those with chronic conditions (Chung et al. 2010).

Increasing attention is drawn to the positive youth development approach, given its emphasis on the strength or capacity building, including a sensitive response to the impact of hospitalization and chronic conditions management on all aspects of life for adolescents. Recent clinical innovations and research findings support the efficacy of the strength-based approach representing a fundamental evolution in the clinical approach to adolescent care (Chung et al. 2010, Canadian Paediatric Society 2008). For adolescents in hospital, they are placed in either pediatric or adult units but require the provision of separate adolescent unit to address their special concerns in aspects of physical environment, staff attitudes, and facilities (e.g., lounge) of their interest (Smith 2004).

As to the case in mainland of China, only one national study was implemented in 2006 to investigate adolescents' needs for health services in three counties representing eastern, middle and western China (Di et al. 2008). Approximately half to 60% of 2,734 subjects of 12~22 years old reported the needs for counseling services about growth, physical examination, reproductive health and sexual organs hygiene, and STIs. However, these findings were somewhat different from the study in the city of Linyi and the county of Mengyin in Shandong Province in August 2010. It was revealed that adolescents around 10 to 20 years old may be at risk of stress (mainly caused by intensive and fiery competitive examination system), Internet addiction, and STIs (Hutton & Grant 2011). In another large scale survey among 4,000 adolescents of 10~24 years old in four districts of Jinan, the capital of Shandong Province, approximately 80% reported the needs for health education classes in school, a mental health counseling center and puberty counseling (Xu et al. 2006). In particular, adolescents in rural areas or those migrant adolescents to urban areas seem to have stronger needs for health services related to STIs and mental health (CYCRC 2008, Hu et al. 2008, Wu et al. 2007). However, no further evidence was available regarding whether the above service needs are now met.

Barriers to adolescent friendly health services

In addition to the structural defect like the lack of a separate space (Smith

2004), there exist many other barriers—legal, physical, economic, psychological and social—in nearly all health systems, which prevent adolescents' needs for health and development from being met. These barriers might be: lack of knowledge on the part of adolescents; legal or cultural restriction such as shameful labeling for those extramarital pregnancy and abortion; physical or logistical restrictions like the long distance between where they live and where to seek support; poor quality of clinical services (e.g., inadequate medical supply, poorly trained or motivated health providers); unwelcomed services projected by supporting staff and health care providers' attitudes; high cost; peer pressure such as prevalent misconception regarding appropriate treatments; and gender barriers (WHO 2006).

Recognising the above situation, the WHO initiates a series of activities including arguing the necessity to pay attention to adolescent health and development, leading to the proposition of AFHS: for the benefit to one's later life and for the next generation, to reduce death and disease in adolescents is one of the essential responsibilities for any government and family; the investment in continuously improving adolescent health and development will definitely contribute to the protection of human capital and the reduction of the diseases burden in one's later life as the majority of chronic diseases in older people are associated with behaviors or lifestyle developed during adolescence (WHO 2002). As usual, the WHO strongly upholds the position statements in the Convention on the Rights of the Child by the United Nations (UN), which articulates the basic right for children and adolescents to life, development and the highest attainable standards of health, to facilities for the treatment of illness and rehabilitation of health in the Article 24 (UN 1990).

The practice of AFHS has been successfully implemented in many developing countries since 1989 when the Costa Rica National Adolescent Health Program was carried out. From 2000 the WHO intensifies advocacy for AFHS hallmarked by the organization of the Global Consultation on Adolescent Friendly Health Services in Geneva in March 2001 (WHO 2001, 2002). It has to be clarified that making services adolescent-friendly is not primarily about setting up separate dedicated services, instead, the greatest benefit comes from improving generic health services in local communities by improving the competencies of healthcare providers to deal with adolescents effectively.

Adolescents are always considered highly valuable as the most positive force representing the future of the society since the establishment of P. R. China. With the growing openness to the world since early 1980s, adolescents are exposed to an increasing number of risks, pressures and threats to their health and development compared with previous generations (CYCRC 2008). Nevertheless, little evidence was identified to suggest the promotion of AFHS in mainland of China, whereas the term AFHS sounds new to healthcare providers including nurses; no literature of relevance was found using the full term or its acronym of AFHS as a key search words in reference databases (e.g., CNKI) in Mandarin Chinese. The impending need thereby is to integrate AFHS into medical, nursing and other health science curricula or training programs to strengthen the health services for adolescents in China.

Priority areas for health and development

Adolescents and health planners have different priority health concerns: for health planners, they showed more concern over STIs/AIDS, injuries, psychiatric problems, too early pregnancy and schistosomiasis; in contrast, for adolescents, they care more about relationships, appearance, bullying, stress (e.g., due to schooling, exams), access to contraception and pregnancy (WHO 2006). This inconsistency could influence the policy generation and improvement which could benefit adolescents' health and future.

The WHO (2003, p. 29) identifies the following priority areas for congruent intervention to address all potential concerns including those among policy makers and adolescents themselves:

a) promotion of healthy development and lifestyles including adequate diet, regular exercise, good oral hygiene, and delayed sexual debut;

b) prevention of health risk behaviours including use of tobacco, alcohol and other substances, and unsafe sex;

c) delay in age of marriage and child bearing;

d) access to appropriate AFHS for family planning, pregnancy and childbirth, prevention and care of STIs including HIV/AIDS, other infectious diseases, nutritional deficiencies, injuries and mental health problems;

e) access to counseling services, including HIV testing and counseling;

f) enhancing capacity of adults, including within the family, to provide caring and responsible relationships with adolescents;

g) promotion of healthy school environments that facilitate the physical and psychosocial well-being of adolescents;

h) opportunities to develop healthy relationships with peers;

i) opportunities to participate in and contribute to pro-social activities in the community;

j) opportunities to continue education or vocational training in healthy (school) environments;

k) protection from hazardous child labour;

l) protection from harmful cultural practices including female genital mutilation and marriage before social and biological maturity.

The above strategic directions reflect the priority health problems with significant impact in adolescent life with attention to the context to create satisfactorily supportive social environment. These priority problems include intentional and unintentional injuries, sexual and reproductive health problems including HIV/AIDS, substance use and abuse (e.g., tobacco, alcohol), mental health problems, nutritional problems, endemic and chronic diseases, which are highlighted by the WHO to encourage and guide changes in any society (WHO 2006). The AFHS goes beyond solving these problems but focuses on the development of essential services packages suitable for adolescents and effective, available, affordable and acceptable in their own society (WHO 2002, 2006). More details will be presented in the next section.

Section 2　AFHS Characteristics

AFHS represents an approach which brings together the qualities that adolescents demand, with the high standards that have to be achieved in the best public health services (WHO 2006). To be considered adolescent-friendly, services should have the following characteristics (EAAAE, the acronym of four key words): a. Equitable, meaning that all adolescents, not just certain groups, are able to obtain the health services they need; b. Accessible, meaning that adolescents are able to obtain the services that are provided; c. Acceptable, meaning that the way to deliver the health services can meet the expectations of adolescent clients; d. Appropriate, meaning that all health services that adolescents need are provided; and e. Effective, meaning that it reflects that right health services are provided in the right way and make a positive contribution to adolescent health and development (WHO 2009).

AFHS characteristics

Three guiding principles underpin AFHS: first, addressing inequalities and facilitating the respect, protection, and fulfillment of human rights; second, taking a life course approach that recognizes the continuum from birth through childhood, adolescence and adulthood; and third, implementing a public health approach by focusing on major health issues that challenge populations as a whole and applying systematic development model to ensure the availability and accessibility of effective, relevant interventions to address them (WHO 2003).

The initial open discussion about AFHS characteristics started in Africa in October 2000 and continued during the global consultation on AFHS in Geneva in March 2001 under the leadership of the WHO. Meantime an agreement was reached that adolescents have the right to access health services that can protect them from any threats to their health and well-being, and these services should be made adolescent friendly and tailored to local needs, taking into account cost, epidemiological factors and adolescent development priorities (WHO 2002, 2006).

The first complete list of AFHS characteristics covers the area of policy, service procedures, healthcare providers, supporting staff, health facilities, adolescent involvement, community-oriented services development and service effectiveness (WHO 2006). Over time the long list of AFHS characteristics is discussed further and then classified into the above five broad dimensions of quality, i.e., EAAAE (see Table 3-2).

Table 3-2 Adolescent-friendly characteristics (WHO 2009, p.2-3)

Characteristic	Definition
Equitable: All adolescents, not just certain groups, are able to obtain the health services they need	
Policies and procedures are in place that does not restrict the provision of health services on any terms.	No policies or procedures restrict the provision of health services to adolescents on the basis of age, sex, social status, cultural background, ethnic origin, disability or any other areas of difference.
Healthcare providers treat all adolescent clients with equal care and respect, regardless of status.	Healthcare providers administer the same level of care and consideration to all adolescents regardless of age, sex, social status, cultural background, ethnic origin, disability or any other reason.
Support staff treats all adolescent clients with equal care and respect, regardless of status.	Support staff administers the same level of care and consideration to all adolescents regardless of age, sex, social status, cultural background, ethnic origin, disability or any other reason.
Accessible: Adolescents are able to obtain the health services that are provided	

Continue

Characteristic	Definition
Policies and procedures are in place, ensuring that health services are either free or affordable to adolescents.	All adolescents are able to receive health services free of charge or are able to afford any charges that might be in place.
The point of health service delivery has convenient hours of operation.	Health services are available to all adolescents during convenient times of the day.
Adolescents are well-informed about the range of available reproductive health services and how to obtain them.	Adolescents are aware of what health services are being provided, where they are provided and how to obtain them.
Community members understand the benefits that adolescents will gain by obtaining the health services they need, and support their provision.	Community members (including parents) are well-informed about how the provision of health services could help adolescents. They support the provision of these services as well as their use by adolescents.
Some health services and health-related commodities are provided to adolescents in the community by selected community members, outreach workers and adolescents themselves.	Efforts are under way to provide health services close to where adolescents are. Depending on the situation, outreach workers, selected community members (e.g., sports coaches) and adolescents themselves may be involved in this.
Acceptable: Health services are provided in ways that meet the expectations of adolescent clients	
Policies and procedures are in place to guarantee client confidentiality.	Policies and procedures are in place to maintain adolescents' confidentiality at all times (except where staff are obliged by legal requirements to report incidents such as sexual assaults, road traffic accidents or gunshot wounds, to the relevant authorities). Policies and procedures address: – registration – information on the identity of the adolescent and the presenting issue are gathered in confidence; – consultation – confidentiality is maintained throughout the visit of the adolescent to the point of health service delivery (i.e., before, during and after a consultation); – record-keeping – case-records are kept in a secure place, accessible only to authorized personnel; – disclosure of information – staff do not disclose any information given to or received from an adolescent to third parties such as family members, school teachers or employers, without the adolescent's consent.

Continue

Characteristic	Definition
The point of health service delivery ensures privacy.	The point of health service delivery is located in a place that ensures the privacy of adolescent users. It has a layout that is designed to ensure privacy throughout an adolescent's visit. This includes the point of entry, the reception area, the waiting area, the examination area and the patient-record storage area.
Healthcare providers are non-judgmental, considerate, and easy to relate to.	Healthcare providers do not criticize their adolescent patients even if they do not approve of the patients' words and actions. They are considerate to their patients and reach out to them in a friendly manner.
The point of health service delivery ensures consultations occur in a short waiting time, with or without an appointment, and (where necessary) swift referral.	Adolescents are able to consult with healthcare providers at short notice, whether or not they have a formal appointment. If their medical condition is such that they need to be referred elsewhere, the referral appointment also takes place within a short time frame.
The point of health service delivery has an appealing and clean environment.	A point of health service delivery that is welcoming, attractive and clean.
The point of health service delivery provides information and education through a variety of channels.	Information that is relevant to the health of adolescents is available in different formats (e.g., posters, booklets and leaflets). Materials are presented in a familiar language, easy to understand and eye-catching.
Adolescents are actively involved in designing, assessing and providing health services.	Adolescents are given the opportunity to share their experiences in obtaining health services and to express their needs and preferences. They are involved in certain appropriate aspects of health-service provision.
Appropriate: The health services that adolescents need are provided	
The required package of health care is provided to fulfill the needs of all adolescents either at the point of health service delivery or through referral linkages.	The health needs and problems of all adolescents are addressed by the health services provided at the point of health service delivery or through referral linkages. The services provided meet the special needs of marginalized groups of adolescents and those of the majority.

Continue

Characteristic	Definition
Effective: The right health services are provided in the right way and make a positive contribution to the health	
Healthcare providers have the required competencies to work with adolescents and to provide them with the required health services.	Healthcare providers have the required knowledge and skills to work with adolescents and to provide them with the required health services.
Healthcare providers use evidence-based protocols and guidelines to provide health services.	Health service provision is based on protocols and guidelines that are technically sound and of proven usefulness. Ideally, they should be adapted to the requirements of the local situation and approved by the relevant authorities.
Healthcare providers are able to dedicate sufficient time to work effectively with their adolescent clients.	Healthcare providers are able to dedicate sufficient time to work effectively with their adolescent clients.
The point of health service delivery has the required equipment, supplies, and basic services necessary to deliver the required health services.	Each point of health service delivery has the necessary equipment, supplies, including medicines, and basic services (e.g., water and sanitation) needed to deliver the health services.

These AFHS characteristics clearly reflects the WHO's effort to strengthen the health system covering the six building blocks (i.e., service delivery; health workforce; information; medical products, vaccines and technologies; financing; and leadership and governance or stewardship) emphasizing the primary care approach (WHO 2007, 2008). Primary health care refers to the essential health care provided in the places where people live or work (WHO 1978, 2008). On the basis of the above list of AFHS characteristics, a series of quality assessment tools (targeting at adolescent clients, healthcare providers, support staff, managers, outreach workers, and community members respectively) have been generated to assist in assessing the quality of adolescent services and identifying the weakness for further improvement (WHO 2009). This marks the other turning point of AFHS from the theoretical and policy focus to the practice-change for quality assurance focus.

Considering the comprehensiveness of AFHS and the large population across the wide geographical areas, it will be a quite long way for mainland of China to make changes to current health service systems. In March 2010, five governmental divisions, i.e., National Population and Family Planning Commission (NPFPC), Ministry of Education (MoE), China Association of Poverty Alleviation & Development (CAPAD), China Association for Science and Technology (CAST), and China Family Planning Association (CFPA) selected eight pilot sites to commence the national action to support adolescents to develop all-around healthy personality characteristics, physically and psychosocially (NPFPC et al. 2010). Although there remains the lack of a core package of essential services for adolescents in mainland of China, the five divisions' action reflect the undergoing cross-sector efforts regarding adolescent development in mainland except that the collaboration requires the partnership with Ministry of Health (MoH) to make the services change to be adolescent-friendly.

Essential services for AFHS

Initially the following essential list of clinical services was proposed (WHO 2002), but later it was argued that the services package can't be fixed menu but appropriate for local needs:

- General health services for tuberculosis, malaria, endemic diseases, injuries, accidents and dental care;
- Reproductive health including contraceptives, STIs treatment, pregnancy care and post-abortion management;
- Counseling and testing for HIV, confidentially and voluntarily;
- Management of sexual violence;
- Mental health services, including the services to address the use of tobacco, alcohol and drugs;
- Information and counseling on development during adolescence, including reproductive health, nutrition, hygiene, sexuality and substance use.

The WHO Pan American Regional Office proposed a core package for improving adolescent health and development through the regional consultation process. The core package should include (WHO 2006):

- Monitor growth and development;
- Identify and assess problem behaviors, managing these where possible or, making referral when they can't;
- Offer information and counseling on developmental changes, personal care and ways of seeking help;

- Provide immunization (e.g., vaccines against rubella, meningitis, hepatitis and tetanus).

Definitely there is no single answer to what constitutes the core package of health services for adolescents in the world. Nevertheless, services for adolescents must demonstrate relevance to their needs and wishes as a special age group. Health services play a critical role in the development of adolescents when they: a. treat conditions that give rise to ill health or cause adolescents concern; b. prevent and respond to health problems that can end young lives or result in chronic ill health or disability; c. support adolescents who are looking for a route to good health by monitoring progress and addressing concerns; d. interact with adolescents at times of concern or in crisis when they are looking for a way out of their problems; and e. make links with other services such as counseling services which can support adolescents (WHO 2006). When developing the services package, these have to taken into consideration.

Section 3   Optimize Adolescent Health Services

AFHS, including preventative, promotive treatment and rehabilitative services, can be delivered in hospital or at health centers, in schools, or in community settings. They may be planned from the top or started by groups of dedicated healthcare professionals who see that the needs of adolescents are not being met, and who believe that services can be more effective. Some examples are provided below mainly by referring to the Orientation Program AFHS module (WHO 2006), suggesting the potential areas for action in a range of different settings (including Youth Center, Apple Home, ect.) in mainland of China.

Services at health centers or hospitals

Basic health services are usually delivered at ordinary health centers in local communities and there is no reason why this should not also meet the needs of many adolescents. One important task is to train and support staff in this setting, to improve skills and to develop an empathetic approach, so that adolescents are willing to attend. These skills can be sustained through regular post-qualification training, and through a system of clinical protocols and guidelines, together with peer assessment and good quality supervision and management. Privacy may be improved by holding special sessions outside normal opening hours, by creating a separate entrance for adolescents or by improving confidentiality once inside. Several hospitals have developed specialist adolescent services or clinics in outhouses or as part of the main building. Hospital based services have skilled specialists on site and can offer a full range of medical services. However, they are limited to centers of population, and may be constrained by competing demands for funds.

There are also dedicated health centers which provide a full range of services especially for adolescents. Such centers may be in large towns or cities, where they are relatively cost-effective, or they may be run by Non-governmental Organizations (NGOs) as 'beacon' services that show what can be done. Such services can provide training and inspiration for other health care providers, but they usually only have an impact in one area, and they cannot be replicated in mainstream services, because of the cost.

Services located at other kinds of centre

Some adolescents are reluctant to visit health facilities that services can also be taken to places where young people already go. In mainland of China, Youth Centers used to be the most popular places for adolescents to undertake a variety of extracurricular activities in holiday or at leisure times. Since last year the Chinese government has started building Apple Homes to help adolescents develop healthy personality (behavioral, social, mental) through the activities of cultural rituals appreciation, peer mentorship, parenting training, health counseling and artistic activities like chess-playing, singing, calligraphy, pottery-making and so forth (Shan 2011). In comparison with Youth Centers, services in Apple Homes put more emphasis on behavioral, social, mental and sexual development for adolescents as a human being, suggesting in the near future it might be more attractive to adolescents if the services could be developed towards adolescent-friendly.

In youth or community centers, a nurse or doctor may hold special clinics, and peer educators can keep adolescents in touch with relevant health or social support services. One advantage is that such centers are already used by adolescents so that they do not have to make a special effort to go there. The drawback might be that a particular centre may only attract part of the adolescent population, being used mainly by boys or by girls or by one age group.

Outreach services

In both urban and rural areas, there is a need to provide services away from hospitals and health centers, to reach out to adolescents who are unlikely to attend. Increasingly in towns and cities, services are being provided in shopping malls, as well as in community or youth centers.

Some countries have promoted services on the Internet to catch the attention of adolescents who have access to computers. Adolescents in remote rural areas are often excluded from routine health services. Health care workers from local centers can take mobile services to visit villages to reach adolescents over a wide area. Services provided in village halls can include screening and immunization with a discrete follow-up appointment service for those who need further treatment or counseling. Visiting healthcare providers can also provide health education talks and materials aimed at adolescents.

Outreach services are also needed for adolescents who slip through the net, although they may be geographically close to an existing health facility. Street adolescents may find it difficult to access mainstream services, but will respond to services targeted on this vulnerable client group. Such outreach services may be run from health clinics or provided by NGOs. Once contact is made with those adolescents who are outside the system, it is important to find a way to create links between the outreach team and mainstream services.

Health services linked to schools

Schools provide a natural entry point for reaching adolescents with health education and services. They are ideal places to screen for or treat a range of common illnesses, to provide additional vaccines (e.g., HBV vaccine to all kids of 15-year old or younger in 2009 in mainland of China), and for health and hygiene education. However, in practice this potential is seldom realized. Schools are short of resources and teachers have neither the training nor the equipment to deliver health education on top of their existing workload. To turn this around requires effective training to build the motivation and skills of staff, and may require outside support for sex education lessons. Some successful schemes train adolescents as peer educators in schools. As with outreach work, it is important to link school health services to local health services so that students who need follow-up care receive it, but efforts are not duplicated.

It is also important to ensure that services provided at school have community support. Many head teachers are concerned that they will open themselves to criticism if they provide services for adolescents. Efforts among the school and community are required to ensure that such moves are supported. There is much evidence that parents welcome other responsible adults talking to their children about sensitive issues, as they often feel unable to deal with these issues at home.

Health services linked to workplaces

Employers and trade unions both have an interest in services that help to keep the workforce healthy, and many workers in workshops and factories are adolescents. Peer education on HIV/AIDS has been carried out in workplaces in some countries. In other countries, the Ministries of Labor provide outreached programmes in boarding houses and factory-based education sessions to meet the reproductive health education needs of young women working in the factories. The Ministries also conduct a general skills course for the large number of female workers.

In particular, nurses are in the unique position by virtue of their education, numbers and diversity of practice arenas to contribute to promote the highest attainable standard of health and development among adolescents. To integrate adolescent health and development components into nursing curricula thereby is necessary for the successful implementation of AFHS. The content areas to be incorporated have been widely investigated in many countries including China (Ju et al. 2009a, b, Liu et al. 2010, Liu et al. 2011, Pan et al. 2010, 2011). Nevertheless, there is still a long way to go for nurses to fulfill their roles in providing health services to adolescents in any settings because of the traditional narrow understanding about nurses' roles and nursing practice.

Section 4   Learning Exercises

The following spot check exercises (see Fig. 3-2~Fig. 3-4) could be used to do self-assessment to see how much you understand about AFHS (WHO 2006).

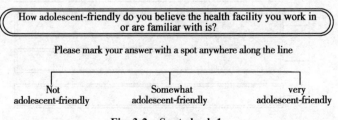

Fig. 3-2   Spot check 1

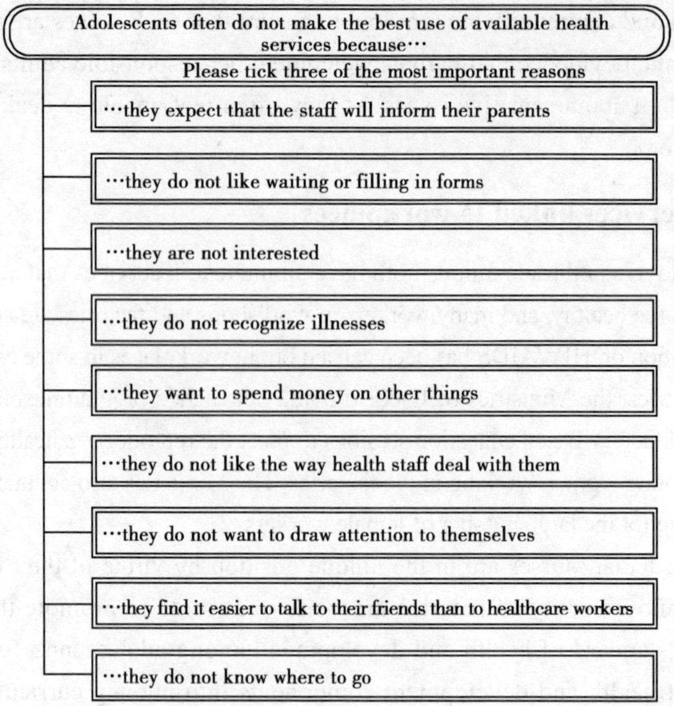

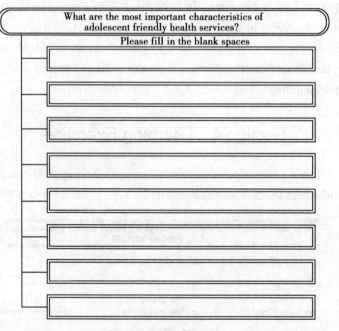

Adolescents often do not make the best use of available health services because…

Please tick three of the most important reasons

…they expect that the staff will inform their parents

…they do not like waiting or filling in forms

…they are not interested

…they do not recognize illnesses

…they want to spend money on other things

…they do not like the way health staff deal with them

…they do not want to draw attention to themselves

…they find it easier to talk to their friends than to healthcare workers

…they do not know where to go

Fig. 3-3   Spot check 2

What are the most important characteristics of adolescent friendly health services?

Please fill in the blank spaces

Fig. 3-4   Spot check 3

References

Bronfenbrenner U. Making human beings human: bioecological perspectives on human development[M]. Thousand Oaks, California: Sage, 2005.

Chung RJ, Burke PJ, Goodman E. Firm foundations: strength-based approaches to adolescent chronic disease[J]. Current Opinion in Pediatrics, 2010, 22(4): 389-397.

CPS. Issues of care for hospitalized youth[J]. Paediatr Child Health, 2008, 13 (1): 61-64.

CYCRC. China Youth Development Report[EB/OL]. China Youth and Children Studies, 2008 [19 May 2011]: http://www.cycs.org/Article.asp?Category=1&Column=389& ID=7869.

Di JL, Wu Q, Wang LH, et al. An investigation on requirement of rural adolescents to contents of health care service in adolescent clinic[J]. Chinese Journal of Women and Child Health Research, 2008, 19(4): 319-321.

Dotterweich J. Positive Youth Development Resource Manual[M/OL]. New York: Cornell University, Family Life Development Center, 2006[5 Jul. 2011]: http://ecommons.cornell. edu/bitstream/1813/21946/2/PYD_ResourceManual.pdf.

Gavin LE, Catalano RF, David-Ferdon C, et al. A review of positive youth development programs that promote adolescent sexual and Rreproductive health[J]. Journal of Adolescent Health, 2010, 46(3, Suppl1): S75-S91.

Guerra NG, Bradshaw CP. Linking the prevention of problem behaviors and positive youth development: core competencies for positive youth development and risk prevention[J]. New Directions for Child and Adolescent Development, 2008(122): 1-17.

Hu XJ, Cook S, Salazar MA. Internal Migration and Health in China[EB/OL]. 2008 [9 Jul. 2011]: http://wwwold.bjmu.edu.cn/extra/col19/1225161485.pdf.

Hutton A , Grant J. Expanding the role of nurses for a rapidly urbanising China[J/OL]. RCNAreport: nursing news, views & attitudes, 2011: http://www.apnedmedia.com.au/ email/rcna-report-feb-11-web-ready.pdf.

Jones R, Bradley E. Health issues for adolescents[J]. Paediatrics and Child Health, 2007, 17(11): 433-438

Ju XL, Zang YL, Lou FL. Necessity of setting up Adolescent Health and Development course in nursing colleges[J]. Chinese Journal of Nursing Education, 2009a, 6(9): 401-403.

Ju XL, Zang YL, Lou FL. A study on the applicability of the Adolescent Health and Development course in China[J]. Journal of Nursing Science, 2009b, 24(2, Surgery Edition): 8-10.

Keeler HJ, Kaiser MM. An integrative model of adolescent health risk behavior[J]. Journal of Pediatric Nursing, 2010, 25(2): 126-137.

Liu T, Pan YY, Zang YL. Investigation on nurses' cognition of competency of adolescent health and development[J]. Journal of Nursing Science, 2011, 26(3, General): 53-56.

Michaud P, Suris J, Viner R. The adolescent with a chronic condition. Part II: healthcare provision[J]. Arch Dis Child, 2004, 89(10): 943-949.

Nelson EE, Leibenluft E, Mcclure EB, et al. The social re-orientation of adolescence: a neuroscience perspective on the process and its relation to psychopathology[J]. Psychological Medicine, 2005, 35(2): 163-174.

Nicol MJ, Manoharan H, Marfell-Jones MJ, et al. Issues in adolescent health: A challenge for nursing[J]. Contemporary nurse : a journal for the Australian nursing profession, 2002, 12(2): 155 - 163.

NPFPC, MoE, CAPAD, CAST & CFPA. Notice to implement healthy pesonality program[EB/OL]. 2010 [25 Jul. 2011]: http://www.hxshdy.com/gwgg/518.html.

Oman RF, Vesely SK, McLeroy KR, et al. Reliability and validity of the youth asset survey (YAS) [J]. Journal of Adolescent Health, 2002, 31(3): 247-255.

Pan YY, Liu T, Zang YL. The integration of adolescent health and development curriculum into undergraduate nursing education[J]. Journal of Nursing Science, 2010, 25(9, General): 64-66.

Pan YY, Liu T, Zang YL. Construction of a tool for measuring undergraduate nursing students' cognition and needs for adolescent health and development and its application[J]. Journal of Nursing Science, 2011, 26(2, Surgery): 65-68.

Rew L, Horner SD. Youth resilience framework for reducing health-risk behaviors in adolescents[J]. Journal of pediatric Nursing, 2003, 18(6): 379-387.

SAM. Transition to adult health care for adolescents and young adults with chronic conditions[J]. Journal of Adolescent Health, 2003, 33(4): 309-311.

Scales PC. Reducing risks and building developmental assets: essential actions for promoting adolescent health[J]. Journal of School Health, 1999, 69(3): 113-119.

Shan J. Press conference for 2010 Survey Report of Adolescent healthy pesonality program[EB/OL]. China Daily, 2011 [8 Jul. 2011]: http://www.chinadaily.com.cn/dfpd/shehui/2011-03/14/content_12168478.htm.

Smith S. Adolescent units—an evidence-based approach to quality nursing in adolescent care[J]. European Journal of Oncology Nursing, 2004, 8(1): 20-29.

Steinberg L. Cognitive and affective development in adolescence[J]. Trends in Cognitive Sciences, 2005, 9(2): 69-74.

Steinberg L. Adolescence[M]. 8th ed. New York: McGraw-Hill, 2008.

Surís J-C, Resnick MD, Cassuto N, et al. Sexual behavior of adolescents with chronic disease and disability[J]. Journal of Adolescent Health, 1996, 19(2): 124-131.

Suris J-C, Michaud P-A, Viner R. The adolescent with a chronic condition. Part I: developmental issues[J]. Archives of Disease in Childhood, 2004, 89(10): 938-942.

UN. Convention on the Rights of the Child [EB/OL]. Office of the United Nations High Commissioner for Human Rights, 1990 [8 Jul. 2011]: http://www2.ohchr.org/english/law/crc.htm.

Wang G, McGrath BB, Watts C. Health care transitions among youth with disabilities or special health care needs: an ecological approach[J]. Journal of Pediatric Nursing, 2010, 25(6): 505-550.

WHO. Declaration of Alma-Ata[EB/OL]. World Health Organization, 1978 [21 Jun. 2011]: http://www.who.int/hpr/NPH/docs/declaration_almaata.pdf.

WHO. Global consultant on adolescent friendly health services: a consensus statement[EB/OL]. World Health Organization, 2001 [8 Jul. 2011]: http://www.who.int/child_adolescent_health/documents/pdfs/who_fch_cah_02.18.pdf.

WHO. Adolescent friendly health services: an agenda for change[EB/OL]. World Health Organization, 2002 [8 Jul. 2011]: http://whqlibdoc.who.int/hq/2003/WHO_FCH_CAH_02.14.pdf.

WHO. Strategic directions for improving the health and development of children and adolescents[EB/OL]. World Health Organization, 2003 [25 Jul. 2011]: http://whttp://whqlibdoc.who.int/publications/2003/9241591064.pdf.

WHO. Orientation programme on adolescent health for health-care providers[M/OL]. Geneva, Switzerland: World Health Organization, 2006[14 Jun. 2011]: http://whqlibdoc.who.int/publications/2006/9241591269_Handout_eng.pdf.

WHO. Strengthening health systems to improve health outcomes: WHO's framework for action[EB/OL]. World Health Organization, 2007 [8 Jul. 2011]: http://www.who.int/healthsystems/strategy/everybodys_business.pdf.

WHO. The World Health Report 2008 - Primary Health Care (now more than ever)[M/OL]. Geneva, Switzerland: World Health Organization, 2008[25 Jul. 2011]: http://www.who.int/whr/2008/en/index.html.

WHO. Quality assessment guidebook: a guide to assessing health services for adolescent [M/OL]. Geneva, Switzerland: World Health Organization, 2009[8 Jul. 2011]: http://whqlibdoc.who.int/publications/2009/9789241598859_eng.pdf.

Wu Q, Di JL, Wu JL,et al. Survey on caring and offer of health among rural adolescents[J].

Chinese Journal of Public Health, 2007, 23(11): 1334-1336.

Xu L, Gong LX, Zhang SP, et al. An anlyais of adolescent needs for reproductive health and related factors[J]. Chinese Journal of Women and Child Health Research, 2006, 21(1): 93-95.

Chapter 4   Adolescent Physical Growth and Development

—— Qinghui Meng, Qian Liu, Yaoyun Pan, Linzhe Pu ——

This chapter will focus on the physical development of adolescents and then present answers to selected common concerns such as menstruation. Nevertheless, to reach a better understanding about adolescents, it must be always remembered that the physical changes are inevitably interwoven with psychosocial changes (Cobb 2010).

Section 1   Overview

Adolescence is a transition from childhood to early adulthood, and it has been described as the time period when an individual is no longer a child, but not yet an adult. It is a time period when an individual undergoes enormous physical changes. Peak rates of growth and development during adolescence are exceeded only by those during fetal life and infancy. But compared with infancy and early childhood, there is much greater individual variation both in the timing of developmental milestones, and in the degree of changes in rates of growth (Berer 2001). These physical changes are accompanied by sexual maturation, often leading to the formulation of intimate relationships, and the development of abstract thinking, self identity, and increasing independence (Steinberg 2008).

Adolescence, thereby, is defined as the progression from the appearance of secondary sex characteristics to sexual and reproductive maturity; development of mental processes and adult identity; and the transitions from total socio-economic dependence to relative independence (Tanner 1990). Although the decade of life from 10 to 19 years provides a time-bound definition of adolescence, it is important to realize that the changes occurring during this period may not correspond neatly with precise ages because of variations in the onset and duration of changes between individuals (Simpson 2001, WHO 2006).

Moreover, this period of transition is perceived differently by different cultures. Its perception is clearly mediated by social, economic and cultural

199

factors. The experience of adolescence, thereby, differs among individuals and by sex in any given society, and by varying conditions and circumstances such as disability, illness, socioeconomic status and poverty (WHO 2008).

WHO clearly recognizes that 'adolescence' is a phase rather than a fixed time in an individual's life, which could be divided into three periods, i.e., early, middle and late adolescence, roughly equivalent to age groups 10 to 14, 15 to 17, and 18 to 21. Although this age-grouping method is not universally accepted, it is practical, providing a basic framework to understand adolescent development. Physical changes accompanying other aspects of developmental changes during the early, middle and late adolescence are presented in Table 4-1.

Table 4-1　Changes during different stages of adolescence (Fleming & Towey 2001)

Characteristics	Early adolescence	Middle adolescence	Late adolescence
Age range	11～13 to 14-15 years	14～15 to 17 years	17～21 years (variable)*
Cognition	• Concrete thought dominant • Existential orientation • Cannot perceive long-range implications of current decisions and acts	• Rapidly gaining competence in abstract thought • Capable of perceiving future implications of current acts and decisions but variably applied • Reverts to concrete operations under stress	• Established abstract thought processes • Future oriented • Capable of perceiving and acting on long-range options
Psychological self and self perception	• Preoccupation with rapid body change • Former body image disrupted • Concerned with privacy • Frequent mood swings • Very self-focused	• Reestablishes body image as growth decelerates and stabilizes • Extremely concerned with appearance and body	• Emancipation completed • Intellectual and functional identity established • May experience "crisis of 21" when facing societal demands for autonomy

Continue

Characteristics	Early adolescence	Middle adolescence	Late adolescence
Psychological self and self perception		● Preoccupation with fantasy and idealism in exploring expanded cognition and future options ● Often risk takers ● Development of a sense of omnipotence and invincibility	● Body image and gender role definition nearly secured
Family	● Defining independence –dependence boundaries ● Conflicts may occur but relate to minor issues	● Frequency of conflicts may decrease but their intensity increases ● Struggle for emancipation	● Transposition of child-parent dependency relationship to the adult-adult model
Peer group	● Seeks peer affiliation to counter instability generated by rapid change ● Compares own normality and acceptance with same sex/age mates ● Same-sex friends and group activities	● Strong need for identification to affirm self-image ● Looks to peer group to define behavioural code during emancipation process ● Cross-gender friendships more common	● Group recedes in importance in favor of individual friendships and intimate relationships

* The upper end depends on cultural, economic, and educational factors.

In fact changes and development occurring during these phases are not necessarily sequential; they may overlap and vary, in relation to gender, cultural, socioeconomic and other factors (WHO 1998). It is important to note that adolescents are not a homogeneous group: their needs vary with sex, stage of development, life circumstances and socioeconomic conditions (WHO 2006). Nevertheless, it is desirable for any adolescent to accomplish all of following developmental tasks: adjust to sexually maturing bodies and feelings; develop and apply abstract thinking skills; develop and apply a more complex level of perspective taking; develop and apply new coping skills in areas such as decision making, problem solving and conflict resolution; identify meaningful moral standards, values and belief systems; understand and express more complex emotional experiences; form friendships that are mutually close and supportive; establish key aspects of identity; meet the demands of increasingly mature roles and responsibilities; and renegotiate relationships with adults in parenting roles (Simpson 3001, Fleming & Towey 2001).

Section 2   Body Changes During Puberty

When a child grows to adolescence, the body starts preparing for parenthood. The chief elements of biological changes in adolescence, often collectively referred to as puberty, involve the changes to breasts, height, body hair and genitalia, denoting a phase in the continuum of the development of hypothalamic-pituitary-gonadal (HPG) feedback system (or called as HPG axis, Fig. 4-1) from the fetus to the attainment of full sexual maturation and fertility (Graber et al. 2010, Steinberg 2008).

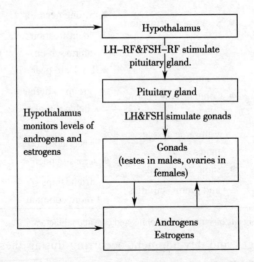

Fig. 4-1   Levels of sex hormones regulated by the feedback system
LH-RF:luteinizing hormone-releasing factor;FSH-RF:follicle-stimulating hormone-releasing factor;LH:luteinizing hormone;FSH: follicle-stimulating hormone (Steinberg 2008)

The HPG axis undergoes an active phase during fetal and neonatal development, enters the resting phase during the remaining childhood, and then moves to puberty. Meanwhile the hypothalamic-pituitary-gonadal axis is activated under the influence of hormones, for instance, luteinizing hormone-releasing factor (LH-RF); follicle-stimulating hormone-releasing factor (FSH-RF); luteinizing hormone (LH); follicle-stimulating hormone (FSH), and the sex steroids (e.g., estradiol, testosterone) bringing about the pubertal manifestations: breast development abbreviated as B, genital enlargement abbreviated as G, pubic hair abbreviated as PH, uterus, ovaries, testes (Brämswig & Dübbers 2009, Steinberg 2008).

The above process lasts for two to five years. Meanwhile there occurs a significant increase in height and weight, and in the musculature (Columbia University 2009). The proportion of body parts changes over time, and these changes appear to be noticeably different between the genders in aspects of height, weight, and secondary sexual characteristics.

In general, the spurt occurs two years earlier for girls than for boys, from the onset of puberty until the end of puberty. Boys can gain an average of 28 centimeters, under the action of male hormones, their weight increases significantly, and muscle tissue develops. Following puberty, boys can gain a higher average muscle tissue mass over girls, and it can continue until adulthood. However, on average, the percentage of body fat for boys remains the same, whereas the percentage of body fat in girls increases significantly (Bordini & Rosenfield 2011a, Brämswig & Dübbers 2009, Hazen et al. 2008, WHO 2008).

Body mass index (BMI), defined as a person's weight in kilograms divided by its square of his height in meters (kg/m^2), is the most commonly used index to classify severe thinness, thinness, normal, particularly overweight and obesity (Reilly 2010, WHO 2011). Table 4-2 lists the global standard of BMI-based classification to facilitate an understanding of adolescents' nutritional status; for those of 19 years old, the cut-offs for adults are referred to: overweight: BMI>25kg/m^2; obesity: BMI>30kg/m^2 (WHO 2011).

Table 4-2   Adolescents BMI screening classification standard (kg/m^2, WHO 2011)

Age (years)	Sex	Severe thinness	Thinness	Normal	Overweight	Obesity
10	M	≤12.8	12.9~14.1	14.2~19.2	19.3~22.5	≥22.6
	F	≤12.4	12.5~13.9	14.0~19.9	20.0~23.7	≥23.8
11	M	≤13.1	13.2~14.5	14.6~19.9	20.0~23.6	≥23.7

Continue

Age (years)	Sex	Severe thinness	Thinness	Normal	Overweight	Obesity
12	F	≤12.7	12.8~14.4	14.5~20.8	20.9~25.0	≥25.1
	M	≤13.4	13.5~14.9	15.0~20.8	20.9~24.8	≥24.9
13	F	≤13.2	13.3~14.9	15.0~21.8	21.9~26.2	≥26.3
	M	≤13.8	13.9~15.5	15.6~21.8	21.9~25.9	≥26.0
14	F	≤13.6	13.7~15.4	15.5~22.7	22.8~27.3	≥27.4
	M	≤14.3	14.4~16.0	16.1~22.7	22.8~27.0	≥27.1
15	F	≤14.0	14.1~15.9	16.0~23.5	23.6~28.2	≥28.3
	M	≤14.7	14.8~16.5	16.6~23.5	23.6~27.9	≥28.0
16	F	≤14.4	14.5~16.2	16.3~24.1	24.2~28.9	≥29.0
	M	≤15.1	15.2~16.9	17.0~24.3	24.4~28.6	≥28.7
17	F	≤14.6	14.7~16.4	16.5~24.5	24.6~29.3	≥29.4
	M	≤15.4	15.5~17.3	17.4~24.9	25.0~29.2	≥29.3
18	F	≤14.7	14.8~16.4	16.5~24.8	24.9~29.5	≥29.6
	M	≤15.7	15.8~17.6	17.7~25.4	25.5~29.7	≥29.8
	F	≤14.7	14.8~16.5	16.6~25.0	25.1~29.7	≥29.8

M=male; F=female.

More significant changes during the period of adolescence are related to the development of secondary sexual characteristics, which projects the growing potential for reproduction mainly resulting from hormonal changes.

Secondary sexual characteristics

Sexual differentiation begins during gestation, when the gonads are formed. General habitus and shape of body and face as well as sex hormones level are similar in pre-pubertal boys and girls. As puberty progresses and sex hormones level rises, gender differences become noticeable, though similar changes occur to male and female bodies.

In males, the increased level of testosterone directly induces the growth of the testicles and penis, and indirectly (via dihydrotestosterone, DHT) influences the prostate. It also directly increases the size and mass of muscles, vocal cords, and bones, deepening the voice, and changing the shape of the face and skeleton. Converted into dihydrotestosterone (DHT) in the skin, testosterone accelerates the growth of androgen-responsive facial and body hair, but may slow and eventually stop the growth of head hair.

In females, breasts are a manifestation of higher levels of estrogens (e.g., estradiol). The increased level of estrogens also widens the pelvis and increases the amount of body fat in hips, thighs, buttocks, and breasts, in addition to inducing the growth of the uterus, proliferation of the endometrium, and menses. More details about the gender differences of typical changes during puberty are shown in Table 4-3.

Table 4-3　Secondary sexual characteristics for female and male adolescents (WHO 2008)

	Adolescent male	Adolescent female
Body hair	● Growth of body hair, including facial, underarm, abdominal, chest, and pubic hair;	● Growth of body hair, most prominently underarm and pubic hair;
Skin	● Increased secretions of oil and sweat glands, often causing acne and body odor; ● Coarsening or rigidity of skin texture, due to less subcutaneous fat;	
Voice vs. breast	● Enlargement of larynx (Adam's apple) and deepening of voice;	● Enlargement of breasts and erection of nipples;
Body composition	● Increased statue, and adult males are taller than adult females ● Increased muscle mass and strength, and greater mass of thigh in front of the femur; ● Heavier skull and bone structure; ● Broadening shoulder, and shoulders wider than hips; ● Higher waist-to-hip ratio than prepubescent or adult females or prepubescent males, on average.	● Greater development of thigh muscles behind the femur, rather than in front of it; ● Widening of hips, and lower waist to hip ratio than adult males, on average; ● Changed distribution in weight and fat, and more subcutaneous fat and fat deposits mainly around the buttocks, thighs and hips.
Sign of reproduction	Nocturnal emission	Menstruation

Tanner stages of sexual maturity

The different phases of secondary sexual characteristics development is conventionally designated as Tanner Stages (Fig. 4-2, Fig. 4-3) or sexual maturity rating (SMR): B1 through B5 for breast development, PH1 through PH5 for pubic hair development, and G1 through G5 for genital development (Brämswig &

Dübbers 2009, Morris & Udry 1980, Tanner 1990).

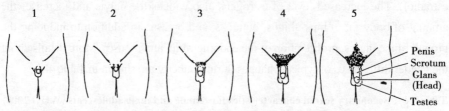

Stage	Pubic Hair(PH)	Penis	Genitlia(G) Testes
1	None	Preadolescent	Preadolescent
2	Scant,slightly pigmented	Slight enlargement	Enlarged scrotum, pink texture altered
3	Darker,starts to curl,small amount	Longer	Larger
4	Resembles adult type,but less in quantity;coarse,curly	Larger,glands and breadth increase in size	Larger,scrotum dark
5	Adult distribution,spread to medial surface of thighs	Adult size	Adult size

Fig. 4-2   Tanner sexual maturity rating for males (Morris & Udry 1980)

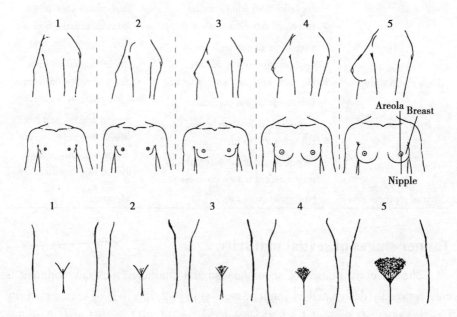

Fig. 4-3   Tanner sexual maturity rating for females (Morris & Udry 1980)

Stage	Pubic Hair (PH)	Breasts (B)
1	Preadolescent	Preadolescent
2	Sparse,lightly pigmented,straight,medial border of labia	Breast and papilla elevated as small mound,areola diameter increased
3	Darker,beginning to curl,increased amount	Breast and areola enlarged, no contour separation
4	Coarse,curly,abundant but amount less than in adulthood	Areola and papilla form secondary mound
5	Adult feminine triangle,spread to medial surface of thighs	Mature,nipple projects,areola part of general breast contour

Fig. 4-3   Tanner sexual maturity rating for females (morris & Udry 1980)(Continue)

Onset of secondary sexual characteristics

On average male sexual development begins at an age of 11.2 years (8.2~14.2 years) during SMR2 and lasts for approximately two to five years (Brämswig & Dübbers 2009, Steinberg 2008). The typical sequence of pubertal events in males is: adrenarche; beginning of growth spurt; testicular development; beginning of pubic hair; and peak height velocity (Fig. 4-4). In particular, the first physical sign of puberty in 98% of males is testicular enlargement; ejaculation often occurs during SMR3 and the first spermatozoa (i.e., spermarche) come at around 13.4 years (range 11.7~15.3 years). Though SMR4 is often associated with fertility but may occur during SMR3.

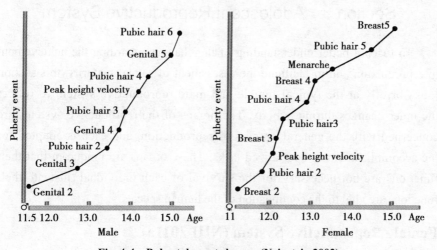

Fig. 4-4   Pubertal events by age (Neinstein 2002)

The mean age of female sexual development starts at 10.4 years (range: 8.0 to 12.6 years) (Brämswig & Dübbers 2009), and the typical sequence of pubertal events is shown in Fig. 4-4. Mostly the beginning of breast bud is the first physical sign of puberty. It was found that the age of the onset of secondary sexual characteristics including menarche decreases over time (i.e., secular trend) due to improved nutrition, increasing obesity, hormonal exposures and other environmental or societal alterations (Zembar & Blume 2007). This secular trend may have an impact on health resulting from the increased risk of sexual activities, pregnancy, abortion, or even breast cancer (Zembar & Blume 2007). On average, the peak height velocity in females comes earlier at SMR2 compared with that at SMR4 in males; the menarche occurs at PH4 for more than half females, but may occur to nearly one fifth at PH3.

The other aspect requiring further investigation is the psychosocial impact related to the onset of puberty. It is consistently found that the impact differs with sex: early-developing males tend to have greater self-confidence and be more likely to achieve better academic, social and athletic success than their peers. In contrast, girls with earlier puberty appear to develop more emotional and behaviour problems and poorer achievement associated with relatively lower self-esteem (Bordini & Rosenfield 2011a, b, Hazen et al. 2008). The other difference is found between late-developing girls and boys: the former do not demonstrate noticeable difficulties in self-esteem compared with the latter (Hazen et al. 2008).

Section 3　Adolescent Reproductive System

To reach a better understanding of the changes regarding the achievement of reproduction and to facilitate the assessment of sexual maturity, this section looks briefly at the typical female and male reproductive system to reflect the inner changes during puberty. The organs of the reproductive systems are concerned with the general process of reproduction, and each is adapted for the accomplishment of specialized tasks. These organs are unique in that their functions are not necessary for the survival of each individual; instead, their functions are vital to the continuation of the human species.

Female Reproductive System (NIH 2011a)

As is shown in Fig. 4-5 (Wikipedia 2005a), the female reproductive system consists of internal organs and external organs. The internal organs are located in the pelvic cavity and are supported by the pelvic floor. The external organs are located from the lower margin of the pubis to the perineum. The appearance of the external genitals varies greatly from one to another, since age, heredity, race, and the number of children a woman has born determines the size, shape, and color.

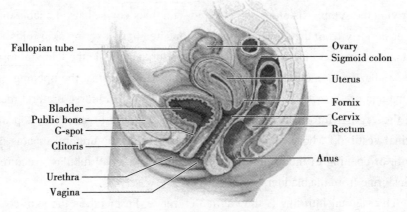

Fallopian tube

Ovary
Sigmoid colon
Uterus
Fornix
Cervix
Rectum

Bladder
Public bone
G-spot
Clitoris

Anus

Urethra
Vagina

Fig. 4-5   Female reproudctive organs (Wikipedia 2005a)

Internal female organs include the uterus, vagina, fallopian tubes, and the ovaries: The uterus is a hollow organ about the size and shape of a pear, located between the urinary bladder and the rectum and suspended in the pelvis by broad ligaments. It is the organ of menstruation (which is to be presented in detail after this session) and during pregnancy it receives the fertilized ovum, retains and nourishes it until the fetus is expelled during labor. The vagina is the thin walled muscular tube about six inches long leading from the uterus to the external genitalia. It provides the passageway for childbirth and menstrual flow; it receives the penis and semen during sexual intercourse.

Each fallopian tube is approximately 4 inches long and extends medially from each ovary to empty into the superior region of the uterus. These two tubes transport ova from the ovaries to the uterus. The ovaries, about the size and shape of almonds, lie against the lateral walls of the pelvis, one on each side, for oogenesis-the production of eggs (female sex cells) and for hormone production (estrogen and progesterone). There is no direct contact between fallopian tubes and the ovaries. When an oocyte is expelled from the ovary, fimbriae create fluid currents that act to carry the oocyte into the fallopian tube. The oocyte is carried toward the uterus by combination of tube peristalsis and cilia, which propel the oocyte forward. The most desirable place for fertilization is the fallopian tube.

External female genitalia include the mons pubis, labia majora, labia minora, vestibule, perineum, and the Bartholin's glands. These structures surround the openings of the urethra and vagina: Mons pubis is the fatty rounded area overlying the symphysis pubis and covered with thick coarse hair; the labia majora run posteriorly from the mons pubis with elongated hair covering skin folds. They enclose and protect other external reproductive organs, while the labia minora are two smaller folds enclosed by the labia majora. They protect the opening of the vagina and urethra. As to the vestibule, it consists of the clitoris, urethral meatus, and the vaginal introitus: the clitoris is a short erectile organ at the top of the vaginal vestibule whose function is sexual excitation; the urethral meatus is the mouth or opening of the urethra; and the urethra is a small tubular structure that drains urine from the bladder.

The vaginal introitus is the vaginal entrance. Perineum is the skin covered muscular area between the vaginal opening (introitus) and the anus. It aids in constricting the urinary, vaginal, and anal opening. It also helps support the pelvic contents. The Bartholin's glands lie on either side of the vaginal opening. They produce a mucoid substance, which provides lubrication for intercourse.

Menstruation (Bordini & Rosenfield 2011a, Brämswig & Dübbers 2009) is the periodic discharge of blood, mucus, and epithelial cells from the uterus. It usually occurs at monthly intervals throughout the reproductive period, except during pregnancy and lactation, when it is usually suppressed.

The menstruation period is controlled by the cyclic activity of FSH and LH from the anterior pituitary and progesterone and estrogen from the ovaries. During the first three to five days (known as the menses phase), a lack of signal from a fertilized egg causes the drop of estrogen and progesterone production, while the drop in progesterone results in the sloughing off of the thick endometrial lining which is the menstrual flow.

Approximately from day 6 to 14 (known as the proliferative phase), the drop in progesterone and estrogen stimulates the release of FSH from the anterior pituitary. FSH stimulates the maturation of an ovum in the grafian follicle. Near the end of this phase, the release of LH increases, causing a sudden burst like release of the ovum, which is known as ovulation.

In the last period of the cycle (day 15th to 28th, i.e., secretory phase), high level of LH causes the empty grafian follicle to develop into the corpus luteum. The corpus luteum releases progesterone, which increases the endometrial blood supply. If the egg is fertilized, the embryo produces human chorionic gonadotropin (HCG). The human chorionic gonadotropin signals the corpus luteum to continue to supply progesterone to maintain the uterine lining. Continuous levels of progesterone prevent the release of FSH and ovulation ceases.

In fact, the length of the cycle highly varies, ranging from 21 to 39 days. Only one interval is fairly constant in all females, the time from ovulation (i.e., the release of an egg cell from a mature follicle) to the beginning of menses, which is almost always 14~15 days. The menstrual cycle usually ends when or before a woman reaches her fifties. This is known as menopause.

Male Reproductive System (NIH 2011b)

The male reproductive tract consists of external genitals and internal organs. These organs are located in the pelvic cavity (Fig. 4-6). The male reproductive system begins to develop in response to testosterone during early fetal life. Essentially, no testosterone is produced during childhood. Resumption of testosterone production at the onset of puberty stimulates growth and maturation of the male reproductive structures and secondary sex characteristics. Testosterone is the male sex hormone secreted by the interstitial cells of the testes.

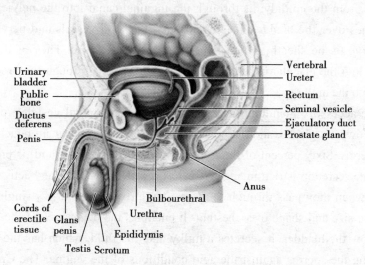

Fig. 4-6   Male reproductive organs (Wikipedia 2005b)

The primary function of the male reproduction system is to produce male sex cells, which are called sperm cells. The primary organs of the male reproductive system are the two testes, where the sperm cells are formed, and the other structures are the duct system and the accessory glandular structure. The testes are two almond-shaped glands whose functions are the production of sperms and testosterone. The testes are suspended in the scrotal sac outside the abdominopelvic cavity. It is believed that the testes lie outside the body cavity because they are very sensitive to heat and the higher temperature in the body is unfavorable for the production of sperm. Each testis is enclosed by a tough, white fibrous capsule called the tunica albuginea. Extension of the capsule divides it into many lobes. Each lobe contains four tightly coiled seminiferous tubules (this is the location of actual sperm production). The seminiferous tubules empty sperms into the testicular network where they travel to the epididymis. The epididymis is located outside of the testis.

The duct system is the passageway for the sperms to exit the body. It contains the epididymis and the vas deferens: the epididymis is a coiled tube about 20 inches long. It caps the superior part of the testis and runs down its posterior side. It forms the first part of the duct system and provides a temporary storage site for immature sperms. When the male is sexually stimulated, the walls of the epididymis contract to expel sperms into the next part of the duct system. The sperms continue their journey through the vas deferens. The vas deferens runs upwards from the epididymis through the inguinal canal into the pelvic cavity and arches over the bladder. It is enclosed with blood vessels and nerves in a connective tissue sheath, which is called a spermatic cord. The vas deferens empties into the ejaculatory duct that carries the sperms through the process to empty into the urethra.

The accessory glandular structure includes the seminal vesicles, prostate gland, Cowper's glands, and the penis: the two seminal vesicles are pouches that store sperms. Sixty percent of fluid volume of semen (seminal fluid) is produced there. The secretion is rich in sugar (fructose), which nourishes and activates the sperms when they pass through the tract. The prostate gland is a single gland about the size and shape of a chestnut. It encircles the upper area of the urethra just below the bladder. It secretes a milky alkaline fluid, which has the role of protecting the sperms against the acid conditions of the vagina. The Cowper's glands are tiny pea-sized glands inferior to the prostate. They form a thick, clear mucus, which drains into the urethra. The secretion is believed to serve primarily as a lubricant during sexual intercourse. And the penis is a cylinder-shaped organ located externally on the mons pubis, immediately above the scrotum. It is made of erectile tissue with cavern-like spaces in it. At the time of sexual excitement, blood fills these spaces, changing the soft, limp penis to an enlarged, rigid, erect organ. The smooth cap of the penis is called the glans penis and is covered by a fold of loose skin that forms the headlock foreskin. Surgical removal of this foreskin, called circumcision, is frequently performed. The penis also serves as part of the urinary tract in the male.

Section 4   Answers to Common Adolescent Concerns

Adolescents in puberty may become concern over the new changes to their body. Through years of global effort, the WHO (2008) identified some common concerns (e.g., delayed puberty) among adolescents and prepared answers accordingly targeting adolescents and their parents. The focus of this section is to present the selected questions and answers surrounding puberty, foreskin, and menstruation from the update WHO document (WHO 2008).

Puberty

As a child becomes an adolescent, the body starts preparing for parenthood. This stage which lasts for two to five years is called puberty. Chemicals produced by the body called hormones, trigger these changes. During puberty, there is an increase in height and weight, and in the musculature. Marked growth and development of the sexual organs is seen, and there are associated changes such as the development of facial and body hair as well as acne.

There is significant variation in the timing of puberty between individuals. Puberty usually begins in boys when they are around 10 years old and lasts till they are 15 or 16 years of age. For most girls, puberty usually begins at around 9 years of age and is usually complete by the age of 14 to 16 years.

Delayed puberty

Puberty is considered later than usual (or is delayed) in a boy when certain changes have not started to occur by a certain age. In males, for example, the sexual organs have not started to develop by the age of 14 or 15 years. In females, the breasts have not started to increase in size before the age of 14 years; there is no appearance of hair near the genital area by the age of 14 years, or periods have not started by the age of 16 years.

The most common cause of delayed puberty is normal variation. Such variation often runs in the family and needs no treatment. However, sometimes poor nutrition or chronic conditions can cause a delay in puberty. It is also important that this is asked about and looked for in history taking and physical examination. When adolescents experience delayed puberty, they may feel anxious and isolated.

Different adolescents go through puberty at different rates depending on their family traits and their nutrition. Almost all adolescents go through the process of puberty with no problems. Health workers should have the capability to do an assessment using some tools or by physical examination, helping adolescents reduce the anxiety caused by delayed puberty. If there exists some underlying problems, referral to specialists is recommended.

Menstrual bleeding

Excessive menstrual bleeding occurs commonly in the first two years after menstruation has started. In most cases, it is not associated with any serious underlying condition. In most cases, heavy menstrual bleeding does not affect adolescents' ability to become pregnant now or in the future. How do we know if the periods are normal? There are three aspects adolescents can keep in mind: Normally periods last between 2~7 days; A 'rule of thumb' is that, normally, seven pads or fewer are soaked daily and need to be changed; and the duration of a cycle is between 21~35 days during adolescence.

Irregular menstrual period

Menstrual periods are irregular when the time between the first day of one period and the first day of the next period is usually less than 21 days or more than 35 days. They are also considered irregular if the time interval between the shortest and the longest menstrual periods differ by more than 20 days (e.g., some periods are 20 days apart, some are 41 days apart). The most common reason for irregular periods is that the body is still developing. After the first period, it takes some time for the periods to become regular. Sometimes irregular periods can be due to malnutrition. Less often, medical conditions, especially those that are related to an imbalance of hormones. Accordingly, if the irregular periods are not associated with underlying causes there are no adverse effects.

If periods are irregular or have stopped due to malnutrition, healthy foods are recommended. If the cause is not due to poor nutrition, referral to a specialist who can advise on appropriate treatment is needed.

Dysmenorrhea

Dysmenorrhea, a very common condition, occurs just before or during the menstrual periods. The pain could be continuous or could come in bouts. It is most severe in the early days of the period and gradually reduces in severity as the period continues. Some adolescent girls may be afraid that something is wrong with the body; while in most cases, the pain is not associated with an underlying medical problem. It is due to a natural chemical substance produced in the body during the periods, which causes the muscles of the uterus to tighten. If the pain is very severe, it may be accompanied by headache, diarrhea, nausea and vomiting. Sometimes it can make it difficult for one to carry out daily activities. It can also affect mood. However, there are no long-term negative effects of the pain or other symptoms.

On account of dysmenorrhea, adolescent girls can take some actions to reduce the pain, e.g., application of hot fomentation like hot water bottle or a warm pad of cloth on the abdomen and back, or taking some medicines to reduce the pain. If the pain is not severe, continuing with daily life will help to focus on other things then soothe the pain. The problem of pain during periods usually declines after childbirth. This is believed to be due to the stretching of the cervix (the mouth of the uterus) during childbirth and the damage to some of the nerve fibers in the area.

Foreskin problems

In contrast to girls' problems related to menstruation, boys show more concern over increased penis and its foreskin. The most common concerns related to external genitalia for male adolescents might be phimosis or paraphimosis. Phimosis is a condition in which the skin in the front of the penis (foreskin) cannot be pushed back or retracted away from the head of the penis, due to the way the foreskin developed, or due to scarring from inflammation or infection. Topical steroids may help to push the foreskin behind the head of penis. If this is a recurrent problem or the medication does not help, referral for circumcision is recommended, which is a surgical procedure to remove the foreskin of the penis.

In comparison, paraphimosis is a condition, in which the foreskin, once pushed back or retracted away from the head of the penis, cannot be pulled forward to its original position over the head of the penis. This may result from the foreskin being forcibly pushed back away from the head of the penis. Paraphimosis may be associated with pain and swelling, and medicines and cold packs will work to reduce the pain and swelling. If pulling the foreskin back over the head of the penis is impossible, surgery is necessary. It is important that this should be treated promptly to avoid any permanent injury to the head of the penis. After the swelling has gone down, circumcision is recommended to prevent this from happening again.

It is important to remind adolescents of the following: when cleaning the penis, gently push the foreskin back to uncover as much of the head of the penis as is comfortably possible and gently wash the head of the penis and the exposed underside of the foreskin; and clean with mild soap and warm water. There may be a little white 'debris' which is normal but also needs to be cleaned and removed. If not doing that, body secretions and urine can accumulate under the foreskin causing irritation and possibly infections as well. When experiencing circumcision, apply soap and wash the penis during the shower or bath, which will help keep it clean. It is important not to use strong chemicals such as disinfectants to clean the penis because these chemicals could damage the delicate skin and result in pain and discomfort.

Certainly there are many others health concerns surrounding the development of external genitalia during adolescence, for example, local pain, sore, or even urination or discharge (vaginal, urinary) problems, which might be the sign of sexually transmitted infections. Concerns in these regards will be answered in the chapter on sexual and reproductive health.

References

Berer M. By and for young women and men[J]. Reproductive Health Matters, 2001, 9(17): 6-10.

Bordini B, Rosenfield RL. Normal pubertal development: Part Ⅱ: Clinical aspects of puberty[J]. Pediatrics in Review, 2011a, 32(7): 281-292.

Bordini B, Rosenfield RL. Normal pubertal development: Part I: The endocrine basis of puberty[J]. Pediatrics in Review, 2011b, 32(6): 223-229.

Brämswig J, Dübbers A. Disorders of pubertal development[J]. Deutsches Ärzteblatt International, 2009, 106(17): 295-304.

Cobb NJ. Adolescence: continuity, change, and diversity[M]. 7th ed. California, America: Mayfield Publishing Company, 2010.

Columbia University. Reproductive Anatomy and Physiology[EB/OL]. Columbia University Mailman School of Public Health, 2 May 2008 [18 Jul. 2011]: http://www.columbia.edu/itc/hs/pubhealth/modules/reproductiveHealth/anatomy.html.

Fleming M, Towey K. Delivering culturally effective health care to adolescents [M/OL]. Chicago, IL: American Medical Association, 2001[23 Jul. 2011]: http://www.ama-assn.org/resources/doc/ad-hlth/culturallyeffective.pdf.

Graber JA, Nichols TR, Brooks-Gunn J. Putting pubertal timing in developmental context: Implications for prevention[J]. Developmental Psychobiology, 2010, 52(3): 254-262.

Hazen E, Schlozman S, Beresin E. Adolescent psychological development: a review[J]. Pediatrics in Review, 2008, 29(5): 161-168.

Morris NM, Udry JR. Validation of a self-administered instrument to assess stage of adolescent development[J]. Journal of Youth and Adolescence, 1980, 9(3): 271-280.

Neinstein LS. Puberty—Normal Growth and Development (A1)[EB/OL]. 2002 [21 Jul. 2011]: http://www.usc.edu/student-affairs/Health_Center/adolhealth/content/a1.html.

NIH. Female Reproductive System[EB/OL]. U.S. Department of Health and Human Services National Institutes of Health, 19 July. 2011 [23 Jul. 2011]: http://www.nlm.nih.gov/medlineplus/femalereproductivesystem.html.

NIH. Male Reproductive System[EB/OL]. U.S. Department of Health and Human Services National Institutes of Health, 19 July. 2011 [23 Jul. 2011]: http://www.nlm.nih.gov/medlineplus/malereproductivesystem.html.

Reilly JJ. Assessment of obesity in children and adolescents: synthesis of recent systematic reviews and clinical guidelines[J]. Journal of Human Nutrition and Dietetics, 2010, 23(3): 205-211.

Simpson AR. Raising teens: a synthesis of research and foundation for action[M/OL]. Boston, Massachusetts: Harvard School of Public Health, 2001[11 May 2011]: http://www.hsph.harvard.edu/chc/parenting/report.pdf.

Steinberg L. Adolescence[M]. 8th. New York: McGraw-Hill, 2008.

Tanner JM. Fetus into man: physical growth from conception to maturity[M/OL]. Revised

Edition. Harvard, Colorado: Harvard University Press, 1990[4 Aug. 2011]: http://www. google.com/books?hl=zh-CN&lr=&id=YxpimctaWd4C&oi=fnd&pg=PA1&dq=Foetus+in to+man:+Physical+growth+from+conception+to+maturity&ots=7tiQkdbK1T&sig=ygsOd w7OqkuMqmDBBXT4yZ8A-7k#v=onepage&q&f=false.

WHO. The Second Decade: improving adolescent health and development[EB/OL]. Department of Child and Adolescent Health and Development, World Health Organization, 2001 [12 Jun. 2011]: http://whqlibdoc.who.int/hq/1998/WHO_FRH_ADH_98.18_Rev.1.pdf.

WHO. Orientation programme on adolescent health for health-care providers[M/OL]. Geneva, Switzerland: World Health Organization, 2006[14 Jun. 2011]: http://whqlibdoc.who.int/ publications/2006/9241591269_Handout_eng.pdf.

WHO. Adolescent Job Aid: a handy desk reference for primary level health worker [M/OL]. WHO, 2008[21 Jul. 2011]: http://www.youthnet.org.hk/adh/4_4Sframework/3_Services_n_ commodities/2_Services/Adolescent%20job%20aid/Adolescent%20Job%20Aid%20-%20 prototype%203.pdf.

WHO. Growth reference data for 5～19 years[EB/OL]. World Health Organization, 2011 [27 Jul. 2011]: http://www.who.int/growthref/en/.

Wikipedia. File:Male reproductive system lateral nolabel.png[EB/OL]. 22 Jul. 2005 [21 Jul. 2011]: http://en.wikipedia.org/wiki/File:Male_reproductive_system_lateral_nolabel.png.

Wikipedia. File:Female reproductive system lateral nolabel.png[EB/OL]. 26 Oct. 2005 [21 Jul. 2011]: http://en.wikipedia.org/wiki/File:Female_reproductive_system_lateral_nolabel. png#file.

Zembar MJ, Blume LB. Middle childhood development: a concextual approach[M]. Upper Saddle River, New Jersey: Pearson Education, 2007.

Chapter 5 Adolescent Psychosocial Development and Health

___Chixun Guan, Miao Huo, Lin Chen, Yunfeng Li, Yongyun Tang___

Psychosocial development is noticeable, like the physical changes during adolescence, representing delicate cerebral development. Stresses increase for adolescents in the face of growth and development, which places adolescents at risk of psychosocial distress or even psychological disorders. This chapter will present the normal psychosocial development as well as common symptoms in relation to mental disorders, moving to a brief introduction to the vague condition of sub-health.

Section 1 Normal Adolescent Psychosocial Development

Adolescence is a life phase between childhood and adulthood, a transition from immaturity to maturity. In this stage, adolescent psychological and physical development have unique characteristics, e.g., multi-faceted psychological development is relatively slower than physical changes, which causes an imbalance between physicality and mentality.

Tasks of adolescent development

Given individual and cultural variability, it is proposed to define adolescence by referral to the tasks of development from distinct domains (e.g., physical, cognitive, psychological, moral) instead of age norms (Hazen et al. 2008). In addition to physical development tasks (e.g., growth spurt, secondary sexual characteristics), major social, emotional and cognitive development tasks during adolescence include: increasing independence and self-regulation (i.e., autonomy), greater sense of personal identity as a sexual being and social identity as a peer and societal member, increased capacity for abstraction, advanced reasoning, risk assessment, and improved language skills (Hazen et

219

al. 2008, Steinberg 2008). Though there exists controversy regarding moral development, it does feature as the stage of adolescence demonstrated through the increased ability to take on others' perspectives, to behave as a good, responsible person guided by abstractive rules and principles (Hart & Carlo 2005, Hazen et al. 2008).

These psychosocial development tasks may appear to be formidable and idealized, but they represent the normal development of adolescent psychology. The following will introduce more about these tasks.

Normal psychosocial development

In adolescence, the major psychological developments include identity, autonomy, and sexuality, which involve the changes in individual's emotions, motivations and behaviours. Although these issues are not unique to adolescence, development in each of these areas takes a special turn during this stage. Understanding how and why such psychological developments take place during adolescence is a special concern of healthcare providers.

Identity development

Identity means the domain of psychological development involving self-conceptions, self-esteem and the sense of who one is. Identity development begins with children's awareness that they are separate and unique individuals and proceeds at approximately the same pace throughout adolescence. It includes the following: What his or her strong points and weaknesses are; ideas about his or her relationship to society (that is, what he or she can expect from it and what it can expect from him or her); ideas about his or her sexual role, and the formulation of a life plan (what niche both personal and occupationally he will occupy as an adult). During this time, an adolescent may wonder who he or she really is and where he or she is headed, this is a time of attempting to discover one's true self (Meeus et al. 1999). Adolescents' description of self expands to include personality traits and attitudes, such as "I'm outgoing" or "I don't like stuck-up people" (Ruffin 2009, Perkins 2008).

Referring to identity development, Erickson's psychosocial theory states that human beings develop according to a pre-set plan which consists of two main elements. First, personality develops according to a predetermined pattern that is maturationally set. Second, each society is structured to encourage challenges that arise during these times (Lewis 1991).

According to Erikson's theory, individuals proceed through eight stages of development which begin at birth and conclude at death. If a particular crisis is handled appropriately, the outcome will be positive. If not, then a negative outcome will be the result. The two stages which involve conflicts that significantly affect early and late adolescent development are stage 4, the latency state (ages 6~11), and stage 5, puberty and adolescence (ages 12~18). Adolescents begin to consider their futures and decide on careers. During this stage they face the conflict of identity versus role confusion. If adolescents formulate a satisfying plan of action about their future, then the outcome is positive and establishment of identity is achieved. Adolescents who do not develop this sense of identity may develop role confusion and aimlessly move through life without any plan of action or sense of security about their future.

From other papers, we know that as individuals mature intellectually and undergo cognitive changes, they come to conceive of themselves in more sophisticated and more differentiated ways. Some adolescents are very conscious of their appearance and inner-self, some may have a high self-esteem, but sometimes their self-confidence is not sufficient and they will easily develop a feeling of inferiority. Also, adolescents tend to imitate certain kinds of people or worship idols in the process of exploring self-identity.

Meanwhile, adolescents may become trendy to acquire peer's acceptance. Sometimes they would even give up or change some of their previous views, behaviours and standards to become similar to their peers, such as becoming materialistic, coveting famous brands, worshipping idols, etc. (School Health Service, SHS 2011).

In addition, an adolescent may pay attention to future orientation, hoping himself or herself able and inclined to think about the potential consequences of decisions and choices. The emergence of abstract reasoning abilities allows adolescents to think about the future and experiment with different identities (SHS 2011).

Autonomy development

During adolescence, there is a movement away from the dependency typical of childhood and toward the autonomy typical of adulthood. For most adolescents, establishing a sense of autonomy is as important a part of becoming an adult as establishing a sense of identity. Becoming an autonomous person—a self-governing person—is one of the fundamental developmental tasks of adolescence, and this process is gradual, progressive, important and relatively undramatic (Zimberoff & Hartman 2000).

Adolescents may seek to question parents' and teachers' authority. But the growth of autonomy during adolescence is frequently misunderstood. Autonomy is often confused with rebellion, and becoming an independent person is often equated with breaking away from the family and building up their own style in this stage (SHS 2011).

Characteristics of autonomy include: 1) emotional autonomy, which is related to changes in the individual's close relationships, especially with parents, 2) behavioural autonomy—the capacity to make independent decisions and follow through on them, 3) value autonomy, which is more than simply being able to resist pressures to go along with the demands of others; it means having a set of principles about right and wrong, about what is important and what is not.

Cognitive development

According to Jean Piaget's cognitive development theory, children progress through four stages in their cognitive development: serimotor (birth to 2 years of age), pre-operational (2 to 7 years of age), concrete operational (7 to 11 years of age) and formal operational (11 to 15 years of age). Each of these stages represents a qualitative leap forward in the child's ability to solve problems and reason logically. The transition from concrete thinking to formal logical operations occurs over time (Lewis 1991).

These advances in thinking process (also called formal logical operations) can be divided into several areas (Ruffin 2009, Perkins 2008, Lucile Salter Packard Children's Hospital 2011): **Abstract thinking** means thinking about things that can't be seen, heard, or touched. Examples include things like faith, trust, beliefs and spirituality. **Reasoning** includes the ability to think about multiple options and possibilities. It includes a more logical thought process and the ability to think about things hypothetically. It involves asking and answering the question, "what if...?" **Ability to think about thinking** is a process known as "meta-cognition". Meta-cognition allows individuals to think about how they feel and what they are thinking. It involves being able to think about how one is perceived by others.

It can also be used to develop strategies, also known as mnemonic devices, for improving learning. Remembering the notes on the lines of a music staff (e, g, b, d, and f) through the phrase "every good boy does fine" is an example of such a mnemonic device.

During this period, adolescents often have conducts like "**Argue for the sake of arguing**" reported by United States Department of Education and American Psychological Association (U.S. Department of Education 2003, American Psychological Association 2002). More details are provided as follows: persistent arguing and pretended wisdom are characteristic features of adolescents. They often go off on tangents, seeming to argue side issues for no apparent reason; this can be highly frustrating to many adults. Keep in mind that, for adolescents, they need the opportunity to practice with these new reasoning skills, which can be exhilarating. **Jump to conclusions.** The early adolescents, even with their newfound capacities for logical thinking, sometimes jump to startling conclusions. With the further development of cognition, the older adolescents are able to suppress impulsive behaviours and be able to manage increasingly sophisticated social situations. **Be self-centered**. Adolescents tend to believe that everyone is as concerned with their thoughts and behaviours as they are. This leads the adolescents to believe that they have an "imaginary audience" of people that are always watching them. On the other hand, the adolescents can be very "me-centered". It takes time to learn to take others' perspectives into account; in fact, this is a skill that can be learned. **Constantly find fault in the adult's position.** The adolescents begin to question adult (especially parental) authority and society standards. Sometimes they will openly question or criticize adults with whom they feel especially safe. They no longer automatically look up to people in authority, but are more selective, giving respect to those they feel deserved. They invariably will resist parental influence and suggestions. **Be overly dramatic**. Everything seems to be a "big deal" to teenagers. For some adolescents, being overly dramatic or exaggerating their opinions and behaviours simply comes with the territory.

Given that physical changes and sexual perspective on puberty and health-risk behaviours are presented in other chapters, Table 5-1 lists major psychosocial changes across three stages of adolescence to help reach an overall and relative simpler understanding (Spano 2004).

Table 5-1　stages of adolescent psychological development (Spano 2004)

Stages of Adolescent Development	Early Adolescence (10~14 years old)	Middle Adolescence (15~16 years old)	Late Adolescence (17~21 years old)
Identity Development and Movement Toward Independence	Emerging identity shaped by in/external influences; moodiness; improved speech to express oneself; more likely to express feelings by action than by words (may be more true for males); close friendships gain importance; less attention shown to parents, with occasional rudeness; realization parents not perfect; identification of own faults; search for new people to love in addition to parents; tendency to return to childish behaviour during times of stress; peer group influence on personal interests and clothing styles.	Self-involvement, alternating between unrealistically high expectations and worries about failure; complaints that parents interfere with independence; extremely concerned with appearance and body; feelings of strangeness about one's self and body; lowered opinion of and withdrawal from parents; effort to make new friends; strong emphasis on the new peer group; periods of sadness as the psychological loss of parents takes place; examination of inner experiences, which may include writing a diary.	Firmer identity; ability to delay gratification; ability to think through ideas; ability to express ideas in words; more developed sense of humor; interests and emotions become more stable; ability to make independent decisions; ability to compromise; pride in one's work; self reliance; greater concern for others.
Future Interests and Cognitive Development	Increasing career interests; mostly interested in present and near future; greater ability to work.	Intellectual interests gain importance; some sexual and aggressive energy directed into creative and career interests; anxiety can emerge related to school and academic performance.	More defined work habits; higher level of concern for the future; thoughts about one's role in life.

Continue

Stages of Adolescent Development	Early Adolescence (10~14 years old)	Middle Adolescence (15~16 years old)	Late Adolescence (17~21 years old)
Ethics and Self-Direction	Rule and limit testing; experimentation with cigarettes, marijuana, and alcohol; capacity for abstract thought.	Development of ideals and selection of role models; more consistent evidence of conscience; greater goal setting capacity; interest in moral reasoning.	Useful insight; focus on personal dignity and self-esteem; ability to set goals and follow through; acceptance of social institutions and cultural traditions; self-regulation of self esteem.

Conflicts during adolescence

Conflicts often arise when inner or external dissonance or disagreement occurs. The significant physical and psychosocial changes pose great challenges to adolescents themselves and those around them, which in turn may influence adolescent development. Ni (2010) summarizes the types of conflicts occurring in adolescence as a follow:

(1) Conflict between adult feeling in mentality and half maturity in physicality, which was caused mainly by physical growth and sexual maturity. Adolescents regard themselves as adults, but their psychological level is still in the transitional stage between the children and the adults;

(2) Conflict between independence and dependence. Feeling self-independent develops rapidly in adolescences: they revolt against the attachment relations with the adult. Along with immature psychology, they cannot solve problems comprehensively, hoping that they can gain support from adults when facing difficulty;

(3) Conflict between being closed and open. The secondary sexual characteristic brings the mystical feeling to youths; they are no longer as frank as before. Meanwhile, they feel lonely, hoping that people care about them;

(4) Conflict between self-abasement and self-conceited. With the limitation of adolescent self-cognitive level, they often rely on temporary feelings to appraise themselves, their mood fluctuates. An accidental success can cause them to feel infallible, and the occasional defeat will also make them suspect themselves,

leading to mood fluctuation;

(5) Conflict between adolescent spurt and social norms. Sexual maturity bring puzzles to adolescents, they admire the opposite sex and have the desire to pursue. But traditional and modern standards often conflict, they cannot coordinate the relationship between sexual strength and social norms.

Section 2　Common Mental Health Concerns

During adolescence, some stressors coupled with changing peer and family interactions, may lead in some cases to mental disorders, such as depression, suicidal thoughts, and anxiety. According to Warren and Broome (2011), the incidence of adolescent psychological disorders is estimated at 10% and the peak time for onset is 14 years old. In China, the ratio is approximately 12.97% in children between 4 to 16 years old (Jing 2010). Understanding the characteristics of adolescent psychosocial development and identifying the signs and symptoms of mental health disorders are important because early intervention is critical to restore adolescent health and to prevent lifelong consequences (Whitlock & Schantz 2008).

Depression

Depression is now recognized as a diagnosable disorder in adolescents. Generally, the proportion of individuals who experience major depression at some points during adolescence ranges from 15% to 20 % (Martin & Milot 2007). It can be defined as feeling sad, hopeless, and (or) unmotivated for at least two weeks or more. It is important to recognize depression because it can lead to suicidal thoughts or attempts, but it is treatable.

Some people who are severely depressed may have suicidal thoughts or may even create a plan to commit suicide. Others will follow through with their plan. Suicide is the third leading cause of death among children and youth, 5 to 24 years old (Martin & Milot 2007). Although females are more likely to be depressed and attempt suicide, males are much more likely to commit suicide.

Adolescents may not show all the symptoms of depression. The most common emotional symptoms include: feeling sad, anxious, or irritable, feeling hopeless or worthless (Liu 2005), a loss of interest in activities or hobbies, a loss of energy and concentration, changes in eating and sleeping patterns, suicidal thoughts or attempts (Martin & Milot 2007). If adolescents want to commit suicide, they also give or throw away favorite belongings, mention the fact that they want to commit suicide, expose themselves to some friends or family who have committed or attempted suicide (Martin & Milot 2007).

When an adolescent is suspected to be experiencing depression, healthcare workers may advise: a. improving family communication: This is to address potentially mental disorders in the context of the family, and is a key to humane care. Improving communication about emotions and involving adolescents in the family in meaningful ways can reduce the consequences of isolation that lead to adverse outcomes (WHO 2003); b. developing self-esteem and self-confidence: Self-esteem is how much persons value themselves and self-confidence, and is the belief in their own ability. Persons with good self-esteem and self-confidence are sure of their own value and strengths and do not fear others knowing their shortcomings (Wang 2005). Adolescents with depression always lack self-esteem and self-confidence, therefore healthcare workers should manage to encourage them to appreciate their strengths, recognize their values, accept themselves, explore their potentia/s, rectify their shortcomings, avoid comparison with others and never fear failure; c. control emotions properly: Adolescence is a period of rapid growing development with stronger and quicker emotional fluctuations (Yan 2009). Healthcare workers can encourage adolescents to express and manage their emotions appropriately. For instance, tell them to express their feelings and analyze the cause of such feelings objectively, such as "I'm very angry because my schoolmates laughed at my shortness", "I'm happy because I made progress in my study".

As a potential concern in association with depression, suicide is among the top 20 leading causes of death globally for all ages and is a global health problem. Every year, nearly one million people die from suicide, 10~20 million attempt suicides, and 50~120 million are profoundly affected by suicide or attempted suicide of a close relative or associate (Hendin et al. 2008). In China, stress and depression cause 70%~80% of suicide in urban area (Centerstone 2008). Mental illness, primarily depression and alcohol use disorders, abuse, violence, loss, cultural and social background, represent major risk factors for suicide.

If healthcare workers suspect an adolescent is contemplating suicide, the National Alliance on Mental Illness (NAMI) recommends that (Martin & Milot 2007): Health care workers should seek professional care for the adolescent immediately. If the threat is immediate, take the adolescent to the nearest emergency room. Do not assume that adolescents who talk about killing themselves will not go through with it. Approximately 80% of all those who commit suicide give some type of warning or message to others. Never assume that someone who is suicidal cannot be helped. Do not be afraid to talk to the adolescent about his or her suicidal thoughts – mentioning the act of suicide will not cause suicide. Open and supportive discussion can help someone contemplating suicide know he or she is being taken seriously and listened to.

Anxiety

Anxiety is defined as having excessive and uncontrollable feelings of fear or nervousness about a future event or an actual situation (Chen 2005). While a small amount of anxiety or stress can be beneficial for development, it becomes a problem if the anxiety is developmentally inappropriate or prevents or limits appropriate behaviour.

Anxiety disorders are the most common mental health problem among children and adolescents. About 13% of children and adolescents between the ages of 9 and 17 experience some kind of anxiety disorders. In general, females are more affected than males (Martin & Milot 2007).

Some of the more common symptoms include but are not limited to extreme, unrealistic worry about everyday activities, such as academic, sport, or social situations, extreme feelings of self-consciousness, tenseness, and a strong need for reassurance, physical ailments, such as stomachaches or other discomforts, panic attacks – periods of intense fear usually involves a pounding heartbeat, sweating, dizziness, nausea, or a feeling of imminent death (Martin & Milot 2007).

When an adolescent is suspected to be experiencing anxiety, healthcare workers may advise the adolescent to control emotions properly, and actions recommended to be undertaken by adolescents may include (Wang & Zhang 2005): a. move away temporarily from the persons or things causing conflict, e.g., go to wash face or drink a glass of water; b. calm down first, analyze the causes of conflicts and then try to shift attention to other things temporarily, or try something relaxing (e.g., listening to music, doing exercises); c. build up a supporting network by talking to others proactively, sharing worries with parents, teachers, schoolmates and friends. Ideally adolescents are guided to understand that there are always ups and downs in life, and it is better to open up feelings, develop an optimistic outlook on life, and never give up hope for the present and future by indulging in the past.

Stressful conditions, sources of anxiety, are inevitable and unpredictable for adolescents in the face of the transition from childhood to adulthood. Gu (2006) proposed a series of methods to prevent the occurrence of stress: a. manage time properly by handling things gradually and step by step or avoiding hasty actions; b. try best without unnecessary worries; c. keep body and mind healthy through maintaining a balanced diet, having sufficient sleep, keeping regular hours, doing appropriate amounts of exercise, developing healthy hobbies, and making good use of leisure time and be optimistic; d. broaden horizon and be well-equipped by reading more books, paying more attention to things around them, and listening to others' experiences and opinions to enhance skills and increase resources to solve problems; and e. establish good interpersonal relationships using proactive communication with others and through strengthening supporting networks.

Alternative ways to be used to relieve stresses include: a. forget frustration temporarily and engage in some leisure activities, such as sports, listening to music, painting; b. talk to people proactively; c. find out the sources of stress; and try different practical solutions and face problem proactively and optimistically (Gu 2006).

Psychotic disorders

Psychotic disorders are severe mental disorders that cause abnormal thinking and perceptions. People with psychosis lose touch with reality, during which delusions, hallucinations and thought disorder may occur (Gelder et al. 2005).

Many studies have shown that the prevalence of psychotic disorders in the whole world varies between 2% and 16% (Zhang 2010), and these disorders usually begin at the age of 12 to 18 (Wang 2005). As psychotic disorders have dramatic impact on an individual, his or her family and the society, attention should be paid to identify the symptoms as early as possible. Identification of psychotic disorders can be drawn from the common symptoms, including delusion, hallucination and thought disorders.

Delusions

Delusions are defined to be false beliefs, such as thinking that someone is plotting against somebody or that the TV is sending secret messages. In psychiatry, it is defined to be a belief that is pathological (the result of an illness or illness process) and is held despite evidence to the contrary (Ellis 2007).

Delusions typically occur in the context of neurological or mental illness, although they are not tied to any particular disease and have been found to occur in the context of many pathological states (both physical and mental) (Matthew & Lisa 2009). However, they are of particular diagnostic importance in psychotic disorders including schizophrenia, paraphrenia, and psychotic depression.

Hallucination

Hallucination is defined as sensory perception in the absence of external stimuli. Hallucinations are different from illusions, or perceptual distortions, which are the misperception of external stimuli (Harper 2010). Hallucinations may occur in any of the five senses and take on almost any form, which may include simple sensations (such as lights, colors, tastes, and smells) to more meaningful experiences such as seeing and interacting with fully formed animals and people, hearing voices, and having complex tactile sensations.

Auditory hallucinations, particularly experiences of hearing voices, are a common and often prominent feature of psychosis. Hallucinated voices may talk about, or to the person, and may involve several speakers with distinct personas. Auditory hallucinations tend to be particularly distressing when they are derogatory, commanding or preoccupying. However, the experience of hearing voices need not always be a negative one. One study has shown that the majority of people who hear voices are not in need of psychiatric help (Honig et al. 1998). The Hearing Voices Movement has subsequently been created to support voice hearers, regardless of whether they are considered to have a mental illness or not.

Thought disorder

Thought disorder describes an underlying disturbance to conscious thought and is classified largely by its effects on speech and writing (Metsänen et al. 2004). Affected persons show loosening of associations, that is, a disconnection and disorganization of the semantic content of speech and writing. In the severe form, speech becomes incomprehensible and it is known as "word-salad". For example, language may be difficult to understand if it switches quickly from one unrelated idea to other or if it is long-winded and quite delayed at reaching its goal or if words are inappropriately strung together resulting in gibberish

(Wikipedia 2011a).

Thought is revealed through speech, observation of patterns of thought naturally involves close observation of the speech of the individual being considered. Possible signs and symptoms of thought disorder may include: 1) Blocking, which is interruption of train of speech before completion, some individuals even cannot recall the topic he or she was discussing. 2) Distractible speech, which means the subject changed in response to a stimulus during mid speech. 3) Echolalia, this may involve echoing of one's or other people's speech that may only be committed once, or may be continuous in repetition, either only the last few words or last word of the examiner's sentences. 4) Perseveration, which means persistently repeating words or ideas (Wikipedia 2011a).

Schizophrenia

Schizophrenia is one of several typical psychotic disorders, often demonstrated through delusion, hallucinations and thought disorders. The onset of symptoms often occurs in young adulthood, with a global lifetime prevalence of about 0.3%~0.7% (van Os & Kapur 2009). A study conducted in 12 areas between 1982 and 1985 showed that the point prevalence rate among schizophrenia patients over 15 years old is 4.75‰ (Ding 2010). Here below (see Box 5-1) is a case example to help the identification of schizophrenia with typical symptoms.

Box 5-1   A case with schizophrenia

Patient LM., a 17 year female unmarried girl was admitted into female psychiatry ward through emergency with complaints of self withdrawn behaviour with self smiling, occasional aggressive behaviour, talking out of context for last ten days. Her history of present illness shows lack of interest in daily household activities with the presence of inflated self esteem with rapidly changing grandiose ideas to the extent of disturbing her social and interpersonal functioning with presence of some odd behaviours like separating garbage into different categories, staring at a particular direction while working reluctantly and speaking unusual things like "she is all powerful and everyone should follow her advice" or "she can destroy the universe with powers bestowed on her by goddess Durga". Her biological functions were altered specially sleep and appetite.

It has to be emphasized that symptoms associated with schizophrenia occur along a continuum in the population and a certain severity must be reached before any diagnosis is made. The diagnosis of schizophrenia should only be made by a mental health professional. Its prevention is somewhat difficult since there are no reliable markers for the development of the disease. Once being diagnosed with schizophrenia, family therapy, assertive community treatment, supported employment, cognitive remediation, skills training, cognitive behavioural therapy, antipsychotic medications or even hospitalization is necessary (Wikipedia 2011b).

Section 3   Sub-health

It is not the case in real life that a person is either absolutely healthy or unhealthy. In the mid-1980s, Prof. Buurman, a scholar from the former Soviet Union, proposed the term of 'sub-health' to describe the edge condition between health and disease (Liang 2009). People with this condition presented neither health nor sickness, but had the bilateral tendencies to convert this condition either to health or to disease. Early detection and intervention could effectively prevent the diseases from happening and improve the quality of life.

Evolution of the concept

In 1995, the broad sub-health concept was confirmed in the conference of the First Sub-health Seminar held in Beijing and it defined sub-health as a transitional condition from the health to disease. Afterwards many scholars described concepts of sub-health as under this condition: There are no apparent diseases found but there are high risks of developing some kind of diseases. Ye Fang described in his Ph.D scientific dissertation that sub-health is a dynamic condition and to some extent it could cause the decline of physiological function, psychological function and social adaptation, but it has not yet reached the diagnostic criteria of any diseases (Ye 2008). There are some terms which are similar to sub-health like chronic fatigue syndrome (CFS) and sub-threshold psychiatric disorders found in the related studies in western countries and Japan.

Incidence

The morbidity of CFS has been steadily increasing in adolescents especially after 11 years old (Chalder et al. 2003). Sub-threshold psychiatric disorders could occur at any ages. According to the studies done by Chinese scholars, there were high incidences of depression among adolescents. In the studies, they found that female students had more symptoms of depression than male students in rural high schools in Hunan Province (Luo et al. 2008). The detected incidence of depression symptoms in students were 11.9% and 8.2% (Xu et al. 2008) respectively in the study of primary schools in Hefei and primary schools in Shenzhen. There are approximately 30 000 adolescents now under sub-health condition according to the study done by the China Association of Prenatal and Postnatal Care in 22 provinces and cities in 2008. The detected incidence of sub-health was 9.5% in another national study on making norms of sub-health for adolescents (Tao et al. 2009).

Hazards

Sub-health affects adolescents in many ways. The anorexia and metabolism disorders could lead the adolescents to malnutrition and thus affect the development of bones and nerves. While the negative moods like pessimism, impatience, low interests could cause unconfident, suspicious and stubborn personality. According to the literature, CFS now has become the main factor for adolescents being unable to maintain a normal daily life and school study, thus it has produced many negative influences and has increased the medical costs (Richards et al. 2005). A study indicated that sub-threshold psychiatric disorders was the prelude of mental disorders and can cause many general mental diseases (Cuijpers & Smit 2004). In conclusion, sub-health can cause many risks to adolescents in the aspects of physiology, psychology, mental and social adaptation.

Assessment

Under the sub-health condition, there are no organic diseases, but the body functions are affected and the adolescents have the notable decline of immunity, physical adaptability and physiological endurance (Briggs & Levine 1994). There are many physical symptoms like sleeplessness, fatigue, weakness and the decline of sexual function, psychological symptoms such as 'blue' mood, low spirits and memory impairment and other social-related problems like coldness, helplessness and loneliness.

Currently there are no approved diagnostic criteria and classification system for sub-health condition. Some countries like US, Australia, the United Kingdom and Japan have made their own diagnostic criteria regarding the physiological sub-health for CFS. But there are some differences between these criteria. According to American diagnostic criteria, if people decrease their activities of daily life to about 50%, it is considered as physiological sub-health while the Great Britain and Australia state that the fatigue should be very severe in their diagnostic criteria for sub-health. There are a few studies about the diagnostic criteria regarding the psychological aspects of sub-health. Judd (Judd et al. 1994, 1997) proposed the concept of sub-general depression which was one of the manifestations of sub-threshold psychiatric disorders. Sub-general depression was defined as approximately 20%~30% population having depression symptoms and these symptoms might affect people's occupational and social function but the dysfunctions have not yet reached to the diagnostic criteria for depression. There are no universal diagnostic criteria established for sub-health currently. Chinese scholars mostly adopt the self-assessment methods and their own definitions to evaluate the sub-health condition, so the results of their studies are significantly different, thus it is difficult to make comparisons horizontally. Now it is very necessary to derive international criteria for evaluation and classification of sub-health condition.

In China, currently the most approved scale for adolescents sub-health evaluation tool is Multidimensional Sub-health Questionnaire of Adolescents (MSQA, Qi et al. 2009). MSQA was compiled and innovated by the research group led by Professor Tao Fangbiao of Anhui Medical University. The reliability and validity of MSQA were very good (Xing et al. 2008) and the retest correlation coefficient, Cronbach's α coefficient and split-half reliability coefficient of the questionnaire was 0.868, 0.957, 0.942 respectively. Taking SCL-90 and Cornell Medical Index (CMI) as criteria, the criterion-related validity was 0.636, 0.649 respectively.

Professor Tao and his research team also developed the national norm for adolescents on the basis of describing the distribution characteristics of physical and psychological sub-health (Tao et al. 2009). They took a sample of 22 325 students chosen from middle schools and high schools in 9 cities of 9 provinces. The MSQA was used for self-rating, and calculated the values of P_{85}, P_{90}, and P_{95} related to physical and psychological domains and six dimensions. Results of this study showed no significant gender difference in the incidence of physical, psychological and total sub-health, but there was significant difference in grades. Based on the study results, they proposed P_{90} as the demarcation value for physical, psychological and total sub-health of different grades and it can be used as epidemiological criteria for sub-health study of adolescents in China. According to this study, the detailed demarcation values for evaluating sub-health in adolescents were published. It included the total 11 symptoms of sub-health in which there were 3 body sub-health symptoms and 8 psychiatric sub-health symptoms respectively. Many subsequent studies indicated that the sub-health condition for adolescents was related to their life satisfaction and some risk behaviours like suicide and self-injuries. Moreover, the demarcation value also could make prognosis for adolescents in the areas like class absence rates, tobacco and alcohol use, the ideas of suicide and some self-injuries (Wan 2009).

The MSQA scale was applied widely after it was published. The study on Wenzhou university students done by Xu Changen (Xu et al. 2010) showed that the detected incidence of adolescents sub-health was 9.3% while the study of Ezhou middle school students and university students done by Liao Xuedan (Liao et al. 2010) showed that approximately 42.7% adolescents were under sub-health condition. Tu Chunyu (Tu et al. 2010) found the physical and psychological symptoms of sub-health were slightly lower than the average national norm in the study of adolescents at Shaoxing universities, high schools and secondary schools. Shao Jixiao (Shao et al. 2011) found that the detected incidences of physical, psychological and physio-psychological sub-health were 13.8%, 13.8%, and 12.6% respectively. In general, MSQA is widely applied in the adolescents' evaluation for sub-health, but it is still at the initial stage. The results are significantly different, so more studies with broad scope are needed to testify its validity.

Interventions

Prompt intervention for sub-health could promote the physiological and psychological development of adolescents. Researchers in some western countries suggested that the sub-health condition should be treated if there were some presenting symptoms (Fulcher & White 1997). In China, Professor Tao Fangbiao (Tao 2009) proposed that the early detection of sub-health should be included in the school health service. Mr. Wang Jinbiao (Wang 2008) found that the sub-health condition of Shanghai University students were related to sports, sleep, diet and leisure model thus they could improve their health level by doing appropriate sports, taking reasonable diet and raising good leisure habits. A traditional Chinese medicine (TCM) study by Liang Xinghua (Liang 2009) found that Chinese traditional herbs could improve the people's health in the aspects of body, psychology and sociology.

Sub-health is a relatively new concept but it is gradually valued by the public and academic researchers. Currently its definition and classification are not clearly defined and the criteria for evaluating and intervening system have not been established universally, especially for adolescents' sub-health condition. It still needs more studies to set its own evaluation and intervention criteria to promote the adolescents health.

References

American Psychological Association. Developing adolescents: a reference for professionals[EB/OL]. American Psychological Association, 2002 [24 Jun. 2011]: http://www.apa.org/pi/pii/develop.pdf.

Briggs NC, Levine PH. A comparative review of systemic and neurological symptomatology in 12 outbreaks collectively described as chronic fatigue syndrome, epidemic neuromyasthenia, and myalgic encephalomyelitis[J]. Clinical infectious diseases.1994, 18 (Suppl 1): S32-S42.

Centerstone. The international crisis intervention symposium[EB/OL]. 30 Jun. 2008 [26 Jun. 2011]: http://wenku.baidu.com/view/8a7ee1649b6648d7c1c746ab.html.

Chalder T, Goodman R, Wessely S, et al. Epidemiology of chronic fatigue syndrome and self reported myalgic encephalomyelitis in 5-15 year olds: cross sectional study[J]. British Medical Journal, 2003, 327(7416): 654-655.

Chen YF. Psychiatric nursing[M]. Beijing, China: People's Medical Publishing House, 2005.

Cuijpers P, Smit F. Subthreshold depression as a risk indicator for major depressive disorder: a systematic review of prospective studies[J]. Acta Psychiatr Scand, 2004, 109(5): 325-331.

Ding D. What is schizophrenia?[EB/OL]. Shandong Red Cross Hospital, 4 Mar. 2010 [25 Jun. 2011]: http://www.sdsmyy.com/jingshenfenlie/leixing/201003041200.shtml.

Ellis HD. Delusions: a suitable case for imaging?[J]. International Journal of Psychophysiology, 2007, 63(2): 146-151.

Fulcher KY, White PD. Randomised controlled trial of graded exercise in patients with the chronic fatigue syndrome[J]. British Medical Journal, 1997, 314(7095): 1647-1652.

Gelder M, Mayou R, Geddes J. Psychiatry[M]. New York: Oxford University Press, 2005.

Gu MS. Personality psychology[M]. Beijing, China: Chinese medicine science and technology press, 2006.

Harper D. Online Etymology Dictionary: Hallucination[EB/OL]. [24 Jun. 2011]: http://www.etymonline.com/index.php?search=Hallucination&searchmode=none.

Hart D, Carlo G. Moral development in adolescence[J]. Journal of Research on Adolescence, 2005, 15(3): 223-233.

Hazen E, Schlozman S, Beresin E. Adolescent psychological development: a review[J]. Pediatrics in Review, 2008, 29(5): 161-168.

Hendin H, Phillips MR, Vijayakumar L, et al. Introduction: suicide and suicide prevention in Asia[M/OL]. Geneva, Switzerland: Department of Mental Health and Substance Abuse, World Health Organization, 2008[26 Jun. 2011]: http://www.who.int/mental_health/resources/suicide_prevention_asia/en/.

Honig A, Romme MAJ, Ensink BJ, et al. Auditory hallucinations: a comparison between patients and nonpatients[J]. The Journal of Nervous and Mental Disease, 1998, 186(10): 646-651.

Jing J. Main mental health problems and strategy for children and adolescents in China[J]. Chinese Mental Health Journal, 2010, 24(5): 321-324.

Judd LL, Paulus MP, Brown JL. Subsyndromal symptomatic depression: a new mood disorder?[J]. J Clin Psychiatry, 1994, 55 (Suppl 4): 18-28.

Judd LL, Akiskal HS, Paulus MP. The role and clinical significance of subsyndromal depressive symptoms (SSD) in unipolar major depressive disorder[J]. Journal of Affective Disorders, 1997, 45(1): 5-18.

Lewis J. The Physiological and Psychological Development of the Adolescent[EB/OL]. Yale-New Haven Teachers Institute, 1991 [7 Jul. 2011]: http://www.yale.edu/ynhti/curriculum/units/1991/5/91.05.07.x.html.

Liang XH. The initial reserach of present sub-health condition in Hong Kong[D]. Nanjing: Nanjing University of Chinese Medicine, 2009.

Liao XZ, Zhang J, Zhang LM, et al. The situation and risk factors of sub-health status of adolescents in Ezhou City[J]. Chinese Journal of Social Medicine, 2011, 27(1): 8-10.

Liu XM. Abnormal Psychology[M]. 1st ed. Beijing, China: Chinese medicine science and technology press, 2005.

Lucile Salter Packard Children's Hospital. Cognitive Development [EB/OL]. Lucile Salter Packard Children's Hospital, [24 Jun. 2011]: http://www.lpch.org/DiseaseHealthInfo/HealthLibrary/adolescent/cogdev.html.

Luo YZ, Wang X, Zhu XZ, et al. Levels of depression symptoms and the risk factors of anxiety in high school students[J]. Chinese Journal of Clinical Psychology, 2008, 16(3): 274-277.

Martin L, Milot A. Assessing the mental health of adolescents: a guide for out-of-school time program practitioners[EB/OL]. Child Trends, Mar. 2007 [18 Jul. 2011]: http://www. childtrends.org/files/mentalhealth.pdf.

Matthew RB, Lisa B. Mental Illness as Mental: In Defence of Psychological Realism[J/OL]. Humana Mente, 2009, (11): 25-43 [25 Jun. 2011]: http://www.humanamente.eu/PDF/ Issue11_Paper_Bortolotti_Broome.pdf.

Meeus W, Iedema J, Helsen M, et al. Patterns of adolescent identity development: review of literature and longitudinal analysis[J]. Developmental Review, 1999, 19(4): 419-461.

Metsänen M, Wahlberg K-E, Saarento O, et al. Early presence of thought disorder as a prospective sign of mental disorder[J]. Psychiatry research, 2004, 125(3): 193-203.

Ni JM. Psychological conflicts in adolescence[EB/OL]. Tonglu Ye Qian Yu Middle School, 13 Sep. 2010 [25 Jun. 2011]: http://www.yqyzx.com/Moral/ShowArticle.asp?ArticleID=209.

Perkins DF. Adolescence: developmental tasks[EB/OL]. University of Florida IFAS Extension, 2008 [24 Jun. 2011]: http://www.education.com/reference/article/Ref_Developmental_ Tasks/.

Qi XY, Tao FB, Hu CL, et al. Study on multidimensional sub-health questionnaire of adolescents[J]. Chinese Journal of Public Health, 2008, 24(9): 1025-1028.

Richards J, Turk J, White S. Children and adolescents with chronic fatigue syndrome in non-specialist settings[J]. European Child & Adolescent Psychiatry, 2005, 14(6): 310-318.

Ruffin N. Adolescent Growth and development [EB/OL]. Virginia Cooperative Extension, 1 May 2009 [25 Jun. 2011]: http://pubs.ext.vt.edu/350/350-850/350-850.html.

Shao JX, Wang H, Li LL. Study on sub-health of adolescents in Chongqing[J]. Modern Preventive Medicine, 2011, 38(9): 1667-1669.

Spano S. Stages of adolescent development[J/OL]. 2004 [23 Jul. 2011]: http://ecommons. cornell.edu/bitstream/1813/19311/2/StagesAdol_chart.pdf.

Steinberg L. Adolescence[M]. 8th ed. New York: McGraw-Hill, 2008.

Student Health Service. Psychological Health of Adolescents[EB/OL]. Department of Health, the Goverment of the Hong Kong Special Administrative Region, 5 Jul. 2011 [7 Jul. 2011]: http://www.studenthealth.gov.hk/english/health/health_ph/health_ph_young.html.

Tao FB. Early detection and intervention in adolescent sub, new areas of school health services[J]. Chinese Journal of School Health, 2009, 30(4): 290-291.

Tao FB, Xing C, Yuan CJ, et al. Development of national norm for Multidimensional Sub-health Questionnaire of Adolescents[J]. Chinese Journal of School Health, 2009, 30(4):

292-295.

Tu CY, Xing C, Fu LJ, et al. Study on the cut-off point of sub-health status among adolescent students in Shaoxing[J]. Chinese Journal of School Health, 2010, 31(12): 1415-1419.

U.S. Department of Education. My child's academic success: how can I help my child to become more confident[EB/OL]. U.S. Department of Education, 11 Sep. 2003 [24 Jun. 2011]: http://www.ed.gov/parents/academic/help/adolescence/part8.html.

Van Os J, Kapur S. Schizophrenia[J]. The Lancet, 2009, 374(9690): 635-645.

Wan YH. Study on relationship between adolescent sub-health and psychosomatic health problems[M]. Anhui: Medical University Of Anhui, 2009.

Wang JB. Self-assessment methods of sub-health status in Shanghai University and lifestyle study of the inter-action of multiple factors[D]. Shanghai, China: Easter China Normal University, 2008.

Wang LL. Analysis of adolescent neurosis and psychotic disorders morbidity[J]. Modern Journal of Intergrated Traditional Chinese and Western Medicine, 2005, 14(18): 2447.

Wang Y, Zhang YL. Nursing psychology[M]. Beijing, China: Chinese Medicine Science and Technology Press, 2005.

Warren BJ, Broome B. The culture of mental illness in adolescents with urologic problems[J]. Urologic Nursing, 2011, 31(2): 95-103.

Whitlock J, Schantz K. Mental illness and mental health in adolescence[EB/OL]. ACT for Youth Center of Excellence, Dec. 2008 [20 Jun. 2011]: http://www.actforyouth.net/resources/rf/ rf_mentalhealth_1208.pdf.

WHO. Caring for children and adolescents with mental disorders[EB/OL]. World Health Organization, 2003 [25 Jun. 2011]: http://www.who.int/mental_health/media/en/785.pdf.

Wikipedia. Schizophrenia[EB/OL]. Wikipedia, 28 Jul. 2011 [31 Jul. 2011]: http://en.wikipedia. org/wiki/Schizophrenia.

Wikipedia. Thought disorder[EB/OL]. Wikipedia, 28 Jul. 2011 [31 Jul. 2011]: http:// en.wikipedia.org/wiki/Thought_disorder.

Xing C, Tao FB, Yuan CJ, et al. Evaluation of the reliability and validity of Multidimensional Sub-health Questionnaire of Adolescents[J]. Chinese Journal of Public Health, 2008, 24(9): 1031-1033.

Xu CE, Wang RJ, Hao JH, et al. Application of new delimitation for students sub-health standard[J]. Chinese Journal of School Health, 2010, 31(12): 1423-1425.

Xu J, Lin DN, Wang JJ, et al. Comparison of influential factors for depressive symptoms among primary school students in Hefei and Shenzhen[J]. Chinese Mental Health Journal, 2008, 22(4): 246-252.

Yan H. Adolescent psychological development and strategies of education[EB/OL]. Shanghai Pudong Institute of Eduation Development, 1 Mar. 2009 [25 Jun. 2011]: http://wenku.baidu.com/view/fba40237ee06eff9aef80767.html.

Ye F. A study on the descriptive definition and evaluation criterion of subhealth using Delphi method[M]. Beijing: Peking Union Medical College, 2008.

Zhang WF. Prevalence of psychiatric disorders among 6～17 year old school children in Liaoning Province[D]. Dalian, Liaoning Province, China: Dalian Medical School, 2010.

Zimberoff D, Hartman D. The ego in heart-centered therapies: ego strengthening and ego surrender[J]. Journal of Heart Centered Therapies, 2000, 3(2): 3-66.

Chapter 6　Adolescent Healthy Behaviour

—— Wen Zhang, Ning Jiang, Hongxia Yang, Na Li ——

Adolescents are viewed by many pediatricians and other health professionals as healthy —that is, they show lower levels of mortality and morbidity compared with children and adults. Most adolescents believe that they are healthy, but there is a growing recognition that some adolescents develop health problems, and many more adopt health risk behaviours that can have a great impact on their health or lead to health problems in well-being adult lives.

Under the leadership of the Ministry of Health, an national survey on adolescent health risk behaviour was conducted in China by the Child and Adolescent Health Institute of Peking University in 2005 (Ji 2007). The survey revealed that in China the prevalence of health risk behaviours was growing, mainly in five aspects which were unhealthy eating, unintentionally injury, suicide, substance abuse, sexual behaviour. Therefore, health care workers should help adolescents to avoid health risk behaviours and establish correct, health behaviours, in order to promote the health of adolescents.

The **Integrative Model of Adolescent Health Risk Behaviour (IMAHRB)** was constructed from a review of the interdisciplinary literature specifically to answer the question "what processes influence and encourage some adolescents to engage in or avoid risky behaviour?" The components of IMAHRB include protective factors, escalatory factors, risk stimulus, judgment, risk-avoidance and risk-taking behaviour and outcomes. Using the IMAHRB, nurses can identify and organize the protective and escalatory factors present in adolescents' lives and have a more comprehensive view of adolescent risk process (Keeler & Kaiser 2010).

This chapter will mainly discuss three aspects of health behaviours of adolescents. They are: healthy eating, physical activity and substance use.

241

Unintentionally injury and suicide will be discussed in other chapters in this book. The following group work can be used by school teachers or health professional educators to inspire students' self-thinking about health behaviours (see Table 6-1).

Table 6-1   Group work

Group work:
    Divide the students into two groups and ask the two groups to discuss the healthy and unhealthy behaviours in our daily life.
    Group 1: Discuss health behaviours and the benefits from them.
    Group 2: Discuss unhealthy behaviours and the outcomes generated from them.
 	
Questions:
    1.   What do you think how to develop health behaviours?
    2.   What do you want to know about healthy/unhealthy behaviours?

Section 1   Healthy Eating

Adolescence is the second peak of growth and development, with total nutrient needs higher than any other period during the life cycle. Adequate intake of nutrients and energy is critical to healthy development (Croll et al. 2001). Healthy eating can optimize health and decrease the risk for chronic diseases such as obesity, heart disease and diabetes.

Healthy diet

Healthy eating is defined as eating more fruits and vegetables, less fat, high fiber, balance and variety (Croll et al. 2001). Adolescents need a healthy diet to grow, to develop, and to function optimally (WHO 2010). A healthy diet consists of sufficient amount of food to meet adolescents' energy needs and a variety of foods balanced across the major food groups. As Fig. 6-1 shows, there are five basic food groups, including starchy food (e.g., bread, rice, potatoes); milk and dairy foods; protein (e.g., meat, fish, egg, beans); fatty foods; fruit and vegetables.

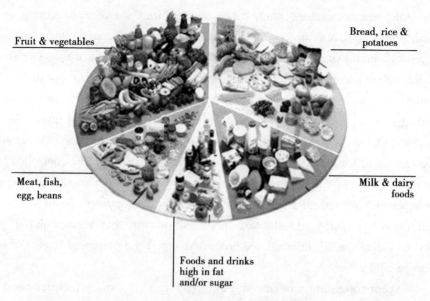

Fig. 6-1 Five food groups (WHO 2010)

Adolescents should eat a diet balanced across the five food groups. They should eat bread, rice and potatoes several times per day, preferably whole grains. Normally one needs 250~400g a day. It is the basis of the Chinese Food Guide Pyramid (Fig. 6-2).

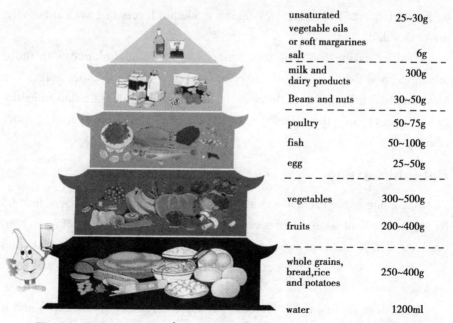

unsaturated vegetable oils or soft margarines	25~30g
salt	6g
milk and dairy products	300g
Beans and nuts	30~50g
poultry	50~75g
fish	50~100g
egg	25~50g
vegetables	300~500g
fruits	200~400g
whole grains, bread,rice and potatoes	250~400g
water	1200ml

Fig. 6-2 Chinese residents' meal pyramid (Chinese Nutrition Society 2007)

Adolescents therefore should eat a variety of fruit and vegetables, preferably fresh and local, several times per day. Fruit and vegetables contain many kinds of vitamins which benefit the health. The recommended amount of the vegetables is 300~500g and fruits is 200~400g per day. Meat is essential in our daily life, preferably lean meat. Replace fatty meat and meat products with fish, poultry and eggs. It is good for adolescents to use milk and dairy products (pure milk or yoghurt) that are low in both fat and salt at 300g per day. Beans and nuts are also recommended for its high quality of proteins. Fat intake should be controlled (no more than 30% of daily energy) and most saturated fats (like animal fat) should be replaced with unsaturated vegetable oils or soft margarines. Besides, a low-salt diet is healthier; total salt intake should not be more than a teaspoon (6g) per day, including the salt in bread and processed, cured and preserved foods (WHO/Europe 2011).

Except for eating a balanced diet, there are still some principles need to know. Food must be prepared in a safe and hygienic way. For adolescents, selecting foods that are low in sugar, eating refined sugar sparingly and limiting the frequency of sugary drinks and sweets will protect their teeth. It is appropriate to maintain body weight between the recommended limits (a BMI of 18.5~25. BMI is derived from a person's weight in kilograms, divided by height (squared) in meters) by taking moderate levels of physical activity, preferably daily.

Healthy eating for adolescents needs to be in accordance with these principles, and they can choose different food in each group as they like. The most important thing for adolescents is that they can integrate daily healthy eating practices into their lifestyles. Then, they can benefit most from healthy eating.

Unhealthy eating

According to the national survey on adolescent health risk behaviour in 2005 (Ji 2007), 19.5% of adolescents never drink milk or soybean milk, 3.6% never eat breakfast, 27.2% often eat sweet desserts, 12.8% frequently drink soft drinks and 4.3% eat fast food 4~5 times per week. These unhealthy eating habits will harm adolescents.

Unhealthy diet is a risk factor for chronic diseases (WHO 2011) and it contains unbalanced diet, excessive food intake, deficient food intake and so on. Unbalanced diet will cause raised blood pressure, raised blood glucose, abnormal blood lipids and so on, while excessive food intake or deficient food intake may cause puberty problems. Unhealthy dietary habits include not eating breakfast, eating fast food and drinking sodas, on diet, dietary bias. These habits will influence the adolescent health and development in different ways.

Breakfast is very important and it has played preventive role on some diseases (Giovannini et al. 2010). Breakfast 'skipping' raise hunger feelings in the morning which can lead to nibbling snacks, particularly those high in sugar and fat (Billon et al. 2002). Eating too much fast food or drinking sodas may cause nutritional disturbance, and snacks could reduce appetite and affect the absorption of nutrient. Fast food can cause obesity which affects health and self-image. Some adolescents on diets do not eat meat or drink milk to lose weight. The lack of protein and calcium may lead to nutritional disturbance or osteoporosis. Some adolescents are 'picky' eaters and always eat the food they like best. Thus, they get the unbalanced diet, where some nutrient is in excess while others are deficient.

Health guidance

Nutritional problems or unhealthy dietary habits during adolescence originating earlier in life can potentially be corrected by following some health guidance. Establishing correct perception about healthy eating and developing healthy habits can prevent diet-related diseases. The whole family, even the society, should involve in the promotion of healthy eating.

Family environment is important in influencing the dietary behaviours of adolescents (Shepherd et al. 2006). Parents should prepare a balanced diet for adolescents, not only based on their preferences, but also on the nutritional and health needs, playing a leading role in eating and set a good example for them. Try to select 'whole foods', such as eating whole wheat bread instead of other bread. Do not use food as the means of reward or punishment. Encourage the whole family to dine together. Besides, families, caregivers, friends, schools, media and so on, should altogether establish a good eating environment for adolescents, as they influence the adolescents' food habits and choices (Roblin 2007).

Adolescents should eat breakfast every day and ensure there are enough carbohydrates and milk or soy milk (Schlundt et al. 1992). Eat snacks in a planned way. Try to reduce the snack intake and eat regularly. Have sufficient fresh vegetables and fruit everyday. Guidelines recommend consumption of at least five portions of fruit and vegetables daily, reduced intakes of saturated fat and salt and increased consumption of complex carbohydrates (Shepherd et al. 2006). Adolescents should also eat less sugar or sweets to protect teeth and maintain the normal blood glucose.

The following case study can be used by school teachers to help adolescents give up some unhealthy eating behaviour by themselves (see Table 6-2).

Table 6-2　A case study with soft drinks

Case study
Some middle school students like cold drinks immediately after exercise or snacks after school, which are not very healthy. They don't realize that this lifestyle is harmful to their body. As a teacher, I think we can do an experiment to test the vitamin C content in the drinks in the practice class. Through the way of doing experiment by students themselves, they can know that vitamin C is very little, not as much as that described in the advertisement. This is a good method to make students resist drinking this automatically.

Section 2　Physical Activity

Physical activities include sports such as football and exercise such as jogging. They also include regular daily activities such as walking to school and doing housework (e.g., fetching water, painting a room).

Benefits

Regular physical activity has important physical, mental and social benefits both during adolescence and later in life. Physical activity not only helps bones and muscles grow and develop, but also helps adolescents remain (or become) fit and trim. Mentally, physical activity helps adolescents build their self-confidence and self-esteem. In addition, adolescents can improve their study and work efficiency. Also, when adolescents feel anxious, sad or angry, they can calm down through taking physical activity. From the aspect of social benefits, participating in sports can help adolescents meet people and develop a sense of camaraderie. Besides, adolescents can learn how to play by the rules, how to cooperate with members of a team, and how to deal with both victory and defeat (WHO 2010).

Lack of physical activity

Lack of physical activity can lead to decreased constitution health of adolescents. Decreased constitution health of adolescents is a global problem. The United States, Japan, Korea and other countries have had a similar situation. Since 1985, China has carried out the National Youth Constitution Health Monitoring five times, and the results show that adolescent health in China is declining generally (Zhang & Zhang 2008). The reason is that lifestyle cannot keep pace with the dramatic environmental changes. Heavy homework for current primary and middle school students have compromised the time for physical activity. Besides, with the rapid development of urbanization, places for physical activity are becoming much smaller. All these factors contribute to the lack of physical activity of adolescents.

Amount of physical activity

It is appropriate to take about 60 minutes in doing physical activity every day. But individuals need to find the tolerable activity intensity and amount according to their own health status. The Central Committee of the Communist Party of China's (CCCPC) "Opinion on Strengthening Juvenile Sports and Building up Juvenile Health" points out that we should ensure students take an hour of exercise every day (CCCPC 2008).

Aerobic exercise

Aerobic exercise is an effective way of taking physical activity. Aerobic exercise takes place under the condition of full of oxygen supply. That is the inhaled oxygen is equal to the demand of the body, thus the body reaches physical equilibrium state. In simple terms, aerobic exercise can be any rhythmic activity, which lasts for a long time (about 15 minutes or more) and whose intensity is moderate or high (Liu 2010). The standardized measurement is heart rate. When heart rate maintains in 150 beats per minute, that is to say, heart rate reaches the maximum heart rate of 75% to 85%, aerobic exercise has been achieved. No less than one hour every time and 3 to 5 times per week is recommended (Qu & Yu 2003). Common aerobic exercises are: walking, jogging, ice skating, swimming, cycling, Tai-Chi, jumping, gymnastic dance, rhythmic gymnastics and so on.

Section 3　Substance Use

Adolescents often experiment with tobacco, alcohol and other substances. They do this for different reasons, e.g., to act older, to fit in with friends, to express their independence, to rebel against adults, or to relieve stress. The use of tobacco, alcohol and other substances can lead to negative health consequences both during adolescence, and into adulthood (WHO 2010, 2011).

Around the world, there is an increasing concern about the use of psychoactive substances by adolescents. In the United States, 65% of adolescents aged 15 to 17 reported by Office of Juvenile Justice and Delinquency Prevention had heavy drinking in the past month (Pacific Institute for Research and Evaluation 2002). In China, the prevalence of current drinking was 36.4% and 23.8% for males and females respectively (Ji 2010). According to the national survey on adolescent health risk behaviour in 2005 (Ji 2007), the rate of smoking was 14.9%, of which 22.4% for males and 3.9% for females. It is reported by China Youth Internet Association that 14.1% of adolescents have Internet Addiction Disorders (CYIA 2010).

What are the substances?

Psychoactive substances (for example alcohol, tobacco, heroin and other drugs), both legal and illegal, are substances which when ingested, can affect the way people see, hear, taste, smell, think, feel and behave (WHO 2006). Common substances can be divided into depressants, stimulants, opioids and hallucinogens. Some substances like alcohol, tobacco are legal while others like heroin, opium are illegal.

The following group work can be used by school teachers or health professional educators to illuminate students and awaken their self-awareness about the substances (see Table 6-3).

Table 6-3   Group work

Group work
Divide the students into 2 groups, and ask each group to list and classify the common substances that they have heard, saw or used, then write down the answers on the whiteboard.

Group 1	Group 2
Type I	Type I
Type II	Type II
Type III	Type III
...	...

Prediction and diagnose

According to Diagnostic and Statistical Manual of Mental Disorders (DSM-IV) written by American Psychiatric Association (APA 2000), substance abuse is referred as that repeated use of alcohol or other drugs leads to problems but does not include compulsive use or addiction, and stopping the drug does not lead to significant withdrawal symptoms. When an individual persists in using alcohol or other drugs, despite problems related to use of the substance, substance dependence may be diagnosed. Compulsive and repetitive use may result in tolerance to the effect of the drug and withdrawal symptoms when use is reduced or stopped.

Substance dependence is a maladaptive pattern of substance use, leading to clinically significant impairment or distress, and having kinds of manifestations. The diagnostic criteria can be found in the book of DSM-IV. Nurses or other health professionals can make a prediction according to the manifestations and recommend or refer the suspicious adolescents to the psychiatrist.

Adverse effect

As the substances will affect the way people see, hear, think, and behave to some degree, substance use may compromise adolescents' mental and emotional development. Therefore, adolescents are at risk of several direct and indirect adverse effects (athealth.com 2007). The adverse effects can be divided into two main parts: physical and mental adverse effects, both of which contain acute and chronic health problems in adolescents, as with adults.

Physical adverse effects include trauma, acute poisoning, organ injury, infection and so on. Substance use leads to mental symptoms, leading to increased incidence of traumatic accidents, such as falls, traffic accidents, drowning and other issues. Nearly 45% of all deaths from traffic accidents are related to the consumption of alcohol. The most common and dangerous hazard is acute poisoning, even leading to death directly. Substance abuse may lead to liver, heart, lung lesions, malignant tumors and infertility. For example, alcohol drinking can lead to cirrhosis, while smoking can cause lung cancer, emphysema and other chronic diseases. Besides, substance abuse may cause AIDS, hepatitis B and other infectious diseases through injection of drugs. It can also lead to localized infections such as abscesses and phlebitis. In addition, excessive substance use (tobacco, alcohol and illicit substances) will increase the risk of cancers, cardiovascular diseases, and respiratory illnesses later in life (WHO 1995).

The direct mental adverse effects can be anxiety, memory and concentration problems, psychotic episodes (fixed false ideas), depression, and suicide. These can lead to family dysfunction, social withdrawal, learning difficulties in school, loss of job and income, criminal behaviour, violence, crimes committed for money to buy substances. The above are the leading mental problems caused by substance use.

Health intervention

If substance use leads to dysfunction, health intervention adolescents should be referred for help to recover. Recovery needs the cooperation of nurses, parents, adolescents and counselors or psychiatrists. The approaches include psychotherapy and behaviour modification and GAPS approach (American Medical Association 1997, Arnett 2007, Yang et al. 2002).

Cognitive therapy is one type of psychotherapy, with the goal of correcting dysfunctional thinking and helping patients modify erroneous assumptions. Teachers and parents should correct adolescents' attitude towards substance abuse and let them realize the harm. Therefore, adolescents may enhance their awareness and control substance abuse behaviours gradually.

Aversion therapy, another type of psychotherapy, connects substance abuse with unpleasant or punitive experiences of adolescents, e.g., pairing the use of an emetic with the experience of alcohol (Wikipedia 2011).

In systematic desensitization and incentives method, another form of psychotherapy, teachers and parents should ask adolescents to gradually reduce the amount of substance abuse every day, and if they reach the day's "target", teachers, parents, or young people themselves should give adolescents some rewards which could consolidate and strengthen the achievements.

In the behaviour modification, according to the individual situation of adolescents, they should take appropriate exercise. In the initial period, they could take low intensity exercise, such as walking in the park, doing exercises indoor and so on. When the condition improves, they could increase the intensity of the activities.

Certain procedures can be followed with the GAPS approach. To begin with, health professionals should gather information, including age, gender, substance abuse time, frequency, quantity and so on. Second, health professionals should assess the extent of substance abuse, situation, literacy and health status, the relationship between family members and colleagues. Third, determine the extent of damage. For the mildly affected, guidance to enhance their confidence is enough. For moderately affected, discussing and consulting on how to quit substance abuse is necessary. For the seriously affected, tracking and providing comprehensive treatment for them is important. After the above procedures, health professionals should discuss the barriers to quitting substance abuse with adolescents and develop a detailed plan for them.

In addition, complications (like withdrawal symptoms, insomnia, restlessness and diarrhea) should be treated carefully, for this can relieve uncomfortableness, bring encouragement and predict the outcome of the treatment. In caring for withdrawal symptoms (Collins & Ellickson 2004, Tang 2006), it is important to provide appropriate comfort to adolescents and alleviate concerns about withdrawal symptoms.

For the adolescents with insomnia, teach them techniques of relaxation, meditation before bedtime. Tell adolescents that a nutrient-rich diet and adequate exercise could help them sleep. Be patient with adolescents who are restless. Encourage adolescents to talk with their parents or peers. For them, going out for a walk or having a warm bath may reduce irritability.

In caring for diarrhea, adolescents should eat nutritious, digestible, low-fat food. Encourage adolescents to drink light salt water and fruit juices to prevent dehydration. Besides, having a good rest and keeping the perineum clean can promote recovery.

The following role play activity (WHO 2006) can be used by school teachers or health professional educators to let the students know the adverse effects and coping skills of substance use, just taking smoking as an example (see Table 6-4).

Table 6-4   A role play about a smoking adolescent

Role Play

You are a young person (boy or girl) of 12 years. You have come to the health center because you have had a cough for the last three weeks and you find it hard to breathe at night.

If the health worker asks you, you say that you have been smoking cigarettes for the last one year. You mostly take them from home where both your parents smoke. You think smoking makes you look cool and feel grown-up. You have friends who smoke. You do not have a boy/girl friend. You used to be good at sports (you choose which one) and wish you had continued. Now you find that you get too breathless.

Through Brain Storm, try to find the answers :

1.   The consequences aroused by smoking in the role play?
2.   In addition, what advices the health worker can give the young person?

Health promotion

As to health promotion, it is important to prevent adolescents from substance use at all different levels (e.g., individual, school, community). It needs the combination of support from schools, families and society. Schools need to strengthen education; parents need to communicate with adolescents and set a good example; while society should create a healthy environment and rely on the power of the media to publicize the harm of certain substances. The following will describe these prevention strategies from these 3 aspects, respectively.

Schools can teach adolescents what the harmful substances are and how to identify them, so as to strengthen education to avoid substance use, using peer education to reinforce the effects. For example, teaching class leaders or team leaders the damage of substance use first, they can then tell the other partners and classmates once they understand the hazard. Teachers should help adolescents establish a correct outlook on life and cultivate an optimistic psychology. Therefore, schools should create a healthy environment for all students.

Prevention within the family is also very important. Parents should create a free, relaxed family environment for adolescents, communicate effectively with them and find out problems early. They should set good examples by their action for adolescents. If adolescents grow up in a healthy environment without smoking or alcohol, it reduces the possibility of being exposed to the substances. For adolescents, they should improve their overall quality continuously, learn about substance use and understand the harm. In daily lives, they should enhance their self-control, establish a correct outlook on life and values and build up good moral.

Society can use the influence of the media. Media is a very important way to affect adolescents' behaviours. For example, in China, we can organize some activities on International Day against Drug Abuse and Illicit Drug Trafficking, to call on the adolescents to stay away from the substances using cards, booklet, video and so on. At the same time, food and drug agencies also need to make an effort to keep adolescents healthy. The overall aim is to create a healthy and harmonious environment.

Against substance use in action

The Chinese Law on the Protection of Minors claims that selling liquor or tobacco to adolescents is illegal. Parents and other guardians have the duty to tell adolescents to keep away from liquor and tobacco. In Shandong Province, the Provincial Minors Protection Regulation enacted by Shandong Province Government Legislation Office (SPGLO 2010) claims that parents and teachers have the duty to guide their children or students to form good habits, and if they find adolescents smoking or drinking, they should correct the bad habits as quickly as possible.

With the spread of Internet, more adolescents have access to computers and are vulnerable to Internet Addiction Disorders, which is also one kind of psychological dependence. Our government also adopts many ways to enhance a healthy web environment for adolescents, so as to promote adolescent health and development. Besides, the state should encourage research networks which are good for adolescents and develop new network technology which is used to prevent adolescents from becoming addicted to the network. For example, it is prohibited to establish Internet bars around primary and middle schools. Internet services in business places should not admit adolescents. It is the responsibility of the whole society to teach adolescents to use Internet appropriately.

To help achieve a better understanding about health risk behaviors in adolescents in local society, Table 6-5 exemplifies the design of social practice activities in this regard.

Table 6-5   Social practice

Social Practice
Select a secondary school where adolescents are the main population and make a survey on unhealthy behaviours and risk factors. **Aim**: Link the theory into practice—make use of the knowledge to identify the unhealthy behaviours, explore the risk factors, and support the health promotion strategy for the students. **Modality**: Make a plan about the practice and obtain the school's approval. Focus on the communicating skills when working with students and try to know about their real thoughts. Analyze the data and help them to develop healthy behaviours. Make a summary after the practice and demonstrate the main experiences.

Summary

This chapter discusses the health behaviours of adolescents, aiming to help adolescents recognize the importance of health behaviours and cultivating them to adopt healthy behaviours and avoid unhealthy behaviours. Adolescent health and development is a social problem and deserves the concern of the whole society. As more countries start to focus on this subject, in the future, adolescents' health will change under the influence of health professionals, teachers, parents and health agencies.

References

American Medical Association. Guidelines for Adolescent Preventive Services (GAPS)[EB/OL]. Department of Adolescent Health, American Medical Association, 1997 [3 Aug. 2011]: http://www.ama-assn.org//resources/doc/ad-hlth/gapsmono.pdf.

APA. Diagnostic and Statistical Manual of Mental Disorders DSM-IV-TR[M/OL]. 4th. Arlington, Virginia: American Psychiatric Association, 2000[3 Aug. 2011]: http://www.behavenet.com/capsules/disorders/dsm4tr.htm.

Arnett JJ. The myth of peer influence in adolescent smoking initiation[J]. Health Education and Behavior, 2007, 34(4): 594-607.

athealth.com. Getting the fact about adolescent substance abuse and treatment[EB/OL]. athealth. com, 15 Jan. 2007 [12 Jul. 2011]: http://www.athealth.com/Consumer/adolescentsufacts. html.

Billon S, Lluch A, Gueguen R, et al. Family resemblance in breakfast energy intake: the Stanislas Family study[J]. European Journal of Clinical Nutrition, 2002, 56(10): 1011.

CCCPC. The Central Committee of the Communist Party of China' s "Opinion on Strengthening Juvenile Sports and Building up Juvenile Health"[J]. Politics Literature Series Glance, 2008, 3(00): 847-851.

China Youth Internet Association. Adolescent Internet addiction survey report on 2009 [EB/OL]. Tencent, 2009 [12 Jul. 2011]: http://edu.qq.com/edunew/diaocha/2009wybg.htm.

Chinese Nutrition Society. Chinese residents' meal pyramid[EB/OL]. Chinese nutrition society, 2007 [12 Jul. 2011]: http://www.cnsoc.org/cn/nutrition.asp?nid=11.

Collins RL, Ellickson PL. Integrating four theories of adolescent smoking[J]. Substance Use & Misuse, 2004, 39(2): 179-209.

Croll JK, Neumark-Sztainer D, Story M. Healthy eating: what does it mean to adolescents?[J]. Journal of Nutrition Education, 2001, 33(4): 193.

Giovannini M, Agostoni C, Shamir R. The relevance of breakfast: concluding remarks[J]. Critical Reviews in Food Science and Nutrition, 2010, 50(2): 129-129.

Ji CY. Adolescent health risk behaviour[J]. Chinese Journal of School Health, 2007, 28(4): 289-291.

Ji CY. Prevalence of drinking behaviour among Chinese secondary school students[J]. Chinese Journal of School Health, 2010, 31(10): 1153-1156.

Keeler HJ, Kaiser MM. An integrative model of adolescent health risk behavior[J]. Journal of Pediatric Nursing, 2010, 25(2): 126-137.

Liu Y. Brief analysis of value of aerobic exercise[J]. Internet Fortune, 2010, 13 (7): 148-149.

Pacific Institute for Research and Evaluation. Drinking in merica: myths, realities, and prevention policy[EB/OL]. Office of Juvenile Justice and Delinquency Prevention, U.S. Department of Justice, 2002 [12 Jul. 2011]: http://www.udetc.org/documents/Drinking_in_ America.pdf.

Qu MY, Yu CL. Practical Sports Medicine[M]. 4th ed. Beijing, China: Peking University Medical Press, 2003.

Roblin L. Childhood obesity: food, nutrient, and eating-habit trends and influences[J]. Applied Physiology, Nutrition, and Metabolism, 2007, 32(4): 635-645.

Schlundt D, Hill J, Sbrocco T, et al. The role of breakfast in the treatment of obesity: a randomized clinical trial[J]. The American Journal of Clinical Nutrition, 1992, 55(3): 645-651.

Shepherd J, Harden A, Rees R, et al. Young people and healthy eating: a systematic review of research on barriers and facilitators[J]. Health Education Research, 2006, 21(2): 239-257.

SPGLO. Shandong Province Minors Protection Regulation[EB/OL]. Shandong Province Government Legislation Office, 6 Dec. 2010 [15 Jul. 2011]: http://www.sd-law.gov.cn/Section/InfoDisplay. aspx?InfoId=fe58007d-eb35-4828-a4be-946bb6e6a9a0.

Tang Y. Nurses' effect in the implementation of smoking intervention[J]. Today Nurse, 2006, 10(10): 4-6.

WHO. The world health report 1995: bridging the gaps[EB/OL]. World Health Organization, 1995 [15 Jul. 2011]: http://www.who.int/whr/1995/en/whr95_en.pdf.

WHO. Orientation programme on adolescent health for health-care providers[M/OL]. Geneva, Switzerland: World Health Organization, 2006[14 Jun. 2011]: http://whqlibdoc.who.int/publications/2006/9241591269_Handout_eng.pdf.

WHO. Adolescent Job Aid Part 3: Information to be provided to adolescents and their parents[EB/OL]. World Health Organization, 2010 [3 Aug. 2011]: http://www.advancefamilyplanning.org/system/files/Adol%20Job%20Aid%20Part%203.pdf.

WHO. Diet and physical activity: a public health priority[EB/OL]. World Health Organization, 2011 [12 Jul. 2011]: http://www.who.int/dietphysicalactivity/en/.

WHO Regional Office for Europe. A healthy lifestyle[EB/OL]. World Health Organization Regional Office for Europe, 2011 [6 Jul. 2011]: http://www.euro.who.int/en/what-we-do/health-topics/disease-prevention/nutrition/a-healthy-lifestyle.

Wikipedia. Aversion therapy[EB/OL]. Wikipedia, 2 Jul. 2011 [26 Jul. 2011]: http://en.wikipedia.org/wiki/Aversion_therapy.

Yang MB, Feng Y, Zhang GB, et al. Rehabilitation model of China-U.S.A Daytop Village on drug detoxification[J]. Soft Science of Health, 2002, 16(5): 23-26.

Zhang Y, Zhang Y. Research on promoting school health and strengthening young peoples physique[J]. Journal of Fuyang Teachers College (Natural Science), 2008, 25(4): 74-75.

Chapter 7   Sexual and Reproductive Health

Ting Liu, Yaoyun Pan, Liyuan Wang, Li Yang

Sexual and reproductive development is an important component integral to the maturation process of adolescents. The environment, in which adolescents are making decisions related to sexual and reproductive health, is rapidly evolving, e.g., greater access to formal education, different job opportunities, more exposure to new ideas from media, telecommunication and Internet, and unsafe food (Laski et al. 2008).

Today's adolescents will determine the societal organization, economic productivity, reproductive health and the well-being of human society in the coming decades (Dixon-Mueller 2008). To improve sexual and reproductive health, thereby, is important for adolescents themselves, their family and society, which deserve appropriate responses in accordance with the changing global context for living (Hindin & Fatusi 2009).

It is reported that the occurrence of sexual initiation and the engagement in premarital sexual activities among adolescents is rising in many countries (Ali & Cleland 2005, Wellings 2006), whereas the prevalence of STIs particularly HIV/ AIDS exacerbates the negative consequence of sexual activities on health (Dixon-Mueller 2009). Adolescent sexual activities, particularly unprotected sex, within or outside marriage, may have a negative impact on reproductive health, increasing the risk of unintended pregnancy, unwanted childbearing and abortion, as well as STIs including HIV/AIDS.

Section 1   Overview

Understanding about sexual health is shaped by political, social and other historical events (e.g., 1960s sexual revolution), ongoing struggle for abortion and reproductive rights, homosexual rights movement, growing population, and altered disease pattern (e.g., increasing number of STIs including HIV/AIDS) (Edwards &

Coleman 2004).

Currently, sexual health is defined as a state of physical, emotional, mental and social well-being related to sexuality; it is not merely the absence of disease, dysfunction or infirmity (WHO 2002). Sexual health requires a positive and respectful approach to sexuality and sexual relationships, as well as the possibility of having pleasurable and safe sexual experiences, free of coercion, discrimination and violence. For sexual health to be attained and maintained, the sexual rights of all persons must be respected, protected and fulfilled (WHO 2002).

Both conceptually and in practice, sexual health and reproductive health overlap. Reproductive health emphasizes reproductive processes, functions and reproductive system at all stages of life. It implies that people are able to have a responsible, satisfying and safe sex life and that they have the capability to reproduce and the freedom to decide if, when and how often to do so (WHO 2011a). For clarification, to support normal reproductive functions (e.g., pregnancy, childbirth) also means to reduce adverse outcomes of sexual activities and reproduction (Glasier et al. 2006).

Common sexual and reproductive health issues

Adolescence is a time of sexual exploration and expression. Many adolescents develop sexual relations during the period of adolescence, before marriage, within marriage or extramarital. The lack of knowledge and skill, limited access to contraceptive methods including condoms, and the vulnerability to coerced sex place adolescents at high risk of STIs including HIV/AIDS. The WHO identified sexual and reproductive health as one of the priority areas for intensive interventions in the globe, and the common sexual and reproductive health concerns among adolescents include early and unprotected sexual behaviors, pregnancy, unsafe abortion and STIs (WHO 2006a).

Prevalence of sex, pregnancy and abortion

It was reported that approximately a quarter (28%) of American girls aging 15 to 19 years old disclosed the experience of sexual behaviors in 1970s, but by the end of the 1980s three fifths disclosed the occurrence. Also being reported was the early sexual debut, for example, the average age for Canadian, British and American girls is approximately 17, and a relative higher percentage of American girls had sex before 13 years (Wu et al. 2006).

Furthermore, approximately 745 000 American youths under 20 years become pregnant every year, and the birth rate among adolescents of 15 to 19 years increased by 3% from 2005 to 2006 (Wang et al. 2007). According to the WHO, approximately 20 millions girls younger than 20 years old become pregnant each year in the world, of whom unsafe abortion occurred to two to four millions (Gao et al. 2002, WHO 2006a). It is estimated that 80 000 women died every year as a result of unsafe abortion, while those who survive the experience probably suffer from immediate or chronic health conditions (e.g., hemorrhage, pelvic infection, infertility, spontaneous abortion in a subsequent pregnancy, psychological distress) throughout the rest of their lives (Huo 2004, Olukoya et al. 2001).

Contributory factors to risky sexual behaviors

The growth of early sex and other health-risk sexual behaviors may result from the puberty and sexual debut at younger age and delayed marriage at older age in comparison with previous generations along with the improved nutrition and health status (WHO 2006b). There exist many ways to experience sexual feelings, which may evoke sexual intercourse as a result.

Many factors, biological, social, cultural, and beliefs about sexual pleasure can influence adolescents' sexual behaviors. In fact, sexual relations during adolescence are often unplanned and sporadic, and sometimes happen because of pressure, coercion or force (Ochieng et al. 2011). Many sexual activities among adolescents are risky, e.g., totally unprotected sex, intermittent use of condoms or other means of contraception, resulting in unplanned pregnancies and unsafe abortions. A number of reasons contribute to such risky behaviors, e.g., have limited knowledge of or access to contraception, worry about negative impact on sexual pleasure or relationships, or behold misconception about pregnancy or STIs from peers, media or Internet (Abiodun & Balogun 2009, Adedimeji et al. 2007, Gomes et al. 2008).

The sexually conservative culture behaves like a double-edged factor: on the one hand, such a culture protects adolescents from the engagement in risky sexual behaviors before marriage, within marriage or out of marriage; on the other hand, such a culture may limit the chance for adolescents to learn safe sexual behaviors and appropriate sexual beliefs, leading to the occurrence of unwanted pregnancy and secrete or unsafe abortion to avoid public shame and social rejection (Yu & Gao 2008, Zheng et al. 2000).

Negative consequences of adolescent sex

Considering that adolescents have still not reached physical, psychosocial and sexual maturity, early, frequent and multiple sexual behaviors involving risk factors (e.g., unprotected sex, promiscuity, unsafe or repeated abortion) during adolescents can have diversified negative effects on adolescents, e.g., poor school performances, emotional disorders, childbirth and pregnancy complication, poor economic or social status, delinquency, substance use, or even premature death (Tao et al. 2010). It was documented that the risk of childbirth and pregnant complication for adolescents under 15 years old is 25 times higher than those over 25 years old (Zhao 2005, Wu et al. 2006).

Thereby, to educate adolescents to keep vigilant to the signs of pregnancy is crucial if unprotected sexual behaviors happened before. Presumptive signs of pregnancy include: the cessation of menstruation, nausea or vomiting (also called as morning sickness), swelling or soreness in breasts, and so forth. Sometimes abdominal pain or vaginal bleeding may occur. In case a safe abortion is not given to adolescents, infection may have set in and adolescent could develop fever, dehydration, or find some contraception products in the uterus (WHO 2006a).

Pregnancy

Pregnancy is defined as the course of embryo and fetal growth and development in uterus. It begins at the fertilization and ends at the delivery of the fetus. Generally, pregnancy is a normal physiological process, but every process is apt to be accompanied by disturbances. During pregnancy, the maternal system may produce a series of changes to adapt to the needs of fetal growth and development influenced by placental hormones and the neuro-endocrine system. The child draws its sustenance from the mother's blood, and the mother has to provide nourishment for two. And, besides providing nourishment, her excreting organs as well as kidneys, must work for two to deal with the child's excretions. Therefore, the pregnant woman is particularly under an artificial unhealthy mode of living, and may be subject to many troubles and disturbances. Various symptoms accompanying pregnancy include morning sickness, pernicious vomiting, capricious appetite, constipation, varicose veins, and so forth (Banerjee & Clark 2009).

However, for adolescents, pregnancy is one of the most difficult experiences a young person might ever face when it interrupts school or other plans. It can create an emotional crisis resulting in feelings of shame and fear. Meantime, because the stress of how to break this news to parents might be even greater, and finding help may seem an impossible task for adolescents, they will crumble under pressures in their environment (Adoption.com 2011). Furthermore, adolescents who become pregnant may not seek proper medical care, and they may not be physically mature enough to handle the stress of pregnancy and childbirth, leading to an increased risk of medical complications (Xu & Shtarkshall 2004).

When it comes to adolescent pregnancy, there is a greater risk of complication for both the mother and child. However, this risk is commonly experienced by younger teens that are not yet fully physically developed. These teens generally suffer the worst complications, such as severe anemia and hypertension due to pregnancy. However, the baby often suffers the most problems. The baby may be born prematurely, suffer from low birth weight, mental retardation or brain damage, with difficulty gaining weight after delivery. Worse still, the baby could be stillborn (Adoption.com 2011).

Abortion

Abortion is the death and expulsion of the fetus from the uterus either spontaneously or by induction before the 22nd week of pregnancy. However, there are several different types of abortion, e.g., spontaneous, and induced abortions. When an abortion takes place by itself, without any outside aid, it is called spontaneous abortion. However, induced abortion occurs as a result of interference which may be medical, surgical or result from the use of herbal preparations or other traditional practices which cause the uterus to expel or partly expel its contents (WHO 2008a).

Generally, abortion is a very safe procedure, but it is still risky for adolescents. In fear of parental notification, adolescents are more likely to resort to unskilled practitioners or to delay seeking a pregnancy termination than older women (Xu & Shtarkshall 2004). When an abortion is performed by an experienced physician, with the observance of the utmost cleanliness (asepsis and antisepsis), then the abortion is accompanied with very little or no danger; but when performed carelessly, by incompetent, non-conscientious physicians and midwives, the operation is fraught with great danger to the patient's health or even life. And abortion is a great cause of premature death and chronic invalidism among women (Robinson 1929).

Symptoms after abortion may include heavy bleeding, lower abdominal/ back pain, vomiting, nausea, painful abdominal cramping, fever, foul-smelling discharge, distension of abdomen, chills or flu-like symptoms (Banerjee & Clark 2009). The most common complications are incomplete abortion, sepsis, haemorrhage and intra-abdominal injury (e.g., puncturing and tearing of the uterus). Common long-term health problems caused by unsafe abortion include chronic pain, pelvic inflammatory disease, tubal blockage and secondary infertility (WHO 2008b).

Section 2　Sexually Transmitted Infections (STIs)

The term sexually transmitted infections (STIs) refers to a variety of clinical syndromes caused by pathogens that can be acquired and transmitted through sexual activity, exposure to contaminated blood, or from a mother to her infant during pregnancy and birth (WHO 2006a, Workowski & Berman 2010). This category of disease include: HIV/AIDS, chlamydial infection, gonorrhoea, genital herpes, human papillomavirus (HPV) infection, pelvic inflammatory disease, syphilis, trichomoniasis and chancroid. Symptoms suggesting the occurrence of STIs include but not limited to urethral discharge, painful urination, genital sores, genital ulcers, lower abdominal pain or tenderness, unusual vaginal discharge or vaginal itching, local skin infection and fever (Altini & Coetzee 2005, WHO 2008a). Of all these STIs, HIV/AIDS might be the most frightening as no cure is available in present. The number of people living with HIV/AIDS worldwide continues to grow. It is estimated that in 2009, 33.3 millions of people may have HIV/AIDS including 2.6 million new infections and 1.8 million HIV/AIDS-related deaths (WHO 2011a).

Some of these infections are life threatening (e.g., HIV, syphilis); others (e.g., hepatitis B, HPV, HIV) predispose to malignancy or destroy fertility (e.g., gonorrhea, chlamydia) (Nelson & Woodward 2006). STIs not only cause physical damages to adolescents, but also cause psychological distress, bring calamities to the partner, children and family, and probably entail great losses to human society like a social disease. Seriously, adolescents with STIs may suffer from chronic conditions, e.g., permanent infertility, chronic pain, cervical cancer, heart or brain damage. Girls with STIs may confront more challenges in comparison with boys with STIs in term of the transmission from mother to infant during pregnancy and delivery, causing severe consequences to the next generation.

Mostly adolescents may think they are too young or too sexually inexperienced to acquire STIs, or misbelieve that STIs only occur to those promiscuous or engaging abnormal sexual behaviors. It has to be emphasized that adolescents are particularly susceptible to STIs because of the lack of information and resources related to STIs prevention and treatment and the reluctance to seek for support due to fear, ignorance, shyness or inexperience (Barnett & Schueller 2002). To provide necessary information and support for STIs prevention, protection and treatment when in need shall be included in the essential service packages for adolescents (WHO 2006a).

HIV/AIDS

Human immunodeficiency virus (HIV) causes acquired immunodeficiency syndrome (AIDS), a condition in humans where progressive failure of the immune system allows life-threatening opportunistic infections and cancers to thrive. Infection with HIV occurs by the transfer of blood, semen, vaginal fluid, pre-ejaculate, or breast milk (Zenilman & Shahmanesh 2011).

HIV infection can be divided into three stages. That is, acute infection (or primary infection), latency and AIDS. As early as 2~4 weeks after exposure to HIV (but up to 3 months later), people can experience an acute illness, often described as "the worst flu ever." This is called acute infection which lasts for several weeks and may include symptoms such as fever, chills, rash, swollen lymph nodes, sore throat, muscle pain, malaise, and mouth and esophageal sores. These symptoms are non-specific and require special awareness to pursue a diagnosis (Nelson & Woodward 2006). The latency stage involves few or no symptoms and can last anywhere from two weeks to twenty years or more, depending on the individual. When HIV infection progresses to AIDS, many people begin to suffer from fatigue, diarrhea, nausea, vomiting, fever, chills, night sweats, and even wasting syndrome at late stages. Many of the signs and symptoms of AIDS come from opportunistic infections, cancers and other conditions which occur in patients with a damaged immune system (AIDS.Gov 2011).

Chlamydia infection

Chlamydia infection is caused by the bacterium *Chlamydia trachomatis*, and is the most reported bacterial infection, with an estimated 2.8 million new cases each year, which can damage a woman's reproductive organs. Adolescents and young adults are most commonly infected with *C. trachomatis* (Nelson & Woodward 2006). The greater the number of sex partners, the greater the risk of infection. Teenage girls and young women are at particularly high risk for infection since their cervix is not fully matured and are probably more susceptible to infection. Since chlamydia can be transmitted by oral or anal sex, men who have sex with men are also at risk for chlamydial infection.

Chlamydia is known as a "silent" disease because the majority of infected people have no symptoms. Symptoms usually appear within 1 to 3 weeks after exposure if occur. The cervix is the most common site of infection for women. Women with chlamydial cervicitis generally are asymptomatic or report only nonspecific symptoms, such as vaginal discharge, postcoital spotting or bleeding, and a burning sensation when urinating. Two-thirds of infected women have no signs or symptoms (Nelson & Woodward 2006). In addition, if the infection spreads from the cervix to the fallopian tubes, some women still have no signs or symptoms; others might have lower abdominal pain, low back pain, nausea, fever, pain during intercourse, or bleeding between menstrual periods. Men with infection might have complaints of dysuria, urinary frequency, a burning sensation when urinating and urethral discharge which is the greatest in the morning. Men or women who have anal intercourse may acquire chlamydial infection in the rectum, causing rectal pain, discharge, or bleeding. Chlamydia can also be found in the throats of women and men having oral sex with an infected partner (Nelson & Woodward 2006, Center for Disease Control and Prevention, CDC 2010).

However, if untreated, chlamydial infections can progress to serious reproductive and other health problems with both short-term and long-term consequences. It can cause pelvic inflammatory disease (PID) and fallopian tube infection without any symptoms. PID and "silent" infection in the upper genital tract can cause permanent damage to the fallopian tubes, uterus, and surrounding tissues. The damage can lead to chronic pelvic pain, infertility, and potentially fatal ectopic pregnancy. Chlamydia may also increase the chances of becoming infected with HIV if exposed (CDC 2010).

Gonorrhea

Gonorrhea is caused by *Neisseria gonorrhoeae*, a bacterium that can grow and multiply easily in the warm, moist areas of the reproductive tract, including the cervix, uterus, and fallopian tubes in women, and in the urethra in women and men. It can also grow in the mouth, throat, eyes, and anus. Any sexually active person can be infected with gonorrhea. Gonorrhea spreads through contact with the penis, vagina, mouth, or anus. It can also spread from mother to baby during delivery.

The range of infections vary by gender but, in general, can vary from isolated self-limited infections to serious, even life-threatening systemic infections. In men, some may have no symptoms at all, and others may have signs or symptoms that appear one to fourteen days after infection, including a burning sensation when urinating, or white, yellow, or green discharge from the penis, painful or swollen testicles. Besides, gonorrhea can cause epididymitis which may lead to infertility if left untreated (Nelson & Woodward 2006).

In women, the symptoms of gonorrhea are often mild, but most infected women have no symptoms. The initial symptoms and signs include a painful or burning sensation when urinating, increased vaginal discharge, or vaginal bleeding between periods. Women with gonorrhea are at risk of developing serious complications, e.g., PID, regardless of the presence or severity of symptoms. In addition, gonorrhea can spread to the blood or joints which can be life threatening. People with gonorrhea can more easily contract HIV (CDC 2010).

Genital herpes

Genital herpes is caused by the herpes simplex viruses type 1 (HSV-1) or type 2 (HSV-2). Most individuals have no or only minimal signs or symptoms from HSV-1 or HSV-2 infection. When signs do occur, they typically appear as one or more blisters on or around the genitals or rectum. The blisters break, leaving tender ulcers that may take two to four weeks to heal the first time they occur. But people would have several (typically four or five) outbreaks within a year. Other signs and symptoms during the primary episode may include a second crop of sores, and flu-like symptoms, including fever and swollen glands. However, most individuals with HSV-2 infection never have sores, or have very mild signs that are not even noticed or be mistaken for insect bites or other conditions (CDC 2010).

Herpes is a chronic, life-long infection; patients can shed virus, not only during outbreaks but also during asymptomatic periods. Genital herpes can cause recurrent painful genital sores in many adults, and herpes infection can be severe in people with suppressed immune systems. Regardless of severity of symptoms, the patients diagnosed with genital herpes may have more difficulty dealing with the psychological impact of the infection than with the physical discomfort. In addition, herpes can make people more susceptible to HIV infection, and it can make HIV-infected individuals more infectious (CDC 2010, Nelson & Woodward 2006).

Genital human papillomavirus infection

Human papillomavirus (HPV) infection is one of the most common sexually transmitted infections. There are more than 40 genital human papillomavirus (HPV) types that can infect the genital areas, as well as the mouth and throat, leading to different symptoms and health problems. At least 13 HPV genotypes can cause cancer. HPV is passed on through genital contact, i.e., vaginal and anal sex, or oral sex and genital-to-genital contact. HPV infection is highly transmissible, and the majority of men and women will acquire HPV infection at some time in their life. However, only a very small proportion will go on to develop cancer (Myers et al. 2000, WHO 2007).

The most important clinical consequence of HPV infection is cervical cancer. Cervical cancer, with the death of approximately 250 000 women each year worldwide, remains one of the leading causes of cancer-related mortality in women (Palefsky 2010). HPV can also cause other types of anogenital cancer, e.g., head and neck cancers, and genital warts, in both men and women. HPV is estimated to cause about half a million new cancers every year, most of them affecting women in developing countries (WHO 2007, Hobbs et al. 2006). Genital warts usually appear as a small bump or groups of bumps in the genital area. They can be small or large, raised or flat, or shaped like a cauliflower. Warts can appear within weeks or months after sexual contact with an infected partner—even if the infected partner has no signs of genital warts. If left untreated, genital warts might go away, remain unchanged, or increase in size or number. But they will not turn into cancer. However, cervical cancer usually does not have symptoms until it is quite advanced (CDC 2010).

Pelvic inflammatory disease

Pelvic inflammatory disease (PID) refers to infection of the uterus, fallopian tubes and other reproductive organs. It is a serious complication of some sexually transmitted diseases (STDs), especially chlamydia and gonorrhea. Sexually active women in their childbearing years are most at risk, and those under 25 are more likely to develop PID than those older than 25. This is partly because the cervix of teenage girls and young women is not fully matured, increasing their susceptibility to the STDs that are linked to PID. Moreover, women who douche or have an intrauterine device (IUD) inserted may have a higher risk of developing PID near the time of insertion.

Symptoms of PID vary from mild to severe. When PID is caused by chlamydial infection, a woman may be more likely to experience only mild symptoms. Women with PID most commonly have lower abdominal pain. Other signs and symptoms include fever, unusual vaginal discharge that may have a foul odor, painful intercourse, painful urination, irregular menstrual bleeding, and pain in the right upper abdomen. Seriously, infection-causing bacteria can silently invade the fallopian tubes and tissues in and near the uterus and ovaries, leading to serious consequences including infertility, ectopic pregnancy, abscess formation, and chronic pelvic pain (CDC 2010).

Syphilis

Syphilis is caused by the bacterium *Treponema pallidum*. Syphilis is passed from person to person through direct contact with a syphilis sore, which occurs mainly on the external genitals, vagina, anus, or in the rectum. Sores also can occur on the lips and in the mouth. Transmission of the organism occurs during vaginal, anal, or oral sex. Pregnant women with the disease can pass it to the babies (Zenilman & Shahmanesh 2011).

Many people infected with syphilis do not have any symptoms for years, yet remain at risk for late complications if they are not treated. Signs and symptoms differ in three stages of syphilis. Primary syphilis is characterized by a chancre, an indurated, nonpurulent, painless ulcer at the site of inoculation; secondary syphilis is characterized by a diffuse, scaling, papular eruption. Typical lesions have a raised border with a rubbery consistency and appear 3 weeks after exposure (Allen 2009). The time between infection with syphilis and the start of the first symptom can range from 10 to 90 days (average 21 days). The chancre is usually firm, round, small, and painless, lasting 3 to 6 weeks.

In the secondary stage, skin rash and mucous membrane lesions are the characteristics. The rash of secondary syphilis may appear as rough, red, or reddish brown spots both on the palms of the hands and the bottoms of the feet, usually without itching. However, rashes with a different appearance may occur on other parts of the body, sometimes resembling rashes caused by other diseases. Besides rashes, symptoms may also include fever, swollen lymph glands, sore throat, patchy hair loss, headaches, weight loss, muscle aches, and fatigue.

The latent and late stage of syphilis begins when primary and secondary symptoms disappear. But without treatment, syphilis will continue to remain in the body even without signs or symptoms, and this latent stage can last for years. In the late stage, the disease may subsequently damage the internal organs, including the brain, nerves, eyes, heart, blood vessels, liver, bones, and joints. The consequences could be difficulty in coordinating muscle movements, paralysis, numbness, gradual blindness, dementia and even death (CDC 2010).

Trichomoniasis

Trichomoniasis is caused by the single-celled protozoan parasite, *Trichomonas vaginalis*. The vagina and urethra are the most common sites of infection in women and men respectively. The parasite is sexually transmitted through penis-to-vaginal intercourse or vulva-to-vulva contact with an infected partner. Women can acquire the disease from infected men or women, but men usually contact it only from infected women.

Most men with trichomoniasis do not have signs or symptoms; however, some may temporarily have an irritation inside the penis, mild discharge, or slight burning after urination or ejaculation. Some infected women have a frothy, yellow-green vaginal discharge with a strong odor. The infection also may cause discomfort during intercourse and urination, as well as irritation and itching of the female genital area. Symptoms usually appear in women within 5 to 28 days of exposure. Having trichomoniasis can increase a woman's susceptibility to HIV infection with exposure, and may increase the chance that an HIV-infected woman passes HIV to her sex partner(s) (CDC 2010).

Chancroid

Chancroid is a highly contagious yet curable STI caused by the bacteria *Haemophilus ducreyi* and is included in the differential diagnosis of genital ulcers. The painful ulcer is a well-demarcated superficial ulceration without induration and is transmitted by sexual intercourse. The incubation period is 3~5 days after contact. The ulcers are accompanied by unilateral, regional lymphadenopathy (Allen 2009). Chancroid is transmitted in two ways, i.e., sexual transmission through skin-to-skin contact with open sore(s); non-sexual transmission when pus-like fluid from the ulcer is moved to other parts of the body or to another person.

Symptoms of chancroid usually occur within 4~10 days from exposure. It causes ulcers, usually of the genitals. The ulcer begins as a tender, elevated bump, or papule, that becomes a pus-filled, open sore with eroded or ragged edges. The ulcers can be very painful in men but women are often unaware of them. Swollen, painful lymph glands, or inguinal buboes, in the groin area are often associated with chancroid. Left untreated, chancroid may facilitate the transmission of HIV (Illinois Department of Public Health 2008).

Section 3   Coping with Adolescent Sexual and Reproductive Concerns

Adolescents look for information and clues about sex from a variety of sources, e.g., parents, siblings, peers, magazines, books, mass media, Internet. However, it is difficult to describe information collected using such channels as appropriate or complete. Many adolescents are found to be ignorant of physical changes, psychosocial implications as well as developmental tasks during adolescence, particularly those changes in association with sexuality.

As was required for being adolescent–friendly (WHO 2006a), health services should help adolescents protect and improve their current health; understand their sexuality and reproductive health needs; learn to take active responsibility for their reproductive health; prevent unplanned pregnancies; prevent serious health problems and premature deaths due to complications from a very early pregnancy or an unsafe abortion; avoid STIs; and make informed choices about reproductive health.

Adolescents' experimentation of risky sexual behaviors exerts threats to their own development and prosperity, and challenges the capacity of family and education as well as health services to cope with. Different strategies and actions can be taken by all relevant personnel in promoting sexual and reproductive health among adolescents. Whatever route is taken, it is always imperative and consistently to emphasize the meaningfulness of taking control over sexual intercourse for adolescents.

Adolescents

Many adolescents have not started sexual intercourse and it is always necessary to teach them to learn to assess their physical and psychosocial maturity to engage in sexual activities and to bear entailed responsibility or even burden, taking immediate and long-term impact of sexual activities into consideration. For those who are already sexually active, attention should be drawn to safe sex (e.g., using condom) and adverse consequences of unprotected sex (particularly unplanned pregnancy, unsafe abortion and STIs including HIV/AIDS). Whenever possible, adolescents should try to keep away from people with sexual intentions or avoid going to places where coerced sex may happen. Some measures may be used to reduce the risk of negative outcomes, e.g., coitus interrupts, condom, emergent contraception, safe period, oral contraceptive medicine. Nevertheless, it has to be borne in mind that the effectiveness of different measures may differ. Once sexual behaviors happen, it is better for adolescents to keep alert to any abnormal changes to their body, e.g., unusual genital or urinary discharges, genital pain, vaginal or urinary bleeding, itching (WHO 2008a).

Parents and teachers

Home and school are the primary settings and the proximate ecological context for adolescents to grow and to learn. A supportive environment is critical for adolescents to seek information and other resources to confront difficulties and challenges and to adjust negative emotional or behavioral reactions to keep on moving forward. Whenever possible, teachers and parents should be equipped with the necessary competencies to help adolescents tackle pubertal changes, sexual identity development, safe sex as well as prevention and protection of risky sexual activities. Open discussion about sexuality should be promoted between adolescents, parents and teachers, which precede the adoption of appropriate values, beliefs, behavioral and attitudes in concert with the society where adolescents are living.

Parents and teachers may not feel comfortable with such discussions. A few ways can be used to start the conversation about sexuality with adolescents, there are different ways that deserve a trial: parents or teachers may share with adolescents what they know, i.e., update information of interest, their own values; 'teachable moments' (e.g., media messages, current events, things happened at school to their friends) may be the other choice; alternatively, parents and teachers could enquire into what adolescents think about what happened regarding specific sexual behaviors or negative consequences (Baber 2005). It is desirable that parents and teachers are capable of dealing with personal sexual problems including discriminations and weaknesses and to express them in a genuine and scientific way, demonstrating respect for the diversity of human beings in terms of sexual beliefs and practices accompanied with the ability to help adolescents figure out different perspectives (Guo 2008).

Under most conditions, parents and adolescents are not so capable that they could simply provide opportunities for adolescents to talk about their interests, feelings and concerns regarding sexual and reproductive health freely, and do listen to them to reach a better understanding. Sometimes parents and teachers can work together with adolescents to find useful resources or to encourage them to seek assistance from relevant others (e.g., school health workers). However, there is no definite way to take to help promote adolescent health and development, what is needed is true concern over adolescent health and development using caring approaches. Support can always be sought from health professionals.

Health professionals for health promotion

As was indicated by the WHO, healthcare providers for adolescents must have the competencies to work with adolescents with adequate time investment and to provide them the required health services using evidence-based protocols and guidelines in a non-judgmental and considerate way that is easy to relate to (WHO 2006a, 2009). The competencies include: having knowledge of normal sexual development; being able to assess prevalent values and practices associated with sexual activity around adolescents; being able to assess the risks of and the responsibilities for sexual activities in adolescents; having the knowledge of prevalent STIs including the sequelae and relevant preventive strategies; being able to assess to resources for prevention and treatment for STIs, and being able to assess pregnancy intention and acceptance in adolescents (Keeney et al. 2004).

Healthcare providers are supposed to be valuable resources for the meeting of adolescents' needs for sexual and reproductive health, particularly for those underserved or marginalized groups (Braeken et al.2007).However, it is somewhat disappointing to find that, in mainland of China, though parents, teachers and healthcare providers perceive the competencies in sexual and reproductive health as important, relatively few would like to develop them, meaning that they are quite weak in this vegard.

Nevertheless, some studies supported the effectiveness of school-based sexual and reproductive health promotion led by healthcare providers in collaboration with school and family (Gavin et al. 2010, Wellings et al. 2006, Zang et al. 2011). It is also revealed that there is no universal approach to sexual and reproductive health promotion and no single-component intervention will work anywhere, so that comprehensive behavioral interventions might be appropriate particularly in relation to curricula (Wellings et al. 2006).

Other successful promotion programs for adolescent sexual and reproductive health are found to be media-, community-, workplace- or health facility-based (Speizer et al. 2003). Of more interest, with the increasing availability of Internet worldwide, the Internet increasingly seems to be a promising site to deal with sensitive topics including sexual and reproductive health. Available evidence seems to support that adolescents prefer to search for health information online with the belief that the Internet is a safe place to ask questions or collect information about personal health concerns (de Nooijer et al. 2008).

In summary, sexual and reproductive health is a sensitive, difficult but important topic area for adolescents and important personnel surrounding them to deal with. Limited evidence is available regarding the appropriate intervention for adolescents in mainland of China, suggesting the need for long and greater efforts.

References

Abiodun OM, Balogun OR. Sexual activity and contraceptive use among young female students of tertiary educational institutions in Ilorin, Nigeria[J]. Contraception, 2009, 79(2): 146-149.

Adedimeji AA, Omololu FO, Odutolu O. HIV risk perception and constraints to protective behaviour among young slum dwellers in Ibadan, Nigeria[J]. Journal of Health, Population, and Nutrition, 2007, 25(2): 146-157.

Adoption.com. Teen Pregnancy [EB/OL]. Adoption.com, 2011[22 Jul. 2011]:http://www. teenpregnancy.com/teenage/are-there-any-complications-that-could-arise-during-or-after-pregnancy.html.

AIDS.gov. Signs & Symptoms[EB/OL]. U.S. Department of Health & Human Services, 20 Jun. 2011[22 Jul. 2011]:http://www.aids.gov/hiv-aids-basics/hiv-aids-101/overview/signs-and-symptoms/index.html.

Ali MM, Cleland J. Sexual and reproductive behaviour among single women aged 15~24 in eight Latin American countries: a comparative analysis[J]. Social Science & Medicine, 2005, 60(6): 1175-1185.

Allen HB. Dermatology Terminology[M]. 1st. London: Springer, 2009.

Altini L, Coetzee D. Syndromic management of sexually transmitted infections[J/OL]. Continuing Medical Education, 2005, 23(2): 62-66[30 Jul. 2011]: http://www.cmej.org.za/index.php/cmej/article/viewFile/599/573.

Baber KM. Adolescent Sexuality[EB/OL]. Center on Adolescence, University of New Hampshire, Jun. 2005[18 Jul. 2011]: http://chhs.unh.edu/sites/chhs.unh.edu/files/docs/fs/adolescent_resources/Adolescent_Sexuality.pdf.

Banerjee SK, Clark KA. Exploring the pathways of unsafe abortion: a prospective study of abortion clients in selected hospitals of Madhya Pradesh, India[M/OL]. New Delhi, India: Ipas India, 2009[30 Jul. 2011]:http://www.ipas.org/Publications/asset_upload_file573_4424.pdf.

Barnett B, Schueller J. Meeting the needs of young clients: a guide to providing reproductive health services to adolescents[EB/OL]. Family Health International, 26 Jan. 2002[12 Jul. 2011]: http://aidsdatahub.org/dmdocuments/A_Guide_to_Providing_Reproductive_Health_Services_to_Adolescents.pdf.pdf.

Braeken D, Otoo-Oyortey N, Serour G. Access to sexual and reproductive health care: Adolescents and young people[J]. International Journal of Gynaecology and Obstetrics:

the official organ of the International Federation of Gynaecology and Obstetrics, 2007, 98(2): 172-174.

CDC. Sexually Transmitted Diseases (STDs)[EB/OL]. Center for Disease Control and Prevention, 4 Aug. 2010 [23 Jul. 2011]: http://www.cdc.gov/std/general/default.htm.

de Nooijer J, Veling ML, Ton A, et al. Electronic monitoring and health promotion: an evaluation of the E-MOVO Web site by adolescents[J]. Health Education Research, 2008, 23(3): 382-391.

Dixon-Mueller R. How young is "too young"?—comparative perspectives on adolescent sexual, marital, and reproductive transitions[J]. Studies in Family Planning, 2008, 39(4): 247-262.

Dixon-Mueller R. Starting young: sexual initiation and HIV prevention in early adolescence[J]. AIDS and Behavior, 2009, 13(1): 100-109.

Edwards WM, Coleman E. Defining sexual health: a descriptive overview[J]. Archives of Sexual Behavior, 2004, 33(3): 189-195.

Gao ES, Lou CH, Tu XU, et al. Status quo, prospect and strategy of adolescents and unmarried youth's reproductive health[M]. 1st. Shanghai, China: Second Military Medical Press, 2002.

Gavin LE, Catalano RF, David-Ferdon C, et al. A review of Positive Youth Development Programs that promote adolescent sexual and reproductive health[J]. Journal of Adolescent Health, 2010, 46(3, Suppl. 1): S75-S91.

Glasier A, Gulmezoglu AM, Schmid GP, et al. Sexual and reproductive health: a matter of life and death[J]. Lancet, 2006, 368(9547): 1595-1607.

Gomes KR, Speizer IS, Oliveira DD, et al. Contraceptive method used by adolescents in Brazilian state capital[J]. Journal of Pediatric and Adolescent Gynecology, 2008, 21(4): 213-219.

Guo BL. To understand school-based adolescent sexual and reproductive health education[J]. The Chinese Journal of Human Sexuality, 2008, 17(3): 23-29.

Hindin MJ, Fatusi AO. Adolescent sexual and reproductive health in developing countries: an overview of trends and interventions[J]. International Perspectives on Sexual and Reproductive Health, 2009, 35(2): 58-62.

Hobbs CGL, Sterne JAC, Bailey M, et al. Human papillomavirus and head and neck cancer: a systematic review and meta-analysis[J]. Clinical Otolaryngology, 2006, 31(4): 259-266.

Huo JZ. Existing problems and rethinking on Chinese adolescent sexual health and sexual health education[J]. Chinese Journal of School Doctor, 2004, 18(4): 379-380.

Illinois Department of Public Health. Chanroid[EB/OL]. Illinois Department of Public Health,

Jan. 2008[30 Jul. 2011]: http://www.idph.state.il.us/public/hb/hbchancroid.htm.

Keeney BG, Cassata L, McElmurry JB. Adolescent health and development in nursing and miwifery education[M/OL]. Geneva, Switzerland: World Health Organization, 2004[25 Jul. 2011]:http://whqlibdoc.who.int/hq/2004/WHO_EIP_HRH_NUR_2004.1.pdf.

Laski L, Schellekens S, Khatib-Maleh M. Generation of change: young people and culture[EB/OL]. United National Foundation of Population Fund, 2008[18 Jul. 2011]:http://www.unfpa.org/webdav/site/global/shared/documents/publications/2008/swp_youth_08_eng.pdf.

Myers ER, McCrory DC, Nanda K, et al. Mathematical model for the natural history of human papillomavirus infection and cervical carcinogenesis [J]. American Journal of Epidemiology, 2000, 151(12): 1158-1171.

Nelson AL, Woodward J. Sexually transmitted Diseases—a practical guide for primary care[M/OL]. Totowa, New Jersery: Humana Press, 2006[30 Jul. 2011]:http://springerlink.lib.tsinghua.edu.cn/content/978-1-58829-570-5/#section=293351&page=1&locus=73.

Ochieng MA, Kakai R, Abok K. The influence of peers and other significant persons on sexuality among secondary school students in Kisumu District, Kenya[J]. Asian Journal of Medical Sciences, 2011, 3(1): 26-31.

Olukoya AA, Kaya A, Ferguson BJ, et al. Unsafe abortion in adolescents[J]. International Journal of Gynecology & Obstetrics, 2001, 75(2): 137-147.

Palefsky JM. Human papillomavirus-related disease in men: not just a women's issue[J]. Journal of Adolescent Health, 2010, 46(4 Suppl.): S12-S19.

Robinson WJ. Woman—her sex and love life[M/OL]. The Project Gutenberg, 1929[22 Jul. 2011]: http://www.gutenberg.org/files/21840/21840-h/21840-h.htm#Chapter_Sixteen.

Speizer IS, Magnani RJ, Colvin CE. The effectiveness of adolescent reproductive health interventions in developing countries: a review of the evidence[J]. The Journal of adolescent health : official publication of the Society for Adolescent Medicine, 2003, 33(5): 324-348.

Tao FB, Sun Y, Hao JH. Early puberty and adolescent sexual and reproductive health services[J]. Journal of International Reproductive Health/Family Planning, 2010, 29(6): 406-409.

Wang FQ, Li Y, Cui HD, et al. Knowledge, attitude and behavior about sex and reproductive health of high school students[J]. Chinese Mental Health Journal, 2007, 21(1): 42-45.

Wellings K, Collumbien M, Slaymaker E, et al. Sexual behaviour in context: a global perspective[J]. Lancet, 2006, 368(9548): 1706-1728.

WHO. Gender and Human Rights—Sexual Health[EB/OL]. World Health Organization, Jan. 2002[17 Jul. 2011]: http://www.who.int/reproductivehealth/topics/gender_rights/sexual_ health/en/.

WHO. Promoting and safeguarding the sexual and reproductive health of adolescents [M/OL]. Geneva, Switzerland: World Health Organization, 2006a[18 Jul. 2011]: http://whqlibdoc. who.int/hq/2006/RHR_policybrief4_eng.pdf.

WHO. Orientation programme on adolescent health for health-care providers[M/OL]. Geneva, Switzerland: World Health Organization, 2006b[14 Jun. 2011]: http://whqlibdoc.who.int/ publications/2006/9241591269_Handout_eng.pdf.

WHO. Human Papillomavirus and HPV vaccines[M/OL]. Geneva, Switzerland: World Health Organization, 2007[24 Jul. 2011]: http://whqlibdoc.who.int/hq/2007/WHO_IVB_07.05_ eng.pdf.

WHO. Managing incomplete abortion[M/OL]. Geneva, Switzerland: World Health Organization, 2008a[24 Jul. 2011]: http://whqlibdoc.who.int/publications/2008/9789241546669_3_eng. pdf.

WHO. Adolescent Job Aid: a handy desk reference for primary level health worker [M/OL]. WHO, 2008b[21 Jul. 2011]: http://www.youthnet.org.hk/adh/4_4Sframework/3_Services_n_ commodities/2_Services/Adolescent%20job%20aid/Adolescent%20Job%20Aid%20-%20 prototype%203.pdf.

WHO. Quality Assessment Guidebook: a guide to assessing health services for adolescent [M/OL]. Geneva, Switzerland: World Health Organization, 2009[8 Jul. 2011]: http:// whqlibdoc.who.int/publications/2009/9789241598859_eng.pdf.

WHO. Reproductive Health[EB/OL]. World Health Organization, 2011a[30 Jul. 2011]: http:// www.who.int/topics/reproductive_health/en/.

WHO. World Health Statistics 2011[M/OL]. Geneva, Switzerland: World Health Organization, 2011b[18 Jul. 2011]: http://www.who.int/whosis/whostat/EN_WHS2011_Full.pdf.

Workowski KA, Berman S. Sexually transmitted diseases treatment guidelines, 2010: recommendations and reports[J/OL]. Morbidity and Mortality Weekly Report (MMWR), 2010, 59(RR12): 1-116[30 Jul. 2011]: http://www.cdc.gov/mmwr/preview/mmwrhtml/ rr5912a1.htm.

Wu J, Xiong GL, Shi SH. Study on sexual behaviors of adolescents[J]. Chinese Journal of Social Medicine, 2006, 23(2): 97-101.

Xu JS, Shtarkshall R. Determinants, outcomes and interventions of teenage pregnancy—an international perspective[J]. Reproductive & Contraception, 2004, 15(1): 9-18.

Yu Y, Gao JR. Analysis on the sex behaviors of adolescents and the influencing factors[J]. Health Education and Health Promotion, 2008, 3(4): 53-56.

Zang YL, Zhao Y, Yang Q, et al. A randomised trial on pubertal development and health in China[J]. Journal of Clinical Nursing, 2011, 20(21-22): 3081-3091.

Zenilman JM, Shahmanesh M. Sexually Transmitted Infections: diagnosis, management, and treatment[M]. 1st. Sudbury, Maryland: Jones & Bartlett Learning, 2011.

Zhao Q. Study situation of adolescent sexual health at home and abroad[J]. Journal of Public Health and Preventive Medicine, 2005, 16(5): 40-42.

Zheng LX, Zhu JM, Tian PL, et al. Sexual behavior and influence factors of young unmarried migratory female workers of Guangzhou[J]. Chinese Journal of Family Planning, 2000, 8(4): 162-192.

Chapter 8　Common Injuries in Adolescents

——— Jie Song, Xiaohong Hou, Chunmei Wang ———

Injury is a major killer of adolescents throughout the world. According to the WHO Global Burden of Disease (WGBD) in 2004, there were approximately 950 000 deaths in adolescents under the age of 18 years annually. China's Health Statistical Yearbook (CHSY) in 2010 showed the death caused by injuries from 10 to 19 years old was 32.58 per 100 000 people, whereas tens of millions of adolescents required hospital care for non-fatal injuries and many were left with some forms of disability, e.g., amputation with lifelong consequences (MoH 2010). Adolescent injury is a major public health problem that requires urgent attention.

With societal development, globalization, urbanization and motorization in association with environment change have grown to be the main factors accelerating adolescents' exposure to risks with significant impact on injuries. Injuries are not inevitable, but preventable or controllable. In this chapter, several common injuries (i.e., drowning, road traffic, poisoning, burns and other injuries like falls, violence) will be introduced, focusing on the epidemiology, risk factors and basic interventions.

Section 1　Drowning

Drowning is the process of experiencing respiratory impairment from submersion or immersion in liquid. Drowning outcomes are classified as death, morbidity and no morbidity (Peden et al. 2002). This definition of drowning was developed by world experts in 2002. In most countries around the world, drowning ranks among the top three causes of death from unintentional injury (Madrid et al. 2010). According to the WGBD, it was estimated that in 2004 approximately 175 000 adolescents under the age of 20 years died as a result of drowning around the world (Peden et al. 2008). Drowning is also one of the leading causes of unintentional injury among adolescents in China (Nong &

Yang 2006).

Prevalence

CHSY in 2010 showed that the rate of drowning deaths in urban residents from 10 to 14 years old was 3.23 per 100 000 people, and residents from 15 to 19 years old was 1.70 per 100 000 people. In comparison, drowning mortality in rural residents was 5. 35 per 100 000 for adolescents aged 10 to 14 years, and 3.38 per 100 000 adolescents of 15 to 19 years old (MoH 2010). It is noticeable from the above that the death rate of drowning among adolescents aged 10 to 14 years in both urban and rural areas is higher than that of among aged 15 to 19 years respectively.

Local data from the studies conducted in China's Zhejiang Province showed 66.7% of all drowning deaths in children occurred among the ages of 6 to 14 years old (Zhong et al. 2008). Boys are overrepresented compared with girls with regard to drowning death rate. The place of drowning mainly includes ponds, reservoirs and rivers, while the absence of pre-hospital care is related to drowning deaths. There is a need to place emphasis on risk factors of drowning, primary prevention, rapid and effective rescue, and immediate resuscitation in case of drowning.

Risk factors

Knowledge of risk factors is a critical prerequisite for the effective prevention of drowning in adolescents. Major risk factors for drowning are described briefly.

Social and demographic factors

Evidence from drowning studies shows that rural adolescents have much higher drowning rates than those in urban areas (Barss et al. 2009). Populations most at risk may be those living in low-income countries of densely populated communities with high exposure to open water (Hyder et al. 2008).

The death rate for drowning is different between age groups. Drowning among those of 1 to 14 years old in China is the leading cause of injury death (Zhang et al. 1998). Adolescents appear to take more risk because of increased independence, increased risk-taking and greater exposure to open water during work or leisure.

Studies (Madrid et al. 2010) suggest that rates of fatal drowning in males are higher than females due to increased exposure to water and risk behaviors, such as swimming alone, indulging in recreation to a greater extent involving aquatic activities.

Underlying medical conditions

Epilepsy, autism and certain cardiac arrhythmias are likely to increase the risk of drowning (Morgan et al. 2008). Children and adolescents with seizure disorder are likely to take more risk of submersion compared with those without epilepsy. Autism is also likely to be at increased risk of drowning according to studies based on a small number of drowning deaths (Sibert et al. 2003).

Agent factors

Lack of safety equipment in water transportation vessels could increase the risk of drowning. The use of blow-up toys, rafts and air mattresses has been recognized as unsafe (McIntosh 2009). Alcohol is linked to approximately 25% to 50% of adolescent and adult drowning in developed countries. Although alcohol increases the risk of drowning due to impaired balance, coordination and judgment, few studies have investigated the effects on alcohol to adolescent drowning in China (Peden et al. 2008). The reason for this may be that adolescents in China seldom drink alcohol.

Environmental factors

Adolescents are prone to drown in natural freshwater sites. Especially in low-income countries, the presence of open bodies of water or a well is strongly related to the risk of drowning. Bodies of such water include ponds, ditches, lakes, rivers, wells and cisterns. A study on adolescent submersion in rural area found that most drowning deaths occurred during daily activities that involve playing, working, washing, collecting water and/or crossing water (Wan 2008).

Inadequate supervision is the most common factor associated with submersions. Swimming in unfamiliar locations, in sites which are not designated as swim areas or not provided with lifeguards probably contribute to many drownings among adolescents (Morgan et al. 2008, Webber 2010). Poor weather conditions (e.g., floods or sea currents) can lead to adolescents drowning even in a single event (Zhong et al. 2008).

Intervention

Environmental improvement

Eliminating hazards is the most effective measure to prevent drowning. In developing countries, building safe bridges or installing piped water systems is found to be an effective factor which can lower down drowning rates significantly (Peden et al. 2008). The other effective measure for prevention is to create barriers between adolescents and bodies of water, for instance, covering wells, creating a fenced barrier near ponds and riverbanks, and building flood-control embankments (Webber 2010).

Swimming instruction

Many studies (McIntosh 2009, Moran 2010) showed that swimming instruction improved swimming abilities. As a result, increased abilities at swimming and survival skills can provide further protection for adolescents. These skills include making sufficient preparation before swimming; swimming safely in open water; identifying dangerous rocks, waves, and poor weather conditions; and mastering self-aid intervention of drowning, and so on.

Effective supervision

Adequate supervision is an important contributory factor for adolescent drowning. Trained lifeguards at swimming pools and on seashores can control risk-taking actions by swimmers, monitor water conditions and restrict swimming in the sea in addition to rescue and resuscitation to reduce the adverse consequences of drowning, e.g., death or brain damage (Peden et al. 2002, Zhong et al. 2008). Furthermore, it is desirable to teach parents and caregivers basic life-saving and first aid skills and to train the general community cardiopulmonary resuscitation (Moran 2010). Nevertheless, the professional rescue from drowning should be emphasized. Educating adolescents about hazards for drowning, recognizing swimming ability and developing rescue and resuscitation skill are good ways to improve ones cognition around water (Barss et al. 2009).

Coping with drowning

The best window of opportunity for rescue is at the site of the drowning (Minto & Woodward 2008). Retrieving patients from water as soon as possible, clearing mouth and pharynx of mud, weeds, vomitus and secretions, expelling the water inhaled in the airway and stomach are carried out to limit the brain damage caused by lack of oxygen.

Immediate cardiopulmonary resuscitation at the scene of an immersion incident is a critical measure associated with much better neurological outcomes in adolescents with submersion injury when breath and pulse are absent (McIntosh 2009). Initial resuscitative efforts by bystanders should include rescue breathing by mouth-to-mouth ventilation and chest compressions (Moran 2010).

In summary, drowning is a public health issue which deserves the worldwide attention. This section briefs some effective interventions to reduce adolescent drowning. More scientific approaches to risk and protective factors in the drowning sequence need to be explored.

Section 2   Road Traffic Injury

A road traffic injury (RTI) is any injury due to collisions originating, terminating or involving a vehicle partially or fully on a public highway and could be defined as fatal or non-fatal injuries incurred as a result of a road traffic crash (Peden et al. 2002 & 2004). It is reported that in most countries around world, road traffic injury is one of the leading two causes of death from unintentional injuries, with the highest occurrence among 15~19 year olds. Globally, road traffic injuries are the top cause of death among those 10 to 19 years old (Peden et al. 2008). As to the occurrence of RTI in mainland of China, it is predicted that the number of road traffic deaths is to increase by approximately 97% in 2020 (Kopits & Cropper 2005).

Prevalence

In 2004, road traffic crashes resulted in more than 262 000 death in adolescents aged under 19 years old (Peden et al. 2008). CHSY in 2010 showed that the rate of RTI in urban residents from 10 to 14 years old was 1.17 per 100 000 people, and the rate of among those from 15 to 19 years old was 3.78 per 100 000 people. As to those among rural residents, RTI mortality rate was 1.73 per 100 000 for adolescents aged 10 to 14 years, and 7.74 per 100 000 for adolescents aged 15 to 19 years (MoH 2010).

A survey from Chinese Center for Disease Control and Prevention (CDC China) showed that in all RTI, more than three quarters occurred on the road. The main causes of RTI are poor bicycling habits and breaking traffic rules (Han 2007). Globally road traffic fatality increases with age, reflecting the different ways of using the road. Adolescents have the tendency to travel more independently, initially as pedestrians, bicyclists, motorcyclists and finally drivers. Surveys in Asian countries showed that RTI was among the first two leading cause for child and adolescents mortality (Peden et al. 2008).

Risk factors

RTI is presently an increasing public health problem. Many factors increase the risk of RTIs for adolescents, for instance, physical and cognitive development, poor supervision, speeding, drink-driving, not using safety equipments and other factors related to vehicle safety and the road environment.

Adolescent-related factors

Age

Some evidences (Kaldy & Kovacs 2003) showed that full integration of visual signals into meaningful contexts was under development when children are around 10 to 12 years old. Some researches (Giedd 2004) suggested that cognitive process in an adolescent brain could affect the risk of road traffic crash in adolescent drivers. Globally, adolescents aged 15 to 19 years old are at greatest risk of RTI as a result of their increased tendency to exhibit risk-seeking behaviors, while the road traffic fatality rate increases with age in low, middle and high-income countries (Sauerzapf et al. 2010).

Gender

A strong relationship between gender and road traffic injury is found with the male-to-female ratio ranging from 3:1 to 5:1 (Peden et al. 2008). A survey for the urban residents of 10 to 14 years old in China showed that the rate of RTI in males was nearly twice that in females, and for those of 15 to 19 years old the occurrence of RTI in males was 5.28 per 100 000, but that in females was 2.20 per 100 000. Furthermore, the occurrence for rural adolescents was higher than that for urban adolescents of 10 to 14 years old (MoH 2010).

Different road users

In many low or middle-income countries, adolescents are at high risk because the road is a shared space for playing, working, walking, cycling and driving (Morgan & Mannering 2011). As pedestrians, risk-taking behavior and peer pressure may increase the risk among adolescents. For cyclists, the risk of RTI is associated with exposure, visibility, cycling on pavements and riding in mixed patterns of traffic. A study in Beijing (Li & Baker 1997) indicated that approximately one third of all traffic deaths were contributed to cyclists. As young drivers, several interrelated factors could place adolescents at an increasing risk for RTI, including drinking and driving, speeding, without using seat-belt, distractions while driving, fatigue and breaking traffic rules (Ghorbanali 2009).

Poor supervision

Lack of supervision has been recognized as a risk factor among adolescents for RTI (Peden et al. 2008). Good supervision could significantly reduce the possibility of an adolescent incurring RTI. Parents or caregivers in special families have a limited ability to supervise adolescents well. Those families might have a single parent, busy working parents, or at least one of parents is sick or depressed (Towner et al. 2005).

Environmental and vehicle-related factors

Poor vehicle design is an important risk factor for adolescent RTI. The standard design of a vehicle with a safer bumper, reverse backup sensors will benefit adolescents (Yeung et al. 2009).

Some environmental factors increase the risk of adolescent carrying out activities in the road environment. For example, volume of traffic, poor land use and road networks planning, lack of playgrounds, sidewalks and bicycle lanes; lack of safe and efficient public transportation systems, or excessive speed (Sauerzapf et al. 2010, Spoerri et al. 2011). Therefore, it is very important to create safe road environments for adolescents to reduce the risk for RTI.

Limited prompt treatment

The availability, accessibility and quality of trauma care services are critical for adolescent with RTI. Numerous adolescents with RTI did not receive prompt medical care and in Beijing, the ratio of those receiving care to those injured was 1:254 (Linnan et al. 2007). The serious problems related to pre-hospital and emergency care include the few trained healthcare and rescue workers, the limited availability of adequate pre-hospital care and acute care, the long-delay between the time of injury and reaching a hospital, or inappropriate referral services (Peden et al. 2008).

Intervention

The holistic measures are of particular value to adolescent road safety, for instance, improving the road environment, training road users to develop standard behaviors, designing appropriate vehicles to protect those inside or outside the vehicle, enforcing road safety regulations and strengthening the emergency health services (Ghorbanali 2009, Peden et al. 2008).

Road environmental improvement

Creating a safe environment for adolescents to walk and cycle should be given adequate attention, while designing space for motorized traffic. In residential areas, play areas and schools, vehicle speeds should be limited to below 30 km/h, which is safe for pedestrians and cyclists (Peden et al. 2008). To achieve this goal, various measures should be taken through essential infrastructural engineering approaches, e.g., designing mini-roundabouts, improving road lighting and creating one-way streets (Lin & Kraus 2009). At the same time, designing safe routes to school should be done together with the provision of buses to transport students to school and the encouragement of walking to school, if possible, accompanied by adult volunteers who may walk along safe routes wearing conspicuous vests. Constructing the infrastructure to separate different types of road users is another measure to prevent RTI, for instance, separate traffic lanes for cyclists and motorcyclists, and sidewalks for pedestrians (Peden et al. 2002).

Education and skills developing

Education plays an important role in RTI prevention. Current research (Bina et al. 2006) on road safety education suggests that developing practical skill is more likely to be effective for adolescents. The most important skill should be problem-solving and decision-making skills. Road safety education could be developed in the classroom and at home. However, adolescence is a difficult age group to reach through the educational approach. Television programs, theatrical presentation, peer education might be better approaches (Shope 2006).

Vehicle designing and safety equipment

Good vehicle design and standards benefit adolescents in and out the vehicles, for example, energy-absorbing crumple zones, redesigning car fronts, using reversing alarms and cameras, alcohol interlock systems. Overwhelming evidences (Hung et al. 2008, Thompson et al. 2009) showed that using appropriate protective equipment was effective for adolescents. Wearing a seat-belt, using bicycle helmets and using helmets for cyclists and motorcyclists are proved to be able to reduce the risk of being ejected from a vehicle and suffering serious or fatal traffic accident.

Road safety regulations

Establishing and rigorously enforcing road safety regulations can prevent nearly half of all deaths and serious injuries of relevance (Stevenson 1997). Raising the legal drinking age, setting lower blood alcohol concentration limits for novice drivers, using appropriate child restraints and seat-belts are key strategies to prevent RTI among adolescents (Hingson et al. 2004). Compliance can be enhanced through the introduction of legislation and enforcement, public awareness campaigns, or making helmets affordable (Peden et al. 2008).

Coping with RTIs

Prompt, efficient and effective pre-hospital care can diminish the number of deaths and injuries from road traffic crashes (Nguyen et al. 2008). Vehicle ambulances need to be equipped with medical devices for adolescents. Health workers need to be trained how to evaluate and manage injured adolescents. Volunteers, young people or emergency responders should be equipped with skills of recognizing an emergency, calling for help and first-aid basics (Sharma 2005).

Effective hospital care after an RTI is crucial for saving life. This could be effected through the provision of adequate resources, e.g., human resources (with appropriate skills, training and staffing) and physical resources (including equipment and supplies), to ensure the delivery of quality services for satisfactory outcomes (Peden et al. 2008).

Section 3   Poisoning

Poisoning refers to an injury resulting from the exposure to an exogenous substance involved cellular injury or even death. Poisons can enter the body through the respiratory tract, gastrointestinal tract, skin or mucous membranes (Peden et al. 2008). Poisoning may be acute or chronic and clinical manifestation may vary accordingly.

Data from the WGBD in 2004 showed that around 45 000 deaths relevant to poisoning were under the age of 20 years (Peden et al. 2008). Among those of 15 to 19 years old, poisoning ranked as the 13th leading cause of death. In general, mortality is the highest in infants and decreases with age until 14 years. After that, there is an increase in adolescents aged 15 years or older, which is caused by the increased exposure to risky workplace (Peden et al. 2008).

The types of poisoning vary considerably, mainly depending on local industrial and agricultural activities. Medicinal drugs are the top cause of non-fatal in children under the age of 5 years in middle and high-income countries (Andiran & Sarikayalar 2004). A survey in a hospital in Harbin China showed that hypnotics poisoning was serious among adolescents due to intentional self harm with the tendency to increase over time (Wang et al. 1999). Adolescents living in agricultural communities are at risk of acute pesticide poisoning and exposure to rodenticides at home or in the field are other reasons for poisoning in Jiangsu (Zhang et al. 1998). Poisoning among adolescents could be caused by carbon monoxide (CO) or alcohol misuse, but a study (Nazari et al. 2010) found that CO poisoning had the greatest risk with older adults.

Local data from studies (Li & Hu 1999) conducted in Xuzhou, China showed 6.38% of all unintentional deaths in children under the age of 5 were due to poisoning. A study (Liu et al. 1999) found that the largest number of poisoning deaths occurred in the age group of 20 to 29 years old. However, Liu et al. (2009) found that peak incidence of poisoning was in the age group of 30 to 39 years old, accounting for 28.0% and 69.7% subjects were between 20 years and 49 years of age. Mostly, poisoning among children under the age of 5 is most likely to be accidental, but poisoning among adolescents is likely to be deliberate and is probably intentional self harm (Peden et al. 2008).

Adolescent poisoning is a public health issue which requires attention. Various measures need to be taken due to the variety of reasons for adolescent poisoning. Strengthening the management of the pharmaceutical market may be an efficient measure to prevent hypnotic poisoning among adolescents. Less toxic pesticides or safe pesticides may be used to prevent cases of acute poisoning. Educating parents and caregivers on how to prevent poisoning has been proved to be a useful prevention strategy aiming to raise awareness and increase knowledge and skills on poison prevention (Nixon et al. 2004). Last, but not least, society should be concerned about the mental health of adolescents. Especially, parents should increase exchange with adolescents and reduce their psychological stress (Wang et al. 1999).

Section 4   Burns

Burns are miserable conditions probably accompanied by intense pain and long-term illness. Usually, adolescents are very curious to gain a little understanding about the world around them, e.g., playing with fire or touching hot objects, which may cause burns. In fact, it was estimated that over 96 000 children under the age of 20 years were estimated to have been fatally injured as a result of burns in 2004 (Peden et al. 2008). In China, burns are considered one of the leading causes of injuries among adolescents, accounting for 28.6% (Wang et al. 2011).

Definition and Classification

Burn is defined as an injury to the skin or other organic tissue caused by thermal trauma. It includes scalds (hot liquids), contact burns (hot solids) and flame burns (flame). Injuries due to radiation, radioactivity, electricity, friction or contact with chemicals are classified as burning injuries too (Wu & Wu 2008).

Burns are distinguished as thermal or inhalational burn by their mechanism or cause. They could be classified as first-degree (superficial), second-degree (partial-thickness) or third-degree (full-thickness) burns based on depth of burns (Bartlett 2002). In medical science, burns are classified according to the extent of burns calling 'rule of nines' (see Fig. 8-1) which assigns 9% to the head and neck region, 9% to each arm (including the hand), 18% to each leg (including the foot) and 18% to each side of the trunk (back, chest and abdomen) (Wu & Wu.2008).

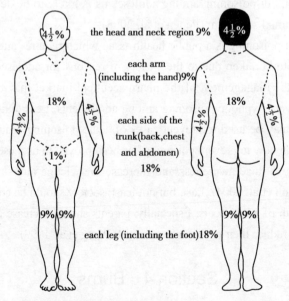

Fig. 8-1　Estimated surface area by 'rule of nines'

Epidemiology

According to WHO statistics, approximately 10% of all deaths caused by unintentional injury are due to fire-related burns and more deaths are from scalds, electricity, chemical burns and other forms of burns (Mock et al. 2008). Overall, children of 1 to 9 years old are at high risk for death from burns, with a global rate of 3.9 deaths per 100 000 people (Peden et al. 2008). Data from a survey among 511 senior high school students in the rural area of Shandong Province China (Jia et al. 2003) showed that 66.7% burned their arms, while 53.8% of all burning injuries were caused by boiling water and 23.2% by hot dietary.

Burns mainly occur in the domestic environment, especially the kitchen, considered as the most common place containing hot liquids, hot cooking oil or stove explosions (WHO 2006). It is worth noting that burns are the only type of unintentional injuries where girls have a higher incidence than boys. The fire-related death for girls is 4.9 per 100 000 people compared with 3.0 per 100 000 for boys (Peden et al. 2008), which is similar to what Guo et al. (2008) reported.

Burns bring about not only deaths, but also lifelong disabilities and disfigurements, which can place a considerable strain on individuals and their families and health-care facilities. Therefore, it is necessary to tackle the possibility of burns.

Risk factors

Risk factors for burns are diverse because of the variety of classifications and different mechanisms of burns (e.g., chemical burn and scalds from boiling fluids). Several common risk factors are introduced, mainly the adolescent-related, agent and environment risk factor.

Adolescent-related factors

Adolescents are curious in nature and eager to try something new and rare, including fire, matches, lighters or fireworks. A report from Hong Kong revealed boys were relatively more inquisitive by nature, resulting in more incidences of burn injuries (Ying & Ho 2001). In comparison, in some countries the occurrence of burns among girls are higher than boys due to increased exposure to the risk conditions such as wearing loose clothes and cooking. This suggests that the prevalence of burn injuries depends on which gender and what age might be more susceptible to burn injuries.

Agent factors

Unsafe equipment, for example, cooking and heating equipment relying on fossil fuels; electrical appliances, plugs and wires, increase the risk of burns for adolescents. In China, for some reasons, flammable substances like kerosene are stored in the house where there is a very dangerous risk of fire-related burn (Zhang 2010).

Many countries celebrate festivals by lighting fireworks that pose a significant threat to adolescents susceptible for burn injuries, especially boys. Studies reported that in Greece, 70% of firework burn injuries involved adolescents aged 10 to 14 years old (Peden et al. 2008). Fireworks have been banned in some areas in China, but careless and unsafe storage and lighting of fireworks contribute a great number of burn injuries, especially damage on eyes each year (Shi & Zhao 2010).

Environment factors

Apart from heating equipment and the kitchen structure, socioeconomic factors (e.g., literacy level, family economic status and relevant laws and regulations) can increase the risk of burns (Edelman 2007). WHO (Mock et al. 2008) reported that the mortality and morbidity by burns were strongly associated with poverty, with a higher incidence caused by burns among adolescents under 20 years old in low and middle-income countries and poor families in high-income countries.

In addition, the failure to provide proper supervision is one of the common factors in adolescent burns. Inadequate water supply to stop the flames spreading and non-functioning smoke detectors are strong risk factors (Peden et al. 2008).

Intervention

Burns may be prevented or minimized by implementing the following strategies:

Environment improvement

Environment improvement was found to reduce the occurrence of burns for adolescents. The following efforts could be taken: have better electronic equipments (e.g., safe lamps, stoves), construct clean and safe kitchens which can meet the building standards, and move dangerous cooking facilities off the ground and out of rooms (Peden et al. 2008). Smoke alarms and residential sprinklers are the other effectives measure to detect the occurrence of fire in time and to stop the flame spreading quickly (Sarma 2011).

Education and Supervision

Studies (Zhang & Ding 2006) indicated that many burn injuries occurred because of careless attitude or lack of sufficient necessary knowledge. To increase adolescents' and their care providers' awareness and knowledge about causes, risk factors, mechanisms, and primary health care methods for burns might be effective strategy to prevent the burns and to reduce the degree of damage (Forjuoh 2006).

Adolescents are curious and inquisitive by nature and enjoy experiencing new things which make them more vulnerable (Ying & Ho, 2001). Through educating their parents, the parental supervision over adolescents can be enhanced (e.g., fireworks use) (Peden et al. 2008). It is desirable to teach their parents to identify possible burns and the condition of the adolescents (Parbhoo et al. 2010), and to take immediate measures to address the burns simply (e.g., pre-hospital) to save the lives and to prevent the infection (Sarma 2011).

Managing burns

Adolescents should be stabilized immediately after a burn before being transported to hospital and this can be done effectively by family members. The purpose is to cool the burned, prevent ongoing burning or contamination (Wu & Wu 2008).

Once the burned adolescent is transported to acute care facilities, the initial assessment should focus on checking airway, breathing and circulation (Peden et al. 2008). There must be a careful and thorough examination from head to toe to find any other signs of trauma. A variety of treatments and rehabilitation measures could be taken according to the extent and depth of burns. If the adolescent is in shock, fluid infusion is essential. Health care workers must know that the first 24 hours is the critical time point (Huang 2008). If the burned adolescent survives the first 48 hours, the risk of death remains because of infectious complications due to the loss of the barrier to bacteria that antibiotics shall be prescribed (WHO 2006).

It has to be emphasized that not all adolescents suffering from burns must be admitted to hospital to receive treatments. In some countries, community health facilities and rehabilitation centers are well established where medical cost is relative lower that the poor families can afford (Mistry et al. 2010).

The occurrence of burns varies according to medical and economic status in the district. Many interventions require rigorous and systematic assessment. More evidence is required for wider implementation.

Section 5　Other Injuries

Apart from the injuries described above, there are some other injuries to adolescents, such as falls and violence, which are also leading causes of morbidity and disability and can result in high social and economic costs (Linnan et al. 2007). In Jiangxi province in China, falls were the fourth leading cause of death (3.1 per 100 000 aged 0~17 years) (Peden et al. 2008). More than one million individuals lose their life as a result of violence, mostly in young ages (Sousa et al. 2010). The injuries are considered as public health problems.

Falls are defined as "an event which results in a person coming to rest inadvertently on the ground or floor or other lower level" (WHO 2011). Youth violence has been considered as "the threatened or actual physical force or power initiated by an individual that results in, or has a high likelihood of resulting in physical or psychological injury or death" by the Center for Disease Control (Centers for Disease Control and Prevention, CDC 2011).

Studies (Rappaport & Thomas 2004) indicated that demographic, social and cultural characteristics had association with fall and violent behaviors. It is estimated that boys fall more frequently than girls, for example, falls occurred 3.5 times more frequently in boys than in girls and higher rates occurred in rural areas than in urban areas (Peden et al. 2008). It is also estimated that adolescents exposed to the violence are more likely to commit violence than those who were not exposed to it (Kennedy et al. 2009).

Different inventions are taken according to the various injuries. Overall, primary, secondary and tertiary prevention are adopted. Primary prevention is to reduce the incidence of problems or pathology by targeting the entire population, not just those who are at risk (Fields & McNamara 2002). Through primary invention achieved by educating all adolescents, future injuries behavior among adolescents can be decreased. Secondary prevention puts the targets on the adolescents with risk behaviors, for example, to prevent injuries from falls, identifying, replacing or modifying unsafe products may be a useful strategy, e.g., helmets and wrist guards are used for adolescents to engage in horse riding or ice skating (Peden et al. 2008). For violence, identifying earlier aggressive behavior, poor social skills, neighborhood deterioration, access to firearms or drugs, and deviant peer groups are very important (Assis et al. 2004). After injuries occur, treatment interventions for youths are characterized as tertiary prevention (Fields & McNamara 2003). Once injuries occur, adolescents should get treatment as soon as possible in hospital or communities. It should be noted that future consequences of injuries, such as disability, psychological condition, need to be emphasized.

References

Andiran N, Sarikayalar F. Pattern of acute poisonings in childhood in Ankara: what has changed in twenty years? [J]. The Turkish Journal of Pediatrics, 2004, 46(2): 147-152.

Assis SG, Avanci JQ, Santos NC, et al. Violence and social representation in teenagers in Brazil[J]. Rev Panam Salud Publica, 2004, 16(1): 43-51.

Barss P, Subait OM, Ali MHA, et al. Drowning in a high-income developing country in the Middle East: newspapers as an essential resource for injury surveillance [J]. Journal of Science and Medicine Sport, 2009, 12(1): 164-70.

Bartlett SN. The problem of children's injuries in low-income countries: a review[J]. Health Policy and Planning, 2002, 17(1): 1-13.

Bina M, Graziano F, Bonino S. Risky driving and lifestyles in adolescence [J]. Accident Analysis and Prevention, 2006, 38(3): 472-481.

Centers for Disease Control and Prevention. Centers for Disease Control and Prevention, America, 26 Jul. 2010 [2 Jul. 2011]: http://www.cdc.gov/ViolencePrevention/youthviolence/definitions.html.

Edelman LS. Social and economic factors associated with the risk of burn injury [J]. Burns,

2007, 33(8): 958-965.

Fields SA, McNamara JR. The prevention of child and adolescent violence: a review [J]. Aggression and Violent Behavior, 2003, 8(1): 61-91.

Forjuoh SN. Burns in low- and middle-income countries: a review of available literature on descriptive epidemiology, risk factors, treatment, and prevention [J]. Burns, 2006, 32(5): 529-537.

Ghorbanali M. Road traffic fatalities among pedestrians, bicyclists and motor vehicle occupants in Sirjan, Kerman, Iran[J]. Chinese Journal of Traumatology (English Edition), 2009, 12(4): 200-202.

Giedd JN. Structural magnetic resonance imaging of the adolescent brain[J]. Annals of the New York Academy of Sciences, 2004, 1021(1): 77-85.

Guo NX, Li JY, Qiu CP, et al. The epidemiological analysis about injuries of 3677 students aged 6~19 old from primary and middle schools[J]. Chinese Journal of School Doctor, 2008, 22(3): 256-258.

Han J. Road traffic injuries, the second causes in all unintentional death among children in China [EB/OL]. Xinhua Net, 26 Apr. 2007 [2 Jul. 2011]: http://news.xinhuanet.com/ fortune//2007-04/26/content_6032438.htm.

Hingson RW, Assailly J-P, Allan WF. Underage drinking: frequency, consequences, and interventions[J]. Traffic Injury Prevention, 2004, 5(3): 228-236.

Hung DV, Stevenson MR, Ivers RQ. Barriers to, and factors associated, with observed motorcycle helmet use in Vietnam[J]. Accident Analysis and Prevention, 2008, 40(4): 1627-1633.

Hyder AA, Borse NN, Blum L, et al. Childhood drowning in low- and middle-income countries: urgent need for intervention trials[J]. Journal of Paediatrics and Child Health, 2008, 44(4): 221-227.

Jia CX, Zhang JY, Bo QG, et al. An investigation on the injuries in 511 students of senior high school in rural areas of Shandong Province[J]. Chinese Journal of Prevention and Contral of Chronic Non-Communicable Dsieases, 2003, 11(6): 263-265.

Káldy Z, Kovács I. Visual context integration is not fully developed in 4-year-old children [J]. Perception, 2003, 32(6): 657-666.

Kennedy AC, Bybee D, Sullivan CM, et al. The effects of community and family violence exposure on anxiety trajectories during middle childhood: the role of family social support as a moderator [J]. Journal of Clinical Child and Adolescent Psychology, 2009, 38(3): 365-379.

Kopits E, Cropper M. Traffic fatalities and economic growth [J]. Accident Analysis and

Prevention, 2005, 37(1): 169-178.

Li GH, Baker SP. Injuries to bicyclists in Wuhan, People's Republic of China [J]. American Journal of Public Health, 1997, 87(6): 1049-1052.

Li H, Hu PZ. Dynamic analysis about unintentional death among teenagers below 10 year olds in Xuzhou[J]. China School Health, 1999, 20(3): 230.

Lin M-R, Kraus JF. A review of risk factors and patterns of motorcycle injuries[J]. Accident Analysis & Prevention, 2009, 41(4): 710-722.

Linnan M, Giersing M, Cox R, et al. Child mortality and injury in Asia: an overview[EB/OL]. UNICEF & Innocenti Research Centre, Oct. 2007 [2 Jul. 2011]: http://www.unicef-irc.org/publications/pdf/iwp_2007_04.pdf.

Liu L, Liu Y, Huang GZ. Analysis of 389 autopsy records of poisoning deaths[J]. Forensic Science and Technology, 1999, (6): 16-18.

Liu Q, Zhou L, Zheng N, et al. Poisoning deaths in China: type and prevalence detected at the Tongji Forensic Medical Center in Hubei[J]. Forensic Science International, 2009, 193(1-3): 88-94.

Madrid C, Maldonado MH, Parra AR, et al. Epidemiology of drowning deaths in Venezuela, 1996-2007[J]. International Journal of Infectious Diseases, 2010, 14(Suppl. 1): e138.

McIntosh G. Swimming lessons may reduce risk of drowning in young children [J]. The Journal of Pediatrics, 2009, 155(3): 447.

Minto G, Woodward W. Drowning and immersion injury[J]. Anaesthesia and Intensive Care Medicine, 2008, 9(9): 409-412.

Mistry RM, Pasisi L, Chong S, et al. Socioeconomic deprivation and burns[J]. Burns, 2010, 36(3): 403-408.

Mock C, Peck M, Peden M, et al. A WHO plan for burn prevention and care[EB/OL]. World Health Organization, 22 Jun. 2008: http://whqlibdoc.who.int/publications/2008/9789241596299_eng.pdf.

MoH. 2010 China Health Statistics Yearbook[EB/OL]. Ministry of Health, China, [25 May 2011]: http://www.moh.gov.cn/publicfiles/business/htmlfiles/zwgkzt/ptjnj/year2010/index2010.html.

Moran K. Child drowning prevention and parental understanding of CPR[J]. Journal of Science and Medicine in Sport, 2010, 12(Suppl. 2): e30.

Morgan A, Mannering FL. The effects of road-surface conditions, age, and gender on driver-injury severities[J]. Accident Analysis and Prevention, 2011, 43(5): 1852-1863.

Morgan D, Ozanne-Smith J, Triggs T. Descriptive epidemiology of drowning deaths in a surf beach swimmer and surfer population[J]. Injury Prevention, 2008, 14(1): 62-65.

Nazari J, Dianat I, Stedmon A. Unintentional carbon monoxide poisoning in Northwest Iran: a 5-year study[J]. Journal of Forensic and Legal Medicine, 2010, 17(7): 388-391.

Nguyen TLH, Nguyen THT, Morita S, et al. Injury and pre-hospital trauma care in Hanoi, Vietnam[J]. Injury, 2008, 39(9): 1026-1033.

Nixon J, Spinks A, Turner C, et al. Community based programs to prevent poisoning in children 0~15 years[J]. Injury Prevention, 2004, 10(1): 43-46.

Nong XQ, Yang L. A prospective study on epidemiology of children drowning[J]. China Public Health, 2006, 22(3): 363-365.

Parbhoo A, Louw QA, Grimmer-Somers K. Burn prevention programs for children in developing countries require urgent attention: a targeted literature review [J]. Burns, 2010, 36(2): 164-175.

Peden M, McGee K, Sharma G. The injury chart book: a graphical overview of the global burden of injuries [EB/OL]. World Health Organization, 2002 [2 Jul. 2011]: http://whqlibdoc.who.int/publications/924156220X.pdf.

Peden M, Scurfield R, Sleet D, et al. World report on road traffic injury prevention [EB/OL]. World Health Organization, 2004 [2 Jul. 2011]: http://whqlibdoc.who.int/publications/2004/9241562609.pdf.

Peden M, Oyegbite K, Ozanne-Smith J, et al. World Report on Child Injury Prevention [EB/OL]. World Health Organization, 2008 [22 Jun. 2011]: http://whqlibdoc.who.int/publications/2008/9789241563574_eng.pdf.

Rappaport N, Thomas C. Recent research findings on aggressive and violent behavior in youth: implications for clinical assessment and intervention[J]. Journal of Adolescent Health, 2004, 35(4): 260-377.

Sarma BP. Prevention of burns: 13 years' experience in Northeastern India[J]. Burns, 2011, 37(2): 265-272.

Sauerzapf V, Jones AP, Haynes R. The problems in determining international road mortality[J]. Accident Analysis and Prevention, 2010, 42(2): 492-499.

Sharma BR. Development of pre-hospital trauma-care system——an overview[J]. Injury, 2005, 36(5): 579-587.

Shi AG, Zhao L. Clinical characteristics of burn for explosion of firecrackers [J]. Jilin Medical Journal, 2010, 31(22): 3648-3649.

Shope JT. Influences on youthful driving behavior and their potential for guiding interventions to reduce crashes [J]. Injury prevention, 2006, 12 (Suppl. 1): i9-i14.

Sibert JR, Lyons RA, Smith BA, et al. Preventing deaths by drowning in children in the United Kingdom: have we made progress in 10 years? Population based incidence study [J].

British Medical Journal, 2002, 324(7345): 1070-1071.

Sousa S, Correia T, Ramos E, et al. Violence in adolescents: social and behavioural factors[J]. Gaceta sanitaria, 2010, 24(1): 47-52.

Spoerri A, Egger M, von Elm E. Mortality from road traffic accidents in Switzerland: longitudinal and spatial analyses [J]. Accident Analysis & Prevention, 2011, 43(1): 40-48.

Stevenson M. Childhood pedestrian injuries: what can changes to the road environment achieve? [J]. Australia New Zealand Journal of Public Health, 1997, 21(1): 33-37.

Thompson DC, Rivara FP, Thompson R. Helmets for preventing head and facial injuries in bicyclists [J/OL]. Cochrane Database of Systematic Reviews, 2009, 1): http://www.thecochranelibrary.com/userfiles/ccoch/file/Safety_on_the_road/CD001855.pdf.

Towner E, Dowswell T, Errington G, et al. Injuries in children aged 0~14 years and inequalities[EB/OL]. Health Development Agency, London, 2005 [2 Jul. 2011]: http://www.nice.org.uk/niceMedia/pdf/injuries_in_children_inequalities.pdf.

Wan Y. Consideration of adolescent submersion in rural area[J]. Swimming Magazine Quarterly, 2008, 3): 14-16.

Wang HJ, Xiao J, Zhang J, et al. Comparable results of epidemiology of children with burns among different decades in a burn unit in Jinzhou, China[J]. Burns, 2011, 37(3): 513-520.

Wang Q, Ge L, Che SH. A survey and analysis on overdose hypnotics poisoning in 103 cases adolescent[J]. Harbin Medicine, 1999, 19(1): 10-11.

Webber JB. Drowning, the New Zealand way: Prevention, rescue, resuscitation[J]. Resuscitation, 2010, 81(2, Suppl. 1): S27.

WHO. Facts about injuries: burns[EB/OL]. World Health Organization & International Society for Burn Injuries, 2006 [22 Jun. 2011]: http://www.who.int/entity/violence_injury_prevention/publications/other_injury/en/burns_factsheet.pdf.

WHO. Violence and Injury Prevention and Disability (VIP): Falls[EB/OL]. World Health Organization, 24 May 2011 [2 Jul. 2011]: http://www.who.int/violence_injury_prevention/other_injury/falls/en/index.html.

Wu ZD, Wu ZH. Surgery[M]. 7th ed. Beijing, China: People's Medical Publishing House, 2008.

Yeung JHH, Leung CSM, Poon WS, et al. Bicycle related injuries presenting to a trauma centre in Hong Kong[J]. Injury, 2009, 40(5): 555-559.

Ying SY, Ho WS. Playing with fire: a significant cause of burn injury in children[J]. Burns, 2001, 27(1): 39-41.

Zhang CP, Ding GL. The prevention of burns[J]. Community Medical Journal, 2006, 4(11): 72-73.

Zhang PB, Chen RH, Deng JY, et al. A prospective study on accidental deaths among 0~

14-year-old children in Jiangsu, 1994~1995[J]. Chinese Journal of Epidemiology, 1998, 19(5): 290-293.

Zhang XZ. Causes and prevention countermeasures of fire disasters for modern family[J]. Fire Science and Technology, 2010, 29(9): 841-843.

Zhong ZW, Zhou ZM, Wang YW. A study on risk factors of drowning deaths and intervention in children[J]. Zhejiang Clinical Medicine, 2008, 10(2): 199.

Chapter 9   Adolescents with Disabilities

—— Yuli Zang, Qian Liu, Jing Liu ——

Disability is a normal constituent of the human phenomenon. Almost everyone is at risk of temporary or permanent impairment at some point in life. Persons with disabilities (PWD)—particularly adolescents—are among the most vulnerable groups in society, while many of them do not have equal access to health care (Schranz et al. 2008, WHO & WB/World Bank 2011). This chapter will bring into surface critical issues surrounding PWD with a particular emphasis on adolescent PWD.

Defining disability

Through a positive bio-psycho-social approach, to function and disability in the continuum of health, the WHO generated a conceptual framework (i.e., International Classification of Function, Disability and Health, ICF) to interpret functioning and disability as a dynamic interaction between health conditions and contextual factors, personal and environmental (WHO 2002, WHO & WB 2011).

In the ICF (WHO 2005,WHO & WB 2011), problems with human functioning are categorized in three interconnected areas: impairments, activity limitation, and participation restriction. Impairments are problems or specific decrements in body function or alterations in body structure (e.g., paralysis or blindness); activity limitations are difficulties in executing activities (e.g., walking or eating); participation restrictions are problems with involvement in any area of life (e.g., facing discrimination in employment or transportation). Disability is the umbrella term for impairments, activity limitation and participation restriction, reflecting the negative aspects of the interaction (i.e., difficulties) between an individual (with a health condition) and that individual's contextual factors (environmental and personal factors). Hereby, health conditions refer to diseases, injuries and disorders (see Fig. 9-1).

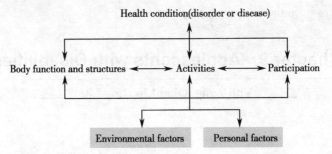

Fig. 9-1   Representation of the International Classification of Functioning, Disability and Health (WHO 2011)

Poverty, disability and health

It is increasingly understood that disability is not only a human rights issue but an important development issue with growing evidence suggesting that PWD may experience poorer socioeconomic outcomes and poverty than those without disabilities. As was articulated (DFID 2000, Schranz et al. 2008), poverty (particularly the severe and multi-dimensional poverty with long duration) and disability reinforce each other, which traps PWD in a vicious cycle and puts them in an ever-worsening double disadvantage involving exclusion and stigma (see Fig. 9-2). In particular, among those with threatening chronic conditions (e.g., cancer), reciprocal (worsening) effects are found between adolescent development and the illness in all aspects, i.e., biological, psychological and social (Michaud et al. 2004, Suris et al. 2004).

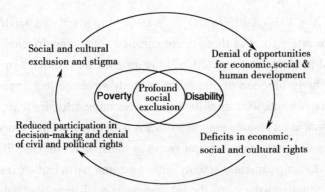

Fig. 9-2   Vicious circle between poverty and disability

Except the assurance of sufficient income from social security, employment and so forth, education and schooling might be the most effective approach to the disruption or even the reverse of the vicious circle surrounding poverty, disability, health and overall vulnerability. The WHO (2010) proposed a matrix to guide the community-based rehabilitation (CBR) for PWD, which highlights the complex of actions covering the areas of education, livelihood, empowerment and social aspect in addition to health. This matrix (see Fig. 9-3) is underpinned by the primary health care principles (including but not limited to being equal, accessible, affordable, available, essential) consistently stressed by WHO to urge all of its member states to reform the health systems for the benefit to health for all (WHO 1978, WHO 2008).

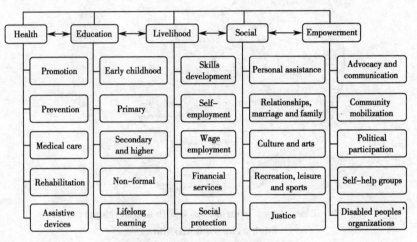

Fig. 9-3　CBR matrix (WHO 2010)

Group features

Similar to the relative neglect of adolescent health and development issues, adolescent PWD drawn limited attention during national and international sampling survey or national census, for example, little data is available to estimate the population size of adolescent PWD. It is conjectured that adolescent PWD aging from 10 to 19 years old may account for around 5% of all PWD (CYCRC 2008,WHO & WB 2011). Using the primary outcomes from 2010 national census and the second national survey about PWD in mainland of China (CDPF 2008, CNBS 2011), it is estimated that approximately 200 million are PWD and of them approximately 8 million (4.13%) are adolescent PWD.

Adolescent PWD faced more challenges compared with those without disability, both physically and psychosocially. In the bioecological approach to holistic health and development including the aspects of body, mind and spirit (i.e., physical, mental and spiritual aspects) (see Fig. 9-4), the immediate biosphere including peers, parents and other adult models plays a significant role in improving adolescent PWD's health and development for a satisfactory transition to adulthood (Bronfenbrenner 2005, St Leger 2006, Wang et al. 2010).

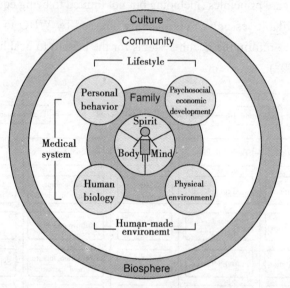

Fig. 9-4 Bioecological approach to health and development for adolescents with disabilities

In particular, sexuality is an integral part of human being, the attitude regarding PWD as asexual is persistent (Esmail et al. 2010, Shakespeare 2009, WHO & UNFPA 2009) that adolescent PWD's sexual maturation during the period of puberty is more likely to be neglected, resulting in more risks of negative consequences of sexual activities, e.g., unexpected pregnancy, abortion, sexual abuse, sexually transmitted infection and so forth (Blum et al. 2001, Surís et al. 1996, WHO & UNFPA 2009). Adolescent PWD often report relatively poorer interpersonal relationship, emotional wellness and academic achievement or lower level of education or employment, but more violence or abuse and suicidal attempts, suggesting the broad areas for intervention (Blum et al. 2001, Lisa Skär 2003, Stevens et al. 1996, Svetaz et al. 2000). Though life skill programs were frequently reported as helpful, the resources constraint, marginal positive outcome and the complexity of intervention may influence the expansion of these activities. Whatever program are developed, it is crucial to have the contribution of adolescent PWD, which is extremely useful when conducting research to identify most effective strategies and measures (Kingsnorth et al. 2007). It has to be remembered by all when developing programs for PWD that nothing is about us without us (Schranz et al. 2008, WHO & WB 2011).

Health care workers' attitudes towards PWD

Considering approximately 5% of all PWD are adolescents (CYCRC 2008, WHO & WB 2011), it is astonishing to find that very limited data are available about adolescent PWD health and development in mainland of China, suggesting the relative little attention to this vulnerable group. As to the health professions, there is a general insensitivity and limited concern over disability-related issues in healthcare education and practice under the long and strong influence of the biomedical model (Matziou et al. 2009, Sahin & Akyol 2010, Shakespeare et al. 2009, ten Klooster et al. 2009). Research shows the poor attitudes among nursing students and nurses, and these attitudes may be worse than those medical students or doctors held, but better than what their peers held (Matziou et al. 2009, Sahin & Akyol 2010, Ten Klooster et al. 2009).

In fact, it was revealed a decade ago that PWD perceived nurses and nursing students' attitudes as demeaning and disempowering (Scullion 1999). Given that enabling PWD is argued as one of the important responsibilities for nurses, particular emphasis on social dimension should be integrated into nursing education and practice to buffer the overemphasis of the biological aspects (Scullion 2000). Only limited education change was reported during the last decade: the trial of integrating a focused disability unit into the revised undergraduate nursing curriculum in New Zealand appeared to have no significant statistical impact over the attitudes towards PWD among a convenience sample of students after the completion of unit (Seccombe 2007). To make more effort to change current healthcare curriculum to enhance students and healthcare workers' competency, thereby, is prerequisite and an urgent need for the high quality delivery of healthcare services to PWD towards the reduction of health disparity (Monsen, 2006, WHO 2009).

Facilitate the transition to adulthood

Adolescent PWD require more support during the transition to adulthood, while nurses were demonstrated to play a crucial role in facilitating the transition (Betz 2007). In general, transition refers to a passage or movement from one state, condition, or place to another (Schumacher & Meleis 1994). For health care workers, the transition services are described as a coordinated set of activities for adolescent PWD within a results-oriented process focusing on the improvement of academic and functional achievements. This set of activities are designed to facilitated adolescent PWD to move from school to post-school activities including post-secondary education, vocational training and integrated employment, continuing and adult education, adults services, independent living, or community participation. The complete transition should cover the aspects of health care, education, social network, community living and job or career preference (Betz 2007, Park et al.2011).

The best practice model of transition comes into being when the following essential features are present: family involvement; interagency interdisciplinary collaboration; self-determination skills; and a transition plan including work-based experiences in inclusive settings (i.e., typical locations such as shelter workshops wherein PWD are considered to be the primary employment setting of choice) (Betz 2007). Nevertheless, in a survey the transition activities were not perceived as satisfactory in the parents' view of adolescent PWD ($n=753$), but health care workers ($n=141$, primarily pediatrician) felt that they provided more than the parents thought (Geenen et al. 2003). Of the 13 transition activities, adolescent PWD's parents seem to rate the majority ($n=7$) as either important or very important, suggesting the great need for transition activities. These activities are: taking care of general health and disability, coordinating health services with other health professionals, help get health insurance, help find health care provider when becoming an adult, teaching to manage own health, and working with the school to coordinate care (Geenen et al. 2003).

To guide health care workers to provide transition services to adolescents with disabilities, the Society for Adolescent Medicine (SAM) states the following action positions: a. ensure a medical home for primary care; b. identify core knowledge and skills for health care workers, adolescents and their parents as appropriate; c. prepare and maintain portable medical summary; d. create a health care transition plan; e. provide primary and preventive care; and f. ensure health insurance (Park et al. 2011, SAM 2003). Accordingly a group of core outcomes are identified by the Health Resources and Services Administration (HRSA), the United State

Department of Health and Human Services to assess the provision of transition services to adolescent PWD and the final outcome is that adolescent PWD receive the services necessary to make transition to all aspects of life, including adult health care, work and independence (HSRA 2008, Park et al. 2011).

In contrast with the significant efforts in developed societies, little was found about the transition services to adolescent PWD in mainland of China. Health care workers could make full use of available evidences from other countries or societies to develop their role in facilitating the transition for adolescent PWD from childhood to adulthood.

References

Betz CL. Facilitating the transition of adolescents with developmental disabilities: nursing practice issues and care[J]. Journal of Pediatric Nursing, 2007, 22(2): 103-115.

Blum RW, Kelly A, Ireland M. Health-risk behaviors and protective factors among adolescents with mobility impairments and learning and emotional disabilities[J]. Journal of Adolescent Health, 2001, 28(6): 481-490.

Bronfenbrenner U. Making human beings human: bioecological perspectives on human development[M]. Thousand Oaks, California: Sage, 2005.

CDPF. 2006 national survery outcomes about persons with disabilities by gender and age[EB/OL]. China Disabled Persons Federation, 12 Aug. 2008[25 Jul. 2011]: http://www.cdpf.org.cn/sytj/content/2008-04/07/content_30336060.htm.

CNBS. #1 Statistics Announcement about the six national population census [EB/OL]. China National Bureau of Statistics, 2011[25 May 2011]: http://www.stats.gov.cn/tjgb/rkpcgb/qgrkpcgb/t20110428_402722232.htm.

CYCRC. China Youth Development Report[EB/OL]. China Youth and Children Studies, 2008[19 May 2011]: http://www.cycs.org/Article.asp?Category=1&Column=389&ID=7869.

DFID. Disability, poverty and development[EB/OL]. UK Department For International Development, 2000[26 Jun. 2011]: http://handicap-international.fr/bibliographie-handicap/4PolitiqueHandicap/hand_pauvrete/DFID_disability.pdf.

Esmail S, Darry K, Walter A, et al. Attitudes and perceptions towards disability and sexuality[J]. Disability and Rehabilitation, 2010, 32(14): 1148-1155.

Geenen SJ, Powers LE, Sells W. Understanding the Role of Health Care Providers During the Transition of Adolescents With Disabilities and Special Health Care Needs[J]. Journal of Adolescent Health, 2003, 32(3): 225-233.

HRSA. The national survey of children with special health care needs chartbook 2005～2006[EB/OL]. U.S. Department of Health and Human Services Health Resources and Services Administration, 2008[3 Jul. 2011]: http://www.uconnucedd.org/actearlyct/PDFs/National.pdf.

Kingsnorth S, Healy H, Macarthur C. Preparing for adulthood: a systematic review of life skill programs for youth with physical disabilities[J]. Journal of Adolescent Health, 2007, 41(4): 323-332.

Lisa Skär RN. Peer and adult relationships of adolescents with disabilities[J]. Journal of Adolescence, 2003, 26(6): 635-649.

Matziou V, Galanis P, Tsoumakas C, et al. Attitudes of nurse professionals and nursing students towards children with disabilities. Do nurses really overcome children's physical and mental handicaps?[J]. International nursing review, 2009, 56(4): 456-460.

Michaud P, Suris J, Viner R. The adolescent with a chronic condition. Part Ⅱ: healthcare provision[J]. Arch Dis Child, 2004, 89(10): 943-949.

Monsen RB. School nurses and health disparities[J]. Journal of Pediatric Nursing, 2006, 21(4): 311-312.

Park MJ, Adams SH, Irwin Jr CE. Health care services and the transition to young adulthood: challenges and opportunities[J]. Academic Pediatrics, 2011, 11(2): 115-122.

Sahin H, Akyol AD. Evaluation of nursing and medical students' attitudes towards people with disabilities[J]. Journal of Clinical Nursing, 2010, 19(15-16): 2271-2279.

SAM. Transition to adult health care for adolescents and young adults with chronic conditions[J]. Journal of Adolescent Health, 2003, 33(4): 309-311.

Schranz B, Shrivastava A, Mohapatra B, et al. Mainstreaming disability in community based disaster risk reduction—a training manual for trainers and field practitioners[M/OL]. New Delhi, India: Handicap International-India, 2008[23 Jun. 2011]: http://www.disabilityindrr.org/TrainingManual_Normal.pdf.

Schumacher KL, Meleis AI. Transitions: a central concept in nursing[J]. Journal of Nursing Scholarship, 1994, 26(2): 119-127.

Scullion PA. Conceptualizing disability in nursing: some evidence from students and their teachers[J]. Journal of Advanced Nursing, 1999, 29(3): 648-657.

Scullion PA. Enabling disabled people: responsibilities of nurse eduction[J]. British Journal of Nursing, 2000, 9(15): 1010-1014.

Seccombe JA. Attitudes towards disability in an undergraduate nursing curriculum: the effects of a curriculum change[J]. Nurse education today, 2007, 27(5): 445-451.

Shakespeare T, Lezzoni L, Groce-Kaplan N. The art of medicine: disability and the training of health professionals[J]. The Lancet 2009, 374(9704): 1815 - 1816.

St Leger L. Health promotion and health education in schools : trends, effectiveness and possibilities[M]. Noble Park North, Victoria: Royal Automobile Club of Victoria (RACV) Ltd 2006.

Stevens SE, Steele CA, Jutai JW, et al. Adolescents with physical disabilities: some psychosocial aspects of health[J]. Journal of Adolescent Health, 1996, 19(2): 157-164.

Surís J-C, Resnick MD, Cassuto N, et al. Sexual behavior of adolescents with chronic disease and disability[J]. Journal of Adolescent Health, 1996, 19(2): 124-131.

Suris J-C, Michaud P-A, Viner R. The adolescent with a chronic condition. Part I: developmental issues[J]. Archives of Disease in Childhood, 2004, 89(10): 938-942.

Svetaz MV, Ireland M, Blum R. Adolescents with learning disabilities: risk and protective factors associated with emotional well-being: findings from the National Longitudinal Study of Adolescent Health[J]. Journal of Adolescent Health, 2000, 27(5): 340-348.

ten Klooster PM, Dannenberg J-W, Taal E, et al. Attitudes towards people with physical or intellectual disabilities: nursing students and non-nursing peers[J]. Journal of advanced nursing, 2009, 65(12): 2562-2573.

Wang G, McGrath BB, Watts C. Health care transitions among youth with disabilities or special health care needs: an ecological approach[J]. Journal of Pediatric Nursing, 2010, 25(6): 505-550.

WHO. Declaration of Alma-Ata[EB/OL]. World Health Organization, 1978[21 Jun. 2011]: http://www.who.int/hpr/NPH/docs/declaration_almaata.pdf.

WHO. Towards a common language for functioning, disabilty and health ICF[EB/OL]. World Health Organization, 2002[28 Jun. 2011]: http://www.who.int/classifications/icf/training/icfbeginnersguide.pdf.

WHO. WHA58.23 Disability, including prevention, management and rehabilitation[EB/OL]. World Health Organization, 2005[25 Jul. 2011]:http://www.who.int/disabilities/WHA5823_resolution_en.pdf.

WHO. The World Health Report 2008 — primary Health Care (Now More Than Ever)[M/OL]. Geneva, Switzerland: World Health Organization, 2008[25 Jul. 2011]: http://www.who.int/whr/2008/en/index.html.

WHO. WHA62.14 Reducing health inequities through action on the social determinants of health[EB/OL]. World Health Organization, 2009[28 Jun. 2011]:http://apps.who.int/gb/ebwha/pdf_files/EB124/B124_R6-en.pdf.

WHO. Community-based rehabilitation (CBR)[EB/OL]. World Health Organization, 2010[25 Jul. 2011]: http://www.who.int/disabilities/cbr/en/.

WHO, UNFPA. Promoting sexual and reproductive health for persons with disabilities[M/OL]. Geneva, Switzerland: World Health Organization, 2009[28 Jun. 2011]: http://extranet.who. int/iris/bitstream/123456789/614/1/9789241598682_eng.pdf.

WHO, World Bank. World report on disability[M/OL]. Malta: World Health Organization, 2011[26 Jun. 2011]: http://whqlibdoc.who.int/publications/2011/9789240685215_eng.pdf.

Chapter 10   Monitoring Adolescent Health and Development

—— **Yuli Zang, Na Li, Liping Hu** ——

Previous chapters present distinctive perspectives on adolescent health and development related to growth, adolescence, psychosocial development and mental health, health risk behaviors, and disability. As proposed by the WHO Pan American Regional Office (WHO 2006), the foremost component of the core package of adolescent friendly health services (AFHS) is to monitor growth and development. This chapter will describe a series of instruments, mostly used world-wide, which have been established with satisfactory psychometric properties among adolescents of 10 to 19 years old in mainland of China to facilitate their wide use and cross-cultural comparison.

These instruments are related to demo-socio-economic characteristics, pubertal development, cognitive development, family dysfunction, strength and difficulties (emotional, behavioural, social), and perceived difficulties in all aspects of social life caused by health conditions. The measurement of knowledge, attitudes and behaviours (KAB) related to puberty is to be introduced to facilitate the evaluation of adolescents' understanding of puberty and adolescence. These instruments will be introduced briefly, one by one, in this chapter.

Section 1   Demo-socio-economic Characteristics

Items related to diseases, problem behaviors, medical insurance, health risk factors, health history, family history and genetics, as well as disability are mainly derived from the basic information part of health records as integral to the National Basic Public Health Services Standard 2009 by China's Ministry of Health (MoH 2009). Other items include whether being a single child or not, growth (i.e., height, weight), educational background of parents, principal caregiver, perceived family income, perceived overall academic score, marital status, and residence. All are shown in Table 10-1. Researchers, teachers or healthcare providers can select

309

some of them for their own purpose.

Table 10-1　Basic personal information for school adolescents

Items	Details
School & grade	School Name: _____Grade:_____
Birth date	_____(yyyy)_____(mm)　　　Age:_____years
Ethnicity	① Han　　② Minor ethnicity (specify)_____
Sex	① female　② male
Single child	① no　　② yes
Growth	height:_____cm　　　　weight:_____kg
Residence place	□urban area　□city skirt　□rural area
Home place	□urban area　□city skirt　□rural area
Mother-education	□no schooling or primary below　　□primary　　□middle school □high school or secondary school　　□associate or above
Father-education	□no schooling or primary below　　□primary　　□middle school □high school or secondary school　　□associate or above
Parent marriage	□harmony　□disharmony　□separate　□divorce　□others
Family type	□nuclear family (including parents and children) □extended family (having more than three generations) □adopted　　□single parent　　□reconstructed family
Family income (relative to the surrounded)	□lowest　□low-middle　□middle　□up-middle　□highest　□not know
Academic scores (relative to the surrounded)	□poorest　□low-middle　□middle　□up-middle　□best
Principal-caregiver	□parents　□grandparents (in-law)　□others_____
Smoking	① never　② almost never　③ sometimes　④ often　⑤ always
Drinking	① never　② almost never　③ sometimes　④ often　⑤ always
Being drunk-before	① never　② almost never　③ sometimes　④ often　⑤ always
Addictive drugs	① no　② yes: □depressant (e.g., hypnotics)　□stimulants (e.g., nicotine) □dissociative (e.g., morphine)　□hallucinogens (e.g., LSD)
Medical-insurance (MI)	① all free　② partly free　③ city employer MI　④ city resident MI ⑤ commercial MI ⑥ new cooperative medical scheme ⑦ poverty security ⑧ others_____
Allergy history	① no　② yes: □penicillin　□sulfonamide　□streptomycin □others_____
Risk exposure	① no　② yes: □chemical　□toxin　□radiation

Continue

Items		Details
Medical history		
Diseases	① no	② yes: Disease 1_____Year of diagnosis _____(yyyy);
		Disease 2_____Year of diagnosis _____(yyyy);
Surgery	① no	② yes: name #1_____Year of diagnosis _____(yyyy);
		name #2_____Year of diagnosis _____(yyyy);
Traumatic wound	① no	② yes: name #1_____Year of diagnosis _____(yyyy);
		name #2_____Year of diagnosis _____(yyyy);
Blood infusion	① no	② yes: cause #1_____Year of diagnosis _____(yyyy);
		cause #2_____Year of diagnosis _____(yyyy);
Family history & genetics	Father ① no	② yes: disease #1_____disease #2_____
	Mother ① no	② yes: disease #1_____disease #2_____
	Siblings ① no	② yes: disease #1_____disease #2_____
Disability	① no	② yes: □hearing disability □speech disability
		□physical disability
		□intellectual disability □visual disability
		□mental disability
		□multiple disability
		severity level_____

For adolescents leaving school but having jobs, items related to school life (i.e., school name and grade, academic scores relative to the surrounded) should be replaced by those items related to jobs, e.g., affiliation name, employee category (i.e., ① manager in governmental/political organization, ② technician, ③ administrative staff, ④ business or service staff, ⑤ agriculture/forest/farm/watering worker, ⑥ industry/transportation staff, ⑦ military staff, and ⑧ others which are difficult to categorise (MoH 2009).

In the updated National Basic Public Health Services Standard 2011, items about living environment are added: a. kitchen airing facilities (① none, ② kitchen ventilation, ③ fan, ④ chimney); b. energy (① liquefied petroleum gas, ② coal, ③ liquefied natural gas, ④ methane, ⑤ firewood); c. watering (① tap water, ② filtered water, ③ well, ④ lake/river, ⑤ pool, ⑥ others); d. toilet (① water closet, ② manure pit, ③ commode, ④ open cesspit, ⑤ shelter toilet); e. livestock place (① separate, ② inside, ③ outside) (MoH 2011). This reflects increasing concern over the impact of living conditions on health. The health concerns for different counties or areas at different periods of time can vary depending on the social, political and economical status and the disease spectrum. It is better to decide which data are really needed for a better understanding of the phenomena in the most cost-effective way.

Section 2   Puberty Development Scale

Apart from direct visual inspection by health professionals, the initial puberty development status assessment can be traced back to Tanner's standard photographs to reflect the progression of sexual maturity over time (Marshall & Tanner 1969, 1970). These photographs were replaced by flow drawings in Morris and Udry's study (1980) to respond to the need to be not so directly linked to sexual body parts (Coleman & Coleman 2002). To make parents and students more comfortable when attending the assessment, the textual Pubertal Development Scale (PDS) was introduced by Petersen and colleagues (Petersen et al. 1988), but their scaling scheme and the scoring strategy was improved by Carskadon and Acebo (1993).

Considering the sexually conservative culture among Chinese, the Chinese version of the textual PDS (abbreviated as C-PDS) using the refined scaling and scoring scheme was developed in Hong Kong. It has been established with satisfactory reliability and validity (Chan et al. 2008). The Manderin (in mainland of China) version of PDS (abbreviated as MC-PDS, see Table 10-2) was derived from the above C-PDS (Chan et al. 2010) to facilitate the evaluation of a school-based health education program among 234 adolescents of 12 to 14 years old. It was found that the Cronbach's α for MC-PDS was 0.66 and 0.80 for boys' and girls' versions, respectively, and the 10-day test-retest reliability (i.e., intraclass correlation coefficient, ICC) was 0.89 and 0.71 for boys and girls, respectively (Zang et al. 2011).

The score scheme (Carskadon & Acebo 1993, Chan et al. 2010) for the MC-PDS is that: for boys version, the first four answer options to each question are give the corresponding point from 1 to 4, and the fifth answer choice of "do not know" is given the point of "0"; for girls version, the scoring scheme for the first four questions is the same as that boys version, but for question 5a, the answer choice of "no" is scored as "0", while that of "yes" is scored as "1".

Table 10-2   Puberty Development Scale (PDS)

Instruction: The next questions are about changes that may be happening to your body. These changes normally happen to different young people at different ages. Please read these questions carefully and select appropriate answers. If you do not understand a question or do not know the answer, please select the answer 'don't know'.

Limited to Boys below

1. Do you have any growth in height?

   ① Not yet started   ② Barely started   ③ Definitely started   ④ Seems complete   ⑤ Do not know

2. Do you have any growth of body hair? (Body hair means hair in any place other than your head, such as under your arms)

   ① Not yet started   ② Barely started   ③ Definitely started   ④ Seems complete   ⑤ Do not know

3. Do have any skin changes? (e.g., acne, pimple)

   ① Not yet started   ② Barely started   ③ Definitely started   ④ Seems complete   ⑤ Do not know

4. Do you have a deepening of your voice?

   ① Not yet started   ② Barely started   ③ Definitely started   ④ Seems complete   ⑤ Do not know

5. Do you have hair growth on your face?

   ① Not yet started   ② Barely started   ③ Definitely started   ④ Seems complete   ⑤ Do not know

Limited to girls

1. Do you have any growth in height?

   ① Not yet started   ② Barely started   ③ Definitely started   ④ Seems complete   ⑤ Do not know

2. Do you have any growth of body hair? (Body hair means hair in any place other than your head, such as under your arms)

   ① Not yet started   ② Barely started   ③ Definitely started   ④ Seems complete   ⑤ Do not know

3. Do have any skin changes? (e.g., acne, pimple)

   ① Not yet started   ② Barely started   ③ Definitely started   ④ Seems complete   ⑤ Do not know

4. Do you have any growth of your breast?

   ① Not yet started   ② Barely started   ③ Definitely started   ④ Seems complete   ⑤ Do not know

5a. Have you begun to menstruate?   ① Yes   ② No

5b. If yes, how old were you when you started to menstruate? _____years

The Pubertal Categorization Score (PCS) is computed as: for boys, totaling the score of #2 (body hair), #4 (voice change) and #5 item (facial hair) and then categorize using the criteria of prepubertal=3, early pubertal=4 or 5 (no 3-point responses), midpubertal=6, 7 or 8 (no 4-point), late pubertal=9~11, and postpubertal=12; for girls, totaling the score of #2 (body hair), #4 (breast development) and #5a item (menarche) and then categorize using the criteria of prepubertal=2 and no menarche, early pubertal=3 and no menarche, midpubertal>3 and no menarche, late pubertal≤7 and menarche, and postpubertal=8 and menarche.

Overall, the textual scoring method could replace the traditional graphical scoring methods during any health screening in school, in communities or at home. Nevertheless, the graphic scoring scheme and a thorough physical examination (e.g., direct visual inspection) are preferable in hospital settings for more accurate clinical judgment by healthcare professionals (Bond et al. 2006, Coleman & Coleman 2002).

Section 3　Zhang Cognitive Development Inventory

The period of adolescence is a crucial stage for significant changes in adolescents' minds regarding cognitive and moral development (Enright et al. 1983, Hart & Carlo 2005, Steinberg 2005, 2008). On the basis of Piaget's stages of cognitive development theory, Perry proposed the theory of intellectual and moral/ethical development to trace the ways of making sense of one's experiences. In Perry's scheme, an individual's forms of reasoning transcend contents, i.e., a person uses ways of reasoning that remain consistent, regardless of the content to be presented; over time one's less adaptive forms of reasoning are replaced by better forms of reasoning gradually, but during a specific period of time, one occupies only one dominant cognitive position; and an individual usually develops from the lower levels of reasoning to higher levels of reasoning (Zhang 2004, 2005).

Recognizing the value of Perry's theory in understanding university students' cognitive development in relation to learning, interpersonal interaction and life meaningfulness, Dr. Zhang and her partners (Zhang 1999, 2002, 2004, 2005, Zhang & Watkins 2001) developed a 75-item instrument (i.e., Zhang Cognitive Development Inventory, ZCDI) to measure students' cognitive development in aspects of education dualism (ED, 20 items), education relativism (ER, 14 items), interpersonal dualism (ID, 20 items), interpersonal relativism (IR, 14 items) and life commitment (LC, 7 items). These aspects are formulated to the five subscales of ZCDI respectively. It was argued that students' cognition develops in sequential from dualism, relativism to commitment, and those at the higher level of cognitive development tend to take the deep instead of surface learning strategies, and to be more legislative, judicial, hierarchical, global and liberal but less executive, local, monarchic, and normative (Zhang 2004, 2005).

Using thousands of university students from mainland of China, Hong Kong and United States of American (USA), the 75-item ZCDI (sample statements are shown Table 10-3) was found to be internally reliable with Cronbach's α ranging from 0.70 to 0.84 (ED subscale), 0.57 to 0.71 (ER subscale), 0.65 to 0.78 (ID subscale), 0.56 to 0.62 (IR subscale), and 0.62 to 0.69 (LC subscale) (Zhang 2004). The content validity was established by the correlation between ZCDI and thinking styles, learning approaches, and self-rated abilities (i.e., analytical, creative and practical abilities) (Zhang 2004, 2005).

Table 10-3　Sample items for Zhang Cognitve Development Inventory

Subscales	Sample statement (i.e., item)
Education Dualism	The key to understanding a course is learning to think the way the teacher wants you to think.
Education Relativism	Selecting a position during an academic debate requires both reasoning and taking risks.
Interpersonal Dualism	I would like to have one close friend at a time.
Interpersonal Relativism	I could get along with people even if the beliefs they hold are very different from mine.
Life Commitment	I have set priorities on my activities so that I could achieve my major goals.

A 7-point scale is used to rate the degree of the agreement with 75 statements/ items respectively ranging from 1=absolutely disagree to 7=absolutely agree, but one of the statements (i.e., item #54) is rated reversely. The subscale score is calculated by totaling all item scores within the subscale. Giving that cognitive development is a continuum, the ZCDI was piloted among adolescents of 10 to 19 years old with the additional scoring point 0 (not applicable or not understand), and the preliminary outcome is to be reported elsewhere by the authors.

Section 4 Strength and Difficulties Questionnaire

The earliest sign of psychiatric disorders for adolescents may be demonstrated through emotional problems, conduct problems, peer problems or attention deficit, but prosocial behaviors may project the inner capacity to overcome the above problems without causing psychiatric disorders. Whether or not these problems reflect psychiatric disorders depends on the social impairment and burden on adolescents, their parents, teachers and others. These ideas lay the theoretical foundation of Prof. Goodman's Strength and Difficulties Questionnaire (SDQ) and the extended version of SDQ (abbreviated as Ext-SDQ), which includes additional social impact items (Goodman 1997, 1999, 2001, Goodman et al. 1998). Both the SDQ and Ext-SDQ can be administered to adolescent of 11 to 16 years old and their parents and teachers respectively, with minor changes to the designation of the corresponding target person. For instance, "you" instead of "your child" is used in the self-report version of SDQ and its extended version.

Over time the SDQ and Ext-SDQ have been shown to have satisfactory psychometric properties, including but not limited to internal reliability (i.e., Cronbach's α), discriminant validity, predicative validity, factoral validity and so forth (Goodman 1997, 1999, 2001, Goodman et al. 2000, Goodman & Goodman 2009). The SDQ (see Table 10-4) consists of 25 items which load on five factors with five items loaded each, i.e., emotional symptoms (item #3, #8, #13, #16, #24), conduct problems (item #5, 7, 12, 18, 22), hyperactivity/inattention (item #2, #10, #15, #21, #25), peer relationship problems (item #6, #11, #14, #19, #23) and prosocial behaviour (item #1, #4, #9, #17, #20). A 3-point scale (0=not true, 1=somewhat true, and 2=certainly true) is used to rate 20 items, but the other five are reverse scored, i.e., do as being told (item #7), have one good friend or more (item #11), being liked by peers (item #14), think before doing things (item #21), finish the work with good attention (item #25). The total difficulty score is the sum of all 20 item scores on emotional symptoms, conduct problems, hyperactivity/ inattention and peer relationship problems (Goodman 1977, 1999, Goodman et al. 1998). An open-end question, i.e., "do you have any other comments or concerns", is added in the end of the SDQ to collect more information for a better clinical implicaiton (youthinmind 2009).

Table 10-4   Strengths and Difficulties Questionnaire (youthinmind 2009)

Item No.	Statement	Not true	Somewhat true	Certainly true
1	I try to be nice to other people. I care about their feelings.	☐	☐	☐
2	I am restless. I cannot stay still for long.	☐	☐	☐
3	I get a lot of headaches, stomach-aches or sickness.	☐	☐	☐
4	I usually share with others (food, games, pens etc.).	☐	☐	☐
5	I get very angry and often lose my temper.	☐	☐	☐
6	I am usually on my own. I generally play alone or keep to myself.	☐	☐	☐
7	I usually do as I am told.	☐	☐	☐
8	I worry a lot.	☐	☐	☐
9	I am helpful if someone is hurt, upset or feeling ill.	☐	☐	☐
10	I am constantly fidgeting or squirming.	☐	☐	☐
11	I have one good friend or more.	☐	☐	☐
12	I fight a lot. I can make other people do what I want.	☐	☐	☐
13	I am often unhappy, down-hearted or tearful.	☐	☐	☐
14	Other people my age generally like me.	☐	☐	☐
15	I am easily distracted, and I find it difficult to concentrate.	☐	☐	☐
16	I am nervous in new situations. I easily lose confidence.	☐	☐	☐
17	I am kind to younger children.	☐	☐	☐
18	I am often accused of lying or cheating.	☐	☐	☐
19	Other children or young people pick on me or bully me.	☐	☐	☐
20	I often volunteer to help others (parents, teachers, and children).	☐	☐	☐
21	I think before I do things.	☐	☐	☐
22	I take things that are not mine from home, school or elsewhere.	☐	☐	☐
23	I get on better with adults than with people my own age.	☐	☐	☐
24	I have many fears, I am easily scared.	☐	☐	☐
25	I finish the work I'm doing. My attention is good.	☐	☐	☐

In additon to the 25 items in the SDQ, the Ext-SDQ includes additional questions: (1) the first asks about the *perceived difficulties* in the area of emotions, concentration, behaviors or getting on with other people using the 4-point scale (i.e., 0=no, 1=minor difficult, 2=definite difficult and 3=severe difficult). If the asnwer is "no", all of the remaining questions about the chronicity, impact, or burden of difficulties will not be asked. (2) The *chronicity* is asked using the question of "how long have these difficuties been present" using the 4-point scale (1=less than a month, 2=1 to 5 months, 3=6 to 12 months and 4=over a year). (3) The *distress* is questioned using "do the difficulties upset or distress you" with the 4-point scale (i.e., 0=not at all, 1=only a little, 2=quite a lot and 3=a great deal), and (4) the same scaling scheme is used to rate the response to the question of "do the difficulties interfered with everyday life" about *social incapacity* in the four areas (i.e., home life, friendships, classroom learning, and leisure activities) respectively (Goodman 1999). Alternatively, responses to questions on distress and social incapacity can be rated using the following 3-point scale: 0=not at all, 0=only a little, 1=quite a lot and 2=a great deal, when being more concerned over the identification of positive cases. (5) The last question is about *burden* using the question "do the difficulties make it harder for those around?" with the 4-point scale: 0=not at all, 1=only a little, 2=quite a lot, 3=a great deal (Goodman 1999, youthinmind 2009).

The SDQ and Ext-SDQ have been translated into more than 40 languages, becoming an internationally used behaviorial screening tool in school, communities and psychiatric clinics (youthinmind 2009). The Chinese version of SDQ and Ext-SDQ has been developed and used in Hong Kong (Lai et al. 2010) and mainland of China with the recommendation of bandings raw scores for Shanghai Chinese of three to 17 years old (Du et al. 2009). Nevertheless, given the existence of traditional and simple Chinese with descent cultural, linguistic and geographical differences, attention has been drawn to the use of the Chinese version for cultural appropriateness and corss-cultural comparison (Toh et al. 2008). Given that no systematic review over the Chinese version occurs nowadays, any interpretation of the SDQ scores, cross-country comparison outcomes and the referal to norms shall be very cautious.

Finally, the format for the SDQ and Ext-SDQ was designed for its purpose, e.g., all 25 items of the SDQ are placed on one side of the sheet, while the additional social impact items in the Ext-SDQ is placed on the other side. More details can be found at the website of youthinmind including the history of SDQ and Ext-SDQ, all available questionnaires in different languages, scoring systems, publications of relevancy, norms and so on (youthinmind 2009).

Section 5   World Health Organization Disability Assessment Schedule Ⅱ

Ideally, there is a universally usable instrument to measure the impact or difficulties caused by diversified health conditions at different severity levels across the life course. Over decades, underpinned by the International Classification framework for function, disability and health, the WHO Disability Assessment Schedule 2.0 (WHODAS 2.0) comes into being (Üstün et al. 2010, WHO 2011). It has been established with satisfactory validity and reliability, for example, factorial structure including factor loadings and test-retest intraclass coefficients (see Fig. 10-1).

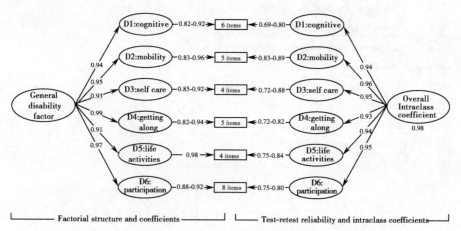

Fig. 10-1   Factorial structural and test-retest reliability of for the 36-item version of WHODAS 2.0 (Üstün *et al.* 2010, WHO 2011)

At present a total of six versions is available for WHODAS 2.0, i.e., self / interviewer/proxy administered 36-item version, self/interviewer administered 12-item version, and interviewer administered 12 plus 24-item version (Üstün et al. 2010, WHO 2011). It should be emphasized that there are relatively strict requirements regarding the use of WHODAS 2.0 in accordance with User Agreement with WHO approval including the use of the indicated structural design, connection sentences, font size and color, as well as underlining key words to increase the understandability and the quality of data to be collected for cross-sector or cross-country comparison. More details are available at the WHO website (WHO 2011). The 36 items in the self-administered version are listed in

Table 10-5 including the introduction for information.

Table 10-5　Unstructured self administered 36-item version of WHODAS (WHO 2011)

This questionnaire asks about difficulties due to health conditions. Health conditions include diseases or illnesses, other health problems that may be short or long lasting, injuries, mental or emotional problems, and problems with alcohol or drugs. Think back over the past 30 days and answer these questions, thinking about how much difficulty you had in doing the following activities. For each question, please circle only one response.

In the past 30 days, how much difficulty did you have in:

Understanding and communicating

D1.1　Concentrating on doing something for ten minutes?

D1.2　Remembering to do important things?

D1.3　Analysing and finding solutions to problems in day-to-day life?

D1.4　Learning a new task, for example, learning how to get to a new place?

D1.5　Generally understanding what people say?

D1.6　Starting and maintaining a conversation?

Getting around

D2.1　Standing for long periods such as 30 minutes?

D2.2　Standing up from sitting down?

D2.3　Moving around inside your home?

D2.4　Getting out of your home?

D2.5　Walking a long distance such as a kilometre [or equivalent]?

Self-care

D3.1　Washing your whole body?

D3.2　Getting dressed?

D3.3　Eating?

D3.4　Staying by yourself for a few days?

Getting along with people

D4.1　Dealing with people you do not know?

D4.2　Maintaining a friendship?

D4.3　Getting along with people who are close to you?

D4.4　Making new friends?

D4.5　Sexual activities?

Life activities

D5.1　Taking care of your household responsibilities?

D5.2　Doing most important household tasks well?

D5.3　Getting all the household work done that you needed to do?

Continue

D5.4   Getting your household work done as quickly as needed?

If you work (paid, non-paid, self-employed) or go to school, complete questions D5.5–D5.8, below. Otherwise, skip to D6.1.

Because of your health condition, in the past 30 days, how much difficulty did you have in:

D5.5   Your day-to-day work/school?

D5.6   Doing your most important work/school tasks well?

D5.7   Getting all the work done that you need to do?

D5.8   Getting your work done as quickly as needed?

Participation in society

In the past 30 days:

D6.1   How much of a problem did you have in joining in community activities (for example, festivities, religious or other activities) in the same way as anyone else can?

D6.2   How much of a problem did you have because of barriers or hindrances in the world around you?

D6.3   How much of a problem did you have living with dignity because of the attitudes and actions of others?

D6.4   How much time did you spend on your health condition, or its consequences?

D6.5   How much have you been emotionally affected by your health condition?

D6.6   How much has your health been a drain on the financial resources of you or your family?

D6.7   How much of a problem did your family have because of your health problems?

D6.8   How much of a problem did you have in doing things by yourself for relaxation or pleasure?

H1	Overall, in the past 30 days, how many days were these difficulties present?	*Record number of days* ____
H2	In the past 30 days, for how many days were you totally unable to carry out your usual activities or work because of any health condition?	*Record number of days* ____
H3	In the past 30 days, not counting the days that you were totally unable, for how many days did you cut back or reduce your usual activities or work because of any health condition?	*Record number of days* ____

A simple scoring scheme could be used mostly, i.e., except H1, H2 and H3, all other 36 questions/items in previous six dimensions can be answered using the

5-point scale each, i.e., 1=none, 2=mild, 3=moderate, 4=severe, and 5=extreme or cannot do, and for each dimension, the dimensional score is the sum of all item scores within this dimension; while the total score of difficulties caused by health conditions are the totaling of all dimensional scores (Üstün et al. 2010). The complex scoring scheme takes account into the weight for different dimensions and the actual meaning of each rating point, e.g., "0" instead of "1" is given to the answer choice of "no" difficulty (Üstün et al. 2010). More details are available from the WHO website or responsible officers.

Over time, the WHODAS 2.0 has been tested and used in more than 16 countries mainly among adults of 18 years old or the above (Üstün et al. 2010, WHO 2011). The first author leads a team to pilot-test the simplified Chinese version among 426 adolescents of 10 to 19 years in urban and rural areas in China's Shandong Province to examine the applicability of the self-administered 36-term WHODAS 2.0. The confirmatory factorial analyses support the factorial structure with CFI of 0.95 ($\geqslant$0.95), RMSEA of 0.08 (around 0.06) and PGFI of 0.62 ($\geqslant$0.50), reaching the bracketed criteria for being a good model fit (Zang 2007); a moderate correlation (r=0.47) is found between the above self-administered 36-item WHODAS 2.0 and the 25-item SDQ; except that for the dimension of "getting along with other people" (α= 0.71), the overall internal reliability (Cronbach's α) and that for each dimension can reach the criteria of 0.80 or greater as a new measurement (Davis 1992), i.e., 0.96 (overall), 0.91 (understanding and communicating), 0.88 (getting around), 0.83 (self-care), 0.93 (life activities), and 0.89 (participation in society). This might be caused by the question on sexual activities (i.e., D4.5): in mainland of China, sexual activities are often considered to be sexual intercourse instead of other sexual expressions such as hug, touch and kiss, therefore, few adolescents really had the experience of sexual intercourse and they may feel discomfort or confused at answering it. Besides, given the relative complicated instruction for items D5.5 to D5.8 (see Table 10-5), there was a lot of missing data, suggesting that it might be better to give some note to these items when using them among adolescents.

Section 6　APGAR to Measure Family Dysfunction

Family has unparalleled influence over children and adolescents growth and development by providing a nurturing social environment. The family function was assessed in aspects of: Adaptation, Partnership, Growth, Affection, and Resolve using one item respectively (see Table 10-6), while the acronym 'APGAR' is comprised of the first letter of these five aspects. The 'APGAR' has been well established and widely used since 1940s when the necessity to view patients in the context of family started to be stressed (Smilkstein 1978).

Table 10-6　APGAR

The following statements are used to measure family functions, reflecting your subjective satisfaction with the family. Please check the appropriate answer to each statement from the options below.

- I am satisfied with the help that I receive from my family when something is troubling me.
  ① Almost always　　　② Some of the time　　　③ Hardly ever
- I am satisfied with the way my family discuses items of common interest and shares problem solving with me.
  ① Almost always　　　② Some of the time　　　③ Hardly ever
- I find that my family accepts my wishes to take on new activities or make changes in my life-style.
  ① Almost always　　　② Some of the time　　　③ Hardly ever
- I am satisfied with the amount of time my family expresses affection and responds to my feelings such as anger, sorrow and love.
  ① Almost always　　　② Some of the time　　　③ Hardly ever
- I am satisfied with the amount of time my family and I spend together.
  ① Almost always　　　② Some of the time　　　③ Hardly ever

In view of Smilkstein (1978), Adaptation is the use of intra- and extra-familial resources for problem-solving when family equilibrium is stressed in crisis; Partnership is the sharing of decision-making and nurturing responsibilities by family members; Growth is the physical and emotional maturation and self-fulfillment that is achieved by family members through mutual support and guidance; Affection is the caring or loving relationship that exists among family members; and Resolve is the commitment to devote time to other members of the family for physical and emotional nurturing, involving a decision to share wealth and space.

Response options are designed to reflect the frequency of feeling satisfied with each questioned aspect on a 3-point scale ranging from 0 (hardly ever), 1 (some of the time) and 2 (almost always) (Smilkstein 1978, Chan et al. 1988).

The scores for each of the five questions are totaled to generate the family APGAR score. A score of 7 to 10 suggests a highly functional family; a score of 4 to 6 suggests a moderately functional family; while a score of 0 to 3 suggests a severely dysfunctional family. Sometimes, according to which member of the family is being interviewed, the word "family" can be substituted by spouse, significant other, parents or children (Smilkstein 1978, Chan et al. 1988).

It was reported that for the 5-item APGAR, the Cronbach's alpha (α) ranged from 0.80 to 0.85, the item-total correlations ranged from 0.50 to 0.65, and the test-retest reliability correlation can reach 0.80 to 0.83. Satisfactory correlation was found between the family APGAR score and previously validated instrument (i.e., Pless-Satterwhile Index, $r=0.80$) and clinical reports ($r=0.64$) respectively (Anonymous 1978, Chan et al. 1988, Smilkstein 1978).

In 1980s the Chinese version of APGAR was developed in Taiwan, Hong Kong and then expanded to mainland of China (Chan et al. 1988, Lv & Gu 1995). Though the wide use of APGAR, a recent survey among 401 pediatricians and family physicians, based on the data collected from 22 059 consecutive visiting by children and adolescents aged 4 to 15 years, seems not to support the effectiveness of APGAR measuring family functioning (Gardner et al. 2001). The use of APGAR in the primary care settings like schools, home or community health facilities thereby shall be careful and it might be wise to use additional family function measures when encountering suspect cases.

Section 7　Puberty Related Knowledge, Attitudes and Behaviours Scale

Puberty refers to the period during which an individual becomes capable of sexual reproduction (Steinberg 2008). In western societies, the history of investigating puberty from biological, physiological and psychosocial perspectives is quite long but accumulated evidence in this regard in mainland of China is relatively limited. Guided by the WHO's competency framework for adolescent health and development (Keeney et al. 2004, WPRO 2002), a series of statements were proposed, revised and finalized using the group discussion and expert panel approach to measure adolescents' knowledge, attitudes and behaviours (abbreviated as puberty-KAB) in relation to puberty and health concerns of relevancy, with the 5-point Likert scale ranging from 1=strongly disagree to 5=strongly agree, was generated through a series of group discussion.

　　This 31-item puberty-KAB scale (see Table 10-7) has been used in a school-based educational intervention study (Zang et al. 2011) to measure students' changes in aspects of knowledge, attitudes and behaviours (KAB) surrounding puberty. In this study, it was found that the Cronbach's α for the boys' (n=102) and girls' version (n=109) is 0.88 and 0.87 respectively, which can meet the rigid criteria ($\geq$0.80) for a newly developed scale (Davis 1992). The 10-day test-retest reliability of ICC is 0.91 and 0.84 for boys and girls version of puberty-KAB respectively (Zang et al. 2011). The items are shown in Table 10-7 for reference. Nearly all items in both boys and girls versions are mainly loaded on only one factor; satisfactory loadings are reached except that of the 20th item on private touch for girls' version. More evidence therefore is required for further evaluation of the psychometric properties of the puberty-KAB scale.

Table 10-7　Measure points and psychometric properties for the puberty-KAB scale

No.	Item statements
1[a]	Know about laryngea (breast) development
2[a]	Know about spermatorrhea (menstruation)
3[a]	Know about external genitalia (health care during menstruation)
4[a]	Accept the physiological changes from spermatorrhea (menstruation)
5[a]	Accept psychological changes from spermatorrhea (menstruation)
6	Wash private body areas frequently
7	Perceive own body changes as natural and normal
8	Expect to change own images
9	Always participate in school physical exercises actively
10	Like doing physical exercise at leisure time
11	Hope to learn a specific sports game (e.g., taekwondo, swimming, tennis)
12	Control the times of having western fast food (e.g., McDonald, KFC)
13	Initiate the communication with parents about health-beneficial diet
14	Parents pay much attention to my diet
15	Conduct in accordance with requirements on boys (girls) by adults
16	Behaviours susceptible to classmates'or friends' influence
17[a]	Feel liking a girl (boy)
18[a]	Desire playing with girls (boys) I liked
19[a]	Female (my) private body areas with my (male) intentional touch
20	Have a good relationship with parents

Continue

No.	Item statements
21	Have good relationships with teachers
22	Much encourage and support from supervisors
23	Tackle interpersonal relationship well
24	Talk with parents about anything including learning and life problems
25	Talk with teachers about anything including learning and life problems
26	Study during puberty of importance to life
27	Always finish study tasks voluntarily
28	Feel forced to study by people around
29	Be satisfied with own development
30	Know how to prevent self from hurt
31	Adjust mood well

a. The item is different for boys and girls version (bracketed).

In conclusion, this chapter presents selected tools for school teachers and healthcare workers to assess adolescents' developmental status, KAB surrounding puberty and experienced difficulties in relevant life domains. It should be clarified that these tools are more appropriate for epidemiological studies or for a general understanding about adolescents without probing into any particular health problems, physical, mental. For any suspect cases, it is necessary to have a thorough physical and psychosocial examination before making any clinical judgment or diagnosis.

References

Anonymous. Family APGAR[EB/OL]. 1978[13 Jul. 2011]: http://www.iprc.unc.edu/longscan/pages/measures/Baseline/Family%20APGAR.pdf.

Bond L, Clements J, Bertalli N, et al. A comparison of self-reported puberty using the Pubertal Development Scale and the Sexual Maturation Scale in a school-based epidemiologic survey[J]. Journal of Adolescence, 2006, 29(5): 709-720.

Carskadon MA, Acebo C. A self-administered rating scale for pubertal development[J]. The Journal Of Adolescent Health: Official Publication Of The Society For Adolescent Medicine, 1993, 14(3): 190-195.

Chan DH, Ho SC, Donnan SPB. A survey of family APGAR in Shatin private ownership homes[J]. The Hong Kong Practitioner 1988, 10(7): 3295-3299.

Chan NPT, Sung RYT, Kong APS, et al. Reliability of pubertal self-assessment in Hong Kong

Chinese children[J]. Journal of Paediatrics and Child Health, 2008, 44(6): 353-358.

Chan NPT, Sung RYT, Nelson EAS, et al. Measurement of pubertal status with a Chinese Self-report Pubertal Development Scale[J]. Maternal and Child Health Journal, 2010, 14(3): 466-473.

Coleman L, Coleman J. The measurement of puberty: a review[J]. Journal of Adolescence, 2002, 25(5): 535-550.

Davis LL. Instrument review: getting the most from a panel of experts[J]. Applied Nursing Research, 1992, 5(4): 194-197.

Du Y, Kou J, Coghill D. The validity, reliability and normative scores of the parent, teacher and self report versions of the Strengths and Difficulties Questionnaire in China[J]. Child and Adolescent Psychiatry and Mental Health, 2008, 2(1): 8.

Enright RD, Lapsley DK, Harris DJ, et al. Moral development interventions in early adolescence[J]. Theory into Practice, 1983, 22(2): 134-144.

Gardner W, Nutting PA, Kelleher KJ, et al. Does the family APGAR effectively measure family functioning?[J]. Journal of Family Practice, 2001, 50(1): 19-25.

Goodman A, Goodman R. Strengths and Difficulties Questionnaire as a dimensional measure of child mental health[J]. Journal of the American Academy of Child and Adolescent Psychiatry, 2009, 48(4): 400-403.

Goodman R. The Strengths and Difficulties Questionnaire: a research note[J]. Journal Of Child Psychology And Psychiatry, And Allied Disciplines, 1997, 38(5): 581-586.

Goodman R. The extended version of the Strengths and Difficulties Questionnaire as a guide to child psychiatric caseness and consequent burden[J]. Journal of Child Psychology and Psychiatry, 1999, 40(5): 791-799.

Goodman R. Psychometric properties of the Strengths and Difficulties Questionnaire[J]. Journal of the American Academy of Child & Adolescent Psychiatry, 2001, 40(11): 1337-1345.

Goodman R, Meltzer H, Bailey V. The strengths and difficulties questionnaire: a pilot study on the validity of the self-report version[J]. European Child & Adolescent Psychiatry, 1998, 7(3): 125-130.

Goodman R, Ford T, Simmons H, et al. Using the Strengths and Difficulties Questionnaire (SDQ) to screen for child psychiatric disorders in a community sample[J]. The British Journal of Psychiatry, 2000, 177(6): 534-539.

Hart D, Carlo G. Moral development in adolescence[J]. Journal of Research on Adolescence, 2005, 15(3): 223-233.

Keeney BG, Cassata L, McElmurry JB. Adolescent health and development in nursing and midwifery education[M/OL]. Geneva, Switzerland: World Health Organization, 2004[25

Jul. 2011]: http://whqlibdoc.who.int/hq/2004/WHO_EIP_HRH_NUR_2004.1.pdf.

Lai KYC, Luk ESL, Leung PWL, et al. Validation of the Chinese version of the Strengths and Difficulties Questionnaire in Hong Kong[J]. Social Psychiatry and Psychiatric Epidemiology, 2010, 45(12): 1179-1186.

Lv F, Gu Y. Family APGAR questionnaire and its use in clinics[J]. Foreign Medical Sciences (Series of Hospital Management), 1995, 1(2): 56-59.

Marshall WA, Tanner JM. Variations in pattern of pubertal changes in girls[J]. Archives of Disease in Childhood 1969, 44(235): 291-303.

Marshall WA, Tanner JM. Variations in the pattern of pubertal changes in boys[J]. Archives of Disease in Childhood, 1970, 45(239): 13-23.

MoH. Ministry of Health Notice of Distributing National Basic Public Health Services Standard 2009[EB/OL]. Ministry of Health/China, 16 Oct. 2009[11 Jul. 2011]: http://www.moh.gov. cn/publicfiles/business/htmlfiles/mohfybjysqwss/s3577/200910/43183.htm.

MoH. Ministry of Health Notice of Distributing National Basic Public Health Services Standard 2011[EB/OL]. 24 May 2011[11 Jul. 2011]: http://www.moh.gov.cn/publicfiles/business/ htmlfiles/mohfybjysqwss/s3577/201105/51780.htm.

Morris NM, Udry JR. Validation of a self-administered instrument to assess stage of adolescent development[J]. Journal of Youth and Adolescence, 1980, 9(3): 271-280.

Petersen AC, Crockett L, Richards M, et al. A self-report measure of pubertal status: reliability, validity, and initial norms[J]. Journal of Youth and Adolescence, 1988, 17(2): 117-133.

Smilkstein G. The family APGAR: a proposal for a family function test and its use by physicians[J]. Journal of Family Practice, 1978, 6(6): 1231-1239.

Steinberg L. Cognitive and affective development in adolescence[J]. Trends in Cognitive Sciences, 2005, 9(2): 69-74.

Steinberg L. Adolescence[M]. 8th ed. New York: McGraw-Hill, 2008.

Toh T-H, Chow S-J, Ting T-H, et al. Chinese translation of Strengths and Difficulties Questionnaire requires urgent review before field trials for validity and reliability[J]. Child and Adolescent Psychiatry and Mental Health, 2008, 2(1): 23.

Üstün TB, Kostanjsek N, Chatterji, et al. Measuring health and disability: manual for WHO disability assessment schedule (WHODAS 2.0)[M]. Malta: World Health Organization, 2010.

WHO. Orientation programme on adolescent health for health-care providers[M/OL]. Geneva, Switzerland: World Health Organization, 2006[14 Jun. 2011]: http://whqlibdoc.who.int/ publications/2006/9241591269_Handout_eng.pdf.

WHO. WHO Disability Assessment Schedule 2.0: WHODAS 2.0[EB/OL]. World Health

Organization, 2011[17 Jul. 2011]: http://www.who.int/classifications/icf/whodasii/en/index.html.

WPRO. A Framework for the Integration of Adolescent Health and Development Concepts into Pre-service Health Professional Educational Curricula WHO Western Pacific Region[EB/OL]. World Health Organization Western Pacific Regional Office, 2002[25 Jul. 2011]: http://www.wpro.who.int/NR/rdonlyres/88E71899-5915-4932-AD47-A78EF3D8E7FB/0/ADHframework.pdf.

Youth in Mind. SDQ: Information for researchers and professionals about the Strengths and Difficulties Questionnaire[EB/OL]. 2009[16 Jul. 2011]: http://www.sdqinfo.org/.

Zang YL. Chinese female nurses' perceptions of and sensitivity towards male genitalia related care[D]. Hong Kong: The Hong Kong Polytechnic University, 2007.

Zang YL, Zhao Y, Yang Q, et al. A randomised trial on pubertal development and health in China[J]. Journal of Clinical Nursing, 2011. 20(21-22): 3081-3091.

Zhang LF. A comparison of U.S. and Chinese university students' cognitive development: the cross-cultural applicability of Perry's theory [J]. the Journal of Psychology, 1999, 133(4): 425-439.

Zhang LF. Thinking Styles and Cognitive Development[J]. Journal of Genetic Psychology, 2002, 163(2): 179-195.

Zhang LF. The Perry Scheme: across cultures, across approaches to the study of human psychology[J]. Journal of Adult Development, 2004, 11(2): 123-138.

Zhang LF. Predicting cognitive development, intellectual styles, and personaltiy traits from self-rated abilities[J]. Learning and Individual Differences, 2005, 15(1): 67-88.

Zhang LF, Watkins D. Cognitive development and student approaches to learning: an investigation of Perry's theory with Chinese and U.S. university students[J]. Higher Education, 2001, 41(3): 239-261.

Epilogue

Yuli Zang

The bilingual book represents an astonishing breakthrough in adolescent health and development in mainland of China using the bioecological approach emphasizing the biological, mental and social aspects of human beings during the period of adolescence.

This book presents the most recent ideas about adolescent development, desired service—particularly adolescent friendly health services—in accordance with primary health care principles, and important issues such as health-risk behaviours, sexual and reproductive health, special concerns for adolescents with disabilities, and screening tools for adolescent health and development in general. Considering the paucity of teaching, research and practice in relation to adolescent health and development, this book is anticipated to lay the foundation of better understanding about adolescent clients as a whole in the face of the challenging transition from childhood to adulthood in any settings, e.g., school, community, industry, judicial arena, welfare institutes.

It took nearly four years for the generation of this book with the collaborative efforts involving the international, national and local partners within the health sector and beyond. A series of activities were implemented to reach a clear understanding about the discrepancy in adolescent health and development status in different geographical areas through systematic measurements and field observations. Some investigations were designed to clarify the interpretation of adolescent health and development competencies for school teachers, health workers (in hospital, communities and schools), nursing students and adolescents' parents in terms of the value and level of competencies, as well as the needs for these competencies.

This book could, thereby, be regarded as evidence-based with confidence aiming to make changes in education and health to improve services to adolescents for a stronger societal pillar force in the near future. To narrow the gap between eastern and western understanding in this area, additional linguistic efforts were made, i.e., the book was written in both Mandarin Chinese and English. It is believed that English speakers could know more about adolescent health and development from the perspective of Chinese in Mainland, while Chinese could obtain more ideas and references to keep abreast of up to date evidence for better service delivery.

This would never have been accomplished without the tremendous editorial and review efforts across the past four years under the strong and continuous sponsorship from the WHO (i.e., pre-registration curricular change for adolescent health and development, improving the quality of health services to persons with disabilities), Shandong University (i.e., Independent Innovation Foundation of Shandong University, disciplinary grant for Asia Pacific Emergency and Disaster Nursing and Partners Network Platform) and participating institutions. Though some authors and reviewers are not involved in writing this book, they contributed a great deal to other activities (e.g., the curricular integration plan, survey on the needs for adolescent health and development competency, systematic assessment of adolescent health and development) at least once in Mandarin Chinese and/or English.

This book simply represents the beginning of advancing adolescent health and development, given that the cross-cutting nature of this area requiring multi-sector efforts including education, health and legislation. Clearly there is no short-cut or any other way to circumvent the responsibility to support adolescents in pursuit of positive development towards a brighter future.

Yuli Zang
PhD, Associate Professor,
Deputy Dean, Shandong University
School of Nursing

Acronym

缩略词

Abbreviation 缩写		Full name 全称
AFHS	adolescent friendly health services	亲青卫生服务
AHD	adolescent health and development	青少年健康与发展
AIDS	acquired immunodeficiency syndrome	艾滋病，全称"获得性免疫缺陷综合征"
APA	American Psychiatric Association	美国精神病学协会
APGAR	Adaptation, Partnership, Growth, Affection, and Resolve	家庭功能量表（适应度、合作度、成熟度、情感度、亲密度）
B	Breast development	乳腺发育
BMI	body mass index	体重指数
CAPAD	China Association of Poverty Alleviation & Development	中国扶贫开发协会
CAST	China Association for Science and Technology	中国科学技术协会
CBR	community-based rehabilitation	社区康复
CCCPC	Central Committee of the Communist Party of China	中共中央
CCYL	China Communist Youth League	中国共产主义青年团
CDC	Center for Disease Control and Prevention	疾病预防控制中心
CDC China	Chinese Center for Disease Control and Prevention	中国疾病预防控制中心
CDPF	China Disabled Persons Federation	中国残疾人联合会
CFI	comparative fitness index	比较拟合指数
CFPA	China Family Planning Association	中国计划生育协会
CFS	chronic fatigue syndrome	慢性疲劳综合征

Abbreviation 缩写	Full name 全称	
CHSY	China Health Statistical Yearbook	中国卫生统计年鉴
CMI	Cornell Medical Index	康奈尔医学指数
CNBS	Chinese National Bureau of Statistics	中华人民共和国国家统计局
CNKI	Chinese National Knowledge Infrastructure	中国国家知识基础设施工程
CO	carbon monoxide	一氧化碳
C-PDS	Chinese version of the textual PDS	港版 PDS
CPS	Canadian Paediatric Society	加拿大儿科学会
CSH	Council of School Health	校园健康委员会
CYCRC	China Youth and Children Research Center	中国青少年研究中心
CYIA	China Youth Internet Association	中国青少年互联网协会
CYL	Communist Youth League	共产主义青年团
DFID	UK Department for International Development	英国国际发展署
DHT	dihydrotestosterone	双氢睾酮
DSM-IV	Diagnostic and Statistical Manual of Mental Disorders	《精神疾病诊断与统计手册》
EAAAE	Equitable, Accessible, Acceptable, Appropriate, Effective	平等、可及、可接受、适宜、有效
ED	aducational aldualism	教育两极性
ER	educational relativism	教育相对性
Ext-SDQ	extended version of Strength and Difficulties Questionnaire	SDQ 扩展版
FSH	follicle-stimulating hormone	卵泡刺激素
FSH-RF	follicle-stimulating hormone-releasing factor	卵泡刺激素 - 释放因子
G	genital enlargement	生殖器增大
GAPS	Guidelines for Adolescent Preventive Service	青少年预防服务指南
HBV	hepatitis B virus	乙型肝炎病毒
HCG	human chorionic gonadotropin	人绒毛膜促性腺激素
HIV	human immunodeficiency virus	人类免疫缺陷病毒（即艾滋病病毒）

续表

Abbreviation 缩写	Full name	全称
HPG	hypothalamic-pituitary-gonad	下丘脑 - 垂体 - 性腺
HPG axis	hypothalamic-pituitary-gonadal axis	HPG 轴
HPV	human papillomavirus	人乳头瘤病毒
HRSA	Health Resources and Services Administration	卫生资源与服务管理局
HSV-1	herpes simplex viruses type 1	Ⅰ型单纯性疱疹病毒
HSV-2	herpes simplex viruses type 2	Ⅱ型单纯性疱疹病毒
ICF	International Classification of Function, Disability and Health	国际功能、残疾与健康分类
ID	interpersonal dualism	人际两极性
IMAHRB	Integrative Model of Adolescent Health Risk Behaviour	青少年健康危险行为整合模型
IR	interpersonal relativism	人际相对性
IUD	intrauterine device	子宫内避孕器
KAB	knowledge, attitudes and behaviours	知识、态度与行为
KFC	Kentucky Fried Chicken	肯德基快餐连锁店
LC	life commitment	生活尽责性
LH	luteinizing hormone	黄体生成素
LH-RF	luteinizing hormone-releasing factor	黄体生成素 - 释放因子
LSD	lysergic acid diethylamide	麦角酸二乙基酰胺, 摇头丸
MC-PDS	Mandarin Chinese version of Puberty Development Scale	简体中文版 C-PDS（臧渝梨博士等）
MI	medical insurance	医疗保险
MoE	Ministry of Education	中华人民共和国教育部
MoH	Ministry of Health	中华人民共和国卫生部
MSQA	Multidimensional Sub-health Questionnaire of Adolescents	青少年亚健康多维评定问卷
NAMI	National Alliance on Mental Illness	国家精神病联盟
NGOs	non-governmental organizations	非政府组织
NIH	National Institutes of Health	美国国家卫生研究院

续表

Abbreviation 缩写	Full name 全称	
NPFPC	National Population and Family Planning Commission	国家人口计划生育委员会
PCS	Pubertal Categorization Score	青春期发育分期分值
PDS	Pubertal Development Scale	青春期发育量表
PGFI	Parsimony Goodness of Fit Index	精简拟合优度指数
PH	pubic hair	阴毛
Ph.D	doctor of philosophy	哲学博士
PID	pelvic inflammatory disease	盆腔炎
Prof.	professor	教授
P. R. of China	People's Republic of China	中华人民共和国
puberty-KAB	Puberty-related Knowledge, Attitudes and Behaviours Scale	青春期知识、态度与行为量表
PWD	persons with disability (or disabilities)	残障人士
RMSEA	root mean square error of approximation	近似误差均方根（或称均方根残差）
RTI	road traffic injury	道路交通伤害
SAM	Society for Adolescent Medicine	青少年医学研究会
SCL-90	Symptom Check List-90	90项症状自评量表
SDQ	Strength and Difficulties Questionnaire	长处与困难问卷（Goodman教授等人编制）
SHS	School Health Service	校园卫生服务
SMR	sexual maturity rating	性成熟评定
SPGLO	Shandong Province Government Legislation Office	山东省政府法律办公室
STDs	sexually transmitted diseases	性传播疾病
STIs	sexually transmitted infections	性传播感染
TCM	traditional Chinese medicine	中医
TV	television	电视
UN	United Nations	联合国
UNFPA	United Nations Fund for Population Activities	联合国人口基金
USA/US	United States of American	美利坚合众国
WB	World Bank	世界银行

续表

Abbreviation 缩写	Full name 全称	
WGBD	WHO Global Burden of Disease	世界卫生组织全球疾病负担
WHO	World Health Organization	世界卫生组织
WHO/Europe	World Health Organization Regional Office for Europe	世界卫生组织欧洲地区办公室
WHODAS	WHO Disability Assessment Schedule	世界卫生组织残障评定表
WHODAS 2.0 WHODAS Ⅱ	WHO Disability Assessment Schedule 2.0	世界卫生组织残障评定表 2.0 版
WPRO	WHO Western Pacific Region Office	世界卫生组织西太平洋地区办公室
ZCDI	Zhang's Cognitive Development Inventory	张氏认知发展量表